sunshine
and friends

THE KALEIDOSCOPE GIRLS

ALSO BY KIMBERLY DIEDE

THE KALEIDOSCOPE GIRLS SERIES
BETTER WITH FRIENDS (BOOK 1)
SUNSHINE AND FRIENDS (BOOK 2)
FIVE GOLDEN FRIENDS (BOOK 3)
with additional books to come...

CELIA'S GIFTS SERIES
WHISPERING PINES (BOOK 1)
TANGLED BEGINNINGS (BOOK 2)
REBUILDING HOME (BOOK 3)
CHOOSING AGAIN (BOOK 4)
CELIA'S GIFTS (BOOK 5)
CELIA'S LEGACY (BOOK 6)

WHISPERING PINES CHRISTMAS NOVEL
CAPTURING WISHES (BOOK 3.5 OF CELIA'S GIFTS)

FIRST SUMMERS NOVELLA
FIRST SUMMERS AT WHISPERING PINES 1980

sunshine
and friends

THE KALEIDOSCOPE GIRLS

BOOK TWO

Kimberly Diede

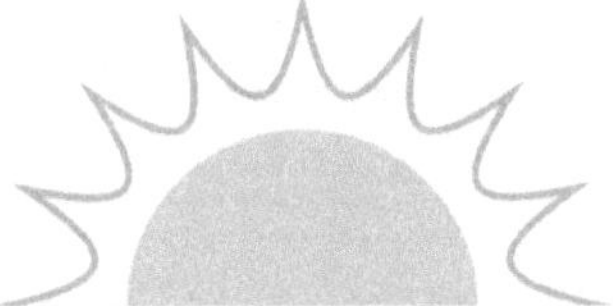

Cover design by Evelyne Labelle at Carpe Librum Book Design – www.carpelibrumbookdesign.com.

Ebook ISBN: 978-1-7351343-7-6

Print ISBN: 978-1-7351343-8-3

To anyone who isn't comfortable
in a swimsuit anymore. Stop stressing.
Neither the sun nor your true friends care!
Take the trip. Wear the suit. Live your life!
And be sure to bring a good book along.

Chapter One

Kit struggled to button her second-most-favorite pair of capris. They didn't have as much stretch as her favorite pair, but she'd already discarded those atop the growing donation pile at the foot of her bed. She hated that she couldn't just assume her clothes still fit. Her weight had only inched up ten pounds in the five years since she'd given up her closet smoking, but everything seemed to have shifted and nothing fit the way it used to.

The open suitcase on top of her bed sat empty, mocking her for getting too lax on her trips to the gym.

It used to be fun to pack. An upcoming trip would mean a new outfit or two, paired with the quality standbys in her closet. But gone were the days when she could pack for a week-long trip in a matter of minutes.

Early in her career, she'd learned the value of buying well-made, timeless clothing. She liked to think her conservative wardrobe balanced out her bright, stylish hairdos, allowing her to maintain a professional look at the office. But this upcoming trip had nothing to do with work, and everything to do with a commitment she'd made to her besties during those last days of their long-ago high school years. They'd promised each other annual girls' trips, starting by the time they turned fifty. As naïve eighteen-year-olds, they'd foolishly assumed the half-century mark would find them all well-established in life with plenty of time on their hands.

Reality looked very different.

But that didn't mean they could shirk their commitments. A promise was a promise.

They were still one year away from black balloons and party sashes sporting logos with *Fifty and Fabulous*, but a soul-refreshing retreat with all five of the Kaleidoscope Girls had reignited their excitement over the idea.

That was six months ago. Kit had accepted the unenviable task of planning this first of hopefully many vacations with the best group of women she'd ever known. They'd rotate the role of travel agent, so she would be off the hook for a few years after this trip.

Kit had invited Jackie, Renee, and Annie to stay with her on Thursday night, given their ridiculously early flight out of Minneapolis on Friday morning. Lynette would meet them in Maui. Kit had picked the early flight, knowing all of them struggled to sleep past five in the morning anyhow, thanks to the insomnia that seemed to accompany middle age.

Thank you, menopause.

She stared at her empty suitcase in frustration. Good thing it was only Sunday. Kit could find time over the next few days to shop. She wasn't in the mood to try on any more clothes tonight. Besides, they'd waited thirty years, and she deserved to feel comfortable and confident on this trip. Her old wardrobe wasn't going to cut it. She shoved the bag back under her bed.

Chloe watched from her perch on the arm of Kit's favorite chair, alternating between preening and glancing with suspicion in her owner's direction. The cat seemed to know the suitcase meant Kit would be leaving her in Dean's hands, and she didn't look pleased about it. Dean was competent in looking after Chloe, but he was allergic to cats. Despite his discomfort, he worked hard to win the pet's affections.

Kit wandered over and dropped into the chair, pleased when the cat didn't bolt. "Don't worry, Chloe. He'll bring treats."

But Kit wasn't optimistic about Dean's chances. Chloe refused to warm up to her fiancé, even though he'd tried every treat and toy he could find, stalwart in his commitment to win her over despite itchy eyes and sneezing fits.

Kit snuggled deeper into her chenille-upholstered chair, scratching behind Chloe's ear. The rumble of the cat's purr helped calm her nerves. Her friends would be upset if they knew how much she'd been stressing over the logistics of this trip, but she couldn't help it. The first trip had to be perfect.

Maybe Jackie would shop with her on Tuesday or Wednesday evening. They could grab dinner, and wine might make trying on clothes less painful, possibly fun. She sent her friend a quick text with an invite, knowing Jackie wasn't likely to see it until after her shift at the animal shelter. The woman often spent seven days a week there, learning all she could about reuniting or finding new homes for abandoned and lost animals. Kit was eager to hear how Jackie's plans were coming together on her alternative career path. Her friend hoped to build a business that matched senior strays with the elderly. It would surely be one of many conversations during their upcoming trip.

Chloe jumped from the armrest and sauntered out of the room. Dean insisted that the reason Kit was a cat lover was because felines were so fiercely independent. He never pointed out the direct correlation between her and her pet, but he didn't have to. She knew he wished she'd rely on him more; however, her childhood had left her scarred.

She didn't need a shrink, or Dean, to tell her she had commitment issues.

Dean was due back from a work trip on Thursday. She doubted she'd see him, with her friends arriving the same night, but he would take care of her cat and keep an eye on her place while she was gone. Jackie had asked more than once why Dean kept his apartment. They'd dated for five years and been engaged for one, and Dean spent many nights at Kit's.

Kit sighed. They would probably get into that topic, too, while relaxing on the beach in Maui.

Her oldest friends knew most of her history—the dark times along with the good. It was both the blessing and the curse of lifelong friends; she couldn't hide the truth from them.

An ominous bleeping sound came from the small television on her dresser, snagging her attention. She'd turned the TV on low earlier to fill the silence before starting the arduous process of packing. A lifetime spent in Minnesota meant she knew instantly what that sound indicated: stormy weather was on the horizon. The remote was within reach, and she turned up the volume out of curiosity. She was at home, her car in the garage, so a severe thunderstorm didn't worry her. If there was a risk of hail, she'd try to pull her pretty planters of flowers up under her patio overhang, though they'd be heavy.

A live weather report was airing, and Kit's favorite meteorologist pointed to an area slightly north and west of Minneapolis. Her stomach did a slow twist when she noticed the flashing red tornado warning, like a bullseye, smack dab over the top of Ruby Shores.

Home.

Even though she'd moved to Ruby Shores at twelve and had lived in Minneapolis since graduating from college, the small town would always mean home to her. After all, her ninety-year-old grandmother and her only aunt still lived there.

"We have confirmation of a tornado on the ground on the northern edge of the small town of Ruby Shores," the meteorologist was saying, a hitch of excitement in her voice. "Stay tuned after these messages for further updates."

The station broke away to commercial and Kit snatched up her phone. The first call to her grandmother didn't go through. Instead, the irritating *all-circuits-are-busy* message ratcheted up her unease.

"Don't panic," Kit said, though no one else was there—not even Chloe. Tornado warnings were a common occurrence in Minnesota, especially in the summer months. But touchdowns were less so. How bad was it back home?

Thunder rumbled outside her window, and rain began to rat-a-tat-tat against the glass. The sun wouldn't set for another hour, but storm clouds were snuffing out its rays.

After the commercial break, a radar graphic on the television revealed a brief thunderstorm in Kit's area, but the flashing red remained over Ruby Shores.

She tried her aunt's number next, but all circuits were still busy.

Chloe streaked back into the bedroom, disappearing under Kit's bed to curl up next to the empty suitcase. The cat hated storms.

Kit took a deep breath and closed her eyes, willing herself not to overreact.

Her mind took her back to the chaos of another Sunday evening when she was just thirteen, still living in her grandparents' house in Ruby

Shores. Her grandmother had sent Kit and her two younger brothers out to the garden to pick carrots and green beans after dinner. Grandpa Walter was nearby, tinkering in his two-stall garage beside the alley. She could still remember how unusually still and heavy the air felt that night, how the buzz and sting of mosquitos tortured them. They must have gotten on Grandma Hazel's nerves, because Sunday evenings usually meant baths and a board game inside after supper. But on that particular night, they were banished to the backyard, despite the oppressive weather. Kit's brothers were nine and ten at the time. She remembered the way Tony balanced the old bushel basket on his head while Kit yanked carrots out of the dry soil, shook most of the dirt off, and tossed them at him. They made a game out of it, but Pete wasn't interested, slinking off when they weren't looking.

Kit could still picture Tony dropping the basket on top of one of their grandmother's prized tomato plants when the wail of a tornado siren cracked the thick air. The noise was earsplitting; the siren hovered high above them, mounted on a pole behind the garage where their grandfather worked.

"Grandma is going to kill you if you broke off that plant," Kit remembered hissing at her brother, just as the sky opened above, sending sheets of rain pounding down on their heads and shoulders. The deluge felt warm for a split second, then quickly chilled. She'd scrambled to pick up the spilled produce alongside Tony, but a firm hand gripped her upper arm and pulled her to her feet.

"Get inside!" her grandfather had shouted. She could barely hear him over the wail of the siren. When Tony reached for the dropped basket, Grandpa Walter yelled to leave it. "Kit, get the boys to the basement!"

Kit remembered thinking her grandfather was overreacting, especially when his face paled as he realized Pete was nowhere in sight. But she'd followed his directions, keeping a death grip on Tony's hand as she dragged him toward the house. Grandma Hazel met them just inside the back door. She'd shooed them toward the basement, making Kit promise to keep an eye on Tony, then hurried out back to help her husband look for Pete.

Kit shivered at the memories of the cool, dank air of her grandparents' basement against her rain-soaked skin, and the grit under her bare, muddy feet as they hurried down the wooden stairs. Tony picked up a sliver along the way, and she was doing her best to pull it out when the solitary lightbulb above their heads flickered off.

With the electricity out and the wind howling beyond the single basement window, the two siblings had sunk down onto the bottom step, unable to see their way forward. Kit was old enough to know she should pull Tony under her grandfather's heavy wooden workbench that spanned the southern basement wall, but she couldn't see her hand in front of her face. They couldn't chance walking barefoot across the basement floor where Grandpa Walter spent the bitter Minnesota winters with his woodworking hobby. A screw or nail would do more damage than the sliver. The wait felt endless, leaving her terrified for the safety of both her brother and her grandparents. Something crashed upstairs and Tony sidled even closer to Kit's side. Her poor little brother's shoulders shook with silent tears.

Was a tornado ripping their grandparents' house apart, right above their heads? Even all these years later, she could remember the way the soundtrack from *The Wizard of Oz* kept playing in her head—the one where the hook-nosed lady rides her bike through a tornado as she transitions into a witch.

The lightbulb above blinked on and off, then back on again. It was eerily quiet above. An otherworldly greenish glow brightened the windowpane. Together, brother and sister tiptoed up the basement stairs and eased open the door into the kitchen. Kit remembered how disconcerting it was to see a bright beam of sunlight streaming through the window over the big white sink so soon after the sky had turned dark as midnight.

The back door burst open just as they stepped into the kitchen, and Pete ran inside, their grandparents close behind. They'd found him in the garage, but the wind had been blowing too hard for them to get back to the house. They'd hunkered down there until the worst of the storm had passed.

The only actual damage to the house on that long-ago night was a broken window at the landing halfway up the staircase leading to the second floor. A tree limb had smashed right through it. Framed family photos lined the wall above the steps, and a finger of the limb reached just far enough to knock the top picture to the floor. Kit remembered putting heavy boots on at her grandfather's direction and heading up those stairs while he went outside to get a ladder. Together, they pushed and pulled the broken branch back out the window, letting it crash onto the lawn below. While she waited for him to return with a piece of plywood to cover the gaping hole, she noticed she'd accidentally stepped on the fallen frame. The glass may have already cracked in the fall, but the break had spider-webbed across her parents' smiling faces on their wedding day.

She realized that was right about the time they'd secretly divorced. It would be another five years before she'd find out how shattered her family had really become.

The severe weather warning sounded again from her TV, pulling Kit back to her adult bedroom and away from that earlier tornado that had wiped out the picnic shelters in the town's park and damaged the roof of her school. Even though she was only thirteen when that first tornado skipped along the outskirts of their town, it had given her an appreciation for the destructive force of nature.

She stared at her phone. Would Grandma Hazel hear the sirens? She often forgot, or avoided, putting in her hearing aids. Kit had no idea if there was still a siren in her grandmother's backyard.

She jumped when her phone vibrated in her hand with an incoming call from Jackie.

"Did you see the terrible weather they're getting back home?" Kit asked the second she answered, skipping right over the hellos.

"That's why I'm calling," Jackie said. "I just heard from Mom."

Jackie's parents lived twelve blocks from Kit's grandmother.

"What did she say? Is everything all right? I tried to call both Grandma and Marge, but I can't get through."

Her question was met with an unwelcome pause. "I didn't know they were getting storms. I'm still at work. I got two calls in a row from a number I didn't recognize, so I thought I better take it. Just in case something was wrong with one of my girls, you know? Or my dad."

Kit waited, impatient for Jackie to get to the point. She'd never had children of her own, but she understood that her best friend's first thought was always about the safety of her twin daughters, off at college. Most parents think that way, but not Kit's.

"I'm glad I took the call," Jackie continued. "Most phones are out in Ruby Shores, but rescue personnel stopped to check on my folks, and they let Mom call me from one of their phones. They must have better service or something."

Unable to take it anymore, Kit cut her off. "Jackie, what's happening back home? Are your parents all right? Is their house still standing? Should I be worried about Grandma and Marge?"

A round of barking started up in the background and she could hear Jackie trying to calm a dog. "Sorry. I think every dog in the shelter tonight, including my Nikki, is terrified of this thunder."

"Chloe is under my bed, too. Come on, Jackie, what did your mother say?"

More barking. "You better pack a bag, Kit. We need to get home as soon as possible. I was already planning to run back tomorrow to give my mom a break with Dad before we go on our girls' trip. I can leave here in ten minutes, and I'll swing by and pick you up. The tornado touched down a block from my parents' house. There are at least three or four homes along Breconwood Road with significant damage. They fear there might be injuries, too."

"God, Grandma's is too close to that area. What if she's hurt or the storm damaged her house, too?" Kit's free hand covered her mouth in horror. The house of her teenage years was only a block behind Breconwood.

"I don't know, Kit, but I bet there will be plenty of cleanup we can help with, regardless. Annie might need help, too. I'm sorry I don't have better news. Was I right to assume you'd want to drive over right away? It'll be dark soon, and we may not be able to do much until morning, but I hate to wait."

The disturbing bleeping sound came from the television again. The meteorologist was still pointing at the area around her hometown, saying, "We have new footage coming in now from a hard-hit neighborhood in Ruby Shores."

"Yes, please, come get me. And hurry, Jackie."

Kit ended the call and dropped the phone onto her bed, her eyes never leaving the television. The footage was jumpy and out of focus—probably supplied by a passerby—but she knew the street. As the video panned across, a voiceover noted significant damage to several homes and businesses. She recognized the house where Jackie's old friend, Owen, used to live. In fact, maybe he still lived there over the summer. A massive tree had fallen across his front yard, but she couldn't see much of the house itself.

She snapped out of the trance the horrifying images had pulled her into, scrambling for the suitcase she'd pushed under her bed in frustration minutes earlier. Chloe hissed, but Kit ignored her. Here she was, worrying about how tight her pants felt and what she'd wear for evenings out with her old friends, while her grandmother might have been scrambling for her life.

Jackie was right. They'd need to check on Annie, too. Their friend lived across town from Kit's Grandma Hazel.

She tossed practical items into her suitcase, including jeans and long-sleeve T-shirts, ignoring the resort-style clothing she'd piled on her dresser. She knew from experience that cleaning up after a summer storm could be dirty, backbreaking work, but her primary concern was for the safety of Grandma Hazel.

CHAPTER TWO

THE SKY WAS BLACK by the time Jackie and Kit rolled into Ruby Shores three hours later. The flashing yellow, red, and blue lights of emergency vehicles overpowered the flicker of receding lightning on the horizon. Shredded leaves and twigs littered the streets, and the occasional larger branch slowed their progress.

Kit lowered her window by a couple of inches so the rain-washed air could chase away the stench of doggy breath that permeated the car's interior. Jackie's poor dog, Nikki, had whined and yelped for most of the drive, the near constant rumble of thunder terrifying her.

"It's quiet now," Jackie said, driving slowly through ponded water at the corner of Main and Fourth.

Kit nodded. "*Too* quiet. Aside from downed tree branches, things look okay on Main. I'm relieved to see the Crystal Café doesn't look damaged. But it's so dark. No streetlights. Power must be out around town. It probably hailed, too, based on all the shredded leaves on the ground."

She continued to study their surroundings, wanting to tell Jackie to punch the gas. They had to get to her grandmother's old house. She needed to know that everyone was okay. Despite their ongoing efforts, they still hadn't been able to reach anyone on the phone during their two-hour drive. But there was a risk of downed power lines in the streets, so Jackie had to be careful.

Jackie reached over to give Kit's hand a reassuring squeeze. "I'm sure she's okay, but there's probably a mess to clean up. It would take more than a tornado to bring Hazel down."

Kit squeezed back, then reached behind her to thread her fingers through the plastic bars of Nikki's dog crate. The whining subsided for the moment and the dog licked her fingers. "It isn't even thundering anymore. What still has her so worked up?"

Jackie used her rearview mirror to glance in the backseat at her border collie. "I don't know. Dogs can sense things."

"I wonder if Chloe's still hiding under my bed back home," Kit said, facing forward again. "She hates storms, too."

Jackie had to slow the car at a barricade placed across the intersection of Main and Breconwood Road. A man wearing a green reflective vest approached. "Sorry, ladies. We've had to close this road to local traffic only. Unless you have identification listing an address in this neighborhood, I'll have to ask you to turn around."

Kit leaned toward the steering wheel to peer out Jackie's window at the man. "We're trying to get to my grandmother's house. We drove over from Minneapolis when we heard about the storm and I couldn't reach anybody on the phone. Please, I need to check on her. She's ninety and lives alone."

"Who's your grandmother?"

"Hazel Campbell. Her address is 1462 Lilac Lane. It's a block off Breconwood."

The man nodded. "I know Hazel. Damn. I didn't realize that was her address. Some homes have significant damage back there. I'll let you through, but be careful. Stay out of the way. If they cordoned off her house, let the experts do their work."

He stepped out of the way and waved them around the orange cones with his flashlight.

"It'll be all right, Kit," Jackie said, easing her car around the barricade.

Kit prayed her friend was right. The pulsing lights atop emergency vehicles were more jarring up close, illuminating downed trees and the occasional knot of bystanders huddled on the sidewalk. It felt like they were moving through quicksand; Jackie could only inch the car forward through the crowded street. Kit rolled her window down the rest of the way and stuck her head out, straining to see in the darkness if there was activity one block east of Breconwood.

A bright shower of orange sparks caught her eye.

"Shoot. You can't take the next right. It looks like lines are down across that street."

Jackie pulled into a nearby driveway, easing to the far right so a car could still get by. Kit looked around at their immediate surroundings. In her anxiety-laced state, she hadn't realized they were coming up to Owen's old place. She couldn't make out much of his actual house in the dark because it sat back a good distance from the street.

"I hope Owen and his boys don't mind if I park here, if they are even home. I don't see anyone. Man, they got lucky," Jackie said, peering ahead at the tree lying across her old friend's yard. "I remember when we used to climb that big old oak. It could have smashed the whole west side of his house, but it looks like it just missed it. Let me get a leash on Nikki, and we'll go to your grandma's place on foot."

Kit rolled her window up and got out, shifting her weight from side to side as she waited impatiently for Jackie to get the dog out of her crate.

"Hey, you can't park there!" Someone had stepped out of Owen's darkened childhood home.

Jackie used her fob to lock the car, then jogged toward the voice with her dog. Kit followed close behind.

"Are you one of Owen's boys?" Jackie yelled as she moved toward the house.

Kit's toe caught on something in the dark, and she stumbled forward, catching herself. She pulled her phone out and turned on the flashlight. "Be careful, Jackie! There are tree limbs down everywhere!"

A young man flicked a larger flashlight on, shining the beam in the women's direction. "Yeah, I'm Adam. Dad is one street over. There are some injuries back there. I came back to grab supplies." He held up a tan leather bag.

"You're the doctor then," Jackie said.

"I'm sorry, do I know you?" he said, shining the light on Jackie as she struggled to step over a large branch. Nikki scaled the obstruction with ease, excited to be free of her crate and straining against her leash toward Adam.

Jackie held her free arm up to balance herself, glancing back at Kit as if to check on her progress before answering the young man. "We haven't officially met, though we sat next to each other on an airplane last year. I'm an old friend of your dad's. Jackie Turner. Can I please leave my car here? I think you can still get a vehicle past it, but based on the size of these branches in your driveway, you won't be moving any cars out of your garage tonight."

He waved. "In that case, sure. No problem. Hey, I gotta get back to my dad and our neighbors. But, um, why are you here?"

Jackie motioned back at Kit. "We're trying to get to her grandmother's house. We're worried about her. She's old and lives alone. When we saw the weather reports but couldn't reach her, we drove over from Minneapolis."

"Where is her house?" the young man asked, already making his way to the corner of Owen's property.

"A block over," Kit answered. She repeated the address.

Adam turned and faced them. "I think that's the house I just came from. I can't remember the woman's name, but she's elderly. Dad stayed with her."

Kit's pulse shot into hyperdrive. "Go! Quick! We'll follow you. You have a better flashlight."

The smaller beam from her phone skipped along the ground at her feet. She could see things on the grass that didn't belong there: A book on its spine, its pages soaked. A brown teddy bear in a puddle of water, gazing up at the sky. The stuffed animal reminded her of the one her friend Lynette used to bring to summer camp. The toe of Kit's tennis shoe caught on a toaster cord and she had to kick it away.

The toy bear caused Kit's worry to extend beyond the fate of her own family. Were any children hurt? Or worse?

"Over here," Adam hissed, crossing the alley behind his house.

They passed through the quiet of someone's shadowed backyard and came out on the next street. Kit's brain fought to process the scene before her eyes. The house they'd just passed looked undamaged in the gloom, but temporary spotlights erected across the street lit up a lot where another house was reduced to rubble. The scattered pieces of someone's home.

"God. Was anyone in there?" Jackie asked, hurrying to keep up with Adam.

"We don't think so," he threw back over his shoulder. He turned to his left and jogged toward Hazel's house.

The house right next to the demolished one was in better shape, though a quick glance revealed broken windows.

Kit spied an ambulance ahead. In front of its open doors, an EMT tended to an injured man. Blood stained the white bandage around the guy's thigh.

What would they find a block over at her grandmother's house?

Adam moved too fast to ask. Kit hurried after him, trying to keep her eyes straight ahead because the surrounding destruction threatened to overload her senses. She needed to stay rational for Hazel's sake.

A patrol car raced past, lights flashing but without a siren—no one wanted to hear more sirens—as the trio crossed the last intersecting road before her grandmother's house. The car's headlights caught the front of Hazel's house for a split second before continuing on. It was still standing. Was it possible the house wasn't damaged? There were fewer emergency vehicles parked at this end of the block. That had to be a good sign.

"Back here," Adam said, his clipped tone winded.

Had he been running around helping the injured for hours at this point? If her grandmother was hurt, why hadn't they sent her in one of the ambulances?

Adam ran around the back of Hazel's toward the old garage and the square garden plot her elderly grandmother still tended. His flashlight beam lit on three people huddled next to a clothesline pole.

"Grandma!" Kit yelled, racing toward them.

The old woman was seated in a wicker rocker that normally belonged on the front porch. She had to shield her eyes from the intense beam of Adam's flashlight. "Get that thing out of my eyes! Kit, is that you?!"

Kit dropped to her knees in front of the rocker and held her grandmother's face, searching it for signs of injury. A small trickle of blood inched down from Hazel's snow-white hairline, but the rest of her face looked uninjured. Kit dropped her hands, then pulled her phone back out and turned the flashlight on low. Her grandmother's arms, always mottled with black and blue bruises, now also bore red slashes across both forearms.

"God, you're bleeding everywhere!"

A heavy hand dropped onto Kit's shoulder. "Not everywhere. Adam doesn't think the cuts are deep enough to require stitches." It was Owen, and he caught Kit under the elbow and applied enough pressure that she stood. "If you'll give my son some room, he'll clean her up. Then Marge can run her in to get looked at."

Kit's knees wobbled as the adrenalin subsided and relief threatened to overwhelm her at finding her grandmother, alive, with only minor injuries. She nodded to Owen, then stepped toward her aunt, arms extended. "You're okay?"

Marge pulled her close. "I'm fine. And I don't even have much damage over at my place. Not like this neighborhood. Mom got lucky, especially since she was outside when it hit."

Kit pulled back and turned toward her grandmother's house. It was too dark to see anything. "Outside? But why? And how bad is the house?"

Marge sighed. "Upstairs windows at the back of the house are damaged. I plan to run inside after I get Mom checked out at the hospital and, hopefully, settled at my house. I hate to think of water damaging the wooden floors up there if they don't get mopped up soon. I'm so glad you're here."

"You need to be careful," Owen cautioned, and Kit glanced over at Jackie's old friend. "It could be worse than just the windows. The storm leveled her garage."

"Leveled?" Kit repeated, spinning to search the darkness. "Grandpa's garage? With all his stuff in there?"

"Wasn't your Mustang in there, too?" Jackie stepped toward Kit and wrapped a supporting arm around her waist. "You keep your car in the extra stall, right?"

Kit drew in a shaky breath. She did store her faded red Mustang—a high school graduation gift from her grandparents—in that garage. She hadn't driven it in years because the motor needed work, but restoring it was still on her bucket list.

If there was anything left of it after tonight.

But before she allowed herself to panic over the classic car, she focused on the fact that her grandmother was going to be all right. That was what mattered.

Hazel groaned, and Kit spun back to face her.

"Dang blasted, what are you doing, boy? It didn't hurt until you started messing with it."

"Hazel, he's trying to help. And that boy is practically a full-fledged doctor," Jackie said. "Pet Nikki, she's worried about you."

Kit spied her friend's dog at Hazel's feet, as if protecting the injured woman. Kit smiled at Jackie, appreciating the diversion. Those cuts had to sting.

"I need to douse these in antiseptic so you don't get an infection. The burning will only last a second." Adam's sure movements as he tended Hazel's injuries hinted at plenty of practice. He may be young, but he looked competent, with a dose of compassion.

"Dad! Over here!" a voice cried from the darkness, somewhere over Kit's left shoulder.

Owen's head swiveled. "That's Logan. My other son. Hazel, you're in excellent hands now. I should probably go see where else I can help."

"Go. Go," Kit's grandmother urged. "Between these three young ladies and your doctor boy, I'll be fine. No need to fuss over me."

But Jackie seemed concerned over Owen's welfare. "You should sit down for a few minutes, Owen," she said. "You look positively beat."

Owen's tired grin spoke volumes. "I'm fine. It's been a long night, but it isn't over yet."

A siren cut through the rain-cooled air, as if punctuating his words.

"At least promise you'll be careful," Jackie said, offering her old friend an encouraging smile. "And thank you for helping with Kit's grandma. And for lending us your son. I can see she's in capable hands."

"All of you need to quit fussing over me," Hazel complained, but she giggled when Nikki licked her hand.

Adam ignored her directive. He got on his knees in front of her, checking her legs and feet for any further injuries. "You are one lucky lady, Hazel. I'm glad you had these sturdy shoes on. They provided you with nice protection. But, I have to ask, what in heaven's name were you doing outside when the storm hit? Warnings went off for a good thirty minutes beforehand."

Hazel shook her head. "Those darn weathermen issue so many warnings, it's like the boy who cried 'wolf.' Figured they didn't know what they were talking about, and if they did, I better get my tomato plants covered up. Last time a tornado went through here, it wiped out my garden."

Kit knew exactly which storm her grandmother was referring to. It was the same one she'd remembered earlier that evening, from the comfort of her bedroom in Minneapolis.

Had that only been a few hours ago?

She opened her mouth to admonish her grandmother for being so foolish, but then snapped it shut again. Hazel was a grown woman. She didn't need to be scolded like a child.

Adam latched his bag shut and got to his feet. "I'd still like someone to look at you down at the hospital to make sure I didn't miss anything. A person can't be too careful."

"With a woman as old as me, you mean?" Hazel quipped.

"Don't you put words in my mouth, young lady."

Marge stepped forward and helped Hazel out of the chair. "We'll go right now. There's bound to be a crowd. Kit, did you want to ride along?"

Hazel shook her head. "I'd rather she run inside and clean up any mess that blasted storm left behind. I'm fine."

"You are our highest priority, Grandma, not the house," Kit said, feeling torn.

Hazel snorted. "The condition of my house *does* impact my well-being. Quit worrying about me. Like this young man said, I got lucky. Go make sure my house did, too. You can come over to Marge's tomorrow and check on me."

Kit sensed her grandmother was going to check out just fine at the hospital. She seemed as spunky as ever. "If you're sure."

"I'm sure. Oh, and stay here. The sun won't be up for hours yet. You aren't going back to Minneapolis tonight, are you?" Before Kit could answer, her grandmother added, "Say, Jackie, are your folks all right?"

"They didn't get hit, Hazel. Thanks for asking," Jackie said. "But we'll go check on them, too. Mom told me they were home and inside when the storm hit."

Hazel nodded as she accepted her daughter's arm. "Your mother is a strong woman, but she never could grow a decent tomato. I doubt she had anything to rush out to save."

Kit rolled her eyes. She'd learned that any filter her grandmother used to possess had dissolved with age long ago. "Grandma, that isn't nice. And you know Jackie's mother grows champion heirloom roses. She was just smart enough not to risk her life to save them."

CHAPTER THREE

KIT LED JACKIE TO the back door of her grandmother's house, careful to avoid any obvious glass shards in the grass. She'd hate for Nikki to cut her paws.

"Owen was right. We need to be careful. Should we put Nikki on the back porch while we check the house? Give her a doggie treat—Grandma keeps a box of them in the cabinet back there. Marge thinks she might have a little something going on with her neighbor who walks his dog by here every day."

Jackie chuckled on the steps behind her. "A little something, huh? I can't even get 'a little something' going with anyone these days, and she's almost twice our age. Go, Hazel! Nikki has to be exhausted given how terrified she was during the long drive over here. Add in a treat, and she'll settle right down."

Once they had the dog safely stowed, the two women entered Hazel's small kitchen. Kit found a heavy flashlight under the sink. The power was still out and they didn't want to run their phone batteries any lower.

"Things look all right in here," Jackie said as Kit swept the beam around the room. The light bounced off the dark window above a white porcelain sink. "Where do you want to check first?"

Kit thought back to the time she'd spent with her brother in the basement of this house so long ago. She'd been terrified in the damp darkness. How much rain had this storm dumped? Was there water in the basement? There wasn't much they could do about it tonight, even if there was water down there. Better to tackle that tomorrow.

"Let's check the rest of this floor, then head upstairs. Marge was right about the hardwood up there. We shouldn't let water sit on them for any length of time. Maybe we should try to board up any broken windows tonight. I don't need any birds flying in, or critters crawling around inside, either."

A flash of lightning, followed by a deep rumble of thunder that rattled the glassware behind cupboard doors, pulled a groan out of Jackie. "Or more rain. Hopefully this won't set poor Nikki off again."

Together, the pair left the kitchen and skirted around Hazel's dining room set. Kit's hip bumped one of the chairs, knocking it against the table. The *crack* was loud in the hushed interior. The flashlight dimmed, and Kit gave it a good shake to try to keep it from going out entirely. The ineffective beam made for an ominous trek through the dark living room.

"I wouldn't have done well in the days before electricity," Jackie said behind Kit, her voice loud in the darkness.

Kit aimed the flashlight toward the open staircase. She noticed Jackie was staying very close on her heels. Maybe she could have a little fun with the scaredy-cat. She pulled up short and Jackie bumped into her. "Wait, did you hear that?"

"Hear what?" Jackie said in a much quieter voice as she grabbed the back of Kit's shirt.

Kit tried to sound terrified as she fought back laughter. "That scratching sound. God, I hated that sound. It used to wake me up at night."

"I don't hear anything," Jackie whispered. "If you're messing with me, Kit, I swear to God I'm going to walk out of here right now and let you deal with the mess upstairs by yourself."

Kit bit back a giggle as she stepped around a low coffee table and tiptoed toward the stairs. "I never noticed that sound until after Grandpa died."

"Knock it off, Kit. Now I *know* you're screwing with me." Jackie slapped her on the back, but her words held no conviction.

Two more steps, and before Kit could continue pranking Jackie, a very real crash had both women bolting for the kitchen and back door. Kit prayed the roof wasn't caving in.

"Grab Nikki," she ordered, shoving Jackie onto the back porch.

"Got her!"

Pulling the door shut behind them, the women sprinted back to Hazel's empty wicker rocker, glowing white in the dappled moonlight. Spits of rain tap-danced on their heads. There wasn't a breath of wind.

"What *was* that?!"

Nikki plopped down on her back haunches next to the wicker, whining as her head swung back and forth between the two women, vibrating with unease.

Kit bent at the waist to catch her breath. Had a tree crashed down on the house? It seemed like the only logical answer, but it was so still outside. At least the flashlight was still working. She ran the beam up and down the back of Hazel's house. Aside from the broken windows upstairs, she couldn't see anything out of the ordinary.

"Hold tight to Nikki. Poor thing! She's trembling. I don't want her to bolt. I need to walk around to the front of the house to see if I can figure out what happened. Are you staying here or coming with?"

She hoped she sounded braver than she felt. She didn't want either of them, or the dog, to step on something sharp in the grass, but she also hated to walk around to the front alone.

Maybe they should just head back to Jackie's car and leave everything until morning, hardwood floors be damned.

Nikki's whine shifted to a low growl, and the hair on Kit's neck prickled when she sensed rather than heard someone coming up behind them. She spun, relieved when her beam fell on Owen's face. His arm sprung up to shield his eyes as he jogged toward them.

"I thought I heard something back here. Or was it the house next door? Are you two okay?"

Kit shook her head. "No."

He sprinted the last few feet to them, reaching for Jackie's hand. Nikki barked in alarm and he snatched his hand back. The dog wouldn't actually hurt a fly, but Owen couldn't know that.

"I meant no, the crash wasn't a house over," Kit said. "It definitely came from Grandma's. We were inside. I was afraid the house was coming down on top of us."

He kept his hands behind his back, out of the dog's reach, as he regarded each of them closely. "You aren't hurt, then?"

Kit shook her head. "We're fine. But I need to figure out what that was. Care to investigate with us?"

"If you want to stay here, I can go look." He wiggled his fingers toward her hand. "I'll need your flashlight."

"We aren't damsels in distress, needing a knight in shining armor," Jackie said, sounding much braver than she had inside the darkened house.

"I didn't mean to imply you were," Owen responded, his words measured. "Just trying to help."

Jackie sighed. "Of course you are. I'm sorry. This is all overwhelming. I overreacted."

Kit cleared her throat. "If the two of you are finished, I'd love to find out what caused that crash."

She suddenly wondered if maybe Jackie had that *little something* they'd joked about earlier going on with Owen, her old grade school friend. Kit knew Jackie had reconnected with him at their class reunion the previous summer.

Interesting . . .

But there would be time to think about that later.

"Follow me," she said, taking charge. With two people behind her, she felt more confident.

They couldn't immediately see the source of the crash until they rounded the corner. The front of Hazel's house no longer looked unfazed by the storm. In fact, a massive tree had smashed down onto the roof of her front porch. It looked like the only piece of porch furniture to weather this storm was the wicker rocker out back. The rest was likely smashed to smithereens.

"That's not good," Jackie said, standing beside Kit as they all took in the damages illuminated by the flashlight.

Not good at all, Kit thought. She knew that tree well, had even spent hours climbing it in her youth. But, she remembered, they never played on it when Grandma's crotchety old neighbor was home, because it wasn't technically in their grandparents' yard. It was Old Man Ezra's tree, and her grandmother had complained about the way it shaded that side of her yard for decades.

"The winds must have damaged it, but it didn't fall right away," Owen said. "Please don't go back in that house tonight. It might not be safe. We need to see how bad things are in the daylight."

And for once, Kit didn't argue.

"Come on," Jackie said, giving Nikki a reassuring pat on the head. "I'm beat. Why don't we head over to Mom and Dad's? We'll come back here first thing in the morning."

Kit jumped when a foot touched the back of her leg, startling her out of a deep sleep. Disoriented, she pushed up onto her elbows, surveying her surroundings. Last night's storm and the aftermath came rushing back to her.

Soft morning light streamed through two windows. Jackie's old bedroom looked smaller than it had when they were kids. The curtain of dark hair, fanned out on the pillow next to hers, brought back memories of their college years. Except they'd each slept in their own beds back then, and the silver streaks threaded through her friend's hair were new.

"Are you touching up those roots before we leave for our vacation?"

Jackie groaned. "I had an eight a.m. appointment for today. Since we are two hours from home, that isn't going to happen. Why'd you have to wake me up?"

"You started it."

Jackie rolled onto her back and checked her watch. "I feel like we just fell into bed. I can't survive on four hours of sleep anymore. I'm sorry again about having to share a bed. Mom thinks Dad does better if she sleeps in another room. She says she got the boot, but Hoover keeps him company. And she's using the other two bedrooms for crafts and storage."

Kit smiled. "I love Hoover. She's such a little firecracker of a dog. I'm glad she's good for your dad. How is he doing? It has to be so hard on your mom."

Before Jackie could answer, Kit's bladder complained. She climbed out of bed and rummaged in her suitcase for a pair of sweatpants.

"It's heartbreaking to see his decline. I notice it more when I haven't seen him for a few weeks. We knew this was inevitable, but it seems like it's happening so fast. Especially since his Alzheimer's had already progressed past the initial stages when my parents finally admitted to me what was happening. I don't envy Mom."

Kit sighed as she left her friend's old bedroom with her overnight bag, shutting the door behind her to keep Nikki inside with Jackie. There was nothing she could say to make Jackie feel better about her father's situation. There was no cure for what he was facing, and it fell to poor Charlotte to serve as his primary caregiver for an unknown period of time, much as her Grandma Hazel had done for her grandfather after his stroke.

Kit hated the idea of ever having to become someone's caregiver or needing one for herself. As she completed a quick and abbreviated morning routine in Jackie's childhood bathroom, she tried to imagine how it would feel to have to rely on someone else for her most basic needs. She didn't think Jackie's father had reached that level of dependency just yet, but she supposed he would eventually. They didn't even leave him home alone anymore.

As she left the bathroom, she jumped for the second time that morning when a voice startled her, stopping her in her tracks.

"Who the hell are you and what are you doing in my house?!"

Kit nodded to Jackie's father as he stood in the hallway outside the bathroom. After their mad rush to town, finding Hazel bleeding in her backyard, and then the crash on or near the woman's house, Kit was getting tired of surprises.

"Good morning, Glen. I'm Kit. Jackie's old friend. You probably didn't recognize me with these glasses on. We drove over last night to check on my grandmother after that storm. It's good to see you up and about. You look good."

He didn't but maybe encouraging words helped someone in his situation. Kit really had no idea how best to interact with Jackie's father.

"Bull. I look awful. Like an old man. Sorry I didn't recognize you, Kit. It's been a long time."

In reality, they'd shared a couple brief discussions the previous summer. But even she had a tendency to forget where she parked the car at the grocery store. How could she fault him, when she knew what was behind his forgetfulness?

"Your grandparents all right over there in that big old house of theirs?"

"Grandma got a little banged up, but she'll be fine. She's lucky it wasn't worse. The storm caught her outside in her garden. There is some damage to the house and garage, though, so I'm heading over there shortly to see how bad it is in daylight. It was hard to tell in the dark." She didn't bother to remind him her grandfather had died when she and his daughter were still in high school.

He nodded. "Mother Nature is unpredictable. Typical woman."

He brushed past her and shuffled down the hallway toward the kitchen. She heard the back door open, followed by the excited yips and deeper bark of two very different dogs.

Someone must have let little Hoover outside, and it sounded like Nikki was tagging along. Either Jackie had beaten Kit to the coffeepot, or Charlotte was up, too. She dropped her things back in Jackie's old room, empty now, then joined them in the sun-splashed kitchen.

It seemed impossible, given the beautiful morning, that a massive storm had blown through only ten hours earlier, disrupting the lives of countless families in town, including her own.

"Will you ladies still be able to leave on your trip?" Charlotte asked.

This exact worry had plagued Kit ever since Jackie picked her up for the dash back to their hometown. They'd avoided the subject during the drive over, as if that would protect the trip Kit and Jackie had both looked forward to for years.

"You're taking a trip? What for? Work?" Glen asked, as his wife slipped a plate of buttered toast in front of him.

Jackie wasn't traveling for work anymore, not since she'd left her corporate job months ago. Kit wondered if Glen remembered any of that.

"No, this trip is strictly for fun, Dad," Jackie said. "We're going to Maui for a week of sunshine and girl time. I'd invite you along, but there are no men allowed."

He harrumphed. "You couldn't pay me enough to go sweat on a hot sandy beach in the middle of the ocean, surrounded by a bunch of harping women. That does not sound like fun."

"We fly out early Friday morning. It's me and Kit, plus Annie and Lynette. Renee, too. She's another friend of ours from summer camp, but I don't think you ever actually met her." Jackie continued speaking as if she hadn't heard Glen. Maybe she found it easier to communicate with him if she acted like there was nothing wrong.

"Annie must be the reason you waited to go someplace as hot as Hawaii in July, instead of escaping Minnesota in the winter," Glen said. "It isn't possible for a high school principal to pick up and leave for a week or two during the school year. That's why your mother and I planned to head south in the winter, somewhere warm, after I retired. Guess we shouldn't have waited so long."

Kit saw a look pass between Jackie and her mother. Before he'd retired, Glen held the job that Annie now filled. Were moments like these, when he seemed to know exactly what was going on around him, a relief for them? Or was it a painful reminder of how much they were all losing as his disease progressed?

"You're right, Dad. We had to wait so Annie could come, too. Years ago, when we were seniors in high school, we promised each other we would take annual trips together when we got older. We didn't want to lose touch the way so many people do after they graduate."

He nibbled his toast but didn't seem interested in his breakfast. "I don't remember you taking any big trips with your girlfriends."

"You're right, Glen," Kit said, filling a cup of coffee and taking the open chair next to him at the kitchen table. "This will be our first. Even back when we promised each other we'd do this, we knew it might be a long time before we'd be able to. We were foolish enough to think that, by the time we turned fifty, we'd have plenty of time and money to take a luxurious and relaxing trip."

"And you aren't even fifty yet," Charlotte said, brushing crumbs from her hands and pushing back from the breakfast table. "Good for you!

I wish I'd have had the time and money at your age to do what you're doing."

Some of the excitement faded from Jackie's eyes. "Honestly, Mom, I've been stewing over this trip. I don't really have the money, or the time, to be gallivanting around the globe. But the time will never be exactly right, so I'm going regardless."

This surprised Kit. She'd assumed the rest of her travel companions were all thrilled about their upcoming trip, and she was the only one with some reservations.

Charlotte waved a dismissive hand. "You two need to stop worrying. If the past year has taught me anything, it's that we shouldn't postpone the important things until some arbitrary date in the future. You never know."

"That's what I've been trying to tell myself, too," Kit said. She knew Charlotte was right. But had the storm changed things? "I'm not sure whether I'll have to stick around here now, though. To deal with Grandma's house."

Glen pushed his plate away, half of his toast remaining. "What day is it?"

"Monday. And you have an appointment with the doctor in twenty minutes," Charlotte said, gathering breakfast dishes.

He nodded. "Right. Monday. Then you have a few days to help your family get situated before you leave, Kit. Do what you can to help, then go live your life. Please. And no matter what happens, make sure you girls take those annual trips. Life can be full of regrets. Trust me. Don't give up on the commitment you made to each other. Now, excuse me. I need to go get poked and prodded so those hacks down at the clinic can pretend there's something they can do to help this old man not forget how to wipe his own ass."

Charlotte shook her head, seemingly resigned to Glen's inappropriate comments. Kit couldn't hold back her grin as she caught the twinkle in his eye. Getting a rise out of his wife might be the only fun Glen still had.

But he was right about one thing. She and Jackie couldn't miss out on their fun vacation. She would work her own tail off over the next few days to make sure she was sitting on the beach with a margarita by Saturday.

Chapter Four

DAYLIGHT REVEALED THE FULL scope of destruction to Ruby Shores. Kit took in the scenes through her open car window as Jackie navigated the blocks between her parents' and Hazel's. She took a few deep breaths to calm her nerves. It would take lots of effort to put this town back together, and many people faced plenty of unanticipated work and expense in their immediate future.

Jackie slowed as they approached Owen's house. The grinding screech of a chainsaw pierced the air, and Kit glimpsed a man's bare back as he nicked large branches off a thick tree trunk that spanned the width of the yard. The dark baseball hat and ear protection the man wore made it impossible to tell whether it was Owen or one of his sons working to clear their property.

"Is that Owen?" she asked, eyeing the man wielding the power tool.

The chainsaw switched off, and the man flipped his earmuffs down to hang around his neck before picking up branches and hauling them to the end of the drive. A pile was growing where Jackie had parked the previous evening.

It was Owen, and Kit gave a low whistle at the sight of his broad chest and flat stomach. "Hmm, he doesn't look like most fifty-year-old men I know," she said, keeping her voice low for Jackie's ears only. "I remember him as a scrawny little kid."

They both knew what she didn't say: that most men their age were going soft around the middle, not unlike themselves.

"He certainly isn't scrawny anymore." Jackie grinned. "Wait. Exactly how many bare-chested, middle-aged men do you hang out with?" She slowed the car even more and gave her old friend a wave.

She assured Jackie she saw her fair share, but didn't elaborate. Didn't the older guys at her gym count? Once his arms were empty, Owen returned the wave. Kit smiled. There was nothing wrong with enjoying a little eye candy, she thought, especially when it wasn't borderline creepy because the guy was twenty-something.

Jackie pulled to the curb and Owen walked over to her car, taking his ball cap off to wipe his brow. Even though his hair was dark with sweat, the silver was still prevalent.

Kit wondered if they'd find the Maui beaches sprinkled with attractive men like Owen. She wasn't single, or looking, but she couldn't deny the heady rush when eyeing a physically fit specimen.

"Morning, ladies. On your way over to Hazel's?"

"We are," Jackie said, bending to address Owen through Kit's window. "I'm hoping things look better in the daylight."

Kit almost laughed, knowing full well that Jackie found their immediate view fine indeed.

Owen shook his head, hands on hips, as his eyes scanned his neighbors' yards. They were all littered with damaged trees from the storm, every single one. He seemed oblivious to Kit's and Jackie's stares. "Don't count on it. But I heard confirmation on the morning news that there weren't any fatalities. Thank God for that."

"I can't thank you enough for helping my grandmother like you did. Both you and your son," Kit said, marveling that he was already outside, cleaning up his own yard before eight. "Were you and both of your sons out all night?"

"Not all night." He shrugged, as if dismissing her gratitude. "Did she check out all right when your aunt took her in?"

"She did. Marge sent me a text this morning, so cell service must have come back up at some point. I'm sure I'll see them both today. I was hoping to figure out what we're dealing with over there before Grandma comes back."

Owen nodded, smacked his palm on the roof of Jackie's car, then stepped back. "This can wait if you'd like me to head over there with you now to check things out."

"Absolutely not," Kit said. "I appreciate the offer, but you've already done plenty. We'll be careful. See to your own place."

He looked over his shoulder, toward the mess in his front yard. "I suppose you're right. The sooner I get back to it, the quicker I can go see where else I can be of service. Adam headed over to the hospital to see if he could help down there an hour before I even dragged my tired carcass out of bed. He left a note. Logan didn't get back here until sunup, so I'm letting him sleep. Though I'm not sure how anyone can sleep through the racket of this chainsaw."

Jackie nodded, then put her car back into gear and crept away from the curb. "I'll call you later and let you know what we find."

"Sounds good. I'll look forward to your call!" He turned back to his fallen tree, slipping the ear protection back into place.

Any other day, Kit would have teased Jackie about the definite back-and-forth flirtation going on between her and Owen, but her mind was already skipping ahead to what they might find at her grandmother's. Given all the damage in town, how long would it take her to hire professional contractors to help with repairs? Someone had said the old garage was likely beyond repair. If that was the case, it would have to be hauled away.

Then she remembered her old Mustang.

In the bright light of day, now that they knew Hazel was safe and no one had died, Kit let herself feel the anguish over likely losing her old car. Even though she hadn't driven it in a long time, she'd imagined it someday restored to pristine condition: a bright cherry red with a spotless white leather interior. She'd imagined driving her old friends out to the beach like she used to when they were teenagers. She'd even researched what it would cost to restore it. Fixing it up might have made for a fun fiftieth birthday present to herself. Now that might not even be possible. What if the damage to the garage also smashed the Mustang beyond repair?

She thought back to her senior year of high school and how hard she'd fought to prevent her father from taking the Mustang when he got out of prison. It was the day after her senior prom, and for Kit, it still ranked as one of the worst days of her life; even worse than the day they sent her father to jail, ripping their family apart.

Her father should have had one year remaining in his ten-year prison sentence, but they released him early. He showed up at Hazel's front door without warning and with a new wife on his arm.

Kit and her brothers had thought their parents were still married.

For Kit, that awful day reinforced one of the hardest lessons every person learned eventually: life could change in an instant. Hazel kept him from stealing her car, but he stole something even more precious.

He'd obliterated the innocent perception Kit had held of him. She'd glamorized her memories of him and all he'd done to hold their family together despite her mother's addictions. But the stranger at the door, all those years ago, bore little resemblance to the father she thought she'd known.

Bless Hazel for stepping in. Her grandmother saved her Mustang that day, much as she'd saved her and her siblings from falling into the foster care system when both of their parents failed them.

It was Kit's turn to step up and help save her grandmother's home. She owed the woman that, and so much more.

"Hazel is going to be *livid* when she sees what that tree did to her front porch," Jackie said, slamming her door and moving to the flower-lined walk that led to Hazel's house.

Kit joined her on the cobblestones. "She certainly is. Her old neighbor is lucky he's in the nursing home. Hopefully she won't take her frustrations out on his poor renters. Come on. Let's see if we can figure out what we're dealing with beyond the porch."

Jackie pulled on the pair of work gloves she'd borrowed from her dad. "Where do you want to start?"

Kit headed for the backyard. Jackie followed her around the side of the house to where they'd found Hazel the night before. Her grandmother was going to be fine, but she still needed to know the state of her old car. "I'm not going to be able to concentrate until I know what happened to my Mustang. Call me selfish, but I can't help it."

"That doesn't make you selfish," Jackie assured her, following close behind. "That makes you human. I've been wondering about it, too. No matter what we find, just keep telling yourself how relieved you are that your grandmother is safe."

"I know. I know."

Kit stepped around a toppled wicker end table that must have blown off the porch when the tornado passed by. She groaned as she rounded the west corner of the house and spied the condition of her grandfather's garage. Even though he'd been dead for decades, she still liked to picture him in there tinkering.

She could no longer do that.

Only the north wall remained standing. The other three were either flat on the ground or jutting out at odd angles, propped up by whatever was still housed inside the old garage. The collapsed roof spanned from the top of the one remaining upright wall to the ground, making the whole mess resemble a decrepit old sailboat.

Three years earlier, after a few too many fender benders, her grandmother had begrudgingly given up her driver's license and sold her Buick sedan. So, other than Kit's Mustang, only old junk remained inside. Tony, Kit's brother, had asked if he could have some of their grandfather's old tools. He'd inherited Grandpa Walter's love of woodworking. This hobby had ultimately saved their grandfather's old tools, and that gave Kit some level of comfort.

"Where was the Mustang parked?" Jackie asked, a hint of confusion in her tone.

Kit was confused, too. "It should have been in the stall along the south wall."

How can that portion of the collapsed building sit so flat to the ground?

"I don't think the Mustang is in there."

"But that's impossible," Kit said, "isn't it?"

But she realized Jackie had to be right. There was no way her car wouldn't be visible in the jumbled mess of lumber and debris that remained.

She picked her way over to the south side of the garage. The yard was a jumbled mess.

"Be careful, Kit. There's some glass and nails in the grass. Your tennis shoes can't protect your feet against that stuff."

"Where the hell is my car?!" Kit asked, moving toward the collapsed structure despite her friend's advice.

The crunch of tires on gravel and the quick *tap-tap* of a horn caught their attention.

Jackie held a hand over her eyes against the bright morning sun. "Who's that?"

Kit didn't recognize the late model Lincoln Town Car rolling up in the alley. "No idea."

They watched as an old man, slightly stooped, eased out of the driver's seat. He waved a greeting once he was upright. "Morning, ladies!"

Kit sighed. How would they get anything done if curious locals started stopping by? She suspected this was one of her grandmother's nosy neighbors, though she didn't recognize him. Maybe he'd move along if she visited with him for a minute or two. She needed to figure out where her Mustang had disappeared to before she lost her mind.

"Good morning. Please, don't come any closer," she said, holding a hand, palm out, to the elderly man. "As you can see, we have a mess on our hands. I don't want you to step on something and get hurt."

A door slammed and Kit saw another white-haired head exit the Lincoln on the passenger's side. "Morning, honey!"

"That's Hazel!" Jackie said, stating the obvious.

The older woman never moved quickly anymore, but the hobble told Kit she was in pain. She hurried through the mess to reach her grandmother's side, forgetting about her missing car for the moment. Hazel rounded the front bumper of the car and leaned against the hood as her granddaughter reached her side.

"Grandma, what are you doing here? It's barely eight in the morning. You never get up before nine, and you had a terrible scare last night! You should still be in bed, taking it easy at Marge's. How do you feel?"

Kit gasped when she caught sight of the greenish-purple bruise covering the upper left portion of Hazel's face, but her grandmother gave her a dismissive headshake.

"Don't worry about me, dear. You know how easily I bruise. It looks far worse than it feels."

"It looks like you went five rounds with a heavyweight boxer, and you didn't come out on top," Jackie said, coming over to stand beside Hazel, too. "I agree with Kit. You should be home in bed."

"*This* is my home," Hazel replied, her arms crossed in front of her chest. "And I needed to make sure it was still standing."

"You knew perfectly well that it's still standing, Grandma. It was still standing when Marge took you to the hospital last night." Kit left out the part about the tree that crashed into the front of the house after Hazel had already left. There was time for that bad news later. "Please. Go to Marge's and rest. Come back later, after I've cleaned things up a little. I don't want you getting upset over this. And speaking of Marge, where is she?"

Hazel stepped away from the car, clucking her tongue at what remained of her garage and ignoring the two younger women.

The mystery man stepped up to her grandmother's side, offering his arm as support. "Oh my. This doesn't look good," he said.

The sound of another car door opening snagged Kit's attention. A teenager climbed out of the back of the Lincoln, flicking his head to flip long bangs out of his eyes.

Who are these people with my grandmother?

Kit cleared her throat as she glanced between the teenager and the old man. "Grandma, I believe introductions are in order?"

Hazel paused, glancing over at her granddaughter. "Of course. Where are my manners? Kit, Jackie, this is Floyd Nelson. A dear friend of mine. And this young man is Isaac, Floyd's grandson. He's staying with him for a bit. Floyd thought we might need a strong young back over here today, so Isaac is here to help." She turned her attention back to her escort, patting his liver-spotted arm in hers. "You were right to insist he come, Floyd. Looks like we have lots of work to do."

There was no way Kit was going to allow her grandmother to stay here. She didn't even know how much damage the house had suffered yet. The old woman would be in the way. Besides, she should be resting after her traumatic night.

Then Kit remembered the perplexing issue of her missing car.

"Grandma, where's my Mustang?"

Her grandmother looked at her in confusion, and Kit's pulse jumped with alarm. Had someone stolen the car right out from under her grandmother's nose?

"The Mustang?" Hazel repeated. "Why, whatever do you mean, dear?"

Her concern over her missing car ramped up even higher with Hazel's apparent surprise at her question. "Grandma, my car has been parked in this garage for years. But I guess I haven't checked on it for quite a while. I knew I couldn't drive it when I was home for the reunion last summer because of issues with the motor, so I didn't think to look in on it then."

"Hello?!" a voice floated back to them from somewhere near the front yard, barely discernable over the squawking of an irate robin above.

Kit nearly growled at yet another interruption. How were they ever going to get anything done if this place turned into Grand Central Station? Unless it was someone from the utility company—that would be good news. Those wires dangling up high, next to the robin, would be dangerous if they were hot.

"I'll run up front and see who that is," she said, pointing at her grandmother and this Floyd fellow. She noticed Floyd's grandson was leaning against the Lincoln, all of his attention concentrated on the phone in his hand. "You three stay put. I'll be right back."

"That sounded like Dean," Jackie said, looking toward the house.

"I thought that, too, for a second," Kit said. "But it can't be. Dean is out of town for work. He isn't even due back to Minneapolis until late Thursday. There's no way he's in Ruby Shores."

She picked her way back the way they'd come, pulling up short when someone rounded the corner and a familiar face came into view.

Jackie was right. *But how? Why?*

"Dean?!"

"God, there you are! Kit, do you ever answer your blasted phone?" the man said, stepping toward her with arms extended.

A rush of emotion crashed into her, and she collapsed into his arms, welcoming their strength as they encircled her waist. She stayed there for a moment, shaken by how much she hadn't even realized she needed him.

After a moment, she pulled back, looking into his face. "What are you doing here?"

"Well, hello to you, too," Dean said, smiling down at her. "You worried me when I couldn't reach you. I got home early—the meeting was a bust—and I wanted to surprise you. I was the one surprised when your house was dark and I couldn't reach you by phone. When I heard about the tornado in Ruby Shores, I took a gamble that you came here for your grandmother."

She shook her head, hardly able to believe he was standing in front of her. "You came all this way, and you didn't even know for sure that I was here?"

"It's only a two-hour drive. And I'm really glad I came. It looks like you could use my help." Nodding toward the ruined garage, his face turned grim. "Is your grandmother all right?"

"Yes, yes, she is. In fact, she's back there, in the alley, on the other side of this mess," she said. "Believe it or not, the storm caught the old fool outside. She was trying to save her tomato plants."

"I heard that!" her grandmother yelled, causing them both to grin.

Dean laughed. "I thought she was hard of hearing!"

"So did I. Come on, I'll take you back to her. I was trying to convince her she should rest at Marge's house, not here. I can deal with this mess for her."

He grabbed her hand. "*We* can deal with this mess."

Nodding to acknowledge his correction, she squeezed his hand and laid her head on his shoulder, again appreciating his surprise appearance more than she would have guessed. Then she remembered the mystery of her missing Mustang.

As she led him toward the alley, she shook her head. "Dean, you aren't going to believe this. I am so ticked. My Mustang. It's gone! I was just trying to figure out what happened to it when you got here. Grandma seems confused. We need to sort this out."

Before she could take another step, Dean paused, tugging her to a stop. Had she almost stepped on something? But the path in front of her looked safe. She tried to pull her hand from his, but he held tight.

"Come on, Dean, I need to talk to Grandma."

"Wait."

Perplexed, she spun toward him. "What? Can't it wait? I don't want Grandma to get too tired standing back there waiting for us."

"*I* took the Mustang."

His simple statement was like an icy bucket of water to the face.

"You what?"

He reached for her other hand again, pulling her a step closer. "Look, Kit, it was supposed to be a surprise. I know how much you want to fix up the Mustang. I thought it would be fun to surprise you with it for your birthday. Your grandmother agreed. I had it hauled out of here a few weeks ago. I know it isn't your birthday for a while, but restorations take time."

"But why would you do that?"

Dean shrugged. The left half of his mouth tilted up. "It isn't every day the woman you are *hopefully* going to marry one of these days turns fifty."

She cringed, though she couldn't say if her visceral reaction was because of his barb about her hesitation to set a wedding date or the reminder of her impending age. At only forty-four, Dean probably didn't grasp the mixed feelings most people feel as they approach the half-century mark.

Finally, she said, "My grandmother is quite the actress, then. She sold me on the whole 'looking confused' act."

"I made her promise not to tell you what I was up to. I bet she was trying to figure out how to spin it so she wouldn't give away my surprise."

Kit breathed a sigh of relief. "You're telling me no one stole my Mustang, then?"

Laughing, Dean released her hands and wrapped an arm around her shoulder, angling her toward the alley. "I'll spin by the shop where they're working on it to make sure their building doesn't look like Hazel's garage after last night, but I'd say the odds are in your favor and your car is safe. Now, we should go let your poor grandma off the hook. It looks to me like she has enough to worry about without having to cover for me."

CHAPTER FIVE

D EAN KEPT HIS ARM around Kit's shoulders as they navigated the debris-strewn backyard toward the alley. He hoped she couldn't sense the way his knees trembled as they walked. He'd been a jumble of nerves ever since coming home to that shocking wedding invitation in the stack of mail in his apartment's mailbox.

It wasn't until his mind registered the significance of the return address label in the upper left-hand corner that he realized why the way his name was scrawled across the front of the envelope looked so hauntingly familiar.

His daughter was getting married.

A daughter he'd never met or claimed.

A daughter Kit knew nothing about.

The girl's mother had chosen to move on without him, all those years ago, before the birth. He hadn't resisted when she faded out of his life, pregnant with his child, but it still weighed heavily on his heart.

Twenty years can feel like a lifetime, but when he held the weighty ivory missive in his hand, his mind took him right back to those turbulent years. It was all he could think about as he raced to Ruby Shores to find Kit. By the time he'd arrived, he'd decided he would tell her everything if things were all right at her grandmother's house. But if she was up to her neck in storm cleanup, or any other drama with the aging woman who'd raised her, Dean might wait to discuss his past with Kit until after she returned from her trip to Hawaii with her old friends.

He knew all too well how heavily family issues could weigh on a person.

After losing his father to cancer at fourteen, Dean had stepped into the role of man of the house, just like he'd promised. His mother, devastated by the death of the only man she'd ever loved, struggled to serve as the sole parental figure to her four sons. She'd needed Dean, her oldest, and he'd needed the distraction of responsibility to help ease the ache in his heart.

For the next ten years, he'd helped his mom keep his three younger brothers from self-destructing. He worked multiple jobs to help with expenses, and earned an academic scholarship to a state university where he scored high enough grades to land a decent tech job when he graduated. Two of his three brothers followed his example, working hard and earning degrees. Only the youngest failed to meet their dying father's wish that all of his sons gain a college education.

"You win some, you lose some," his brother Nick would say when Dean reminded him of their dad's wishes.

Then things took that complicated twist he'd come to regret.

He'd met Erin Morales at a work conference. They were colleagues. Erin was a few years older, and even more driven to succeed in her career than Dean, which wasn't easy given the way men dominated the field twenty years ago. They dated for a few months before she took a promotion that required her to move across the country. Dean still felt obligated to stay near his family. They weren't done raising his youngest brother yet, and it would take a miracle to get him through high school.

And so, her move marked the end of what wasn't much more than a casual dating relationship.

That would have been the end of it, if not for that other letter he'd received from Erin, a few months after she'd moved away. She'd felt compelled to let him know she was pregnant. He was the father, but she wanted absolutely nothing from him, other than for him to know that they'd created another life together.

The letter arrived the same week he was battling with school officials to allow his kid brother to graduate. Their mother had fallen into a well of depression, sure her deceased husband was frowning down on her from the heavens over her inept parenting abilities. To her, it wasn't enough that she'd managed, with Dean's help, to get the oldest three through both high school and college just fine.

Dean remembered the confusion he'd felt when he first read Erin's letter. It took him completely off-guard. His confusion turned to anger. How dare she decide he couldn't play a role in the child's life? His own father had been an amazing role model, and Dean knew he wanted to be a father to his own children someday.

He just hadn't planned on "someday" coming so soon. Shouldn't he be more involved in such a critical decision regarding his child?

But as he watched his brother saunter across the stage at graduation with a false sense of confidence on full display, Dean sensed more trouble ahead within his immediate family. The family he'd promised his father to help raise.

Anger morphed to a deep sense of shame. Erin's stance to take one hundred percent responsibility for the child they'd conceived together let him off the hook, and he was relieved. When he was finally honest with himself about this, he felt guilty.

That might have been the end of it.

It wasn't.

He never forgot he had a child out in the world somewhere. It was years before he even found out if Erin had given birth to a girl or a boy. He didn't reach out to her, telling himself he was following her wishes, but the guilt still consumed him. He didn't say anything about Erin or the baby to his mother or brothers. He told himself he'd have a family of his own someday—when the time was right, and the right woman came along.

Then he met Kit.

Kit was the right woman for him in every way—except one.

She didn't want kids.

But he'd seen the way she was with children. When the two of them would visit her friend Jackie and spend time with her twin girls, Kit lit up. They wouldn't ever have a family biologically, given Kit was approaching fifty years old, but there were other options.

When it became apparent that they would build a life together, Dean should have told Kit about the child. But it was easier to leave it in his past.

He forgot that the past has a funny way of butting its head into the present.

Like Erin, Dean also met Kit through work, but in a less direct way. Kit's role with the environmental consulting company where she worked as a conservation biologist was to help restore and protect natural wildlife habitats for a variety of species. Her passion was butterflies. Dean's employer used artificial intelligence to monitor for changes in butterfly migration patterns to help determine the "why" behind the shifts.

Two years into his relationship with Kit, Dean found himself on a new project, and his professional path crossed with Erin again.

This time Erin was in a different place emotionally. Amazingly, she was interested in trying again with Dean, after all these years. But he was fully committed to Kit.

Erin told him all about Summer then, their sixteen-year-old daughter. He'd done his best to hide his emotional turmoil over the details she finally shared with him about the child, worried his old flame might use it to pull him back to her. He was tempted to ask to meet the girl, but he knew there would be a price to pay for such a meeting, and he wasn't willing to pay it.

Still, word of Erin's interest in Dean got back to Kit at one of his company's summer picnics. It proved to be a rough patch for the couple, but he stayed focused on his current relationship, and eventually they saw their way through Kit's jealousy. He still didn't tell Kit that he shared a child with the other woman—though *share* wasn't quite the right word.

Summer would be twenty years old now, and she was getting *married*. Wasn't she too young? Not that he had any right to voice his concern.

Erin had included a brief note in the wedding invitation, encouraging him to attend because their daughter wanted to meet him. In the note, Erin mentioned that she'd be there with her own fiancé. She was a smart woman, and probably assumed Dean would be more likely to attend if he wasn't worried about her pressuring him to reignite their relationship again. Erin promised that this was all about what Summer wanted. The young woman wanted to meet her father, but with no strings attached.

He thought Summer sounded far more mature than her twenty years. Maybe she *was* ready for marriage.

Dean realized he needed to finally be honest with Kit about everything. The invitation was a sign that the time had come. If Kit was going to be his wife, she deserved to know that he had a daughter.

He hated to dump this bombshell on Kit right before her long-awaited girls' trip. But maybe the timing was actually good. She could talk through all the ramifications that Dean's long-lost daughter could have on their relationship with her best girlfriends. He knew Kit would need time to process something so significant, and who better to do it with than her besties?

Regardless, he had to tell her, because he wasn't sure he could continue to go through life ignoring the daughter he'd never met. Especially knowing she would now likely be the only child he'd ever have, given Kit's stance on a family.

He'd hurried over to Kit's place, expecting to find her at home on a Sunday evening, and probably packing. But she wasn't there. Then he heard about the storm that hit her hometown.

Now he was going to have to wait to tell her again. Kit was notably upset about the situation with her grandmother. It would be better to keep the news to himself until she got home from Hawaii. He'd pick a more opportune time to fill her in. Summer's wedding wasn't until August, so he had an entire month.

He felt the tightness in Kit's shoulders and across her back when they'd hugged in her grandmother's yard. *Yes, she has enough to deal with right now.* He hated keeping secrets from her, especially one of this magnitude. If he didn't play things right, he could lose her. Kit expected honesty. She'd grown up without enough of it, and she deserved it from him.

He worried he might have waited too long.

"Kit? Was Jackie right? Was that Dean we heard?"

Despite his internal battle, Dean grinned at Hazel's voice. "She sounds pretty spunky to me."

Kit shook her head as she squirmed out from under his arm. "Not only is she spunky, she showed up with some old guy named Floyd this morning who I've never met."

"Really? Floyd, huh?" Dean asked, intrigued. He'd never known Kit's grandmother to spend time with a man. Her husband had died while Kit still lived here, before she'd even graduated from high school. That was a long time to be alone.

Hazel threw her hands up in the air when she spotted them. "As I live and breathe! Good to see you, Dean. Kit here was just asking about her old Mustang."

Dean tried not to laugh at the suggestive lift of Hazel's eyebrows, as if she were silently pleading with him to clear up her granddaughter's confusion. He stepped forward and gave the stocky older woman a warm hug. His own grandparents were all long gone, and he considered her family. "Don't worry, Hazel. I fessed up. She knows I took the Mustang in for an overhaul."

"Mustang?" A young man Dean hadn't noticed looked up from his phone. "What year?"

Dean kept one hand on Hazel's shoulder as he turned to the boy. He looked thirteen, maybe fourteen. "A classic. A '66."

The kid nodded. "I prefer the '65, but '66 was a good model year, too."

Kit gave the boy a sideways look. "You think you know cars, do you? I'm sorry, what was your name again?"

The teen pushed away from the car he'd been leaning against and dropped his phone into his pocket. Dean braced for the vintage car lecture he feared Kit might launch into while wondering who this kid belonged to.

"Isaac," the boy said. The grin he offered Kit seemed to take the punch out of her. "And I was just kidding. Everyone knows 1966 was the best year for muscle cars, including the Mustang. Yeah, I know a little about cars. I used to work on them with my dad."

Dean picked up on the past tense.

"My grandson here tells me he wants to work on old cars for a living," Floyd said, smiling at the young man.

Floyd earned himself an eye roll.

Kit cleared her throat. "I appreciate you bringing Grandma by, Floyd, and bringing your grandson to help, but I'm afraid I'm not quite ready for another set of hands quite yet. Maybe tomorrow?"

Dean noticed a look pass between Hazel and her friend, this Floyd guy. Something was up. "Kit's right, Hazel. You should rest," he spoke up. "I'm going to head back to Minneapolis tomorrow afternoon for a work dinner, but I could pick you up in the morning. I'll bring you back here so you can see what kind of progress we're making. How does that sound?"

Hazel let out a lengthy sigh. "All of you need to quit treating me like a child. I'll rest later. Right now, we were hoping to go play brunch bingo at the senior citizen's center. It starts at ten."

Isaac groaned. Dean caught the pain in the boy's eyes. He obviously had no desire to chaperone his grandfather and Hazel over a hot game of bingo. Dean wanted to protect the kid from such a boring fate, but he also suspected Kit didn't want the boy hanging around here, getting in her hair. A quick glance at his watch told him the garage where he'd taken the Mustang should be open by now.

He had an idea.

"Say, Isaac, if you like old cars, you should see the collection over at the garage where they're working on the Mustang."

The smile was back. "That sounds better than bingo. But I doubt they'd want a kid like me showing up and asking to see their cars."

Dean couldn't have said why the simple statement about a *kid like me* tugged at his heart. "After last night's storm, I have a legitimate excuse to stop by the shop and make sure they didn't suffer any damage. Why don't you ride along with me and check things out? Unless you'd rather go play bingo? And as long as it's all right with your grandfather, of course."

Isaac snorted. "It's not like I need his permission for every move I make."

Floyd looked stricken at the boy's sass. Hazel's hands came up to rest on her hips. "Isaac, we've talked about this. You need to treat Floyd with respect."

It was Isaac's turn to look surprised—embarrassed, even. "Yes, Ms. Hazel. You're right. Sorry, Floyd."

It surprised Dean when the teen didn't call the older man Grandfather, but he didn't comment on it. "Mind if he bums around with me for an hour or two, Floyd?"

Floyd checked his watch. "Don't mind a bit. As long as he won't be a bother to you?"

"He isn't a bother. Kit, Jackie, how about you ladies? I really am curious about the state of things over at the shop. Mind if I go check things out? Then I'll come back here and start cleaning things up outside."

Kit nodded, pulling a pair of gloves out of the pocket of her jeans. "That would give Jackie and me a chance to see what we are dealing with here and make a game plan. Go, we'll see you all later."

Dean glanced at Isaac, about to tell him to buckle up as the boy settled into the passenger seat. But it wasn't necessary. He supposed kids these days grew up wearing seat belts.

That reminded him. He needed to ask the guy doing the restoration job to replace the frayed belts in the Mustang with new ones.

"He isn't really my grandpa."

Dean started the car, not sure he'd heard Isaac correctly. "What's that?"

"Floyd. He isn't really my grandpa. But he likes to say he is."

What was Dean supposed to say to that? All he wanted to do was let the kid see some cars and give Hazel a break.

"Okay," he hedged, considering whether to pick up the thread of conversation Isaac offered or change the subject completely. The kid had something he wanted to say, clearly. Dean's years in the Big Brother program had taught him you need to listen when teenagers are ready to talk. You might only get one shot at hearing them out on what's bothering them. "If he isn't your grandfather, who is he to you?"

Isaac picked at a hole in his jeans. Was the rip part of the design, or were the pants simply falling apart? "He's my stepmother's father. I'm an orphan, kind of."

Dean's heart skipped a beat. What makes someone *kind of* an orphan? He nodded, waiting to let Isaac take the conversation at his own pace.

The light turned red, and Dean watched three massive dump trucks filled with broken tree branches pass through the intersection; limbs waved as if part of a parade rather than heading for the landfill.

"Did you know my left eye isn't real? It's a prosthesis. Pretty cool, huh? Most people can't even tell. Want me to take it out and show it to you?"

Dean smirked. Isaac reminded him of his little brothers. They never shut up when they were younger. Some kids are tight-lipped, especially as teenagers, but those rare few are an open book. At least about some things. "No, I don't want you to show it to me. What happened to your real one?"

"Lost it. Car accident."

The light turned again and Dean continued in the shop's direction, one hand draped over the steering wheel. He wondered what else the boy might have lost in the accident, given his earlier comment about being an orphan. *Kind of.*

Isaac didn't keep him guessing. "I lost my eye and my mom. I was only three, so I don't really remember her much. Only from pictures."

"Oh, man . . . I'm sorry to hear that, Isaac. It sucks to lose a parent, especially so young."

The boy's hand moved to the window control, lowering it a few inches before putting it back up and reaching for the radio. The air-conditioner was already battling the summer heat and humidity, and Dean was glad he didn't have to ask the kid to leave the window alone. "I'm not looking for sympathy. I told you about my eye and my mom because it's why I want to work on old cars."

Not following the line of reasoning, Dean hoped the kid would clarify. Either the boy lacked in the storytelling department, or the situation with Erin and Summer had him too distracted. And what would Kit's reaction be when she found out about his secret? He couldn't go five minutes without his brain flipping back to that worrisome topic.

"Are you going to ask me why the accident makes me want to work on old cars?"

Strange kid. But he'd play along. "What's the connection?"

"My dad knew everything there was to know about muscle cars. He could take them down to the frame and then rebuild them, all without looking in a manual. When he didn't know how to fix something, his partner at the shop usually did."

Dean had to slow the car when he encountered a downed oak tree sprawled across the road. Two city employees worked to move it out of the way. "And?"

"And Mom was driving an old Camaro that Dad had rebuilt for her. A drunk driver hit us head on. I was in the backseat. The trunk lid had stuck, so she piled the groceries next to her. I was in a booster seat. Those old cars don't have much for safety features. Definitely no air bags. Mom hit her head on the side window, and then the steering wheel. She never had a chance."

Dean winced, sparing a glance at his passenger. "Man, that's awful. How do you know all this? You were so young when it happened."

Isaac's expression soured. "I know. I *wish* I didn't know so much. But after the accident, my dad was obsessed about what he should have done differently to save her. At first, I thought it was just grief, and over time he'd move on. And in a way he did. He married again when I was ten. But he never quit talking about the accident. They made older cars with more steel than cars today. Less plastic. In theory, wouldn't that make them safer if they could incorporate some of today's safety equipment into those earlier models?"

The shop that held Kit's Mustang came into view. Dean sighed in relief when the only obvious storm damage he could see was a peeled-back section of metal roofing. During the drive from Hazel's, he'd noticed heavier damage on the occasional building, as if the tornado had skipped along, wreaking havoc, then bounced up out of harm's way before descending again, farther down the street.

Isaac was still talking. "He didn't figure out how to make those old cars safer, but I will. I'm going to get my engineering degree, gain some tech skills, then build a business that retrofits as many cars that are out on the road without modern safety features as I can. My mom would probably feel like that was an admirable career path, don't you think? Hey, is this it?"

"Yep, this is it. And I think she'd be proud of you, no matter what kind of work you choose."

Dean parked and got out, not bothering to wait for Isaac. He wasn't far behind, still talking.

The kid had brought up an interesting topic, though. What if they could do more than just replace seat belts to make Kit's Mustang safer? He knew she'd love to drive it around Minneapolis, especially in the summer. So the safer, the better.

By the time he reached the front entrance, Isaac was at his side again. "I doubt they've actually started working on Kit's car yet, but there are lots of vintage models in here at all different stages of restoration. Plenty for you to see."

The teen nodded. His eyes flashed with interest, but his mouth had finally stopped talking.

Dean nodded to two technicians inside, but kept an eye out for the owner. Isaac was already wandering around the front portion of the building that served as a showroom. Dean left him to explore, figuring he couldn't get into too much trouble, and wandered toward the back shop area. The racket of an impact wrench filled the air. The whole place smelled of oil, old leather, and fresh paint.

Here they made old things new again.

That was when he understood Isaac's vision. There had to be a way to make these cars *better* than when they rolled off the assembly line decades ago. Isaac didn't have the knowledge to pull it off yet, but maybe Dean could help him. It certainly piqued his interest.

"I've never seen anything like this," Isaac said, catching up with Dean. "Dad worked on old cars, but he only kept a few in his shop at a time. And their equipment was secondhand, or even thirdhand. I had no idea there were so many vintage models around this part of the state."

Dean remembered feeling a similar sense of awe on his first visit. "I did research before bringing Kit's car here. I wanted to take it to the best place I could find. I was willing to haul it somewhere else in the country, even, but it turned out that wasn't necessary. This guy's reputation is first class. They're booked out for months, but since Kit grew up around here and they'd done a little work on the Mustang way back when her grandfather was still alive, they squeezed me in."

A car door slammed and footsteps approached.

"Dean Adams. Good to see you, man. Did you swing by to make sure your little lady's wheels are still in one piece after that mother of a storm last night?"

Dean turned to the voice and gave the short, wiry man a fist bump. "Gibb. Glad to see your place is still standing. Be a shame to lose any of these beauties."

"They've survived this long. A little wind and rain aren't gonna take 'em out. My building took a bit of a beating, but we can fix it."

Isaac took a step forward and held a hand up in greeting. "Hi, I'm Isaac. Great place ya got here."

Gibb narrowed his eyes at the boy, as if just realizing Dean wasn't alone. He looked between his paying customer and Isaac. "Yours?"

"Nope. He stopped by Kit's grandmother's place to help with storm cleanup. Say, that reminds me. Good thing her car was in here. The garage where Kit stored it came down in that storm last night. I doubt even *you* could have fixed the old girl up if she'd still been parked inside." Dean motioned toward the boy. "Wolff Gibb, this is Isaac. Seems he inherited a love of old cars, so I let him tag along. His dad used to work on them, and now he wants to, too."

Gibb's eyes swung back to Isaac. "What's your old man's name?"

Isaac shuffled his feet. "Kane Nash."

The shop owner's expression softened and he shook his head, as if the name meant something to him, too. "Nash was a master with motor rebuilds. Met him at a swap meet years ago. We did business together a time or two. Hell of a thing that happened. My condolences."

A shiver of unease hit Dean. Isaac had suffered even more loss than his eye and his mother.

"Thanks," the boy muttered. "Wish I'd have learned more from him before he died."

Gibb nodded, keeping a close eye on Isaac. "I know Dean lives over in Minneapolis. What about you? Do you live around here?"

Isaac shrugged. "I do now."

Gibb seemed to consider this. After a beat, he shoved his hands in the back pockets of his oil splattered jeans and rocked back and forth on the balls of his boot-clad feet. "You need at least a high school diploma to work here, but if you get bored and want to learn a few things, pop in and watch. Just don't get in the way."

Dean found Gibb's comment about high school graduates interesting. It reminded him that looks can be deceiving. Even though Gibb could be mistaken for a high school dropout himself based on his unkept appearance, Dean knew he was a well-educated man, including a master's degree from a prestigious university. It wasn't something the shop owner was likely to bring up in conversation, but his set of framed diplomas hung directly behind his desk in the shop's main office.

Isaac straightened at Gibb's offer, his shoulders pulling back and an eager expression stealing over his face. Here was another important reminder for Dean—even if a kid loses his parents, others can step up and offer guidance. He used to be better about doing that kind of thing himself, but he'd gotten slack. Had anyone stepped forward to play the role of father for his own daughter, when Dean hadn't bothered?

"I'd like that," Isaac was saying. "I know how to stay out of the way. You won't even know I'm here."

But as the boy uttered that last sentence, his expressive face changed yet again, his eyes growing shuttered.

What secrets does this poor kid carry? Dean wondered. *Secrets eat away at you, kid.*

It was a fact Dean knew all too well.

CHAPTER SIX

WHILE KIT APPRECIATED THE offer of a strong, young back to help with the storm cleanup, she needed time to assess the damages and formulate a game plan before she could put Floyd's grandson to work. Dean came to the rescue again by inviting the boy to go with him to check on her Mustang. He'd already driven the two hours to Ruby Shores, just in case Hazel needed help and Kit was already there. As if all of that weren't enough, he'd even arranged to have her Mustang refurbished for her birthday. She was lucky to have a standup guy like Dean in her life. He'd proven time and again that he'd do anything for her.

She'd watched Floyd drive a drooping Hazel away, wishing her grandmother was going back to Marge's house to rest instead of heading to brunch bingo. She'd managed to pull Floyd aside, while Hazel was talking with Dean, and she asked him to avoid driving by the front of the house. She couldn't prevent her grandmother from finding out about her wrecked porch forever, but she could try to delay the discovery while the older woman recovered physically from her ordeal.

After they left, Kit scanned the toppled garage and the back of Hazel's house, trying to decide where to start. "We should get a better idea of what we are dealing with. Come on."

She and Jackie picked their way through the yard and up the littered back stairs. Kit was eager to check the second floor. She moaned when she spied the cracked front window in the living room. Bent tree branches pressed against the glass, threatening to thrust their way in if the weakened glass gave way. Last night's storm kept finding new ways to leave damage in its wake. Jackie looked concerned, too, and Kit held her breath as she crossed the room, praying the window wouldn't give way and pepper them with sharp pieces of broken glass.

"Are you coming? I want to see how many windows need to be boarded up on the second level."

Her friend paused. "I'm going to run back to the kitchen for something I can take notes with. We need to get a rough estimate of how much plywood to pick up. Then I'll run and see if I can still find any. I'm sure they'll sell out at the local hardware store soon, if they haven't already."

Kit climbed the stairs, her footsteps silent on the carpet. Jackie laughed from the base of the stairs. "I bet you don't even realize you still avoid the squeaky board on the fifth step. Just like we did when we were teenagers."

"Some habits die hard," Kit said, grinning over her shoulder.

As Jackie went searching for a pen and paper, Kit continued upstairs, letting her fingertips trail over the many framed family photos lining the stairway, the glass unbroken. She noted both the differences and the similarities between the current photo gallery and the one that used to hang on the wall during that earlier tornado that kept springing forth from her memory. All the pictures of her parents were gone. The kids' high school graduation pictures now held the places of honor at the very top.

On the landing halfway up, the stairs turned at a ninety-degree angle. Kit sighed in relief when the window there was still intact, but she knew they'd find a different story in the bedrooms. She'd spied broken windowpanes from out back.

The air was hot, already sticky with humidity, as she reached the top of the stairs. With the power off the air-conditioner was useless of course, but that alone couldn't explain the sheer weight of the air. There had to be multiple broken windows up here based on the amount of air flowing in.

During her teen years, Kit had claimed the small bedroom to the right. She froze outside the open door, shocked at the state of her old room. The busted upper pane of the double-hung window was at least one of the culprits behind the telltale humidity. Half of it lay splintered in worrisome puddles of rainwater on the hardwood floor. The more tenacious glass, still clinging to the window frame, jutted out in jagged shards.

The broken window was a problem, but the overall state of her room was even more worrisome. Her bed used to sit below the now-ruined window, and it would have caught the broken glass and rainwater, but it and its frame were gone now. Just last summer she'd slept on that aged mattress while home for her class reunion. The lumpy old thing should have been hard to sleep on, but her body unconsciously adjusted to the most comfortable position, like muscle memory. And, somehow, her back had felt fine each morning.

Where was her bed? She hoped her grandmother hadn't felt the need to order a new one. She was fairly certain she hadn't complained about its sorry condition when she was here. Hazel, like so many seniors, lived on a very limited budget and couldn't afford to be replacing beds in rooms people seldom used anymore.

Cardboard boxes were strewn around the room, some taped shut and labeled with bold black marker, while others remained open and half-filled. A glance inside the closet revealed an empty rod and upper shelf, but a tangle of old shoes still littered the floor.

What was Hazel up to?

With a sigh, Kit kept moving. She'd have to solve the mystery of her old room later. Right now she needed to get the floors mopped up. Hopefully the water hadn't already damaged the wood beyond repair.

The door across the hall was closed. Kit held her breath as she opened it, unsure what she would find in her grandmother's room. Warm, stale air, with an undercurrent of lavender and talcum powder, wafted out, devoid of the humidity prevalent in her childhood room and the hallway.

All the curtains were closed, cloaking the room in shadow. Kit flipped on the wall switch out of habit, and it took her a second to realize that when the light flooded the bedroom it meant the electric company had managed to get the power turned on.

She crossed to the window beside Hazel's bed and pulled the curtain back, thankful to see the glass was still intact. Her grandmother's bed was right where it was supposed to be—though she couldn't actually see it under the piles of clothes stacked on top.

Was her grandmother in the middle of a massive decluttering project? Or was it possible she'd finally accepted their ongoing advice to move into assisted living, where she wouldn't have to work so hard to keep up this big old house all on her own? It would explain what appeared to be an interrupted packing session.

Relieved not to find storm damage in her grandmother's room, Kit pulled the door closed, leaving yet another mystery for another day. She still had to check the third bedroom—the one her brothers had shared as kids—and the bathroom. There could be problems in the attic, too.

Her brothers' old room revealed another mess. Located in the back corner of the house, the bigger bedroom sported not one but two broken windows. The mattresses under the damaged windows—her brothers', still there, unlike her own—had soaked up the rain and caught most of the broken glass. At least the floors were dry.

"What's with your old room?" Jackie asked, appearing in the doorway.

Kit jumped at the sound of her voice, not having heard her coming up the stairs.

"I have no idea. Maybe Grandma finally decided to move somewhere that's easier to keep up."

"If this storm doesn't convince her of that, nothing will. Dean called. Your ringer must still be off. He and that kid finished up at the garage where they're working on your Mustang. He's going to find one of those big roll-off dumpsters to help with cleanup."

"That's a good idea," Kit said. She removed the broken glass before stripping the bedding off the mattress closest to the door, grinning when she noticed her brother's initials carved into the twin bed's headboard. "I never knew Pete did this."

Jackie smiled as she entered the room. "Pete wouldn't even fit in that bed anymore. He's way taller than six feet, isn't he?"

Kit nodded. "I think he ended up five inches taller than Tony. He's, like, six-four or something."

As Kit tossed the mattress pad onto a growing heap of wet bedding, Jackie set a small notebook and pencil on a nearby dresser, then pushed her palms against the mattress top. "This thing is sopping wet. Are you going to keep it? It's seen better days."

The old mattress was stained. It would be tough to dry inside, and if she had it hauled outside, it wasn't going to be worth bringing back in. She sighed. "I don't think it's worth saving. I'll ask that kid—Isaac—to haul it out and toss it for us."

They decided the second mattress, also wet, couldn't be saved either. Kit was sorry they hadn't been able to board up the broken windows the night before.

As the two women continued to check the house, they found undamaged windows in the bathroom at the end of the hall. The attic also looked free of any obvious storm damage, aside from half-filled, strategically placed buckets that meant the roof was already in need of repairs *prior* to the previous day's events. The storm may have only made the roof worse.

Kit filled her arms with the wet bedding from her brothers' old room. "My gut tells me we aren't going to be as lucky in the basement as we were in the attic—if you can call a leaky roof 'lucky.' "

"Hello! Anybody home?" a voice drifted up the stairs.

"Oh wow, it's Annie!" Jackie cried, scooping up a wet comforter and two pillows before heading for the stairs. "I called her earlier this morning to check on them. She said they were heading back from out of town and didn't know if they had any damage at their house or over at the high school yet."

Kit felt the prick of guilt. She'd been so worried about her grandmother that she hadn't even thought to check in on their old friend and her family.

Sometimes she was such a crappy friend.

She was eager to talk to Annie now. Following Jackie down the stairs, Kit vowed to try—again—to keep a broader perspective instead of obsessing with her own issues. It was a nasty habit, as Dean occasionally pointed out to her.

"There you two are," Annie said. She'd let herself in through the back door. Hazel had always insisted the girls come and go like it was their own home. It was nice to see some things hadn't changed. "Is Hazel going to be all right? Jackie thought so when we talked this morning, but I've been worried."

Kit dropped the soiled bedding on the bench beside the front door and gave Annie a quick hug. "She's as ornery as ever. She has cuts and bruises, and they want her to rest because she took a nasty bump to the head, but they don't think she has a concussion. Believe it or not, she already stopped by this morning. I sent her back to Marge's. Doctor's orders. Though I think they're taking a bingo detour first."

Annie's shoulders had visibly relaxed, and she smiled at this last part. "Bingo, huh? That's a relief. When I saw that huge elm on top of her porch, I didn't know what to think."

"She was actually off at the hospital when that sucker came down last night," Jackie said, adding her armload of wet linens on top of Kit's. "We were in here, checking the house, when it came crashing down. I think I might have wet myself. That was scary."

"Heck, I *laugh* and I get a little leakage these days," Annie said, winking at Jackie. "My kids ruined me."

"But we wouldn't trade them for the world, would we?" Jackie said.

Kit felt the familiar sting of exclusion. She would never experience that deep connection that so many women shared, because she'd never be a mother.

"What did you find at home?" Jackie asked. "I'm guessing it wasn't too bad, since you're here."

Annie shook her head, eyeing the front window. "We got lucky. Lots of debris in the yard, but the house is fine. At least at first glance. Henry is going to check the shingles, but I wanted to get over here to help if needed, and to check on Hazel."

"What about the school?" Kit asked.

"I'm assuming, since no one's called me yet, that it's still standing. The maintenance guy stays on top of things for me. I mentioned swinging by there on the way to our house when we pulled into town, but Henry reminded me that a principal's primary responsibility is the kids, not the building. He says I take on too much," she said, waving her hands as if dismissing his observation. "Now, what are we dealing with here? We probably need to at least clip those branches away from this front window, even if we can't move the tree away on our own. That's a lot of pressure."

Kit loved the way her old friend slid right into her helpful mode. She could learn things from Annie.

"Three broken windows upstairs and water to mop up, but otherwise most of the mess is outside. The old garage fell down. That building won't be salvageable." Jackie turned to Kit. "Where can we be of the most help?"

Kit sighed. "Come with me to check the basement? I'm afraid of what I might find."

Clapping her hands, Jackie laughed. "That's right. I forget how creeped out you always get when you have to go down to the basement. Why is that?"

Kit shrugged, brushing past her two friends to head for the door to the lowest level. "Today I'm just worried about water down there. But I blame my mother. She used to say it's haunted. It was probably her twisted way of keeping us in line, and I know better than to believe anything she says, but that one stuck. Plus, it's always so musty."

She tugged at the door, not surprised when it took extra effort to yank it open. Expecting damp air to hit as she descended the stairs, Kit was pleasantly surprised when she could barely detect the musty smell she knew so well.

"It's not that bad," Annie said from a step above. "It just smells like an old basement."

"You're right, this is better than it used to be." A soft hum caught Kit's attention. "Looks like Grandma put a dehumidifier down here. Wonder why she never thought of that before."

Jackie was the last one down the stairs. "What are we looking for?"

"Ghosts," Annie said, wriggling her eyebrows.

"Cute," Kit said, turning her back to them. "I'm hoping this corner over here stayed dry. Water used to seep in through the foundation."

"I actually can't remember ever coming down here." Annie wandered over to an old dresser that matched her in height. "What's in here?"

Kit shrugged. "Like I said, I never liked to come down here. I almost had a heart attack the one time I looked in those drawers. One was full of old wigs that Grandma used to wear. You can imagine what I thought when a bunch of hair popped out at me."

This drew a laugh from both Annie and Jackie.

"I would have loved to have seen that," Jackie said. She ran a hand over the scarred wooden top of Grandpa Walter's old work bench.

"You probably heard me scream all the way over at your house."

"Someday you are going to have to go through all this stuff," Annie said. "Are all these totes full? They don't look very old. Smart not to use cardboard boxes down here if it's usually damp."

Kit eyed the stacks of black totes with surprise. "I have no idea. It's been a while since I've been down here, but those definitely weren't here the last time." She took a step toward the mysterious containers but paused when Jackie groaned. "Did you find water?"

"Yep, you were right, Kit," her friend said. "This whole corner is wet. What's back here?"

Kit would check the totes later. She moved over to stand beside Jackie. "The root cellar. When we were kids, Grandma kept the shelves in there stacked with all the pickles and jellies she canned. I remember helping her. She always picked the hottest days in August to do the canning. I hated it, but no one makes chokecherry jam like Grandma Hazel. I'm actually not sure if she does any canning anymore, now that she lives alone. That little room might be empty." She pulled at the oblong door handle. It wouldn't turn. "That's weird. It feels like it's locked." Additional tugs proved fruitless.

"Let me try," Jackie said, bumping Kit out of the way.

"Be my guest. Just don't break that handle off. It's pretty rusty."

Jackie did everything but brace her foot against the doorjamb as she yanked and pulled, but still the door didn't budge. "I hope there's nothing on the floor in there. Canned goods would probably be fine if there are still some on the shelves. You'll have to ask your grandma for the key."

Kit nodded, then started moving items away from the puddles of water on the floor.

"Hey, Kit, come here," Annie said from the opposite corner of the basement. "You'll want to see this."

"Can it wait? I should get this stuff off the floor."

"Well, it could, but I'm dying to find out why your grandma has a neat stack of men's tighty-whities on her *dry*... ."

Kit frowned as laughter choked off Annie's words. The woman wasn't making any sense. She dropped a dripping plastic laundry basket full of towels onto the workbench, knocking a roll of paper towels off as she hurried over to the washer and dryer. "Hazel is thrifty with her money. She has to be. Maybe she's using Grandpa's old underwear as cleaning rags."

"Wasn't your grandfather a big man?" Annie asked, shaking out a folded pair of underwear and holding them toward Kit with both hands. "These are mediums, and they don't look like rags. See, the tag still looks new."

"Eww, put those down!" Kit slapped at Annie's hand. "Maybe Marge did some laundry over here. Grandma has a hard time getting down these stairs. Her knees give her trouble. I bet Marge is doing laundry for both of them now, and it's easier to do it over here."

"Last time I talked to Marge, she was blissfully single."

Kit groaned, her mind grasping for any plausible explanation. "Well, it's not like my ninety-year-old grandmother is in a relationship with a man where he's sleeping here and leaving his underwear for her to wash."

"Are you sure?" Jackie said, sneaking up behind them. "Seems like we might have stumbled onto a little senior hanky-panky here. What about that man who drove her here this morning? He was on the smallish side."

Kit shook her head. "I'm sure there is some other logical explanation—one that can't possibly involve Grandma having a boyfriend."

"Shame on you, Kit!" Jackie headed back to the wet corner of the basement. "Would it kill you to hope your grandma has found love again? You may not have a romantic bone in your body, but some of us do."

Kit shuddered as she picked up the underwear Annie had dropped, shivering as she refolded them. "Why do you always insist I'm not romantic? I have my moments."

"Eww," Annie said, mimicking Kit from a moment earlier. "I like Dean, but don't be putting pictures of your 'moments' into my head."

"If you two would stop goofing off, we could clean this up before I faint from starvation," Jackie said. "I spoke too soon when I said there weren't any cardboard boxes down here. There are a few of them on the floor, and they're falling apart in this water."

The bottom of a water-logged box gave way as she attempted to hoist it onto the workbench. Old photographs spilled across the basement floor, causing all three women to gasp.

"Oh no, those are going to be ruined!" Kit cried, dropping to her knees to gather the photographs. She ignored the moisture that seeped through the knees of her jeans, grabbing for the roll of paper towels on the floor. "Quick. Paper towels might help."

She went to stand, but miscalculated, and smacked her head on the bottom of the workbench.

"Don't break the bench," Jackie teased.

Kit ignored her, rubbing at the sting. But before she could get up, she spied a set of keys hanging from a nail behind the vice that was mounted to the side of the bench. She wouldn't have noticed them if she hadn't been down on her knees. "Hey, look. I recognize this key chain. It used to be Grandpa's. I wonder if one of these keys unlocks the root cellar." She grabbed the keys and slowly straightened, squinting as the pain ebbed away.

Annie was holding out her hand. "Let me check. I'm good with keys."

Kit handed them over and stretched her head from side to side, praying she hadn't screwed up her neck. Once she felt clear-headed, she started to blot any water she could see from the photos with a paper towel. "Who locks a root cellar? They never locked it when I lived here."

It took Annie multiple tries, but eventually she was able to turn the lock. The key grated, and then the door swung toward her, rusty hinges screeching in protest. "It's dark. I can't see anything."

Kit pulled out her phone and flipped on the flashlight. "Here."

Taking the light, Annie took one step into the previously sealed-off room. "Hmm."

"What? Are there canned goods that we need to move? Or toss?"

Annie popped her head out. "It doesn't look like Hazel has done any canning lately. Kit, you aren't going to like this."

Kit felt a shiver down her spine, picturing her imaginary ghosts again. She knew it was ridiculous. She was a *scientist*. But she'd never been able to shake the feeling that this place had a dark energy to it.

"How bad can it be after discovering men's underwear on the dryer?" Jackie asked, trying to see into the root cellar from behind them.

Kit snatched her phone back, using its light to pan from top to bottom, and into all four corners of the root cellar. Annie was right. None of this stuff belonged to Hazel.

CHAPTER SEVEN

K IT DROPPED ONTO THE passenger seat as Dean tossed his suitcase into the trunk. After missing out on sleep when she had to share a bed with Jackie the first night, Kit had slept like the dead at the hotel. She was so incredibly thankful for Dean. Displaced townspeople filled most of the hotel, but he had used his loyalty status with one of the hotel chains in town to snag the last available room. Kit wasn't sure whether it was all her physical labor or simply sleeping next to Dean for the first time in two weeks that allowed her to sleep so deeply—maybe both—but she was grateful for the rest.

She laid a hand on Dean's thigh when he settled into the driver's seat. "I hope you know how much I appreciate you coming down here like you did. Don't feel like you need to come back to Grandma's after lunch. I know you have that client dinner in the city tonight."

Dean started his vehicle, laid a hand over Kit's, and backed out of his parking spot. "I wish I could stay and help with more cleanup. I know you need to get back home, too, to prepare for your trip. When is your flight again?"

Kit removed her hand to snap her seat belt in place, then leaned her head back with a tired sigh. "Early Friday morning. I haven't even packed yet. What does the rest of your week look like?"

"It'll be busy," he replied, as he drove out of the parking lot and headed toward Ruby Shore's downtown area. "I'm hoping we'll get the go ahead on the St. Louis project at dinner tonight."

Kit nodded, only listening to Dean's response with half an ear as he launched into his level of involvement in the proposed project. Her eyes took in the remaining storm damage in many of the yards as he drove. The destruction magnified her growing apprehension over leaving town before her grandmother's place was cleaned up.

Dean must have picked up on her silence as he turned onto Main. "You alright?" he asked, glancing her way with concern.

She shook her head. "Dean, I've been thinking. Maybe I shouldn't go."

Dean pumped the brakes and hit his blinker. They were still a block short of the Crystal Café where they were meeting Hazel for brunch.

"Dean! We'll be late," Kit warned, checking that no one was close behind them. "Grandma doesn't like to be kept waiting."

"We'll be on time. Only *you* think being ten minutes early is the same as being on time. Besides, Marge is working. She'll keep Hazel occupied until we get there. We have to talk about this. It's important."

He pulled into a parking spot that overlooked the town square and killed the engine. Through the windshield, Kit could see sparkling water droplets spurting into the air against the sunny morning sky. The old fountain beneath the droplets had served as the park's anchor for as long as Kit could remember.

You'd never guess a terrible storm barreled through here two days ago, she thought. The public works department—or maybe an army of volunteers—already had Emerald Park back to normal. Only a few raw spots, high up on trees, gave any hint as to the havoc the wind had played. If only Hazel's place was back in this kind of shape already. Then she might feel better about leaving on vacation.

"See? This is what I mean," she said, motioning toward the windshield.

Dean looked between her and the view beyond the glass. "You're going to have to be more specific."

"Look how they already have this place back to the way it was before the storm. Grandma's is a long way from looking this good. Her neighbor's tree is still on top of her porch, and I'm sure the city will insist we haul the garage away before too long."

Dean settled back into his seat, as if they didn't have to be somewhere in a few minutes. It made Kit want to scream. Nothing rattled the man.

"How long will you be gone?" he asked.

"Ten days. Two travel days and eight days on the island. But do you see? It's too long to be gone right now."

He shook his head. "Actually, the timing is good. How soon can you get someone over to take care of that fallen tree?"

"At least two weeks, but maybe we could do it ourselves. If you came back after work on Friday, we could get a sizeable chunk of it taken care of over the weekend."

Dean looked skeptical. "You saw the size of that tree trunk. It's going to take some heavy-duty saws, and I hate to admit it, but I haven't touched a chainsaw since I was a teenager. While I love your grandmother dearly, I don't feel like giving up a hand or foot—or worse—to get that tree moved out."

Kit crossed her arms and turned to look out her side window, not caring that she was pouting. She thought back to the previous morning when they'd spotted Owen hard at work with a chainsaw in his front yard. Dean had many amazing qualities, but he was no handyman.

"The only way those garage walls are coming out is with a tractor and dump truck. Kit, this is not do-it-yourself work. Hazel's is only one of many damaged homes and buildings in the area. Work with Marge to get on the contractors' calendars, then go home, pack, and take that trip you've been talking about with your girlfriends since you were eighteen years old. This will still be here when you get back. Don't you always give up some of your vacation time every year because you don't use it?"

Kit snorted. "Yeah, and my boss wasn't happy when I had to take this week off without notice, given I'll be out for another week and a half yet for my trip."

"Screw him," Dean said with a wave. "That grouch is lucky to have you."

She laughed. "Down, boy. You haven't had your coffee yet today, have you?" She teased. Her unease over leaving was loosening its grip under the assault of Dean's logic. "So, you don't think it's selfish of me to go?"

"Absolutely not. I'd tell you if I did."

This was true. She could count on Dean to be straight with her, even if what he said was sometimes painful to hear. This time, his guidance was easy to receive.

But there was still one big question.

"Where will Grandma stay until her house is back in livable condition?"

Dean shrugged. "There are options. Marge's house would be the most logical place."

"They may kill each other if they have to live under one roof for long. Why do you think Grandma never asked Marge to move in, even though things are tough for her around the house?"

Dean's grin dropped away. "Maybe this will be the push Hazel needs to move somewhere else. I know that isn't what she wants, but it might be what she needs."

Kit had fallen asleep with the same thought the night before. It was a wonder she hadn't tossed and turned all night, imagining Hazel's reaction to the notion. "Do you want to tell her that over caramel rolls and coffee?"

Dean gave her a wink as he started the car back up. "That would be better coming from family."

"Nice try. She's thought of you as family for years, and you know it."

The scent of coffee and fresh baked goods assailed them as they entered the Crystal Café.

Marge was behind the register, ringing up a customer. "I thought maybe you got lost on your way over," she said. "You're never late."

"Blame *him*," Kit said, poking her thumb in Dean's direction, who shrugged shamefacedly.

The stern look on her aunt's face fell away. "Mom's waiting in the back. But I should warn you. She's not alone."

Kit's stomach jumped, and she remembered the odd assortment of things they'd found the day before. She'd avoided her mother for the past ten years, but the fact her grandmother's locked room in the basement contained items from Kit's childhood—things only her mother could still possess—meant she was back. If she wasn't physically in town, she'd at least had some kind of contact with Kit's grandma.

Mia was like a bad penny. She kept showing up, about once every ten years, at the most inopportune times. The last time was at her aunt's husband's funeral, and Marge hadn't been happy to see her sister, either.

Kit would be content to never cross paths with that woman ever again. A girl can only take so many betrayals.

"Is it that old fella she was riding around with yesterday morning?" Dean asked, oblivious. Kit had failed to mention anything to him about the items she'd found in the basement with Jackie and Annie, so he had no idea to suspect Hazel might be about to drop *the bomb that was Kit's mother* on them. "I can't remember his name."

"Sure is," Marge said.

Kit's shoulders instantly sagged with relief. A polite old man would be easier to deal with than a long-absent mother. Even if it meant thinking about those tighty-whities in the basement.

Dean nodded, placing a hand on the small of Kit's back. "Is Isaac here, too?" At Marge's confused look, he nudged Kit forward and said, "Never mind. Best not keep Hazel waiting."

As they approached the table, the man seated beside Kit's grandmother stood, nodding expectantly at them. "Good morning!"

Kit grinned when the man pulled a chair out and motioned for her to take a seat. Chivalry wasn't dead yet. Not in Ruby Shores, at least.

"Morning," she said, settling in. Her eyes scanned her poor grandmother's bruised face. It looked worse than the day before.

"I know, I look awful," Hazel said with a shake of her head. "I didn't even bother to conceal it with makeup. What would be the use? Floyd says it's barely noticeable, but he is just being nice."

"Hazel, that shiner gives you the perfect opportunity to milk your granddaughter and daughter for anything you want today. There's always an upside." Dean's grin told Kit he wasn't overly concerned with the state of her grandmother's face.

Healing would take time, she reminded herself.

"Anything I want?" Hazel parroted. "What I want is to go home. Did you get that tree off my porch yet?"

Kit sighed. "I was hoping you didn't see that."

"I'm old, Kit, but I'm not blind. Or stupid. All that weight is hurting the integrity of my house."

As Kit leaned back so a waitress could refill Hazel's and Floyd's coffee cups, she thought back to her conversation with Dean in the car. "Grandma, that tree is humongous. We're going to have to hire professionals to haul it away. Everyone with tree damage—and that's basically everyone—is trying to do the same thing right now. You're going to have to be patient."

Hazel's grunt spoke volumes.

After placing their food order, Kit's eyes sought her grandmother's again. She'd have preferred to have this conversation in private, but that didn't seem possible. She needed some answers.

"You had water in the basement again."

Kit swore she saw her grandmother's face blush, but the bruising made it hard to be sure.

"You were in the basement?"

"I was. Me, Jackie, and Annie."

Her grandmother sighed, then pulled her shoulders back and returned Kit's gaze, her eyes no longer wavering. The look reminded her of the no-nonsense woman who'd raised her. "Did you get things cleaned up?"

"Yes. Since you've stored most of the things on the floor in those heavy-duty black totes—which I'd never seen down there before—cleanup wasn't too bad. And the humidifier should help, too. That was smart, by the way."

"I have Floyd to thank for that."

Kit shot the older gentleman a thankful grin before once again addressing her grandmother. "We had to access that back storage room where you usually keep your preserves. It disappointed me not to find my favorite chokecherry jam on any of the shelves."

Hazel squirmed. "Been years since I did any canning. No one around to help me anymore."

"You know I'd come help. Just ask." Kit decided it was time to get to the point. "Grandma, how long have you been storing Mia's things in your basement?"

Hazel's eyes jumped up from Kit's face to a spot behind her, face flushed with guilt.

Someone was standing behind Kit.

"That worthless sister of mine better not be back."

Kit hated the pained look that flitted across her grandmother's face. She could have kicked herself for putting it there.

"What are you talking about?" Dean asked, his tone concerned.

Kit turned just as the plates in Marge's arms wobbled. She reached up, helping to stabilize the stack of dirty dishes.

Marge didn't even seem to notice. "Mom, tell me Mia isn't back."

"She isn't back."

Marge looked just as relieved as Kit felt. The last thing Kit needed was for her pitiful excuse of a mother to stir up more trouble than they were already dealing with this week.

"Hey, Marge," a male voice cut through the cloud of drama hovering over their table. "I've been waiting twenty minutes for my eggs. What's the holdup?"

"We will discuss this later, Mother," Marge said, spinning away to see to her impatient customer.

"I think you all forget who you are talking to," Hazel said, facing Kit with a stubborn expression. "I'm not an old woman you can push around."

Their food arrived, giving them all a second to catch their breath.

"I'm sorry, Grandma. But you can imagine my surprise. None of that stuff used to be in your basement." Kit cut into her gooey caramel roll, the scent of it reminding her of long-ago days. Her grandmother used to bring them here every Sunday after church.

"In fact, some of her things have been down in that root cellar for almost three years. She dropped off the black tubs more recently."

Kit's fork slipped from her fingers. "Three years?" How long had her grandmother been in contact with Mia? She felt a surge of resentment. "Why?"

The older woman shook her head as she picked up her own fork. "This isn't a conversation I want to have in front of an audience, Kit. But I appreciate you cleaning up the water. When do you think I can move back home?"

Kit opened her mouth to protest, but Dean caught her left hand and squeezed it.

"Hazel, what Kit is trying to tell you is that it's going to be a while before your house is safe to live in again. I think now might be the time to consider whether going back home is the best idea. Maybe this storm was a sign that you should consider other options."

Floyd, so far quiet during the exchange, cleared his throat. "I've been trying to tell her that, too. Kit, your grandmother is a stubborn woman."

Kit thought the look Floyd shot her grandma looked more flirtatious than reprimanding, and it reminded her of what Annie had found. Her grandmother probably wouldn't be any more excited to discuss the underwear than she was the topic of Kit's mother, but Kit was dying to know. "Fine. We'll talk about Mia later, but you have to tell me why we found three pairs of men's underwear on your dryer."

A speck of egg shot out of Dean's mouth.

Her grandmother didn't look nearly as amused. "You know I hate it when you call your mother by her name."

"If she acted like a mother, maybe I would call her Mom," Kit shot back. "The underwear?"

"For Pete's sake, you have a dirty mind, girl."

Kit threw up her arms in exasperation. "A dirty mind? Why do you say that? I was just asking why you have men's underwear in your laundry. Grandpa's been gone for over thirty years, so they couldn't be his."

Floyd slapped a palm lightly against the table. His eyes disappeared as his wide grin crinkled his face into a mass of deep wrinkles. "Hazel, I told you when my washer went on the blink that your assistance with my dirty laundry would start rumors. But you never listen to me, do you, young lady?"

The mood around the table lightened almost immediately. Kit decided she liked Floyd. The scowl on her grandmother's face softened, and her chuckle loosened the tension in Kit's chest.

"Now that we've solved *that* little mystery," Dean said, scooping up a big forkful of eggs while giving Kit a pointed look, "why don't we all enjoy our meals and give Floyd a chance to tell us a little about himself. And Floyd, tell us more about Isaac. He seems like a good kid."

Grateful for the reroute of the conversation, Kit ate her roll and kept an eye on her grandmother while Floyd talked. She seemed to watch her male friend with genuine warmth.

I shouldn't have come down on Grandma like that, Kit chided herself, savoring the smooth caramel on her tongue. *I owe this woman so much.*

They'd discuss Mia later. They'd also figure out her grandmother's living situation. For now, Kit just wanted to enjoy time with Grandma Hazel—the woman she respected most in the world—and ignore the tickle of betrayal she felt when she wondered how long her grandmother had been talking to Mia behind her back.

Chapter Eight

Marge appreciated Kit's assurances that she'd get contractors lined up to handle the fallen tree and garage, as well as the broken windows and roof damage. She'd told her aunt it was the least she could do, since Marge already did so much for Hazel. And Kit always kept her promises. She maintained high standards on that front. It was the only way she could live after years of betrayal by her own parents.

It took hours to line up the professional help, but once it was done she felt better about leaving for vacation. Jackie had already returned to the city and her job at the animal shelter. Even though Dean had returned to Minneapolis the day before, too, she'd kept his hotel room. He also arranged a rental for her so she could get home after focusing on the logistics of getting Hazel's house back in order. Her morning was split between cleaning up the yard and arranging contractors. At noon she returned to her hotel for a shower.

As she was wrapping a towel around her head, her phone buzzed on the nightstand next to the king-size bed. Her grandmother's number flashed on the screen.

"Hey, Grandma, what's up?"

"You should come to the park."

Kit didn't like the worry in her grandmother's voice. "The park? You mean downtown? Are you there now? Are you all right?"

"For heaven's sake, girl, I'm fine. But your friend's dad is standing in the water fountain. I'm afraid he's lost his marbles."

Kit's heart sank. "Glen? Jackie's dad?"

"Yup. Poor man. Not sure where his wife is. This guy needs help."

Kit used her shoulder to keep her phone against her ear and let the towel fall to the floor so she could fluff her wet hair. She'd planned to fix it, apply a little makeup, and find lunch somewhere. Her grandmother's phone call changed all that.

"I'll call Jackie's mom right away and throw some clothes on. I just got out of the shower. Are you at the park alone? How did you get there?"

Her grandmother's sigh was staticky through the phone. "Quit worrying about me, Kit. How do you think I manage when you aren't in town? Help poor Glen if you can. I'll be here."

Click.

Kit stared at the phone, her grandmother's words echoing in her head. Hazel could take care of herself . . . most of the time.

Her call to Jackie's mother went straight to voicemail. Kit donned the only clean clothes left in her suitcase. She'd try to call Jackie from the car.

By the time she reached the fountain downtown, a uniformed police officer sat next to Jackie's father on the waist-high ledge that ringed the landmark. A puddle of water darkened the concrete around Glen. Both men were smiling, and Kit exhaled a sigh of relief. She spotted her grandmother on a nearby bench, a paper coffee cup from the Crystal Café in her hand.

Kit had gotten ahold of Jackie, and she knew her friend was frantically trying to reach Charlotte at this very moment. Hazel looked relaxed as Kit approached the chatting pair at the fountain.

"Hey there, Glen. Officer. Everything all right?"

The officer got to his feet. Kit didn't recognize him, which wasn't surprising given how long she'd lived away from Ruby Shores. The uniformed man tucked his thumbs in the front of his belt, giving her a welcoming nod before glancing back at Glen. "Mr. Turner here is just waiting for his wife to come pick him up. I thought I'd visit with him while we waited for her."

"Did someone call her, then? My grandmother got ahold of me, but I couldn't reach Charlotte. Mrs. Turner."

The officer nodded, motioning to the bracelet on Glen's arm. "She's on her way. His emergency contact information is on that. Mr. Turner and I go way back. This isn't the first time we've had a little chat down here at the fountain."

Glen smirked. "You were always a handful in school. How many times did I have to haul *you* to the office?"

"More times than I care to remember," the younger man admitted. "And there's your wife now."

Kit heard footsteps hurrying their way and Jackie's mother rushed past her, arms extended. Her hair was rolled up in tight rows of curlers and a towel draped over her shoulders. Kit caught a whiff of the unmistakable scent of perm solution.

Charlotte grabbed her husband's hands. "Glen, you can't keep doing this. I'm afraid Mrs. Miller isn't going to be willing to keep you company anymore when I have to go out." She turned to Kit. "Thank you for looking out for him."

"Don't thank me. Thank Grandma," Kit said, motioning to her grandmother on the park bench. "She called me, and by the time I got here, this nice officer was already visiting with him."

"I'm sorry this keeps happening, Officer. The doctor adjusted Glen's medication, but it doesn't seem to help with his confusion."

Jackie's father stood, brushing off the seat of his pants. Charlotte sighed when she noted the state of his clothes. "No need to talk about me like I'm not here," he said. "I headed to the square to stretch my legs. It's always a pleasant walk on nice days like this."

Charlotte looked as tired as Kit felt.

The police officer pulled a small notebook out of his shirt pocket, scrawled something on the top page, then tore it out and handed it to Jackie's mother. "It might be a good idea to call these folks," he said, motioning with his pen toward the slip of paper in Charlotte's hand. "I always enjoy our little visits, but there are safety concerns."

After a quick glance, Charlotte stuffed the paper in the pocket of her skirt. "I'll look into it," she said, moving to lead her husband toward their car. She assured Kit she'd call Jackie, and all three went on about their day, leaving Kit, her grandmother, and the gurgling water fountain behind.

"Poor man. Mrs. Turner probably needs to look into getting him a room over at the memory facility. When people reach a certain level of decline, they aren't safe in their own homes anymore."

Kit sank down on the bench next to her. She couldn't help but wonder if Hazel was nearing a similar stage. She had a growing list of physical ailments, but her mental health seemed solid.

As if she could read Kit's mind, Hazel held up one hand and shook her head. "I'm not ready to leave my house yet."

Kit sighed, wondering how hard to push her grandmother on the topic. She'd start with a few simple questions. "Grandma, why are you so adamant about staying in your house? Isn't it lonely? Doesn't it get hard for you, traipsing up those stairs to your bedroom every night?"

"I can manage," the older woman insisted.

"But why do you want to? I guess that's what I don't understand. There are places where you can live in your own apartment, but you don't have to cook anymore. You can go to a community room to eat and play games."

A car honked on the street behind the women. Two kids whizzed by on bicycles.

Her grandmother shifted on the park bench, turning her body to face Kit. "I've considered a place like that. And maybe someday it will feel right. But not today."

Kit did her best to stay calm and rational, despite her rising frustration. "Why? Why do you think you wouldn't enjoy it?"

"I didn't say I wouldn't enjoy it. I might. But I can't afford it."

Kit nodded. She had already given the financial implications plenty of thought. "You could afford it if you sold the house. Grandma, the market is hot right now. You're within walking distance of the lake. That's prime real estate! With money from your house, you could live comfortably in a place where people are available to help as much or as little as you like."

"But I can't sell."

"Can't? Or won't?"

Hazel crossed her arms over her chest, a familiar gesture that Kit knew meant the woman wouldn't change her mind. At least not today. "Won't, I suppose, if you want to get technical."

"Marge is the only family in town these days, and she has her own house. If you wanted to live together, you would have already moved. I know you love your house, but I worry about you, all alone. What if you fall?"

She shrugged and said matter-of-factly, "Then you find me in a heap at the bottom of the stairs someday."

Kit could feel a headache forming as the muscles tightened in the back of her neck. "Grandma, that isn't funny."

"Believe me, I know that."

Frustrated but resigned to yet another stalemate, Kit watched a fat bumblebee dart in and out of a nearby flower garden.

"Kit, I'm actually glad we have a few minutes alone. I wanted to talk to you about the things you found in my basement."

Kit, however, did *not* want to talk about Mia. She closed her eyes, envisioning her toes in the sand and a cool glass of white wine in her hand. Or maybe a margarita. A double. Nothing could drive her to drink like the subject of her mother.

Unless it was the tighty-whities her grandmother wanted to discuss. That would be more entertaining.

"Mia's things?" Kit asked, fearing she already knew the answer.

Hazel sighed, then began. "Your mother has worked very hard through the years to overcome her addictions. I think she's finally found her way to peace."

Kit snorted. She couldn't help herself. Mia had tried rehab more times than Kit could count. Or so she claimed. But it never stuck. Kit had resigned herself to the fact that her mother would likely die from alcoholism.

"I talked to her last night."

Shocked, Kit spun toward her grandmother. "Last night?"

"I called her. We talk every Tuesday evening, so she was expecting my call."

Kit let the words sink in. "How long has this been going on?"

"A while. I told her you found her things."

A mosquito stung Kit on the back of the neck, and she slapped it away, annoyed. "Why is that stuff even down there? I didn't think she kept any of it."

"She loves you and your brothers."

"No. She doesn't. If she loved us, she wouldn't have stayed away for all these years. She wouldn't have treated us like castoffs, dumping us at your house and taking off like she did."

Hazel picked at a piece of lint on her black linen skirt, flicking it into the grass. "Kit, I think it's time you heard the full story of your mother's early years. She made me swear to keep her secrets, but all that is doing is widening this chasm between the two of you."

Kit bent down and plucked a single, lonesome yellow dandelion from under the bench. "I suppose this is where you try to tell me she's just misunderstood."

"You know me better than that," Hazel said, shaking her head. "No. My Mia has had her fair share of missteps and failures. But not everything is her fault. Things happened when she was young that left scars."

"Grandma, we're all scarred. In my case, it's thanks to her."

Hazel bent low, looping her fingers through the handles of her purse. "If you are going to keep interrupting, I think I'll just meander on home—I mean, to Marge's. I don't have time for this."

Kit wondered what her grandmother had to do that was so pressing, but she knew that wasn't the real issue. "No. Stop. I'm sorry. If you have something you think I need to hear, I'll be quiet and listen."

Hazel straightened, leaving her purse at her feet. "Without interrupting? You know how much I hate to be interrupted."

Kit laughed, despite her trepidation over whatever it was that her grandmother wanted to share. "I promise."

Hazel crossed her legs and settled back against the bench. All was quiet around them, and Kit considered poking the woman to get her started, but she'd promised to behave.

"I've told no one what I'm about to tell you. Not even Marge. Not even your grandfather, God rest his soul. But I think you need to hear it. It might give you a smidge more empathy for your mother. Believe me, I know what a mess she made of her life. And yours. Lots of the chaos was because of her own poor choices. However, I firmly believe there were two contributing factors that set her down a hard path, one it has taken her years to steer away from."

Kit bit back a humph. Her grandma made it sound like Mia had found her way back. She'd heard that song and dance before.

As if sensing her granddaughter's thoughts, Hazel paused, eyeing her closely. "Remember, hold your tongue until you hear me out."

Kit nodded, biting her tongue. She'd listen. But if Hazel didn't get to the point, she'd have to find a bathroom soon. Too much coffee while arranging contractors earlier. Or maybe fear over what the older woman was about to tell her was affecting her bladder.

"As I was saying, Mia started her young adult life with two strikes against her. The first was in her genes."

"Her what?" Kit asked, surprised. "Do you mean jeans like pants, or genetics?"

"Genetics. I'm not sure if you ever noticed, but your grandfather never drank any kind of beer or liquor. Not a drop. That's because too many in his family suffered from alcoholism. He believed that if he ever started, he might not stop, and he didn't want to live life like that. That's why Marge doesn't drink, either."

Kit grimaced. "How did I not know this? Grandma, you know Pete has a drinking problem. You should have told us!"

Her grandmother let her head fall back to stare at the fluffy white clouds above. "Actually, I pulled Pete aside when I noticed an issue during his senior year in high school. But I'm afraid my warnings fell on deaf ears." She brought her chin back down. "The family weakness was something your grandfather hated, and he made me promise not to talk about it freely."

"That's ridiculous!" Kit said, earning herself a reprimanding look. "I'm sorry. I know I promised not to interrupt. But I'm not going to give my mother a pass for all the awful things she's done to our family, simply because we *might* be genetically predisposed to alcoholism."

Hazel vented another heavy sigh. "That's your prerogative. I choose to believe it contributes to my daughter's problems."

"You said there were two things."

"I did. The second thing is harder to talk about." The old woman rubbed her arms, as if chilled, despite the eighty-degree heat of the summer day. "Something awful happened to Mia when she was seventeen."

A shiver passed through Kit, as if the dark memory her grandmother had summoned was weaving through them both. She shifted on the bench but remained quiet.

"Mia dated a boy. We only met him once. Your grandfather knew of the family. They were a rough bunch . . . from the 'wrong side of the tracks,' Walter used to say. We made the mistake of telling her she couldn't see him."

Kit didn't think that was a mistake. "You were trying to protect her."

"We were. But Mia took directives as a challenge. Initially, we thought she obeyed our wishes, but we came to find out later that she was still sneaking out to see him. Then, one Sunday morning, she came down for church with a shiner. Worse than this one I'm sporting now. She claimed she smacked her face with a cupboard door, but we knew better. Your grandfather disappeared for an hour after that, and we never made it to church that day. He refused to talk about where he'd gone. But I knew. After that, Mia stuck pretty close to home. We thought the trouble was behind us. We didn't realize it was only beginning."

While the bit about family alcoholism was a surprise, this litany about her mother's bad choices in men wasn't. History had proven she had yet to pick a winner where men were concerned. Unless she'd broken that losing streak in the ten years since Kit had last seen her, which Kit very much doubted.

"Let me guess," she said, slinging an arm behind her grandma's shoulders. "Mom kept sneaking out to meet the loser, even after he beat her up."

"No, she didn't. I kept a very close eye on her. But the damage was already done."

The chill was back. "Wait. Don't tell me that loser was actually my father?"

"Of course not. You weren't born for another three years. But, unbeknownst to me, Mia *was* pregnant. Then the foolish girl snuck off and had a back-alley abortion. Didn't even tell her sister. I doubt she'd have told *me*, except there were complications. Mia couldn't stop the bleeding. The doctor—if that miserable excuse for a man she saw was even properly trained—did a terrible hatchet job on your mother. I rushed her in to see our pediatrician. We didn't know if she'd ever be able to have children after that."

Kit felt a strange sense of unease. There'd been a very real possibility that she might never have been born. Her grandmother was right. Mia had suffered. No seventeen-year-old should have to face the horrors of physical abuse or a dangerous, illegal abortion.

"That's awful," she whispered.

"It was awful."

"Did Grandpa know that part?"

Hazel shook her head. "No. It would have killed him. Or worse, he'd have ended up in prison for killing the monster who put her in that predicament in the first place. She swore to me that the boy pressured her to have sex, but she wouldn't allow me to take it to the police. I wish I'd have gone to the authorities regardless. We learned later that they sent the kid away soon after for raping another girl."

Hazel caught her breath, then continued.

"This all happened the spring of Mia's junior year. After that, it took Herculean efforts to keep your mother engaged enough during senior year to get her through graduation. She was spiraling, and nothing we tried seemed to help. We knew that she'd moved on from drinking to drugs when I found marijuana in her bedroom."

Another surprise. Kit knew her mother nearly drank herself to death on more than one occasion, but she hadn't known there'd been drugs, too. Was her mother a drug addict, besides being an alcoholic? Nothing would surprise her when it came to Mia.

A low buzzing caught her attention, drawing her eyes to a fragrant rose bush behind their bench. As the bee floated between the blossoms, a flutter caught her eye. It was a big monarch butterfly, larger than she could ever remember seeing in nature, though she'd worked with bigger specimens in the lab.

When she and her friends were young girls, they'd learned about the metamorphosis a caterpillar went through when it transitioned into a butterfly. She felt like the story her grandmother had just shared represented the opposite type of transition: that of an innocent young girl into a trainwreck of a woman, defiled by men and weakened by substance abuse.

Why had she never questioned how her mother ended up being such a mess?

Suddenly, her headache bloomed into a full-blown migraine. She needed time to process everything her grandmother had told her.

Hazel touched her fingers to Kit's cheek. "Not all of your mother's problems were her fault, dear. At least initially. Can you see that now?"

Kit rubbed the back of her neck. It did nothing to relieve the pressure behind her eyes or in the center of her chest. She didn't want to hear any more. It was easier to blame her mother—and her father to a lesser degree—for her own messed-up childhood than it was to think about the impressionable young girl Mia was and the damage that had been inflicted upon her.

Mia's sad tale seemed to have taken the starch out of her grandmother as well. Hazel slumped back against the bench and used a tissue to dab at her brow.

Kit needed time, and her grandmother needed to get some place cool.

"Thank you for trusting me with this, Grandma. But we should get you out of the heat. I'll give you a ride back to Marge's. I've lined up contractors for the work on your house, but it'll take at least a month. Will you be all right for now? I'm going home tomorrow, and I have a flight to catch on Friday. But I promise I'll be back as soon as I can. We'll talk more then."

The older woman bent to pick up her purse and got to her feet, wobbling as she straightened. Kit slipped a hand under Hazel's elbow, thinking of how her grandmother had supported her and Tony and Pete when Mia failed to be a proper mother.

Whatever "a proper mother" is, Kit thought. She knew mothers came in all different shapes and forms, with many different abilities. She sighed. "I know I'm not the only one Mia hurt over the years, Grandma. She hurt you, too. But despite everything she's done, it seems like you've forgiven her."

Her grandmother patted a hand against Kit's own. How could the woman be so composed when Kit felt shattered?

"I'm her mother," Hazel said, her chin held a notch higher than was natural. "What choice do I have?"

CHAPTER NINE

K IT WASN'T SURE WHAT to do with all the family history her grandmother had dumped in her lap. Sleep eluded her after their visit in the park, but at least her migraine was gone by the time the sun appeared again on the horizon.

Was it reckless of her grandmother to let Mia back into her life? Kit had never planned to give the woman any leeway after the years of heartache she'd caused. But maybe her grandmother had one thing right: it was different for a mother. Maybe Hazel couldn't help but forgive her own child, no matter what she'd done.

Kit shifted in the driver's seat of the rental to avoid staring at the splattered moth on the windshield. She realized with a start that Mia would be nearly seventy years old now. In her mind's eye, her mother would always be that thirty-something-year-old woman with a drink in her hand, stumbling around their house while Kit's once attentive father tried to hold the pieces of their family together.

They'd both failed Kit and her brothers.

She'd also been able to put a name to another of her jumbled feelings during the darkest hours of her nearly sleepless night. She felt betrayed by her grandmother. Shouldn't Hazel support Kit, her only granddaughter, above even Mia? Kit had never broken Hazel's heart.

The gas light on the dash blinked on, and even though Kit wasn't far from home, she pulled into the next gas station. She had too much to do before her friends arrived that evening to wind up out of gas and stranded on the side of the road. Her unexpected dash to Ruby Shores ruined her plans to squeeze in a little shopping to fill her suitcase with better-fitting clothes. She'd pack what she had and do any necessary shopping in Hawaii instead.

That would be more fun anyhow.

Fifteen minutes later, she was back on the road with a full tank of gas and a fresh cup of coffee. With luck, she'd soon be packed and relaxing on her patio with the first glass of wine of their vacation, awaiting Annie, Jackie, and Renee.

Then she remembered Dean had her favorite carry-on bag back at his apartment.

Maybe he'd be a good sport and drive it over to her place so she wouldn't have to make a detour. She checked his location with their family share app, disappointed but not surprised to see he was at his office. It was still early on a Thursday afternoon, after all.

She tried calling him, but it went straight to voicemail. "Hey, Dean. I hoped to catch you, but you're probably busy. No problem. I'm just going to swing by your place and grab my carry-on. It'll make navigating through the airport so much easier. Hope you don't need it next week. I don't think you're flying again until after I'm back. We really should pick up a second suitcase like that. It's the perfect size. Anyway, thanks again for driving over to Ruby Shores to help, and if I don't talk to you before we fly out tomorrow morning, I'll call you to let you know when we get to Maui. Oh, and don't worry about the rental. I called and they are sending someone to my place this evening to pick it up. And thanks again for promising to check on Chloe while I'm gone, too. I'll clean her litter box tonight and leave a fresh bag of her favorite food on the counter. Try not to spoil her too much. Love ya."

A motorcycle zipped past and swung into the lane directly in front of her. Her heart leapt as she hung up and then turned off the radio. Traffic was heavy and she needed to concentrate. She hoped her friends wouldn't have trouble getting in. Jackie would be fine, but Annie was coming over from Ruby Shores, and Renee's resort was almost three hours from Minneapolis.

The parking lot in front of Dean's apartment had plenty of open spots. She found the key ring with his spare at the bottom of her purse and let herself in to his building, holding the door for the mailman as he exited the apartment's foyer.

Dean was notorious for letting his mail pile up, so she used the smaller key on the ring he'd given her to check his mailbox. The few pieces of junk mail and one envelope from his bank meant he must have grabbed it himself for a change, in the last day or two. She glanced again at the letter from his bank. He'd talked to her recently about opening a joint bank account, but they hadn't actually done it yet. She supposed it was a logical next step as they worked toward marriage and a combined life.

Once inside his unit, she groaned at the mess. "He didn't know you were stopping by," she muttered, doing her best to cut him some slack. Her anxiety was already high after the bombshells her grandmother had dropped. She didn't need to add to it by dwelling on Dean's irritating little habits that grated on her nerves. "It's not like *I'm* perfect."

As her words echoed around the empty kitchen of her fiancé's apartment, she almost laughed. At least Dean wasn't one to talk to himself.

The air felt stuffy. Condensation dripped from the air-conditioning unit into a gaudy ceramic bowl on the floor. Dean had told her once that his oldest niece gave him that bowl for Christmas when she was five. Cute, but he was going to need to call his landlord again about the ineffective cooling unit.

She made her way to his cluttered desk under the window that looked over the green space on the backside of his building. Personally, she'd hate to live somewhere with no access to the outdoors—not even a balcony—but she knew Dean just thought of this place as a handy crash pad near the airport.

Speaking of the airport. If the apartment wasn't so messy, maybe she would have suggested she and her friends sleep here, given how early their flight would go out in the morning. But it was definitely a bachelor pad. Plus, there weren't any extra bedrooms.

She noticed the cell phone bill on top of a stack of mail on the desktop. When her phone conked out the previous year, Dean insisted she jump on his plan. They'd save money, and he didn't mind paying it. She'd protested, but he'd tapped the diamond he'd slid onto her finger weeks earlier, reminding her that eventually they'd combine most everything. He'd paid their cell bill for a year now. It would be a nice surprise for Dean if she paid the bill for once. She'd tell him to take the money he saved and do something fun with it. He was always making nice gestures like that for her. She knew she wasn't as good at those spontaneous little surprises as he was, but she could change that. For starters, she could do this for him.

As she picked up the bill, her hand brushed the paper beneath it. The texture felt different enough that it piqued her interest.

She picked up the piece of mail, squinting to make out the fancy font. It was a wedding invitation. The names meant nothing to her, and she wondered if someone Dean worked with was getting married. She knew many, but not all, of his coworkers.

Or . . . did the bride-to-be's last name sound vaguely familiar?

"Summer Morales," she said. "Morales. How do I know that name?"

A picture flashed in her mind then, like a still photograph one might capture of a pivotal moment.

They'd been at Dean's summer work picnic—the type of thing she hated, but he'd convinced her to go with him with the bribe of ice cream later. She replayed one particular scene of a woman she'd never met, hanging on Dean's arm and looking up at him in a smiling way that had the unmistakable air of intimacy to it. No one else seemed to notice, but Kit remembered the way the hair on her arms had prickled. Dean made introductions, looking unaffected by the woman's attention.

Later, when Kit stepped into the dessert buffet line, Dean's administrative assistant had leaned close and whispered that it was nice that Kit wasn't put off by Erin's presence. Kit remembered asking the woman who Erin was, and the uncomfortable wave of jealousy she'd felt when the story came out. She'd been right. Dean had dated the woman in his past. Why was he allowing her to flirt so blatantly with him at the picnic, when he'd brought Kit as his date?

Armed with the truth, Kit remembered feigning a headache and insisting they leave early. They'd fought that night, and for the first time since she'd started dating Dean, she'd questioned the depth of their relationship. Dean insisted Erin meant nothing to him. Kit wanted to believe him, but there was something he wasn't telling her. She was sure of it. But, with time, they eventually found their way back to a more solid footing, and the woman's name had never come up since.

"Her name was Erin *Morales*," Kit said aloud, the thick paper stock creasing in her tight grip.

Keys jangled in the lock.

She spun to face the door.

Dean rushed in, his expression tense. His eyes flitted between the paper she held and her face.

"Who the hell is Summer Morales?" Kit blurted. "And why did she invite you to her wedding?"

Dean hurried through the door, letting it slam behind him as he tossed his keys on the small table he ate at during his limited stays in his apartment. He held his hands out toward her, his gaze holding tight to hers.

"I can explain. I wanted to tell you, but the time never seemed right."

Instead of making her feel better, his words slammed against her chest, causing her heart to race. Anger that an old girlfriend had the nerve to invite him to her daughter's wedding had spurred her knee-jerk reaction. Logically, she knew Dean couldn't have prevented his old flame from sending it. Maybe the woman was tenacious, even after all this time. That didn't mean that Dean had encouraged her.

But his reaction was all wrong.

The only time Dean's cheeks ever flushed was when he was guilty of something. Until now, it was never anything serious, just simple things like putting a nearly empty carton of milk back in the fridge or using the last of the toilet paper.

His cheeks flamed red.

He ran his hands through his hair, leaving it sticking up at odd angles.

Kit felt lightheaded. Whether it was her lack of sleep, the stuffy air, or her system being overwhelmed from too many shocks, she couldn't be sure. All she did know for sure was that Dean was keeping something important from her.

"I need to sit down."

"I'm sorry it's so hot in here. I'd open the window, but that would only make it worse," he said, flipping on the ceiling fan above her as she sank onto his couch.

Her eyes went back to the wedding invitation. It was still clutched in her hand, even though she wanted nothing more than to throw it at him. Something was very off here, and she suspected it had everything to do with the bride's mother.

But at Dean's next words, she realized she couldn't have been more wrong.

"Summer is my daughter."

This was so much worse than an old girlfriend who still wanted him back.

The room spun. Nothing was making sense.

"Kit? Are you all right? Should I get you water?" He collapsed into a matching chair across from Kit, the bright flush of his cheeks draining away to an unhealthy pallor.

"Am I all right?" She hated the hysterical note in her voice. She'd never been prone to hysterics. Even through the worst of dealing with her mother. But this . . . "No, Dean, I'm not *all right*."

Unable to stay seated, she popped back to her feet, finally tossing the invitation at his face. She took a deep breath, tilted her head back, and focused on a burned-out lightbulb in the fan while she tried to settle her racing heart.

When she felt steadier, she lowered her eyes to his. "Your daughter? Do you mean to tell me that after all this time, when I've felt awful about depriving you of being a father, you already had a child?! You've been a father *all along*, and you never told me after all these years? How could you lie to me about something this important?"

The invite had landed on his thigh. He didn't touch it, and when he stood to catch her by the shoulders, it fluttered to the floor. "She's never been a part of my life. It was what her mother wanted, and I never argued. We were kids. In our twenties. But my blanket acceptance of Erin's wishes cost me more than you can ever imagine."

She wriggled away from him. His arms fell helplessly to his sides, and she could see the tears swimming in his eyes.

"Erin," she whispered.

"Yes. You know we dated. We've talked about that. It was nothing, really, but sometimes life has a way of turning nothing into an enormous pile of something."

She scoffed. "And that pile of something is a *child*."

He rubbed both hands on his cheeks. "That didn't come out right. Can we sit down and have a civil conversation about this?"

If her system wasn't already on overload, Kit might have agreed to an adult conversation. But her earlier heart-to-heart with her grandmother had left her feeling like a raw, wronged child again, and this was all too much.

She stared at the man she'd thought she could trust.

How did I fall for the lies again?

Hadn't she lived through enough dishonesty to know it wasn't safe to trust anyone?

They would have to talk about this eventually. She knew that. But, for now, she needed to leave before she said something she couldn't take back.

She felt the old walls settle back into place somewhere deep inside her—the walls she'd constructed as a teenager. The ones she'd needed to survive. The ones she'd worked so hard to put behind her so she wouldn't end up living life alone.

Her legs felt like wood as she walked back to Dean's desk. She picked up the cell phone bill. "My turn to pay this."

She knew this was a ridiculous thing to say at such a crucial time. But she'd reached full capacity. There was zero room to take in anything more.

He just stared at her with fear in his eyes.

After shoving the bill in the small purse still looped over her shoulder, she moved to his bedroom. Her steps felt robotic. The carry-on was in his closet.

My friends will help me through this, she thought, threading stiff fingers through the case's handle and making her way back through the apartment to the front door.

"Kit, we have to talk about this," Dean said, shuffling sideways beside her. "It isn't as bad as you think. Believe me."

Believe him. She couldn't bring herself to meet his eyes again. She shook her head, glanced at her set of spare keys she'd dropped on his counter when she'd entered—so long ago it seemed, before her world crumbled—but didn't pick them up.

"We'll talk when I get back," she said, letting herself out and closing the door behind her. As she walked toward the elevator, she prayed he wouldn't come after her.

He didn't.

CHAPTER TEN

K IT DIDN'T WANT TO acknowledge the pointy elbow nudging her right arm. After another restless night—thanks to both Dean's bombshell and someone's snoring—she needed sleep. The one thing she'd decided during yesterday afternoon's drive from Dean's apartment to her blissfully quiet and cool townhouse was that this girl's trip wouldn't suffer for all her current drama.

"Kit, I'm sorry, but I need to go to the bathroom," Jackie said, keeping her voice low in the shadowed cabin.

A quick glance up showed Kit that the pilot had turned off the seat belt sign. She must have fallen asleep after takeoff. "I told you not to drink two cups of coffee, Jackie."

Jackie popped her seat belt off and stood. "I thought we promised each other there'd be no lectures on this trip."

Kit snorted. "I think that was regarding no limits on fun things—like shopping, dancing, and wine consumption."

"Trust me, I'm much more fun when I have my morning coffee," Jackie said. "Scooch your legs to the side so I can get out."

Kit did her best to give Jackie room, and Renee did the same in her aisle seat.

"I'm so glad you guys let me crash your party," Renee said to Kit once Jackie was free. "I know making travel arrangements for five is tougher than four, especially for rooms."

Kit rearranged her legs to get comfortable. "Quit worrying about it, Renee. We love that you could get away. Besides, Lynette insists on having her own room—God knows she can afford it—so it wasn't even a wrinkle in my planning. By the way, who is watching Whispering Pines while you're away? July must be peak season for a lake resort in Minnesota."

Renee sighed. "It *is* peak season. It was almost impossible for me to get away when I first reopened the resort. But my oldest is able to run things for a week at a time now. I wouldn't turn it over to her for the entire summer season—she's not quite twenty-two—but she's a big help. Home for the summer. And my husband, Matt, will be around, too, when he isn't on duty."

"Ah, yes. Your hunky sheriff husband. I'm still sorry none of us could make it to your wedding."

"Don't be silly! Everyone is so busy, especially in the summer. I'm just glad we'll all get to reconnect on this trip. We're on a plane to *Maui*! I still can't believe it. I've never been to Hawaii. Have you?"

Kit shrugged. "First time for me, too. But I thought you met Matt on a tropical vacation. I remember your story of a romantic kiss at midnight on New Year's, complete with a sandy beach, waves, and moonlight."

The moment the words left her mouth, Kit felt a twinge of dismay at the memory of her awful fight with Dean.

They let Jackie crawl back to her seat and buckle in again. Sunlight streamed into the cabin through a few unshaded windows.

Renee smiled at Kit. "You have an excellent memory."

"That's not exactly something someone would forget," Kit said, doing her best to push all thoughts of Dean out of her mind.

"What wouldn't someone forget?" Jackie asked.

"Renee's never been to Hawaii. I remembered what she told us about how she met her new husband in a tropical paradise. I just couldn't remember where she found him."

"You make him sound like a lost dog," Jackie said.

Kit rolled her eyes. "Leave it to you to equate a sexy sheriff with a *dog*."

"I met him on a trip," Renee chimed back in. "In fact, this early morning flight reminds me of that plane ride I took with my two kids. It was to Fiji. That's where I met Matt. I was laid off from my job after twenty years, and I didn't know what I would do. I didn't know my Aunt Celia had left me the resort yet, but I found out when I was on that trip."

This surprised Kit. "I didn't know that part of the story."

Renee pulled her large purse out from under the seat in front of her, and rummaged through it. "It's been an incredible few years for me. My life looks totally different from what it was in late 2015, when we flew to Fiji. For a while, it felt like I was getting pummeled with one shock after another. But I'm happy to report that I survived the storm, and I've never been happier."

Kit understood how the storm felt.

Renee offered Kit and Jackie what looked like miniature breakfast bars, wrapped in pink cellophane. Kit accepted one. "These are cute. What are they?"

"Energy bars. My sister and mom sell them. They're kind of taking off. At first, they just offered them to resort guests at Whispering Pines, but now they can't keep up with demand."

Jackie unwrapped her bar and took a tentative bite. "Oh wow. That's good!"

"Jess makes these?" Kit asked, pleased with herself for remembering Renee's sister's name.

"No," Renee said. "Jess doesn't care much for cooking. She's too busy with other things. Our youngest sister, Val, is the baker in the family. She spent lots of time in the kitchen with our mom growing up. Now Mom insists that Val's culinary skills have exceeded hers."

Jackie took another bite of her bar, smiling as she chewed. "And your mom and sister are in business together?"

"I guess you could say that. Val has four boys, but they were struggling financially, so she wanted to do something while still being there for her kids. That was part of it, at least. She wanted to be more than a wife and mother. Our aunt—the same aunt who left me Whispering Pines—she left Val some financial backing to start a business. So that's what she's trying to figure out. Mom's helping."

Kit thought back to her discussion in the park with her grandmother. Had that only been two days ago? She wondered if Renee had any idea how lucky she was to have a supportive mother. "It sounds like your family is pretty great."

Renee nodded. "We are all really close. I know that isn't very common these days. I've got a lot to be thankful for. But it hasn't always been easy."

No one gets to be our age without some heartache along the way, Kit thought.

Jackie folded the pink wrapping from her bar and tucked it into the seat pocket in front of her. "Life can be tough," she said, echoing Kit's thoughts. "But a week on the beach will be the perfect time to hash through our troubles and figure out some answers. Isn't that what friends are for?"

Kit wasn't sure it would be that simple, but she appreciated feeling like she had somewhere to turn if she wanted to talk about her troubles. She'd have to decide whether she wanted to or not. Could she handle all the revelations she'd discovered over the past couple of days on her own?

Annie waited for them as they exited the plane in Kahului.

"You look well rested," Kit said, stiff and tired after her hours back in coach.

Renee, looking stiff as well, rushed off to find a bathroom.

"I *feel* rested," Annie said with a satisfied grin. "My husband earned back a few points with that surprise upgrade to first class. It was a first for me."

"What did Henry do this time that he had to earn back points?" Jackie asked, adjusting the straps on what looked like a very heavy backpack.

Annie seemed to deflate at the question.

Kit grabbed her arm and angled her toward the baggage claim sign. "Don't answer that, Annie. There will be plenty of time for talk later. For now, we're going to enjoy the tropical air and hope to God the rental I reserved is big enough to hold our luggage."

Annie's grin returned. "That might not have been an issue if you hadn't brought a suitcase big enough to hold a stowaway."

"Touché. The cleanup back home in Ruby Shores cut into the shopping I'd planned to do. And I'll admit, I wasn't as efficient with my packing as usual. I wasn't sure what things in my closet even fit anymore, so I just dumped. But my suitcase isn't even full. I want to do some shopping here, and I wanted to have room to take things home."

Renee returned from the lady's room. "Did I hear something about shopping?"

Kit dipped her head and extended her arm like a chauffeur might do. "Of course. Again, this is a *girls'* trip. But first, we need to get settled at our hotel. Assuming I can find it. Let's go."

The foursome made their way to baggage claim, exchanging high-fives when all their bags appeared, and then went to claim their rental. It wasn't long before Kit was driving them all down a winding highway that hugged a breathtaking shoreline.

"Can I just say that you knocked it out of the park, Kit?" Jackie said, lowering her window. "If you ever tire of counting butterflies at work, you could start a new gig as a travel agent."

Kit slowed when a gaggle of chickens strutted onto the highway. Once the oncoming traffic was past, she eased around the birds, thankful the road wasn't too busy. "I'll have you know I do lots more at work than count bugs. And no thank you to the travel agent gig. Not to complain, but planning this trip was a real pain in the butt. I'll gladly turn over the reins to someone else for next year's trip."

Annie tapped Kit's headrest from behind. "I nominate Lynette since she's not here to decline."

"What time does she get in?" Renee asked from her seat beside Annie.

Kit shrugged. "I was going to check the email she sent me last week, but I forgot. See? Some travel agent I'd make. Maybe she's already landed. Her arrival time wasn't too far off from ours, but there was enough of a difference that she didn't want to make us wait at the airport."

"I still can't believe this worked out." Jackie captured her blowing hair in one hand. "All five of us, together again. It'll be like summer camp all over!"

Annie laughed. "Only better. Summer camp for grownups. I'm hoping we aren't in bunk beds, and don't have to worry about spiders crawling in our sheets."

Kit held up one hand, keeping the other on the steering wheel. "I can promise there will be no bunk beds or spiders at the hotel I booked for tonight."

Kit laid her forehead on the cold marble of the resort's front desk. She was exhausted, and they'd already hit their first travel snag.

"I didn't realize when you promised no bunk beds or spiders that you were comfortable saying that because there are no *rooms*," Jackie said. She emphasized her last word by bumping against Kit's thigh with her hip.

Kit groaned without lifting her head. "Cute, Jackie. Instead of figuring out how to open a business to unite senior dogs with the elderly, try your hand at comedy. Because you are *so* funny."

"Who's ready for a piña colada?"

Annie's words were enough to make Kit stand up straight, despite the fact that another migraine was threatening. "Why aren't any of you worried that we don't have rooms?" She rubbed her temple with one hand while she accepted a frosty drink with the other. A trickle of the white, slushy concoction dribbled over her fingers. She licked at the mess, and the taste on her tongue reminded her that life wasn't all bad. She was in the tropics, for God's sake.

Annie raised a plastic flute she still held. "Because the woman at the front desk didn't seem overly concerned. I'm sure her manager will be over shortly with some answers."

A second woman in a well-tailored, short-sleeved black suit approached, her heels clicking on the cool marble at their feet. "I'm so sorry for the confusion, ladies. We do, in fact, have rooms for you. One guest in your party called earlier this afternoon to make some changes, and they ended up changing the name on the reservation. That's why my employee couldn't find your records immediately."

"Changes?" Kit asked, her overtaxed brain failing to connect the dots.

"Lynette must have called in," Renee said.

"That's correct. A Ms. Lynette Howe phoned in and requested room upgrades. She also left a message for all of you." The manager held up a folded black card. "Would you like me to relay it to you now?"

"An *upgrade*?" Kit repeated.

This pulled a groan from Jackie. "Please ignore her. I think she left her brain on the plane. It's been a long day. It may only be four o'clock here, but it's already nine at home, and I'm afraid we're going to need a little time to adjust. What did Lynette say?"

Kit was happy to let Jackie take charge.

The woman slipped a slim set of readers onto the bridge of her nose and referenced the note. "Lynette is sorry to let you know travel complications will delay her arrival until tomorrow afternoon, but she insists you enjoy some extra pampering while you wait for her. P.S. If you discuss anything juicy, be prepared to repeat everything when she gets here." The woman grinned at them over her glasses. "It sounds like the five of you have a fun vacation planned."

The growl of someone's stomach could be heard over the hushed conversations of other nearby guests. Kit noticed Renee blush and push a hand against her stomach. Her blush brought to mind Dean's flushed face from the day before, and another wave of exhaustion hit her.

The woman assisting them must have heard Renee's stomach, too. She tucked Lynette's message into her jacket pocket and clapped her hands. "You ladies must be tired, and you are obviously hungry, so we should get you settled. You can leave your bags. I'll have someone bring them up for you."

It felt odd to leave her bag, but the woman was walking away at such a brisk clip, Kit had to hurry to keep up. She looked at her friends and felt some of her weariness ebb away. "I'm sorry Lynette is losing a day."

Annie drained the last of her piña colada and handed the flute to an employee balancing a platter of similar empties. "I am, too. I can't wait to see her and catch up. I also can't wait to learn more about this *upgrade*."

Kit noticed a smile flit across the manager's face as she entered an elevator and held a button to keep the doors open long enough for all four friends to enter.

"Are the two new rooms near each other?" Jackie asked, stepping back against the wall of the elevator to give everyone room.

The woman nodded. "They are at the same end of the hallway. Two have an ocean view. The other two face a lovely golf course. Lynette said you could decide who gets which room, but I can assure you, they are all equally lovely."

"Wait." Kit shifted her purse strap up on her shoulder. "Did you say *four*? There must be some mistake. I had two rooms booked for us, plus a separate suite for Lynette."

With a shake of her head, the woman pushed another button on the elevator's control panel. "There's no mistake. Your friend requested that each of you have your own personal suite. And don't worry, she's already covered the cost of the rooms for the next four nights. Oh, and I forgot to read you the last line in her message. She said to 'just say *thank you*.'"

Everyone but Renee laughed. She glanced around. "Why is that funny?"

"That was something our favorite lunch lady used to say to us when she'd save us the best slices of pizza or chocolate cake. *Just say 'thank you'!* I can't believe Lynette remembered that."

Renee shook her head, tapping the wide silver bangle on her wrist. "You aren't going to believe *this*. I ordered this bracelet from Lynette's company, and they inscribed those very words on the inside. I guess those words must have meant something to her."

"I guess they did," Kit said.

"This way, ladies."

They filed out of the elevator and followed the woman down a nearby hallway. Her heels were silent against the thick carpet. She stopped near the end of the hallway and used a card to open a door. Light flooded the hushed hallway, and the *click-clack* of her shoes started up again as she showed them inside.

The last threads of jetlag tore away from Kit's brain as her senses fought to take in the beauty. Cool shades of cream and white, punctuated with turquoise and pink, surrounded them on all sides. The brightest swath of bluish-green was the wide expanse of ocean, visible through open doors leading to a roomy balcony. Spilling from a white vase on a low coffee table, tropical blossoms perfumed the air.

"Oh my" was all Kit could manage as her feet carried her toward the balcony. She felt as if she were floating.

"I vote Kit gets this room," Jackie said, trailing behind her. "None of the other rooms could be this perfect, and she earned it with the work she did setting up this trip."

With a flick of her wrist, the manager filled the perfumed air with the soft strains of a violin. "I can assure you, all four rooms are equally lovely. I'll open the other three for you as well, and then I'll give you a chance to settle in. We offer a delicious menu selection in our open-air restaurant downstairs if you are interested in coming down for a meal."

Kit spun slowly, taking it all in. "That all sounds lovely, but I'm not sure I'm ever going to want to leave these rooms. Do you offer room service?"

The woman grinned. "Of course. Anything and everything to make your stay more pleasant. And please, here is my card. My direct number is there if you need anything. Ms. Howe asked that I take extra special care of all of you, pending her arrival. You girls certainly have a generous friend."

Jackie bent to smell one of the wide, blood-red blossoms in the white vase. "We certainly do. We've waited thirty years to take this vacation together, and it looks like Lynette is pulling out all the stops."

Chapter Eleven

THE SAND PULLED AT Kit's bare feet, cold and gritty beneath a top layer of sunbaked warmth. She stepped forward with trepidation, her eyes seeking Dean where he waited for her beneath a floral arch of blood-red blooms and greenery. The ocean crashed endlessly in the background. The heavy sand slowed her progress. She watched as her fiancé checked his watch. She could sense his impatience, even from the distance that still separated them, but she couldn't seem to get any closer.

A light tapping sound emanated from nearby, out of place and barely discernable.

Music from a hidden violin morphed into the familiar strains of Canon in D, and rows of guests rose from white plastic chairs and turned to face her in unison. Something wasn't right. She didn't know any of these people. When her eyes darted back to Dean, his back was to her as he scuttled away across the sand toward the meandering line where water lapped across the shore.

The bouquet in her hands shifted into a wedding program sporting a snapshot of a much younger couple. Kit still wore a white gown—the one she'd thought was her wedding dress—but she could see now that it was a simple, flowing summer dress.

This wasn't *her* wedding. She wasn't the bride.

A hand pulled her from the aisle. Her eyes met Jackie's stern gaze. She felt the reprimand of her tardiness without her friend having to utter a word.

The tapping grew louder.

"What is that noise?" she whispered, but a glance in Jackie's direction revealed nothing more than an empty row of white chairs.

Banging replaced the mysterious tapping sound. Kit's eyes fluttered open, allowing a sea of white to flood in.

"Kit! Are you awake in there?"

Kit grabbed a pillow and dropped it on her face, molding it down over her ears with bent arms. It blocked out the white light, but not Jackie's hollering.

"Come on, Kit. Get up! We're going down for breakfast and we only have forty minutes until our appointments start in the resort's spa!"

Did she say spa?

Kit tossed the pillow aside and checked her watch.

It was only twenty after seven.

"Go away. I'm on vacation and vowed not to get up before eight!"

The handle of the outer door leading into her suite jiggled. Her friends weren't going to leave her alone.

What was Jackie saying about a spa?

Kit swung her feet out of bed, immediately recoiling from the shock of the icy, smooth tile below. She'd woken during the night, she remembered, her body soaked with sweat. A change of the thermostat to its coldest setting had seemed like a brilliant solution at the time, but now her bedroom felt like a meat locker.

More jiggling.

"I'm coming! Hold your horses!"

She shrugged into the decadent white robe she'd dropped on the end of her bed following her shower the night before to wash away the travel grime.

A yank brought the wider-than-average door swinging silently inward—too fast for her to prevent the inevitable crash against the wall. But there was no crash. A hefty, rubber-tipped doorstop sent the door swinging back toward Jackie's smiling face. An extended hand stopped the freewheeling door, then her three chattering friends who'd successfully kept her up well past her bedtime filed into her room, looking much too awake.

"This time difference has me all messed up," Kit complained as she tagged along behind the other women. "How can you all look so chipper?"

"I just talked to my son. It's twelve thirty in the afternoon back home," Annie said, sliding the door open to Kit's balcony. "He made me promise to bring him back a fun pair of board shorts."

"That does not explain why you don't look as tired as I feel," Kit groaned.

"Get dressed, Kit," Jackie said. "We have reservations at the resort's restaurant in five minutes. We talked about breakfast last night. Did you forget to set an alarm?"

Kit rubbed her eyes. "I'm sorry, guys. I'm sure I missed half of what we talked about in Renee's room last night. I haven't gotten much sleep lately, and I think it all caught up with me. Tell me I didn't plan a day packed solid with touristy crap for us today."

Jackie held up one hand. "We promise. Don't you remember? We all agreed to take today and ease into vacation mode. Besides, Lynette isn't due in until this afternoon. We don't want her to miss out on too much."

"Other than our morning at the spa," Renee chimed in.

"Did we talk about the spa last night?" Kit asked. "I don't remember, but I wouldn't say no to a massage."

Annie checked her watch. "No. Lynette is still spoiling us. I was up before the sun and found an invitation under my door to a morning of pampering at the resort's spa."

"We *all* got one," Renee said, heading back to Kit's door. She returned a moment later with a pale turquoise envelope in her hand. "Here's yours."

Kit took it from her and started to open it, but Jackie snatched it away. "Kit, you never like to be late. Go. Throw an outfit on. If we don't hurry, we'll all have rumbly stomachs during our massages."

"Fine, fine, give me two minutes," she said, rushing past Jackie toward her suitcase.

She still felt grouchy, but she had to admit—dressing for a spa visit held vastly more appeal than attending the strange beach wedding from her dream minutes before.

Kit tossed the last corner of her toast to the persistent bird that had squawked at her throughout her breakfast. She knew better, but she couldn't resist.

They'd opted for a table on the edge of the patio to enjoy an unobstructed view of the ocean waves. The salt of the sea blended with the aroma wafting from the flowers and steaming coffee on their table, making for a heady mix.

"A massage is the *only* thing that could pull me away from this relaxing breakfast," Annie said, tilting her face up to the warm morning sun.

Everyone agreed. Kaanapali was living up to its hype.

"Is anyone else feeling a little weird about all this money Lynette is throwing around on us, and she isn't even here yet?" Annie asked, tapping a nail against her coffee cup.

"Not as weird as I felt thirty minutes ago when I went from being the bride on the beach down there to a tardy wedding guest."

Jackie frowned, her eyes darting to the glass of orange juice next to Kit's coffee. "Is there champagne in that?"

Kit laughed. "No. It was a dream I was having when you all showed up banging on my door. It was the weirdest thing."

Annie nodded, a knowing look on her face. "I'm sure this beautiful location has your subconscious toying with the idea of a destination wedding. It makes sense. I can't see you going the traditional church route."

Kit knew the more likely cause was that shocking wedding invitation she'd found on Dean's desk, coupled with the impatience she sensed in him over her failure to set a date. She hadn't said a word about the invite or Dean's shocking revelation to her friends, but she would. When the moment was right. She needed more time to think through what it meant first. She'd need a glass of something stronger than orange juice in her hand when she discussed Dean's betrayal.

Their waiter brought their tabs, and they dashed off their signatures and room numbers before scraping back their chairs and heading for the standalone building that housed the resort's spa.

As they walked, Jackie spoke up. "Annie . . . getting back to your question about Lynette spending money on us. Remember how she hated all the times she didn't have enough lunch money during school? Things were really tight for her and her mom. She told me once that her dream was to pick up the tab for something fun for all of us. Her online boutique is doing really well. Treating us like this is a dream come true for her."

"And me," Kit muttered as the foursome entered the hushed interior of the spa.

The air smelled even better here than it did at breakfast. The peaceful sound of gurgling water paired nicely with the dainty, slow twang of a ukulele. It reminded her of the times her grandfather picked at an old ukulele he claimed to have won in a poker game as a young man in the Army.

"All that's missing is a pretty Hawaiian woman in a grass skirt," Renee said, swaying her hips to the calming music.

"Aloha, ladies." A fresh-faced young woman greeted them, appearing from behind a bamboo divider. It was as if Renee's words had conjured her out of thin air, but she wore a pale pink uniform rather than a grass skirt and coconut bra. "We have a morning of luxurious treatments planned for all of you."

Jackie groaned. "I've waited my whole life for someone to say those words to me."

A ripple of soft laughter followed.

"Please follow me. I'll show you where you can change." The woman led them into the depths of the spa, much as the other woman had guided them to their gorgeous rooms the day before. "Our goal is to help each of you feel lighter, brighter, and more peaceful by helping you release tension and troubles from your body and mind."

"That's an ambitious goal," Kit said.

The woman paused, looking back over her shoulder at Kit, a challenging glint in her eye. "We are *very* good at our jobs."

Someone whistled, and Jackie elbowed Kit when they started moving again. "Why so cynical today? Lighten up. This is going to be fun."

Jackie was right, of course. Quiet time to reflect under the expert hands of professionals in a gorgeous setting was just what she needed to put her troubles aside.

At least until she had to go home.

Kit could have easily dozed off under the strong hands of her masseuse as the younger woman kneaded tension from her neck and shoulders, but she hated to miss a moment. She'd already enjoyed a facial, hand and foot massages, and a seaweed wrap, and her nails sported a deep aqua polish that reminded her of the ocean. Rumbling stomachs weren't a concern either. Light, tasty treats awaited them at opportune times and locations as she and her friends rotated through their morning activities.

She'd needed this. All of it. Time with old friends who already knew most of her secrets and loved her in spite of it all. They expected nothing from her except friendship. None of these women had betrayed her—which was more than she could say for nearly everyone else in her life.

As the last vestiges of tension released from her body, a wave of emotion washed up in her. Her body's reaction confused her, and she tensed.

The hands massaging her left shoulder paused. "Does something hurt?" the demure woman asked, her voice low and quiet to match the peaceful atmosphere of the room. "Am I applying too much pressure?"

The concern in the woman's voice was too much. Kit's shoulders shook as silent tears wet the silky fabric beneath her cheek. She shook her head, wanting the woman to continue, but she didn't trust her own voice.

"Nature does not like a vacuum. I felt the tension . . . the unease . . . ebb from your muscles. From your body. I think perhaps what you are feeling is simply your spirit, your soul, working to purge the negative emotions you were holding deep inside. Don't hide your tears. Your reaction isn't as uncommon as you might think. Now, if there is no physical pain, just try to relax. I have a special oil here that can help with the release of negativity."

All Kit could manage was a nod. She tried not to feel foolish, and she clung to the woman's words as she cried.

The only way to heal old wounds was to let the poison go.

What was released could no longer hurt her.

Kit shivered as she emerged from the cool, hushed atmosphere of the spa into the hot Hawaiian sun. She shouldn't have doubted their promise of relief. While she wasn't exactly at peace, she did indeed feel lighter for the first time in three days. She could even pull a deep breath into her lungs and hold it without feeling like she would suffocate.

There was no need for her to rush. They'd agreed to meet on the stunning beach behind the resort when they finished up. The sun was shining, a refreshing breeze caressed her pampered skin, and there were zero expectations of her for the afternoon. The sensible part of her brain considered an afternoon in the shade, away from the damaging salt and sun. She hated to undo the benefits of the various treatments she'd enjoyed that morning. But then she remembered that the words *vacation* and *sensible* didn't belong in the same sentence.

After changing into the only swimming suit and coverup in her suitcase that she actually liked, she grabbed her new paperback and made her way to the water. She was the last one, aside from Lynette, to reach the beach.

"Any word from Lynette yet?" Kit asked her friends. "I hate that she's still not here."

Jackie tilted back her large-brimmed straw hat so she could see Kit. "Well, hello. We thought you got lost. And, no, no word yet."

Kit grinned. "Nice hat. You look like Mrs. Howell from *Gilligan's Island*."

Jackie's bottom lip popped out. "It's your fault I have to wear it."

"My fault?"

She nodded. "After pointing out my scandalous roots in bed the other morning, I ended up paying double to reschedule my hair appointment before we left. So there's no way I'm letting this expensive hair fade in the sun," Jackie said with just the right amount of dramatic flair to be funny.

Annie looked up from the book in her lap, her eyes darting between Kit and Jackie. "In bed?"

Renee laughed.

"Get your mind out of the gutter, Annie," Jackie said, dropping her hat onto the sand next to her lounge chair. "We had to share my old bed the night of the storms in Ruby Shores."

Annie shrugged. "Isn't the whole point of a girls' vacation to let our hair down? Be inappropriate? I, for one, am sick and tired of being all buttoned-up and proper. If I want to let my mind dip into the gutter, so be it."

Kit dropped into one of two open chairs. "That sounds like a fabulous idea." She grabbed the hem of her coverup and yanked it over her head. The thin material caught on one of her diamond studs, trapping her for a second. Once she was loose, she tossed the coverup on top of Jackie's discarded hat.

"A bikini?" Renee clapped her hands. "I love it! You go, girl. I haven't had the nerve to wear one of those in twenty years."

Kit tugged at the high waistband of her bottoms, smoothing it over the extra roll of flesh that she didn't remember being there the last time she wore this suit. "I probably shouldn't wear one either, but screw it. It's not like you three care what I look like, and I don't know anyone else here. I get so blasted hot in a one-piece."

Annie reached for the strings of her coverup, untying it and throwing it on top of Kit's. "You girls are good for me. I want to go home with a nice tan."

"You're good for me, too," Renee said. "I watch the girls and younger women traipse around Whispering Pines in skimpy swimsuits, and I miss the days when I looked good in things like that. But when I look at the three of you, all I see are strong, seasoned women who glow. No one is paying any attention to us. Why do we worry so much about what we look like?"

"Because society is obsessed with youth," Annie said, a bitter edge to her voice. She lowered the back of her lounge chair, untied the strap around her neck, and held the top in place while she flipped onto her stomach. Kit grinned. If she sat up too quickly, she'd flash the beach.

"Do you ever feel invisible?" Jackie asked, hiking up the short skirt she wore over her swimsuit so her thighs were bare.

Kit pulled Jackie's hat out from under the two discarded coverups. "I'm sorry I teased you about your hat. I love that shade she used on your hair this time. Put this on so you don't ruin it. What do you mean, invisible?"

Jackie shoved the sunhat back on her head with a shrug. "I mean exactly what I said. Invisible. Years ago, my mom complained about that to her sister, and it stuck with me. I hated the dejection I heard in her voice when she said it. I used to think she was oversensitive, but now I know she was right."

Renee pulled a tube of sunscreen out of a canvas bag and squirted a dollop of lotion into her palm. "My aunt used to say that some women fade into the background as they age. I think it was at her eightieth birthday party. She had a bright, flowy dress on, and it made her eyes sparkle. When I complimented her on it, she told me she refused to be invisible. And believe me, no one would have ever accused my Aunt Celia of fading."

"She sounds like the woman *I* want to be at eighty," Jackie said, tucking her darkened locks behind her ears and adjusting her hat.

Renee nodded. "You would have all loved Celia. She was an amazing woman."

"Did I hear someone say 'amazing woman'? Because I'm looking at four of them right now!"

Kit whipped her head around at the fresh voice and scrambled out of the low-slung chair as fast as she could. "Lynette! You made it!"

As Lynette rushed toward them, a surge of joy washed through Kit at the sight of the woman. Her smiling face, the bright caftan she wore, and the way her signature salt-and-pepper curls danced on the ocean breeze. The two grabbed each other in an enthusiastic embrace.

"I hope you ladies saved some wine for me, because it's been a heck of a travel day!" Lynette said, still holding tight to Kit's hand as she hugged each of the other three women with her free arm. "I didn't think I'd ever get here!"

After assuring Lynette there was plenty more wine—and fun—Kit kicked her way back to her chair through the hot sand as the greetings continued. She noticed two men, both shirtless and attractive and at least ten years younger, saunter by along the water. Here was the eye candy she'd hoped to see. One of the men gave a friendly wave and whispered something to his friend.

After giving their group the once-over, the other man yelled that they'd send drinks over to get their party started, then they continued on their way.

Renee stared after them. "Did those two just hit on us?"

Kit laughed. "Yes, I think they did. Hey, maybe we aren't so invisible after all!"

Chapter Twelve

BY Sunday morning, Kit was ready to explore the island. Her body was finally past the jetlag, and after a day of pampering and relaxing on the beach, she needed to move.

As a group, they planned to alternate between lounging by either the pool or the ocean at the resort, and playing tourist on the island. Kit knew Jackie had visited Kauai with her girls and Ben once. Only Lynette had been to Maui before.

"But remember, one of the main reasons we're doing this is so we can reconnect," Jackie had reminded them all at breakfast that morning. "I don't know about the rest of you, but I've missed our long talks under a hot summer sun!"

Sunday, according to their plan, would be a touristy day. They would explore old Lahaina and wrap the day up at the traditional luau that evening. Their resort offered bus transportation into town, so no one needed to drive the rental.

"I'd forgotten how many little shops line Front Street," Lynette said as they stepped off the air-conditioned bus. "If any of you plan to take souvenirs home to family, this will be the perfect time to get that done early."

Kit's eyes scanned the area. The mighty Pacific Ocean lay off to their left, with plenty of commerce on their right. "We could have skipped breakfast this morning. These hole-in-the-wall eateries look adorable. We can get everything from coconut shrimp to shaved ice to Hawaiian coffee, all within a few yards of each other!"

Annie rubbed her hands together. "I hope some of the shops carry baby clothes."

"*Baby* clothes?" Kit asked, wondering why Annie would be interested in bringing home souvenirs for an infant.

Unless . . .

"Wait. Do you have news?! Is Ava expecting?"

"I am! I mean, *she* is!" Annie laughed. Her excitement over a brand-new chapter in life gave her a definite glow. She bounced up and down. "I've been dying to tell you. Can you believe it?"

Her announcement was met with hugs and squeals all around.

"That was fast," Jackie said. "They've been married for, what . . . a year?"

Annie shook her head. "Two years. But it still doesn't feel real. They're both only twenty-four. They seem too young to have kids already."

Lynette grabbed Annie's hand. "I know just the place. My CFO had a baby two weeks before I came here the last time, and I found the cutest shop a block off Front Street. I might have gone a little overboard. Come on, ladies, let's start there. This is a momentous occasion! I hope they're still in business. Who would have thought, when we planned these trips way back when, that one of us would be a grandma already?"

"*Almost* a grandma," Annie said, skipping to keep up with the longer-legged Lynette. "It doesn't feel real yet. And I'm still so nervous for Ava and her husband."

"Oh, it'll feel real the minute you hold that little one in your arms," Jackie said.

All five of them headed in search of the store. After a bit, Kit, Renee, and Jackie fell back, and as soon as there was a distance between them and the other two, Kit sighed.

"Can you guys believe this? We aren't old enough to be grandmothers."

She noticed Jackie and Renee exchange glances.

"What? Don't tell me one of *you* has news, too?"

Renee snorted. "No! Not me, at least. But my daughter is twenty-one and my son is almost nineteen. Neither has a significant other, but, knowing they date, I worry about it happening. And I say 'worry' only because neither is ready to have kids yet. Parents have worried about their babies having babies since time began. At least Ava is married."

"I second that," Jackie said. "My twins aren't ready for babies yet, nor am I. But you never know. I'm excited for Annie, though. You know, it's weird. I thought Annie was acting strange, like she had something on her mind. I'm glad it's good news."

Kit agreed, still processing Annie's news. Her own decision to never have kids would also mean no grandkids. It was something she hadn't really thought about, and she felt a pang of disappointment in her heart. During her harried drive home from Dean's on Thursday, she kept replaying that momentous decision about kids. Was she too old to change her mind? Yes, given her age. Now, here was Annie, facing the prospect of being a grandmother! It felt surreal.

Lynette held open the boutique door, waving for them to hurry. "Ladies, we have shopping to do! Annie said her daughter is expecting a girl. The Kaleidoscope Girls can surely get that little peanut off on a stylish foot."

The shop was long and narrow. Plenty of pinks and purples hung on the right, with more gender-neutral and boyish outfits down the center and to the left. Kit couldn't resist running her fingers over the soft muslin of a darling white blanket sprinkled with tiny butterflies in pastel colors.

Lynette's comment about the Kaleidoscope Girls sent Kit's mind way back, to the first summer she'd met these women at summer camp. She'd had zero interest in attending. But these girls had welcomed her with open arms—at least, eventually—and their friendship had survived for nearly forty years.

Sometimes the things we fear the most turn out to be the greatest blessings.

As she watched Annie flit from display table to hanging racks to cubbies full of every kind of baby trinket and bauble imaginable, Kit got caught up in the excitement with the others. None of them could resist. After an hour of picking from the darling assortment of merchandise, the five agreed they'd done enough damage to their pocketbooks. They needed coffee.

Given their piles of purchases, the shop owner graciously offered to ship it all to Annie's home back in Ruby Shores, free of charge.

"It's our job to spoil that little girl," Lynette said later, as they came to a bakery they'd passed earlier. "After my first time visiting that boutique, I went home with the idea of adding an infant line to our business, but we ultimately decided against it."

"Why?" Jackie asked.

"Mother convinced me it could dilute our brand. In hindsight, I can see she was right. But how fun would it be to go to market and pick out precious little outfits like those?"

At the counter they got their pick-me-up beverages, but there were no open tables, so they took their treats to go. With steaming paper cups of coffee and fresh pastries in hand, the women then made their way to benches in Banyan Tree Square.

Kit kicked off her sandals as she nibbled on a macadamia-encrusted scone, her eyes taking in the hustle and bustle around them. "What will Henry say when those boxes of baby goodies arrive?"

The smile Annie had worn since revealing her big secret faded at Kit's question, and before responding she took a sip of her pale coffee. Annie always added plenty of cream to every cup. "I doubt he'll notice," she said.

It seemed like a strange response, but then Kit remembered Henry wasn't the father of Ava and Colton, Annie's two oldest kids. "What does he think about the baby news?"

Coffee sloshed over the rim of Annie's cup, and she set it down, shaking off her hand. "Good thing that cooled down," she said, her smile looking forced. "Actually, I haven't told him. She isn't due until early March, so my daughter asked me to keep it to myself for a while yet. She knows Henry isn't too fond of her husband. But I wanted to tell you four. You don't count."

Lynette laughed. "Only old friends can say something like that and not offend each other."

"You know what I mean," Annie said, sipping her coffee again. "But enough about me. What are we shopping for next?"

Renee crinkled an empty sheet of wax paper and brushed a muffin crumb from the corner of her mouth. "I have explicit directions to bring both Julie and Robbie sweatshirts. I would like to get that done today, so I don't have to be searching for those during the rest of the trip."

Lynette nodded. "Good plan. How old are your two these days? What are they up to?"

"Julie is running things at Whispering Pines for me while I hang out with you. Believe it or not, she'll turn twenty-two next month. She'll wrap up her undergraduate degree soon, and then I'm not sure what her plans will be. She had a tough freshman year, so she feels like she's a semester behind. After Celia left me the resort, Julie was an enormous help. I couldn't have reopened without her."

"Hey, maybe we should visit Whispering Pines for one of our annual girls' trips," Jackie said. "I know we spent that one weekend there last year, but it wasn't summertime. Renee, you always light up when you talk about your resort. It must be a very special place."

Renee's head tilted, as if considering Jackie's suggestion. Then she sighed. "I'm not sure about that. Don't get me wrong, I love our resort. To me, it's the most special place on earth. Repeat customers say the same thing. But it's small and rustic. There isn't a bar or restaurant anymore, though there used to be, way back when. I couldn't compete with this."

Activity continued around them, and the ever-present whisper of the ocean provided background to it all.

"It isn't a competition, Renee," Lynette said, downing the last of her coffee. "Yes, Maui is breathtaking. Big trips like this can be a treat. But do you guys feel like we have to do something *this* extravagant every year?"

The other women all shook their heads.

"It's not about the location as much as the company," Annie said, holding her coffee high as if in a toast. "But any trip is better if there's water involved. I don't care if it's an ocean, a lake, or even a swimming pool. Water and sunshine are hard to beat. I'd love to visit Whispering Pines in the summer."

Renee grinned, her appreciation for her friends' flexibility and interest reflected in her eyes. "You girls are the best."

"What about your son? How old is he?" Kit asked, bringing the conversation full circle. Of the four other women in their group, she knew the least about Renee's story. Their paths had crossed much less frequently since that first year at summer camp.

"Oh, yes, Robbie. My little guy who grew too quickly into a young man. Believe it or not, he'll turn nineteen this fall. We *all* survived his freshman year of college. It took time to find the right balance between fun and his studies, but he got there . . . *eventually*. I hope."

Jackie laughed. "I know exactly what you mean. Both my girls struggled with that, in different ways, last year. I'm hoping our kids' second years go more smoothly."

Kit took another sip of her cooling coffee, enjoying but not truly feeling a part of the conversation as it focused on kids and eventual grandkids. She glanced Lynette's way, wondering if her one other childless friend was feeling the same way. But Lynette seemed fully engaged in what Renee was saying. That was the thing about Lynette. When she gave someone her attention, she was all in.

Jackie stood and tossed the paper products from her midmorning snack into a nearby garbage can. "I vote we make our way up and down the street and hit every tacky souvenir shop Lahaina has to offer. But we can't only buy for our families. I have an idea. Remember how I said yesterday that I sometimes feel invisible these days?"

Kit got to her feet, disposing of her garbage, too. "I have a theory about that, Jackie. Maybe you feel invisible because you're spending all your time with dogs now, whereas you used to work in a corporate office with lots of people. It's not like a collie can ask you how your day was or compliment you on your new dye job."

"Ha-ha," Jackie shot back. "To be honest, I feel more at home with the dogs these days. But seriously, I think we should all shop for a fun new dress to wear to the luau tonight. Something more colorful than the clothes we packed in our suitcases. Maybe a little more revealing, less conservative."

Lynette looked enthralled with the idea. "No one has ever accused *me* of being conservative."

Jackie waved a hand as if sweeping away Lynette's words. "I agree, hon. You have amazing clothes. You should—you've built a very successful career selling fabulous clothes to women. But when was the last time you wore something that didn't come from your company? I bet even *you* could use some fresh inspiration some days."

"Oh, you have no idea," Lynette said. "I'm in. But we vote on the dresses for each other, right? That way no one will wimp out."

"You're on," Jackie said. "Let's go."

Kit spun her sweating cocktail between her fingers, enjoying the way the sunlight glinted off the glass. It would feel good to sit after a full day on her feet, but there was more for them to do before dinner and the hula dancing started.

This group knew how to shop. They'd purchased the trinkets and clothes to take home for their families, but finding the dresses proved to be the most fun.

Lynette, an expert in clothing women's bodies, had been correct to insist they all weigh in on each other's selections. It proved to be an eye-opening experience.

"I've never worn a dress like this," Annie said as they strolled along the sidewalk that rimmed the beach. She motioned down at the deep V neckline and mid-thigh length of her new wrap dress. "I somehow don't think this is normal attire for a grandmother-to-be."

"We need to reinvent clothing for grandmas," Lynette joked. "Mom would be more likely to approve of a new line for mature women than for babies. That feels like an idea that still fits in our wheelhouse."

"And you could help keep us all in style with that line," Renee said. "I need to do a better job of updating my wardrobe."

Kit shook the ice cubes in her glass, not wanting to waste any of her tasty drink. A well-built, shirtless young man passed by, wearing the relaxed uniform of the staff. It consisted of nothing more than a yellow-and-green-print cloth tied around his waist. She couldn't help but wonder what he wore underneath. The man-boy whisked her empty glass away, freeing her hands.

This is so fun, she thought. *I don't ever want to forget today.*

"We all look great tonight, and the sunset over the ocean is gorgeous," she said. "We need a group photo with the water as our background."

Kit searched for someone who could take the shot. A woman, wearing a dress that matched the earlier man's "uniform," stood nearby, taking pictures for another group. Kit caught the woman's eye, passing her phone to the quasi-photographer.

"Come on, girls, everybody needs to squish together so we all fit in the picture," Kit said, doing her best to get the distracted women lined up as quickly as possible.

"Maybe I could just use this as our Christmas card this year," Annie said with a laugh, tugging at the hem of her short dress. "People would sure wonder about that, wouldn't they?"

After a series of shots, Kit retrieved her phone and thanked the woman. They still had fifteen minutes until the buffet would open, so they continued down the sidewalk.

"I know your outfit isn't technically a dress, Renee," Jackie was saying, "but that jumpsuit is timeless. Didn't you say your husband has property on Fiji? Do you ever go?"

Renee nodded, preening in her vivid aqua pantsuit sporting slit legs and tropical flowers splashed across the fabric. "We are hoping we can get away in 2020—so next summer—to celebrate our wedding anniversary. This little number will definitely be in my suitcase for that return trip. Oh, say, look at these cute totem poles. I should take one back to the resort and mount it along the beach. They're supposed to chase away evil spirits."

Jackie frowned. "You have evil spirits at Whispering Pines?"

Renee laughed. "No. But we do have a couple of mischievous ghost boys said to roam the beach and hide sand toys."

"That sounds like a ghost story best told around a campfire," Lynette said, bending down to study one of the handcrafted poles.

Kit watched as her friends debated over which locally crafted totem pole would be best for Whispering Pines. Maybe she should pick up a small one for her front patio, too. It would be a fun reminder of the trip.

Eventually, they found their way to the open buffet line. When Kit had made their reservations, she'd selected the more expensive seating option that placed them near the stage. As she set her full plate on their table and got down onto a low pillow, she hoped she'd be able to get back off the ground again at the evening's conclusion.

When she voiced her concern, Annie shot her a squinty-eyed look. "Didn't we agree to avoid saying anything negative about our aging bodies for the rest of our trip? Quit it, Kit. If I can get down here and risk flashing my unmentionables at the table behind us, you can, too."

The laughs continued. These women fed Kit's soul. She'd needed this more than she'd even imagined.

Eventually, Lynette pushed her empty plate away. "Does tonight remind you of anything, girls? The dressing-up-and-going-out-for-a-night-of-dancing part, I mean."

Renee held up a hand in protest. "I went along with buying slinky dresses, but I draw the line at getting up onstage to dance. My hips weren't flexible enough for the hula dance at eighteen, let alone at forty-nine. Besides, these dancers tonight are professionals."

"I'm with you on that," Lynette said. "Tonight, we only have to *watch* the dancing. But it still reminds me of our senior prom. Remember how fun that was? We got all dressed up in our pretty gowns and spent the evening dancing."

Jackie shook her head as she adjusted the strap on her new sundress. The matching flower bloom—tucked behind her right ear to communicate to anyone who knew the distinction that she was single and available—added the perfect touch. Her eyes sparkled as she shook an accusatory finger at Lynette. "You did not dance that night away. I specifically remember you spending most of the evening making out with your hot date like a couple of teenagers."

Lynette shrugged, her yellow dress glowing in the setting sun. "To be fair, we *were* teenagers. Man, I haven't thought of Storm in years. I wonder whatever happened to him."

"Storm. What kind of name was that?" Kit said, thinking back. Jackie was right. That dark stranger Lynette had met through her job at the pizza shop *was* hot. "You never kept in touch with him?"

"No. Things went pretty haywire after that. Prom night was the calm before the storm. Pardon the pun."

A swell of groans met Lynette's play on words, followed by a moment of quiet as everyone seemed lost in their memories of that long-ago night.

"Whatever happened to *your* date, Kit?" Jackie asked.

"Charlie? My lab partner? I have no idea."

Jackie looked confused. "No, that wasn't who I was thinking about. It was that other guy you were chasing. My friend's brother. He wasn't your actual date, but you liked him. What was his name?"

The memories flooded back for Kit. "Bruce? God, I haven't thought of him in years either. All I remember is your brother Ronnie mentioning something about being the best man in his wedding. We lost touch. Not that we were ever really friends. He was four years older than us, which was a big deal when we were only eighteen."

Not one to be left out of a conversation, Renee set down her fork and leaned forward. "Hey, whatever happened to that guy you guys set me up with? Owen? Anyone stay in touch with him?"

Kit's eyes swung to Jackie. "Ah, yes, our old friend Owen. Why don't you tell our friends about Owen, Jackie? He's pretty handy with a chainsaw."

Jackie gulped down the remainder of her drink at Kit's question. "I don't know what you're talking about."

"Bull," Kit shot back, enjoying herself. "To answer your question, Renee, Owen still spends his summers in Ruby Shores. He's some hotshot entrepreneur these days. Single with two grown sons. We actually ran into him last year at our class reunion, and then again last week. He doesn't live far from my Grandma Hazel, and after the storm hit, he was one of the first to help her out."

Renee nodded. "I could tell he was a nice guy but his heart belonged to someone else. Are you saying that you are finally reciprocating his feelings, Jackie? Owen would have loved to be your prom date instead of mine, but I couldn't get a read on how you felt about him."

Jackie chewed on her lip. "I don't know what you're talking about," she repeated.

Kit smirked. "You might not have been smart enough to realize Owen liked you when we were kids, but I sense a definite attraction between the two of you now."

Jackie could say whatever she wanted, but Kit knew her old friend was definitely intrigued by the rich, single bachelor. It had just taken her thirty years to notice him in that way.

A rhythmic beat began, and dancers in grass skirts and flamboyant headdresses made their way onto the stage.

"Saved by the drums," Jackie said, tossing her napkin playfully at Kit.

Kit turned her attention to the show as it began, allowing herself to fall into the brilliant spectacle. Renee was right. The elegant routines and the undeniable talent of the performers created a mesmerizing experience.

The night sky darkened and an ocean breeze continued to ruffle everything it touched, adding to the incessant movement of the dancers and causing the flames of the tiki torches rimming the grass carpeted stage to bow. Young women and men moved with an organic sensuality like nothing Kit had ever witnessed before. The show unfurled against the backdrop of pulsing drums, punctuated with the occasional whoop from a dancer, and even a few catcalls from those in the audience.

Colorful costumes added to the timelessness of the dances. Flowing fabrics fashioned into barely there shifts and loincloths complimented the lithe moves of the performers. Grass skirts rustled. The flicks, rolls, and undulations of supple hips and balletic hands captivated the attention of all.

While a few of the women stood tall and willowy, sporting defined midsections that gave evidence to the countless hours they'd spent perfecting their art, others were curvier with softer middles, as if their bellies would provide the perfect spot to nuzzle a child. All moved in perfect rhythm, taking part in a dance passed down to them through the ages.

Who had taught these talented dancers to move with such precision and grace? Or did a deeper and more ancient knowledge spur them on?

A master of ceremonies shared snippets of history about the area surrounding the luau, and talk of lovers of all ages journeying here pulled at Kit's battered heartstrings. But the more primal beats, gestures, and passages sung in a mysterious foreign tongue conveyed the most powerful messages embedded in the evening's magical performance.

When the show wrapped up, Kit felt as if she were emerging from a trance.

"That was fabulous," Annie said. She stretched and got to her feet, careful to hold the skirt of her dress down as she rose. "You did a great job picking this one, Kit. How do those dancers move like that? This was all so fun. If you aren't careful, we're going to insist you plan our trips *every* year."

"Oh no, you don't," Kit said, getting slowly to her feet and refusing to grimace when her knee tried to lock up. "I don't know which of you gets the honor of planning next year's trip, but it won't be me. I've done my heavy lifting for a while, and now I'm just going to relax and enjoy the rest of this week."

Who knows what my life will look like by next year? Kit thought. *Everything might be different.*

But the one constant she could always count on, no matter what was happening in her personal life, were these four women. Sharing this amazing, breezy evening with them was proof of how lucky she was to call them friends.

Chapter Thirteen

K IT SLID HER GLASS doors leading to the balcony open, enjoying the solitude. A soft ocean breeze caressed her face and body, reminding her of the way it had made the torches dance at the previous night's luau. Dawn was agonizingly slow to arrive. She couldn't sleep. The rising sun painted puffy clouds with the soft colors of cotton candy. She thought she caught the scent of pineapple on the air, but it might have been the air freshener she'd spotted just inside the door to her balcony.

It would be fun to tour a pineapple farm while on Maui. She'd have to send Dean pictures. A pizza with Canadian bacon and pineapple before a movie was often their go-to date night.

The pain of Dean's betrayal came crashing down on her again, much like the insistent waves against the smooth sand below. When they first started dating, he'd never hidden the fact that he wanted to be a father. Once he'd accepted her stance on the issue, he avoided the subject, but Kit had often worried he was settling in his relationship with her.

Apparently he wasn't as committed to being a father as he'd led her to believe. Not if he could walk away from a child he already had.

How dare he make her feel guilty about not wanting children, like she was keeping him from fulfilling some lifelong dream, when he'd had a child all this time? How dare he keep such a monumental secret from her?

And for him to still keep this secret even after receiving the wedding invitation . . . to allow this to blow up on the eve of her special trip that had been thirty years in the making?

At least she'd managed not to think about it this morning during the minute it took her to go from her sumptuous bed with its ridiculously comfortable sheets to her balcony with this stunning view. An improvement over the day before, when it was the first thing she thought about upon waking.

She needed advice. Was she overreacting?

Maybe if Dean hadn't known about the child. But that wasn't the case. He admitted he'd known, he'd known all this time, but he'd walked away.

A gust of wind pressed her short silk nightie against her frame. She shivered. She should probably go grab her robe. What if someone saw her?

Then again, if they were as invisible as Jackie seemed to think, now that they were well into middle age, no one would notice anyhow.

Screw it. The breeze felt wonderful.

She stepped to the rail surrounding her balcony. Despite her shaky sense of bravado, she was glad she wasn't backlit by any lights inside her room. The small refrigerator next to the hot tub was well stocked, so she helped herself to a bottle of guava nectar. Renee had raved about it after finding one in her own minifridge.

If it wasn't so early, she'd climb into that hot tub right now. It was so inviting. The jets would feel wonderful on her sore feet. Their shopping had left them blistered.

But she didn't want to disturb the peaceful morning. Instead, she draped a fluffy cotton towel on the lounge chair beside the tub and settled down on it, juice in hand. She took a sip. The liquid was thicker than she'd expected and tasted a little like strawberries.

Would it be fair for her to discuss Dean's situation with her girlfriends, or would she be betraying her fiancé? On the other hand, if she didn't find her way through this cloud of doubt, he might not be her fiancé for long.

Was this why she'd been reluctant to set a wedding date? Had she always known on some subconscious level? Lynette would probably say it was her intuition. She was woo-woo like that.

Maybe she should have at least called Dean, let him know she'd made it safely to Hawaii. She hadn't been able to bring herself to reach out, and he'd been equally quiet on his end.

"He probably spent yesterday shopping for a father-of-the-bride suit," she muttered.

Her eyes trailed a trio of fishing boats on the horizon. At least she thought they must be fishing boats, given the hour.

"Good morning, Kit."

The disembodied voice shocked her out of her self-induced pity party. Her slack grip on the juice caused it to slip from her fingers. The plastic bottle spewed sticky pink liquid under her chair.

"Annie?"

A hand reached around the wall that separated Kit's balcony from the one on her right, fingers waving. "I can't see you, but I can hear you," her friend said. "You couldn't sleep either?"

Kit laughed, despite the mess under her chair. "Nope. You might as well come have a cup of coffee with me so I quit talking to myself."

"I thought you'd never ask!"

Careful to avoid the spill, Kit stepped back into her room to grab her robe and a hand towel to clean up the mess. She'd just pressed the ON button for the small coffee pot when Annie tapped on her door.

"That was fast," Kit greeted her friend, still tying the belt around her hotel robe.

"Who is buying a father-of-the-bride suit? Does one of your brothers have a daughter getting married?"

Kit flipped the extra lock back in place above the doorknob. "You heard that, huh? No, neither of my brothers. It's a long story. I didn't want to get into it before. I'm still shocked by it all."

Annie, looking more like a teenager in her collegiate T-shirt and terrycloth shorts than a woman pushing fifty, steepled her fingers together and shot Kit a mischievous smile. "I sense a story here. Do tell!"

"Not without coffee. Take this one, and I'll make another. I added cream for you. Be careful on the balcony. I just spilled my juice out there. I need to clean it up."

Her friend took the white paper cup, then wriggled the fingers of her free hand at Kit.

"What? You want sugar, too?"

Annie grinned. "No, give me that towel. I'll wipe up the mess quick."

Kit let her friend take the hand towel she'd draped over her shoulder. "It sure is nice to hang out with a bunch of women who think to help out," she said. "Thank you."

Annie touched the towel to her brow before spinning toward the balcony. "Queens help queens."

Kit grinned as she switched out the coffee pods. "Hey, I like that! Maybe that should be our motto."

The hand towel was draped over the hot tub's ledge when Kit stepped back outside. Pink splotches marred the previously pristine white cloth. The floor didn't even feel sticky under Kit's bare feet. Two fresh bottles of juice sat on the small table between their chairs.

"That stuff is so yummy," Annie said. "I thought we both needed a bottle. It's not like we get pampered like this at home."

"You can say that again. Do you feel guilty for letting Lynette foot the bill on these upgrades? Because I do."

Annie took a sip of her juice while still holding her coffee. "Look at us, two-fisted drinking at six in the morning." She giggled as she set the bottle back down. "I felt a little guilty at first. Then I talked to my daughter. Since she's pregnant, I check in with her every day. I never expected to be this nervous during her pregnancy. Anyway, I told her about Lynette upgrading our rooms and paying for our spa visit. Ava has met Lynette, of course, but she knows you and Jackie better. She's never met Renee. She said not to overthink Lynette's generosity. 'Don't protest, but let Lynette know how much you appreciate it.' When someone doesn't graciously accept an unexpected gift, it can tarnish some of the glow the giver might be feeling."

Kit sat with that for a moment. "Wow. When did Ava get so smart?"

"I'm telling ya, that kid was born with an old soul. Did you know that my great-grandmother died on the same day Ava was born? I swear Matilda jumped bodies that day," Annie said with a wriggle of her eyebrows.

"We'll know for sure if she feels compelled to name her baby Matilda."

Annie cringed. "I don't remember my great-granny as being a warm and fuzzy woman, but I'm trying to practice being nonjudgmental where my first grandchild is concerned. So, even if . . . God forbid . . . they name her Matilda, I won't say a word."

Kit set her coffee down before picking up her juice. She didn't want to risk wasting another one. "I still can't believe you are going to be a grandmother. Can you?"

"Nope. Ava is barely showing, so it doesn't feel real."

"If she isn't very far along, how can they be certain it's a girl?"

"I asked that, too. I have another friend whose daughter was expecting last year, and they got the sex wrong based on an ultrasound. She had to scramble to redecorate the nursery before the happy new parents brought the baby home. But Ava said now they can do a blood test early in the pregnancy. That gives them a definitive answer. Despite that assurance, if I do any decorating for them, I'll be sure to keep the receipts."

Kit smiled as the blush of the sunrise strengthened. This topic was so much more fun than the one she'd been ruminating over. "Just think—a queen decorating a room for a princess."

"Careful, you're going to make me cry!" Annie tapped at the corners of her eyes in jest. "Now, what were we talking about before we got off on that tangent?"

"I'd rather keep talking about you," Kit said, relaxing back against the lounger.

"Now that you mention it, you've been kind of quiet, Kit. Not your normal boisterous self. Is something up?"

Knowing she needed to talk to someone, and appreciating that Annie didn't know Dean as well as Jackie did, Kit decided it was time to seek some advice. "I'm not exactly sure where to start."

"Is there a beginning?"

"Not really. This isn't a linear-type issue. It's more complicated than that."

Annie shifted to give Kit her full attention. "I can handle complicated. God knows I've been doing enough of that for the past thirty years."

Kit saw an opening. "Is it something you want to talk about?"

"Nice try. We are talking about *you*, and I won't let you sway me, even if you try to wrap the conversation back around to my precious future granddaughter. Start wherever you please. I'll catch up. Remember, queens helping queens."

Annie wasn't going to give up.

"Fine. I guess I've been kind of slow to set a wedding date."

Annie snorted. "No need to state the obvious, hon. We actually talked about that when we were waiting for you to join us at the beach after the spa, me and Renee and Jackie. We vowed to get you to set a date as soon as we get home from our little getaway. Dean loves you. You love him. What the heck are you waiting for?"

If only it were that simple, Kit thought. She understood why her friends would think that. Especially Annie, who couldn't know how badly Dean wanted to be a father.

Or did he?

With a growl of frustration, Kit sat forward, dropping her feet onto either side of her lounger. "I never wanted to have kids."

"I know that, Kit. You've never tried to hide your feelings on that topic, so I'm sure you were very open about that fact with Dean. Though I always thought you'd make a fabulous mom. You practically raised your little brothers."

"No, Grandma raised them. I just helped a lot. Dean has always wanted kids. I didn't. I was afraid he'd resent me."

Voices floated up to them from below. The resort was slowly waking up.

Annie seemed to consider Kit's statement. She twirled her ponytail, reinforcing Kit's earlier thought that she looked like a kid. After some time, she sighed. "Dean is a grown man. You've been together a long time. If that was a deal breaker for him, he wouldn't have proposed."

"Yeah, I was wrong about that whole 'father' thing. In fact, I found out on Thursday just how wrong I was."

After tightening her ponytail, Annie dropped her hands into her lap. "That sounds ominous."

"Everything I thought I knew about Dean was a lie."

Annie got to her feet, then bent over to rummage through the minifridge.

"What are you doing?" Kit said.

"Looking for alcohol. That sounded like a very loaded sentence."

Kit gave Annie's butt a soft kick. "Stop! Sit down. It's too early to drink anything other than juice or coffee. I don't want to start this early. Today is a beach day."

"Who said the alcohol is for you?" Annie joked, brushing at her bottom before sitting back down, empty-handed.

"Do you want to hear this?"

"Of course I want to hear it. I can hear how heavy your heart feels. Tell me as much, or as little, as you want. But if Dean dared to cheat on you, I'm a bit of an expert in infidelity, so I might be able to help."

Annie's words reminded Kit of how much her friend had suffered throughout her first, short marriage. She shook her head. "No. Dean didn't cheat on me, but he kept an enormous, life-altering secret from me. I honestly don't know if he'd have ever told me the truth if I didn't find that damn wedding invitation."

Confusion marred Annie's features. She made a circular motion with her finger. "Is this taking the story back to the father-of-the-bride comment you made earlier?"

Kit nodded. "Dean has a daughter. And she's getting married next month."

Silence. Annie's mouth fell open but no words came out, even though her eyes held countless questions.

Kit sighed. "I'm screwing this up. Even *you* couldn't keep up with this disjointed telling of the mess I fell into on Thursday. Let me back up."

"Take your time." Annie took a sip of her neglected coffee. "We have all day."

"No, we don't. I don't want to give any more vacation time to this issue than is absolutely necessary. But I do want to tell you everything. I need your advice."

Not wasting any more time, she told Annie about the way she'd stumbled across the wedding invite, as well as the fights they'd had about the girl's mother earlier in their relationship. Annie didn't interrupt.

Once she'd shared the whole sordid tale, Kit finally asked, "Am I being ridiculous?"

"You are not being ridiculous. Dean failed to tell you a very important detail about his past."

Kit was more than a little relieved that Annie was seeing her side of things. "Right?! And the topic of kids is still an issue."

"This daughter who suddenly wants some type of relationship is also part of the puzzle. Have you thought about her in all of this? You could be her stepmother."

"Oh lord," Kit moaned, dropping her head into her hands. "The nasty old stepmother. Did you know I'm older than Dean?"

Annie laughed. "There isn't enough of an age difference between you two to matter."

"Honestly, I haven't given the girl too much thought. Why has she suddenly reached out to him? Maybe she just found out about him herself? I guess I didn't ask."

"How does Dean feel? About the way you left things, I mean."

A worm of guilt wriggled in Kit's stomach. "I don't know. I haven't talked to him since I left his apartment."

"On Thursday? Do you guys often go days without talking?"

"Of course not," she said, feeling childish. "I don't know what to say."

"Oh, honey, avoidance isn't the answer. You should call him. I doubt he shared everything with you during the heat of the moment. You might feel better after you give him a chance to explain himself."

Kit caught herself chewing on the edge of her thumbnail, a nasty habit she thought she'd given up years ago. She made a fist and tucked it into the middle of her stomach, trying to quell the ache there. "You're probably right. Maybe I should try to call him."

Annie slapped her thighs, then stood. "I think that is an excellent idea. Try him now! If he has time to talk, great. If not, I'm heading back to my room to change into my running clothes. You can join me if you like."

"I hate running, and I already have blisters from yesterday." But Kit knew she was just pouting. She dreaded the idea of making the phone call, even though she knew she needed to.

"Then we walk. It's still early. Maybe we'll find some pretty shells on the beach. Do you want me to clean up these drinks before I go?"

Kit smiled up at her friend, appreciating her unquestioning support. "No, for once let's let the maids do that. If you don't hear from me in ten minutes, run without me. I'll find you later."

Annie paused long enough to give her a quick hug, then she skipped back into Kit's room, angled for the door. "Sounds good. Give him a chance to speak his piece, and then let's get back to our vacation. Life's problems can keep until we get home."

Kit couldn't help but wonder, as Annie's words faded and the door opened and closed behind her, what problems her friend might have waiting at home for her, too.

CHAPTER FOURTEEN

K IT SPENT MONDAY FOLLOWING Annie's advice and enjoying her vacation, despite not being able to get ahold of Dean. When he didn't pick up, she'd reminded herself it was already early afternoon in Minneapolis and the first day of every week was always busy for Dean. Had he gotten the go ahead to proceed with the St. Louis project? She left a message asking him to call her and then put it out of her mind. No matter how heavy their troubles might seem, she needed to trust in the strength of their relationship.

She didn't join Annie for a run, however, figuring her blisters gave her a valid excuse. There was no way she wanted to have sore feet for their entire vacation. Later, she split her time between the swimming pool with a book and lounging along the beach with her travel sisters. She snuck in a nap in her tranquil hotel suite before dinner. If she could, she'd slow down time. Their week was going too fast.

The relaxed pace of island life was allowing her to catch her breath. She was starting to go hours without her troubles with Dean—or the impending doom she felt when she thought about her mother—even crossing her mind.

Over dinner, her friends mentioned similar experiences. They all appreciated the rare treat of no one having any expectations of them. Despite their different lives back home, none of them could escape the demands on their time the way they could here.

I'll miss this place, Kit thought as she strolled toward her favorite restaurant at their resort on Tuesday morning. The scent of bacon mingled with chlorine and flowers as she passed the swimming pool, her eyes finding what had become "their" set of recliners.

Would she ever come back here? It wasn't likely, and she felt the familiar bittersweet twinge she often felt while traveling. It was hard to leave a place like this, even when you reminded yourself that the world was full of wonderful destinations.

"Good morning," a familiar voice called.

She turned to see Lynette and Jackie approaching. She was glad to see that Lynette no longer wore the harried look she'd arrived with, and Jackie wore a wide grin.

"Morning. Don't you both look chipper this morning!"

"Lynette was just telling me about some of her recent online dating escapades. Uff da!" Jackie laughed. "How are you this morning? You don't seem to be in a hurry, so we must not be late."

Kit checked her watch. "We agreed on eight thirty, right?"

"Nope. Quarter after," Lynette said.

"Oh. Shoot. Hopefully Renee and Annie haven't given up on us."

Jackie motioned around them. "I guarantee they are perfectly content sitting with fresh coffee and a view of the ocean."

Renee and Annie did in fact appear relaxed, laughing and chatting as Kit approached with the other two latecomers.

"I'm so sorry. I thought we'd decided on eight thirty."

Annie motioned to Kit to take the seat next to her. "I figured it was something like that. You're never late, Kit. But no worries. Renee was just telling me about some of the clandestine hookups she's witnessed at that resort of hers."

Lynette flagged down a passing waiter to request more coffee as she took one of the two remaining open chairs. "Now that's the kind of girls' trip gossip this week has been missing. Spill it."

A pink flush appeared on Renee's cheeks, and Kit didn't think it was sunburn from their hours outside the previous day. They'd all taken care to slather their faces with plenty of sunscreen.

"I shouldn't gossip about our guests. Whispering Pines really caters to families," she said, picking up a laminated menu card and fanning herself. "My Aunt Celia is probably shaking her finger at me from heaven, scolding me for my loose lips."

Lynette poured herself a cup of steaming coffee from the fresh pot the waiter just set on their table. "I'm not so sure about that. From what you've told us about your aunt, she wasn't a prude."

"You're right. She wasn't. And my sister Jess and I are convinced that Celia had at least one romantic relationship at the resort. We found some old photographs, and even a set of initials carved into the wooden stairs in front of the old duplex out there. My dad filled in a couple of blanks, but not many. Certainly not enough to satisfy our curiosity."

"Here's to women with an aura of mystery around them," Lynette said, holding her coffee high before taking a sip.

Renee nodded. "Now that you mention it, Lynette, you remind me of my Aunt Celia. Successful, single, business-minded. You would have loved her."

"I still can't believe she left you a lake resort," Annie said. "All my aunt left me when she died was her snippy little dachshund. I was still in college and in no position to own a dog, but I was the only one who could stand Winnie. I had to make the woman a deathbed promise to take care of her dog."

"Ouch! Winnie the Wiener Dog sounds like a lot for any kid to take on!" Renee laughed. "Breathing life into an abandoned old resort wasn't exactly a picnic, either. Some days I was sure attempting it would be the biggest mistake of my life."

"Do you still feel that way?" Kit asked.

"Now? No. I still have my moments, but that's just part of the hospitality business. The good far outweighs the bad."

Annie freshened her coffee, adding in a packet of sugar and a dollop of fresh cream. "Tell them about the couple you caught hooking up on the beach."

Renee shrugged. "What can I say? There is always a touch of romance in the air at Whispering Pines. The moon was full, and the beach is relatively secluded. There used to be a row of cabins right next to the water when my aunt first spent time there with friends, but a storm took those out. I have to admit, Matt and I even sneak down there sometimes for some privacy. College kids home for the summer come and go at all hours, so we have to get creative."

Kit snorted. "You probably don't need to be so secretive. They're kids. They don't pay any attention to what you are doing behind closed doors."

"Kids know way more than we give them credit for, Kit," Jackie said. "My girls used to plan to be out of the house some evenings when Ben would come over. They weren't subtle with their innuendos, and they weren't even in college yet."

Kit felt herself withdraw from the conversation. She knew Jackie never meant to hurt her feelings, but sometimes her comments about how little she knew about raising kids stung. She didn't need any reminders that she was childless, especially with her recent discovery that not even her Dean held that title anymore. Aside from Lynette and her Aunt Marge, practically every other adult Kit knew was a parent.

The conversation meandered on to funny stories of the times Annie and her big sister had walked in on their parents while they'd been on a family vacation—not once, but twice.

"I swear it scarred me for life."

By the time they'd finished their breakfasts, Kit's good mood had returned.

"We better finish packing, ladies," Lynette said as they settled their breakfast tab. "It's almost ten."

They were on the road within the hour, all crammed into one car. As she turned onto the highway that would take them south along the coast before turning inland, Kit had to laugh when she caught Annie's eye in the rearview mirror.

Annie rolled her eyes. "I don't see why I'm always the one who gets shoved into the middle. And tell me again why I need to hold your suitcase, Lynette?"

"Because you have the shortest legs and Kit's big suitcase takes up most of the trunk space. She can't hold my bag, she's driving," Lynette said without an ounce of apology in her tone. "Say, Kit, I got in touch with the car rental. They're going to swap out a larger SUV for this one this afternoon. I hope you don't mind."

It delighted Kit that Lynette had thought about trading up. "I think that's an excellent idea. Our dear Annie might vomit again, especially if she gets woozy on the Road to Hana."

Annie expelled a dramatic sigh. "One puking episode in the backseat of your Mustang, Kit, and you never let me live it down. Remember, you're the one who made me drink half a bottle of Boone's Farm that night."

"That wasn't me, that was Jackie!"

Jackie smirked. "I've always been a wine connoisseur."

"Lucky for us, your taste in wine has improved," Renee said. Kit glanced in the mirror again and noticed Renee edge closer to the back passenger door. "Annie, put your right leg down here."

"Don't worry, ladies, this drive shouldn't take us more than an hour. The traffic isn't too bad."

"Thanks again for driving, Kit," Jackie said, smiling over at her from the front passenger seat.

"After you almost killed us last summer on the way home for the reunion, I thought I better not hand *you* the keys."

"What?!" Annie laughed from the backseat. "You never told us about that!"

Jackie waved a dismissive hand. "Kit exaggerates. If anyone died, it would have been the fool on the motorcycle. But I was too observant to let that happen."

The badgering and visiting continued, and Kit couldn't believe how fast a sign for Haiku appeared on the side of the road.

Time flies when you're having fun.

"Do you know the street address?" Jackie asked, peering around at the lush vegetation that was starting to make Kit feel claustrophobic. "My phone's reception is terrible right now."

Kit nodded. "That can be a problem, especially when we take the Road to Hana later this week. I printed out the confirmation to be on the safe side. Pull it out of my purse, would you?"

Annie shifted behind the large suitcase on her lap. "No cell service means no GPS. I hope we can find it."

If anyone should feel claustrophobic, it's Annie, Kit thought, hoping she could find the rental she'd painstakingly picked out.

The hula gods were smiling down on them. After only two wrong turns, Kit found the street, and then the house itself.

"This isn't on the ocean, then?" Jackie asked, a tinge of disappointment in her voice.

"Afraid not. Those can run a thousand dollars a night, so I found us something here in Haiku instead."

Lynette whistled. "This will be just fine."

"Wait until you see the pool in the backyard." Kit eased the car to a stop in front of the plantation-style home and rolled down her window to better view the property. "If it's as nice as the pictures made it look, we might never want to leave."

Jackie opened her door but glanced at Kit before getting out. "And even if it's not perfect, nothing is going to put a damper on this trip. Thank you for finding this place, Kit. I know it's hard to wade through options based on nothing more than pictures on the internet."

Kit climbed out, crossing her fingers that the house looked as nice inside, and in the backyard, as it did from the front. The curb appeal was over the top.

"Get out," she heard Annie demand, and laughed as Lynette practically fell out of the backseat.

Once inside, they all quickly agreed that Kit had outdone herself with this arrangement. Jackie disappeared in search of a bathroom while Renee and Annie took everyone's luggage back to the bedrooms.

"Looks like I won't need you to help me out with this piece of our itinerary, Lynette," Kit said. "The rental car and our double rooms might have been too small, but this place more than makes up for it."

"It sure does," Lynette said, breezing past her in a blue and white caftan that billowed out behind her. She headed straight for the double doors leading to the backyard. "This looks like something you'd find at a five-star resort!"

Kit exhaled as she followed Lynette out the doors. "What a relief."

Lynette glanced her way. "You did good. And not just with this. With everything."

"And *you* made it better." Kit captured Lynette's hand in her own. "We make a great team, old friend."

"Be careful who you're calling 'old,' " Lynette said, but her grin and the squeeze she gave Kit's hand before releasing it meant she wasn't offended. None of them were eighteen anymore.

"Can you believe we pulled this off?" Kit asked. "It only took thirty years, but here we are."

"Here we are," Lynette echoed, shrugging out of her caftan and dropping it over the back of a red Adirondack chair that paired nicely with the backyard décor. "Can you feel that?"

Kit wasn't sure what she meant. "Feel what?"

Lynette opened her mouth but then closed it, as if hesitant to say what she'd been thinking. She shook her head, then meandered over to the pool. "This looks like it's straight out of a travel brochure. And I love that there isn't any traffic noise."

"How do you like New York?" Kit asked. She was dying to hear more about her friend's day-to-day life. Lynette hadn't said much about it since they'd been together.

"Oh, wow—check this out," Lynette said, giving no sign she'd heard Kit's question. "It's like walking into the water from a beach. I bet it's salt water, too."

"It is," Kit said, thinking back to the property overview and reviews she'd read during her planning phase. "Since an ocean-side property was over budget, this is the next best thing."

"What other surprises do you have up your sleeve for us, Kit?"

She shrugged. "I guess you'll just have to wait to find out."

"Where did you learn to cook like this, Kit, and how on earth did you have everything you needed? We didn't even go to a grocery store!"

Kit laughed as she handed her plate to Renee, who'd insisted on cleaning up. "Trust me. I can make three things, and that spaghetti and meatball recipe was one of them. Grandma Hazel refused to eat spaghetti sauce from a jar. As far as groceries, I took the property owner's advice. She warned me that the shopping options are limited around here, so I ordered ahead. Besides, I knew none of us would want to spend part of our day food shopping."

"Good call," Annie said as she helped Renee clear the table. "I admit, after four or five days of eating out, a homecooked meal tasted fabulous. What are you cooking for us tomorrow?"

"Well, since the other two things I know how to make are wintery comfort foods, I'm tapped out."

"I'm just teasing," Annie assured Kit as she opened the dishwasher and started stacking plates inside. "Dean cooks, right?"

Was her friend nudging her to tell the others about her troubles with Dean? She held her breath, but Annie simply smiled at her when their eyes met. Maybe Annie had more confidence in Kit's ability to iron things out with Dean than she did.

"He does," she said, hating the hitch she felt in the center of her chest at his name. She still hadn't been able to reach him and now she was worried that he was avoiding her. Could she blame him?

"I don't know about you, but I could use a swim after that meal," Lynette said. "I'm going to put a suit on. Anybody care to join me?"

Annie laughed. "After that enormous plate of pasta I just ate? Your eyes would burn if you had to look at me in a swimsuit right now."

Lynette frowned. "I didn't think we were doing that this week."

"Doing what?" Annie said as she wiped the table with a dishrag.

"Body shaming."

Annie looked at Lynette. "But I wasn't. Was I?"

"That's what it sounded like to me." Lynette shrugged. "We get enough of that out in the real world. We don't have to tolerate it here. Annie, your body is beautiful and strong and everything still works. Am I right?"

Annie looked uncomfortable. "Well . . . yeah . . . I guess everything still works."

Lynette sighed and stood. "Annie, repeat after me. 'I am a strong and beautiful woman.'"

"I'm not going to say that."

Kit feared an argument was brewing. "Why don't we take our wine and head outside?"

Lynette flicked an irritated glance her way before crossing her arms over her chest and pinning Annie with a more intense gaze. "How many amazing children did that body of yours grow?"

Annie took a deep breath. "Three."

"And how far did you run yesterday morning?"

"I don't know. Four miles, maybe," she said, still looking uneasy.

"And you're worried about a little bloat because you just enjoyed a scrumptious meal with your old friends?"

"My *best* friends," Annie clarified, earning a tiny smirk out of Lynette. "Look, Lynette, I see what you're trying to do. Let's get real here for a minute. None of us have the shapes we used to have. It's normal for us to be a little self-conscious, especially in bathing suits."

"Is it?" Lynette's arms were still crossed. "Or are we just buying in to society's brainwashing? We need to change what we consider normal."

Annie threw her dishcloth into the sink. "I'm not sure I have the energy to take on that battle."

"Do you ever get tired of shrinking?"

The woman's unwillingness to back down surprised Kit.

"Lynette, what's going on?" Jackie asked. She'd been watching quietly from the head of the table, sipping her Chardonnay. "All Annie said was that she's too full to put on a swimming suit."

Lynette shrugged again. "I guess I'm sick and tired of being marginalized simply because we now fall into the category of 'women of a certain age.' We need to stop being our own worst enemies."

Kit pushed away from the table. "All right. This discussion would be better around a sparkling swimming pool with plenty of wine. Something is bothering you, Lynette, and I've had a feeling all week that something is up with you, too, Annie. Let's go outside and see if we can't clear the air a little."

Annie rounded on her. "It's not like *you* aren't keeping secrets, too, Kit."

Kit held her hands up. "Whoa. Down, girl. Yes, I have plenty of problems, too, but at least I was open with you about what was bothering me."

Jackie set her wineglass down and opened a cupboard. She sent Kit a questioning look, then pulled out five plastic wine goblets and emptied her glass into one of them. "I am officially moving this discussion outside. *Now*. Before someone says something that they'll regret. Everybody grab one of these cups. If we can't be here for each other, then let's just climb into that big new vehicle they dropped off an hour ago and head back to the airport. What's the matter with all of you?"

Chapter Fifteen

K IT OPENED THE DOOR for Jackie. "Why are you taking an empty wine bottle out back? The point of the plastic glasses was so we wouldn't have anything breakable around the pool."

"You'll see," Jackie said over her shoulder. "I'll be extra careful with the bottle, but I need it for something."

Kit shook her head as she headed for the red chairs. She started rearranging them to better facilitate a conversation, surprised at their heft. "I think these babies are solid wood. None of that composite stuff in paradise, apparently."

"Don't hurt your back," Jackie warned. She settled into her chair, careful not to spill her wine, the bottle tucked firmly under one arm.

"Hey, no body shaming," Kit shot back, wriggling her eyebrows. The second the words left her mouth, she glanced around, hoping Lynette wasn't within earshot yet. If she overheard her, the woman might think she was mocking her. She wasn't, but Kit was curious. "What do you suppose has her so uptight? She seemed perfectly fine until Annie made that comment about a swimming suit."

"No idea." Jackie sighed as she tilted her face up toward the sky. "What is it about this weather? When I close my eyes and allow myself to be still, it feels like the breeze is caressing me."

Kit had an idea, but she kept it to herself.

"What? I can see you smirking, Kit."

"The breeze feels nice. Like you said!"

"Knock it off. You have something on your mind."

Lynette's discarded caftan from earlier draped over the back of Kit's chair. She threaded the silky fabric between her fingers. "This is so soft. I love the vibrant blue. Do you think this is part of her current line?"

"You're impossible, Kit."

She laughed. "I was just thinking, when you commented on the breeze, that it's high time you found a man to caress you again. Instead of relying on Mother Nature. No matter how seductive she might seem in this paradise."

Jackie regarded her with one eye, the other still shut, as if Kit's teasing only deserved half of her attention. "I've given up on men."

"Oh, really? I doubt that."

That brought both eyes open. "What's *that* supposed to mean? I'm doing just fine without a man."

"Hmm, I'm not sure you should settle for 'fine.' I think you already have your eye on someone. An old friend, perhaps?"

Jackie sighed, her eyes drifting shut again. "All my *old* friends are right here, and while I love you all dearly and I may give up on men, I'm still not into girls."

Kit could see right through Jackie's feigned ignorance. "You know exactly who I'm talking about. Owen still thinks about you. I can tell."

"Owen? As in my old prom date?" Renee said as she breezed onto the patio in a bright red one-piece. "*Tell* me the two of you have finally acknowledged how attracted you are to each other!"

Jackie's eyes remained closed. "Ignore Kit. She doesn't have a clue."

"No clue, huh?" Kit sat up. "I saw the way the two of you were eyeing each other the night of the storm."

Renee dipped a toe into the pool water. "Oh, this feels delicious. It's like bath water. I admit I'm disappointed, though."

"In this place?" Kit said, surprised.

"Of course not! People *dream* of places like this. If you ever visit Whispering Pines in the summer, don't expect something like this," Renee warned, wading in farther. "No, I'm disappointed that you still haven't let anything develop with Owen, Jackie. I knew way back when that his heart already belonged to you. Kit said the two of you have been talking?"

Jackie set the wine bottle down next to her chair. "Kit, what lies have you been telling?"

Her comment offended Kit. "I never lie, Jackie. You know that."

"Chill, girl, I was kidding. There is *nothing* going on between Owen and me. Not now, not when we were kids."

Renee faced the other two women, easing onto her back in the pool. "That's a shame. Kit said he's even cuter now than he was when we were kids."

"Well, maybe *Kit* should date him then," Jackie said. Kit heard the irritation in her tone, despite the plastic smile on her face.

Annie joined them, looking uncomfortable in her bathing suit. Kit hadn't heard the door open. "Kit! I don't think you should give up on Dean that easily. I know you are probably joking about dating someone else, but don't you think that's a little harsh? You two are facing an enormous challenge, but you shouldn't give up so easily. Have you even talked to him since you've been in Maui?"

Jackie sat forward in her chair. Her foot bumped the glass bottle. It teetered precariously, the glass sounding brittle against the concrete, but she stabilized it before it could fall and break. "Oh, I see. Something has come up between you and Dean, so you're trying to deflect by teasing me about Owen."

Annie scrunched her face. "Sorry. Did I say too much?"

It was Kit's turn to sigh. "Don't apologize. Problems with Dean were going to come up this week. In fact, I could use all of your advice. But let's wait until Lynette gets back. I don't want to share the sad tale three times. I already bent Annie's ear about it."

The patio door opened and Lynette walked out, wearing a bikini not unlike the ones she wore to the beach back in Ruby Shores when they were kids.

"Oh, wow," Kit said, taking in the sight of her friend. "You look amazing."

Lynette stopped at the edge of the pool and spun slowly. "Actually, I can read your mind, Kit, and you think I've lost *my* mind. This suit—which cost me two hundred bucks, by the way, and promised to 'enhance my curves'—wasn't quite the magic bullet they promised. I'm wearing it regardless. And not for the first time. I wore it when I went to Tahiti with Wyatt two months ago."

"You're clairvoyant now, are you?" Kit said, watching Lynette wade into the pool with unabashed admiration. She looked perfectly at ease in the swimming suit that did little to hide the fact that Lynette wasn't a scrawny eighteen-year-old anymore. The stylish, flowing outfits her friend designed, sold, and wore so well camouflaged an expanding middle and dimpled thighs.

Jackie frowned. "Wyatt? I thought you two had broken up when we were at the retreat at Whispering Pines last winter."

Lynette slapped at the water. "What can I say? He missed me."

"And did he like your swimming suit?" Kit asked with a grin.

"Apparently not. We didn't fly home together from that trip. And I'll never take him back ever again.. Even if he begs."

"Damn," Kit whispered. "What a loser."

Lynette dove under, her barely covered rear end poking out of the water before she disappeared entirely. Kit and Jackie exchanged concerned looks before she resurfaced.

"Did you have a boob job?" Annie asked, eyeing Lynette from the edge of the pool.

"I did. And I regret it."

"Why? They look great. I can't believe I didn't notice them last summer when I took you out on the pontoon."

"Because they aren't *me*. I let other people convince me I wasn't enough. I know some women have plastic surgery because it's what *they* want. More power to them—it should always be that way. It wasn't for me. I'd have them removed, but since the implants haven't given me trouble, insurance wouldn't cover it. So, unless I want to pay out of pocket for the surgery, I'm stuck with them."

Lynette swam to the far side of the pool and hoisted herself out. Water sluiced off her. They all watched as she made her way toward a small building with a POOL HOUSE sign across the door. It looked more like a shed to Kit, but she supposed an upscale property like this needed fancy names. "I am going to look for floaties back here."

The minute the screen door slapped shut, Jackie let out a huff. "Do you think she's upset about Wyatt? Maybe she really liked him if she took him back once. If he dumped her because she wore that suit out in public, he's a dick."

"I can hear you, Jackie," Lynette cried from inside the pool house. "Hold that thought."

"Nice, Jackie," Kit hissed. She hoped Lynette's feelings weren't hurt.

Jackie shrugged. "What?"

A minute later, Lynette came back out carrying an inflatable chair. Once she set it in the water and climbed on, she paddled around so she could face Jackie, who was sipping her wine.

Kit thought Jackie looked embarrassed.

"Wyatt and I had an understanding. We both knew we'd go our separate ways someday. Did he leave me because I embarrassed him? Maybe. I was getting tired of him, anyhow. He wasn't satisfying me in bed anymore."

Jackie choked on her wine.

"You really need to lighten up, Jackie," Lynette said. "Look, I'm sorry if I'm a bit much today. Annie, I apologize for jumping down your throat earlier. I shouldn't have done that. I'm just tired, that's all. Tired of feeling like I'm losing my edge in my business these days. Tired of hearing women our age moan about growing older. I don't know about all of you, but I believe we are just reaching our prime. Life knocked all of us around through the years, but we always got back up with lessons learned. The little things barely even faze us anymore. Why would we allow other people to convince us we aren't as worthy as we used to be?"

"Amen, sister," Renee chimed in, slapping the water in front of her. "Do you ladies have any idea how many naysayers I encountered when I was working my butt off to get my resort up and running again? People thought I was crazy. They thought a single, middle-aged woman with two teenagers had no business running a lake resort in the middle of nowhere."

"You proved them wrong, though, didn't you?" Lynette said, nodding in Renee's direction. "That's exactly what I'm talking about. People should fear us for our internal fortitude, for our breadth of knowledge, and for our empathy. Instead, they try to write us off."

Kit appreciated the fire behind Lynette's words, but she worried something serious might be wrong. "How is work, Lynette?" she asked. "Your company seems to be bigger than ever. I see lots of posts about your online store on social media. You're doing amazing things, but you seem kind of upset."

"You'd be upset, too, if the board of directors at the company you built from scratch tried to work you out of a job."

There it was—the true cause of Lynette's tirade.

Everyone took a beat, absorbing Lynette's announcement.

"Tell me you didn't let that happen," Jackie said.

"Of course I didn't allow it!" A grim grin widened across Lynette's face. "But that doesn't mean they won't try again."

Jackie stood, scooping the empty wine bottle off the ground. "We're going to need another bottle. It sounds like we have lots to talk about."

"I still don't understand why you brought that empty bottle out here," Kit said.

Jackie shrugged. "I was going to spin it. You know, like spin the bottle? Whoever it landed on was going to have to spill whatever's bothering them. The truth is flowing now. We don't need to make it a game."

She was back quickly with a new, uncorked wine bottle.

Annie held up her plastic goblet for Jackie to fill. "I'm going to regret this in the morning."

"You'll be fine. I brought an extra-large bottle of aspirin on the trip," Jackie said with a grin.

Once everyone had a fresh goblet of wine, Jackie waved at Lynette. "Continue."

Lynette shook her head. "I don't want to get into all the sordid details. But I was late getting to Hawaii because Mom and I were busy putting a new board in place. We retained the right to do that, thankfully. Things will still be tricky when I get back to the real world."

Kit was jealous of the fact that it was still Lynette and her mom. They'd been inseparable for as long as she'd known her. "What's it like, working with your mom every day?"

The slight change in the conversation brought a smile to Lynette's lips. "It depends on the day. Mom has jammed a lot of living into her seventy years on this planet."

"Are you saying she's learned to crawl up from even more body blows than you?"

"That's exactly what I'm saying. And that makes her an even bigger force to be reckoned with."

Jackie shook her head. "I wouldn't bet against the two of you in a fight. But that reminds me. Forgive me, Lynette, but you seem to be ready to talk about something else, too. Kit, I want to hear what your grandmother had to say about the stuff we found in her basement. And what happened with Dean?"

"What stuff in the basement?" Lynette and Renee asked simultaneously, looking between Kit and Jackie.

Annie laughed. "You mean the tighty-whities on Hazel's dryer? Or your mom's things?"

"Wait," Lynette said. "Is Mia back in Ruby Shores?"

Kit took a large gulp of her wine. "Supposedly, the men's underwear Annie found on the dryer belong to Grandma's man friend. She was helping him out because his washer broke. The discussion we had about my mother's things raised more questions for me than answers. No, Mia isn't back in town. At least Grandma said she wasn't. But I found out that they talk every week."

Renee waved her hand. "I'm sorry. I guess I'd forgotten you lived with your grandmother as a girl. You're estranged from your mother, right? When did you last see her?"

Kit snorted. "Mia pops back into our lives about once every ten years. It's been a little longer this time around. I can tell my grandmother is softening to her again. Marge, my aunt, still hates Mia. They're sisters."

"That sounds ugly."

"Yeah, not all of us come from perfect families like you, Renee." She immediately regretted how harsh that sounded. "Oh, wow, I'm sorry. That came out all wrong."

Renee laughed, and Kit could see she wasn't upset.

"What questions did your talk with Hazel bring up?" Jackie asked. "Did you talk to her about your mom the same day she spotted Dad in the fountain?"

"Your dad was in the fountain?" Annie asked.

Lynette rolled off her floating chair, moved out of the pool, and reached for the caftan on the back of Kit's chair. She wrapped it around her waist and settled into one of the open chairs, never spilling a drop of her wine.

"Impressive," Kit said.

Lynette raised her glass in acknowledgment.

As Jackie explained that her father's dementia was getting worse, Kit thought about her promise to her grandmother to keep Mia's history to herself. How much should she share with her friends?

"I'm not sure how much longer Mom will be able to care for him at home," Jackie was saying.

Renee shook her head. "That's tough. It's hard to watch our parents getting older. Mine are still doing well—other than Mom's knees giving her trouble—but I always wonder."

"Then there's *my* mom," Lynette said. "She still beats me into the office most mornings."

"Is she slowing down at all?"

Lynette grinned at Annie. "Not really. Are your parents doing all right?"

"They are. Thanks for asking. But, Kit, I'm really curious what you found out about your mother's things."

Both Annie and Renee left the pool and sank into chairs. The evening air was still warm enough that they didn't look chilled, despite their wet suits.

Kit sighed. "Grandma felt it was time to share some things with me about Mia's past. Things she thinks contributed to her addictive behaviors."

"From the look on your face, I guess you're still trying to decide if she gave you valid reasons or just more excuses," Jackie said.

"I'm that easy to read, huh?" Of the women seated around her, Kit had always felt closest with Jackie. She couldn't hide things from the woman. "It's weird, you know? I feel so protective of Hazel. Mia hurt us all, badly, but I think it's been hardest on Grandma. Hazel basically wrapped up our conversation by saying Mia is her daughter and she doesn't really have any other option than to forgive her. Again."

"Do you want to talk about what Hazel said about Mia's early years?" Jackie asked, concern shining from her eyes.

"She asked me to keep the worst of it to myself, so I won't get into all the ugly details. I guess she never even told my grandpa all of it. She also told me that alcoholism runs pretty rampant on my grandpa's side of the family. Grandpa never drank a drop of alcohol because of it. I was still a teenager when he died, and I never really realized that about him. I'm sure that was one reason I always felt so safe in my grandparents' house. It was the only place where there wasn't any drinking."

Jackie set her half-empty cup at her feet. "When you think about all the heartaches alcohol causes, it makes this wine taste a little bitter. So Hazel thinks Mia's alcoholism was inevitable? Because it ran in her father's family? I know studies show there are links, but that doesn't excuse her for walking away from her children."

Kit swirled the wine that remained in her own glass, staring down into the maroon liquid as she weighed Jackie's words. She again felt a surge of protectiveness for her grandmother. "No, Grandma just thinks that's part of the puzzle. She claims Mia has been clean for a long time. But, again, I've heard that before."

"And you are hesitant to believe it now," Lynette added, finishing the thought in Kit's head.

"Exactly. Do you guys think I should?"

She scanned the faces of her friends. No one looked convinced that it was time for Kit to give her mother another chance. They all knew, with the exception of Renee, just how much Kit had suffered due to Mia's neglect.

"Trust is a really tough thing to earn back," Lynette eventually said. "Kit, no one would blame you if you never let your mother back into your life. Everyone in your family, including Hazel, has the right to make their own decision on this. Now, I don't know about the rest of you, but I'd be more comfortable if I changed out of this damp suit and we moved this conversation inside. It's still hot out, even though it's getting late."

Everyone agreed.

By the time they'd all dressed for bed, Annie suggested a card game they played way back at summer camp. "Ladies, I get that one of the reasons we are here is to help each other out with some tough topics, but I think it's time we had some fun."

Later, when Kit's exhausted head finally hit the pillow, she realized she still hadn't told anyone but Annie what was happening with Dean.

CHAPTER SIXTEEN

Kit wouldn't allow herself to look at anything other than the next step. She was afraid that if she looked down, she might throw up her breakfast on top of Jackie's head, after which her friend would toss her over the railing to her death below.

"I can't believe I let you guys talk me into letting Jackie plan today's activity," she said through gritted teeth, catching her breath. "Ziplining? Really? You know I'm not a fan of heights."

Annie glanced down at her with a grin. "You'll be fine, I promise! If you'd loosen up a little, you might even enjoy this. I *love* ziplining."

"Just what the world needs—more ziplining grandmothers."

"Kit, quit your complaining and get moving," Annie said, her grin fading. "We aren't the only group up here."

Eyes back on the next step, Kit moved, afraid she'd go down with the smallest misstep.

"Did you see how cute our guides are?" Lynette was saying from behind Jackie. "Any of them would be hunky enough to be on this year's 2019 Ziplining Hunks calendar."

Despite her death grip on the ropes lining the stairs, Kit couldn't help but grin. "I doubt there's such a thing."

"We could make it a thing," Lynette shot back, her voice slightly winded from the climb. "Should I ask them if they'd be interested?"

Out of the corner of her eye, Kit could see Jackie's shoulders shaking below her. Her friend's laughter eased a little of the tension from her neck.

"What," Jackie said, "are you going to produce a hunky calendar full of ripped twenty-something-year-olds now?"

"Nope, I'd focus on the more mature guides. The older I get, the more those under forty look like silly little kids to me," Lynette said. "Why not at least consider the calendar? I'm always keeping my eyes open for new products that might appeal to my clientele."

A chunk of bark skipped down from above, startling Kit. "Hey, watch it, Annie!"

"Sorry! These big old trees take a beating from us humans climbing around on their trunks."

She huffed. "The only living things that should be climbing these trees are monkeys."

"Almost there, Kit. We'll be at the top in a few more feet."

"Great," she yelled back to Annie. "And explain to me why I couldn't stay at the bottom like Renee? Why didn't *she* have to do this?"

Jackie swatted at Kit's foot from below. "Because *you* don't let fear win, Kit. Jeez, quit being such a baby and try to enjoy this, would you? Annie was excited about ziplining, and you're going to ruin it with your complaining."

Kit clamped her mouth shut. The logical part of her brain knew that Jackie was right. Annie had been so excited when they added ziplining to their list. Kit still thought something might be up with her, but she wouldn't talk about it. The least she could do was let Annie have her fun.

Even if it endangered Kit's life.

"You realize you can't really fall, right, Kit? That harness they clipped on you will catch you if you slip," Jackie pointed out.

"So they say," Kit said. She refused to put as much faith in the safety harness she wore as her friends seemed to. "But you're right. I'll try to relax and have some fun."

The words had just left her mouth when she reached the first platform. A beautiful sea of green jungle stretched out before them, the breeze making the treetops wave like the ocean. The sight stole her breath.

Jackie jostled her from behind. "Can you give the rest of us a little room, Kit?"

"Oh, oops, sorry!" She moved closer to the solid trunk of the tree to give the rest of her friends more room on the platform. She refused to move closer to the railing.

"That was the hard part," Annie said, shooting her a reassuring look. "Getting up is hard. Getting down—that's a whole different ballgame. Ready for the thrill of a lifetime?"

Kit spied a rope that extended away from the platform to disappear into the treetops. "Let's just hope this isn't the *end* of my lifetime."

"It won't be. I promise. Jackie did her research and this guide company has one of the best safety records around. They've only lost two customers so far this year."

The words startled Kit out of her fear-induced daze, but when she swung her eyes to Annie, she could see her friend was only teasing.

The older of their guides stepped up onto the platform.

"Ladies, how are we doing up here? Everyone is comfortable with how high we are? Subsequent platforms will be a little higher."

He turned toward Kit's groan.

"Oh, boy—I can see from that lovely shade of green you're sporting that this activity isn't your favorite." His eyes crinkled at the corners of his lined, bronzed face. "Don't worry. I won't let anything happen to you."

Ordinarily, when Kit's feet were planted firmly on the ground, she took exception to a stranger assuming she was a wimpy female needing help. But high above the forest floor, where only monkeys truly belonged, his reassurances acted like a balm to her frayed nerves. "Promise?" she managed to eke out, keeping her back flat against the thick, solid tree trunk.

"I promise, sugar," he drawled. "Now, come here. Give me your hand. The young lady ahead of you looks like a pro at this. After she goes, I'll help walk you through exactly what is going to happen. By the end of today, you'll love ziplining as much as she does."

But grabbing his hand meant removing her palm from the sense of security the old tree provided. She shook her head.

"Oh no, come on." His voice took on a sterner but still warm tone. "You can trust me."

She glanced over his shoulder to see one of the other guides hooking Annie up to the rope she'd spied a minute ago with some type of hook and strap system. Her friend was all smiles.

"It's been nice knowing you, Annie," Kit said. Sarcasm had always been her go-to in times of high stress.

"See you on the other side, Kit!" Annie hollered back, whooping as she stepped off the platform, her guide giving her a little shove.

"Now I *know* I'm going to throw up," Kit said, bending at the waist to try to fend off the nausea. She was careful to keep her butt pushed against the tree trunk.

Strong fingers pulled at her shoulders. "Come on. You can do it," the older guide said as he pinned her with his forceful gaze. "Just try this one jump. I promise, if you hate it, I'll escort you to the end of the course, where you can wait for your friends."

"Will that escort be on the ground? Because once I get down, my feet won't leave the ground again until it's time to catch our flight home."

He laughed. "You are a stubborn one, aren't you?"

Jackie snorted next to her. Kit had forgotten she was even there.

What choice do I have? she thought.

She couldn't very well stay on the rickety platform all day. Another group was coming up behind theirs. The next activity on their day's agenda was snorkeling. The idea of entering the ocean with flippers and a snorkel had cost her sleep. Now snorkeling sounded easy compared to flying around in the treetops.

She took a deep breath and grabbed his hands, feeling a modicum of comfort as his warm, callused fingers closed around hers. She squeezed them so tightly that he grimaced, but he kept his encouraging smile in place.

"I can do this," she said, nodding.

"Yes. Yes, you can. Now, if you'd give me back one of my hands, I can get your harness ready."

Two hesitant steps forward led to one backward step, until the guide tugged gently at Kit's hands.

"What if I throw up?"

"Honey, the forest won't care. The only real danger is if you accidentally spray one of your friends here with puke, but I expect they would forgive you. Come on, ma'am. If you're brave enough to color your hair that shade, like the inside of a ripe mango, nothing can really scare you."

Her left hand shot to the back of her neck, where her hair was peeking out from under the unflattering helmet. "You don't like my hair? And please, don't call me 'ma'am.' It makes me feel old."

"I didn't say I didn't like your hair. And I grew up using 'ma'am' as a sign of respect, nothing more."

Kit hadn't noticed that he'd slowly inched her toward the platform Annie recently jumped from. He gently but firmly extricated his other hand from her grip and got down to business, efficiently readying Kit for her first jump.

"Do you ever jump with someone, you know, on their first time?" she stammered.

Somewhere in the treetops, a bird squawked, as if laughing at her.

"Only with the little kids who don't weigh enough to slide all the way to the other end. You'll do fine."

Kit braced her feet, shaking her head from side to side. "You make fun of my hair and then you call me fat."

The guide, who was probably close to her age, threw up his hands in frustration, his patience worn thin.

"Ignore her," Jackie said from behind. "She always gets irrational when she's scared. Can I just give her a little push?"

Knowing Jackie, she'd do it.

"Push me and die," Kit ground out. "Fine. I might as well get this over with. Am I good to go? How do I stop on the other end?"

"You're good to go. Hold on tight to both handles. It will help prevent you from spinning. Ready?"

Sunlight glittered on the diamond in her engagement ring. "What if my ring falls off?"

"Is it loose?" he asked.

She tested it. "No. I think my fingers are swollen from the humidity."

"It won't fall off. Now, grab hold."

If I lose the ring, it'll be a sign, she thought.

"Go, Kit! Go, Kit! Go, Kit!" Jackie and Lynette clapped and chanted behind her.

"God help me," she whispered.

Then she stepped away.

The platform disappeared behind her, but her feet still kicked, instinctively reaching for solid ground. She heard Jackie yelling to relax, and she fought the urge to keep kicking. She felt utterly alone as the air rushed past. The views were breathtaking, and gravity had no hold on her. She threw her head back and howled to the treetops, her joy over conquering her fears spilling out of her. The action caused her to lose some of her equilibrium, and she fought to pull her head back up.

Another platform, similar to the last, came into view and she slowed as if by magic. A different guide was waiting. She remembered his role was to help her up onto the next platform. Behind him, she could see a beaming Annie, bouncing on the balls of her feet in excitement.

And just like that, Kit was standing on the next platform, her first ziplining experience behind her.

"That was amazing," she shouted, feeling as excited as Annie looked. "Can I go again?"

The air was steamy by the time they finished with the last zip line. Renee waited for them at the bottom, one hand over her eyes to block the strong sun, and relief bloomed on her wilted expression when they appeared.

"Did everyone survive?"

After her hesitant start, Kit discovered she loved the feeling of freedom as she zipped down the lines. If it wasn't so hot, and she wasn't so hungry, she'd have considered trying to convince at least one of her friends to go through the course with her a second time.

"Are you glad you agreed to this, Kit?" Annie asked, falling into step beside her as they made their way back to the rental car.

Kit stuck both arms out and spun in one slow circle as she walked. "So glad. I'd go again!"

"What were you so afraid of?" Jackie asked, tugging on the tail of Kit's T-shirt.

"Death," Kit joked.

"The guide thought you were cute," Lynette said as she caught up with them all. "Did you notice?"

Kit dropped her arms, only to stumble forward on a tree root. She caught herself before she went down. "Which one?"

"Duh," Lynette said. She pulled the tie out of her hair and let her curls blow in the breeze. "The older guy on the first platform. The one I'd pick for the month of February in that calendar I suggested. Maybe you shouldn't have put your brave on and jumped. You could have walked the forest floor with him."

Jackie snickered. "I don't think Kit's fiancé would appreciate her walking through this dense vegetation with a rugged Hawaiian guide."

Some of Kit's elation evaporated at the mention of Dean. "Screw him," she bit out, unzipping the pocket in her capris to fish out the car keys.

"Who? The guide?" Jackie asked. "He was amazing with you! He knew exactly what to say to get you to jump."

"No, not him. He was great, even if he was hard on me. Screw *Dean*. He doesn't get to dictate what I do on this vacation."

They'd reached the car. "Wowzah," Jackie said, jumping away when she leaned against the car door and her skin touched the hot metal surface. "What did Dean do that has you so uptight? You've been belly-aching about him this whole trip."

"Dean kept an important secret from me. I'll tell you the whole ugly story soon."

After a moment, Jackie nodded. "I hope you do . . ." she said, her voice trailing off.

"Look. I'm sorry. This has been so fun, and it's only noon. I think today could turn into one of those magical memory-making days. Let's not ruin it with talk of our problems. I'd love to set mine to the side and forget about them for today. Who's with me?"

A round of "Absolutely!" and even one "Hell yes!" met her question.

Jackie bowed her head to Kit, lowering her voice. "I'm here whenever you need to talk," she said. "You gave me a safe place to land last fall when I upended my life. Let me return the favor."

Kit nodded, then raised the keys into the air. "Which one of you beautiful women would like to drive us to the beach? My hands are shaking like a leaf, either from hunger or adrenaline, but either way, I don't think you should trust me with your lives right now."

Lynette snagged them from Kit's hand and climbed behind the wheel. "I didn't think you'd ever ask. You've been driving us around since we were kids. It's time you gave up a little control."

Kit opened the passenger door behind Lynette. "Should I assume there is a euphemism buried in that statement? I can let go, too, you know."

Lynette threw her head back as far as the headrest would allow and her laughter filled the interior of the plush SUV. "I wouldn't have believed that an hour ago when you were fighting to keep your feet planted on that first landing. But once you loosened up and let Mr. Mature Hot Guide Man talk you down, we could barely catch up!"

CHAPTER SEVENTEEN

K IT CLOSED HER EYES against another wave of nausea as Lynette took a tight curve faster than was necessary. Kit usually drove because she often got carsick in the back, though she kept that little secret to herself. They were all lucky her stomach was basically empty, or she might have made an awful mess of things.

They'd decided to wait to eat their picnic lunch on the beach. It had turned out to be the right call, even though she was so hungry she would have gnawed on the leather armrest if it wasn't so firmly attached to the door.

"You still look a little green," Annie said, tilting her head toward Kit. "You all right?"

"I'll be fine. I think it's just system overload from our little ziplining adventure."

Annie patted her knee. "I'm proud of you, you know. Despite how scared you felt, you took a chance, and then you realized how much you loved it."

As Annie pulled her hand back, Kit inhaled deeply, followed by a slow exhale. They were coming out of the dense vegetation of the jungle and the sky was visible once more. She bet if she rolled down her window—which she wouldn't because it provided a glass barrier between them and bugs as big as her fist—she'd be able to smell the ocean.

Jackie shifted around to look at the three women in the back. "On to our next adventure! I already know Kit gets nervous snorkeling, but she said she'd do it. What about you, Renee? Please tell me you aren't going to sit on the sidelines this afternoon, too."

Renee stretched the seat belt away from her chest. "Nope. I'm hot and sticky from this morning. You couldn't keep me out of the water if you tried! I've actually done both scuba diving and some snorkeling down in Fiji, so I'm looking forward to this. After we eat, that is. I'm *starving*. Lynette, you put the cooler in the back, right?"

Lynette glanced in the rearview mirror, opening her mouth in mock horror before her expression shifted into a smile. "You can trust me to never forget the food. And beverages. Both alcohol and kid-friendly."

Renee tapped her on the shoulder, grinning. "Since there aren't any kids with us, should we assume you might try to pick up some other cute young hotties for your upcoming calendar? We know you like them young."

Lynette shook her head at the same time she flipped on the left blinker. "*Liked*," she corrected. "Past tense. No more immature men for me. In fact, I might be done with men entirely."

Doubtful laughter followed her declaration. They knew that even if Lynette were ready for a change, it wouldn't be *that* drastic. Lynette loved men.

"Jackie claims to be done with men, too, but I don't believe her either. How much longer? I'm starving, too," Kit said, her stomach growling.

"If we can find a place to park, I'd guess five minutes per the sign we just passed," Lynette answered. "If you can't wait that long, I might have gum in my purse."

Kit smiled but shook her head. "I'll make it."

It turned out to be fifteen minutes. But it took them no time at all to get the heavy cooler propped open in the middle of a large blanket they'd borrowed from a closet at the rental house, and they all soon held paper plates weighed down with slices of meats, cheeses, and imported olives. Cold cans of seltzer rested beside them.

They didn't have the beach to themselves, which wasn't a surprise given the pristine swatch of sand that lined a calm expanse of water. Two different families with young children cloistered by the water's edge, and other knots of people lounged here and there.

Annie tapped the top of her can. "Only one of these before scuba diving, ladies. We need to keep our wits about us in these shark-infested waters."

Jackie laughed, knocking her sweating can against Annie's in a mock toast. "We're snorkeling, not scuba diving, but I agree we need to limit the alcohol before this next adventure. The waters are *not* 'shark-infested.' I checked. This is a relatively safe area as far as sharks are concerned."

"Let me guess," Kit said, leaning over to gaze at Jackie pointedly. "More research?"

Jackie popped a purple olive in her mouth. She nodded as she pulled the pit out from between her teeth. "Way back when, a great white bit a guy swimming near us on our honeymoon. I'll never forget his panicked screams. I can't imagine the pain the poor guy must have suffered. Let's just say it's made me more cautious."

"You've got to be kidding! On your honeymoon with good old Todd?"

"Yep." She selected another olive from her plate. "I should have realized it was my new husband who was the shark, but the fact escaped me for a few years."

"At least you got Mack and Hailey out of the deal. Todd *is* a shark, but his sperm made quality kids." Kit winked.

Lynette tossed her empty plate into a sack and reached for the zippered bag of rented snorkeling equipment, pulling out a set of goggles. "Men have to be good for something, right?"

"And sometimes that's all they're good for," Annie chimed in, disposing of her plate, too. She got to her feet and held her arms wide. "I apologize to all of you men," she yelled, spinning in loose circles, "but this girls' trip has been thirty years in the making and it wouldn't be complete without man-bashing!"

Her foot tangled in the blanket and down she went amid fits of laughter.

A man got up from his blanket a few yards away, but Jackie waved him back. "She's fine! She was our star gymnast as a kid. They teach you how to fall with grace."

He shrugged, grinned, and lay back on his towel, giving the women their space.

Jackie turned back to Annie, where she still lay on her side, her shoulders shaking. "Tell me you're laughing."

Annie collapsed onto her back, hiccupping with giggles. "I'm laughing. Though you have more faith in my training than you probably should. *Shit*, that hurt."

"Are you sure you've only had *one* of those seltzers? You seem kind of loopy."

She pushed up onto her butt, hanging her wrists over bent knees. "I'm fine, I'm just having fun. I needed this week with you girls even more than I realized. Thank you *all* for making it happen."

There was a brief pause at this statement, then Jackie asked, "Annie . . . are things all right back home?"

Renee held up a hand in protest. "No, no, no! No talk of problems, remember?! Come on, ladies. Finish eating. I can hear the mermaids calling us now. They want to play! And I, for one, plan to heed their siren song."

Jackie dumped the rest of the snorkeling equipment onto the blanket. "As long as those mermaids aren't Fran and Ivory, back from our girlhoods to torture us again."

Lynette slipped thick, yellow-framed goggles into place. They covered her eyes and nose. "It wasn't *your* lives those little bitches tried to ruin, it was *mine*. And Kit's. And if they are out there now, they won't get back to this beach in one piece if I get my hands on them."

Everyone dissolved into more giggles at Lynette's nasally words. The goggles were pinching her nose, and she sounded like she had a terrible sinus infection.

"Hey, would you mind watching our stuff while we swim?" Kit hollered over to the man on his towel. She wasn't sure why she should trust a stranger, but her gut told her he was honest.

"I'm not good enough to come to your friend's aid, but I'm good enough to play 'watch dog' over your stuff?" His mock indignation was watered down by a chuckle.

She grinned at him. "Something like that."

"Fine. Go have fun! I'll make sure no one wanders off with your seltzers or your olives."

She picked up her flippers and walked to the water's edge. "I was more worried about the car keys and phones, but thank you."

She plopped onto her bottom and struggled to get her feet into the awkward black contraptions.

Jackie sat next to her and snapped her own flippers into place. "Jeez, Kit, why don't you just invite him to steal our rental while you're at it?"

"Oh, chill. He's fine. I trust him."

"Why? You don't even know him."

"Not sure, I just do."

"Whatever you say." Jackie struggled to her feet, turned her back to the water, and waded in backward, disappearing under a wave.

Kit watched her friends, enjoying the tropical sun on her back and in no particular hurry to get in. The water was already cooling her off as it lapped against her bottom and legs. She could only get one flipper on. She set the other one aside and leaned back on her hands, feeling her worries slip away with the gentle waves.

"Are you coming?" Renee yelled.

Kit gave her a thumbs-up, but she didn't try her flipper again.

"Looks like you might be having some trouble," an older woman said as she sank onto the sand next to her.

Kit hadn't noticed her approach, but she returned the woman's friendly smile, admiring her bright yellow and black two-piece suit that accentuated a muscular physique. From the neck down, the woman could have been any age, though sunspots stood out against her sun-bronzed skin. But her deeply lined face and blondish-white hair made Kit suspect she was at least seventy.

Goals, Kit thought. She wondered if the woman lived nearby, close to the beach.

"The strap broke," she said, motioning to the flipper she'd given up on.

"Mind if I take a look?"

Kit handed it to her. "Do you live around here?"

The woman glanced up from the flipper, then settled her gaze on the water. "Why? Do I look like a beach bum?"

Her words held no animosity, and Kit laughed. "Honestly, you look at home here. I want to be just like you when I grow up."

"Oh, dear, never aim to grow up. Life is more fun when you maintain the heart of a child. Here you go. It wasn't broken. Just being difficult."

"Thanks." Kit took the flipper back, but she was in no hurry to end their conversation. "I'm Kit Robinson. I'm here on vacation with a group of girlfriends. We actually planned this girls' trip when we were kids."

Kit wasn't sure why she felt inclined to share so much.

The woman grinned. "I heard your friend's declaration about men earlier."

"That's Annie. I think something is up with her at home, but she won't talk about it. Yet." Again, Kit wondered at how much she was sharing.

The woman nodded, her eyes scanning the horizon. Kit turned to look, too, and saw her four friends floating on their backs and playing in the water. She suspected they'd come back to shore soon and collapse on their towels in exhaustion.

"I'm sorry," the woman said, breaking the companionable silence. "How rude of me. You gave me your name, but we got on a tangent before I could properly introduce myself. My name is Nancy Drew."

Kit narrowed her eyes at her, trying to tell whether she was kidding. "No, it's not."

The woman calling herself Nancy Drew laughed. "I can assure you that it is most definitely my name. My mother was a librarian. I suppose she thought she was clever naming me after the teenage sleuth."

"I'm sorry," Kit said. "Now *I'm* being rude."

"Don't worry, I'm used to that kind of reaction to my name. Growing up I hated it, but now I embrace the novelty. I didn't even take my husband's last name when we married. That was rare back then."

Kit sat with that for a moment. She watched her friends play out in the water while also thinking back to some of her favorite mysteries from the beloved *Nancy Drew* series.

"You said you and your friends have been planning this trip since you were kids? What's the occasion?"

Kit gasped as a larger than average wave surged across the sand and hit her in the chest. Laughing, she scooted a few feet back. "Friendship, I guess."

"Sounds like the perfect excuse for a trip to me. I'm here with an old friend, too. My best friend's husband, actually. The two of them insisted I join them on their annual trips here to escape the brutal winters back home after my husband died. That was eleven years ago."

Kit sensed there was much more to this friendly woman's story. She stayed quiet, hoping Nancy would continue.

"Over time, our one-month long vacations extended, until eventually we stayed all winter." She lapsed into silence, as if lost in the memories. Then she gave her shoulders a shake. "Pardon me. Too much history to sift through."

"I'm sorry," Kit said. "I hope I didn't cause you to dwell on any painful memories."

Nancy Drew straightened her legs, allowing the waves to run up to her waist. "I've discovered that the best memories are richer *because* they're colored with a few shadows. The bad times make us appreciate the good. Without them, we take too much for granted. But heavens, listen to me waxing poetic when you probably want to sit here and enjoy a bit of quiet. Or, don't let me hold you here if you'd like to join your friends."

Kit would rather hear the rest of the woman's story—or at least the abbreviated version—than swim out to the rest of her party, where the water would be deep. Her aerial tricks through the treetops had provided enough excitement for the day. She wasn't sure her nerves could take much more. Plus, admittedly, Jackie's comment about sharks still lingered.

"You aren't keeping me. I'm enjoying our visit, in fact. If you don't mind, I'd love to hear more about your lovely friends. Unless you don't want to share anymore."

Nancy bent her legs and perched her chin on top of one knee. "We lost Sally to breast cancer. She held the dratted disease off for a few years, and I suspect the beauty of Maui had a lot to do with that. But eventually she tired of fighting. Before she went, when the end was near and our hearts were breaking, she made us promise we'd keep coming here for as long as we're able. It's been four years now. It was awkward at first, both of us having lost a spouse. But over time we realized what a gift she'd given us. We both sold our homes back in Wisconsin and bought a lovely bungalow near here. I suspect we'll be here until we, too, move on to whatever comes next after this lifetime."

Kit was fascinated. She tried to imagine what it would be like to build a life with a best friend's husband. The pain of loss had to be great. But this woman—named after one of Kit's favorite childhood book characters—didn't look like she was suffering. She practically glowed.

"Your friends are coming back," Nancy said. "They're probably coming to check on you. Thank you for the chat. Give that flipper a try. Even if you don't like the deeper water, you shouldn't miss the beautiful corals and colorful fish closer to shore. And enjoy your girls' trip. Maybe you can come back again. Maui never gets old."

As the woman stood, Kit had to know. "Did you marry your best friend's husband, then?" She doubted anyone Nancy's age would shack up with a guy, but she was learning to question her assumptions. People were full of surprises.

"Oh no, dear. One marriage was plenty for me. And for him."

Kit considered this, getting to her feet as well. "Oh, so it's platonic, then."

Nancy's bright blue-green eyes twinkled above her broad smile, and Kit realized they matched the ocean stretching to the horizon. "I didn't say that either. But a girl should never kiss and tell."

The woman headed off down the beach with one final wave.

"Who was that?" Jackie asked, struggling out of the water in her flippers. Her eyes followed the older woman down the beach. "I love her suit. Props to her for wearing a bikini at her age. What's her story?"

Kit grinned, locking the highlight reel of the woman's story in her brain. "I'll save it for later." It was a story best repeated on a moonlit evening with a glass of wine in hand and friends to share it with.

Chapter Eighteen

When Kit rolled out of bed the next day, her body let her know the ziplining had required muscles she'd apparently ignored for too long. After surviving such an adventure-filled Wednesday, she appreciated their plans to relax today. It would give her a chance to recover before they attempted the Road to Hana.

She'd done a little snorkeling close to shore yesterday, as Nancy Drew had suggested, and avoided any snorkeling-related mishaps, but poor Lynette gained a nasty scrape down her stomach when a rogue wave pulled her across an outcropping of coral in shallow water. The stubborn woman raised her middle finger to a star-studded sky, declaring to the universe and anyone listening that she refused to heed conventional opinions that reserved bikinis for younger women, and they'd all laughed at her. She probably would have escaped the coral without injury if her suit covered her stomach, but that wasn't going to change her mind. Lynette would wear whatever she damn well pleased, and she'd sell attractive swimsuits for women over forty through her company, too. As an entrepreneur, lines were often blurred between her real life and her business.

Lynette's declaration last night reminded Kit of her visit with the real-but-not-real Nancy Drew. After she'd shared what she could remember with the rest of the Kaleidoscope Girls, as they'd relaxed around the lighted pool, the modern mystery novel next to her bedside felt lacking. She might have to scour some used bookstores when she got home. It would be fun to revisit some of her favorite titles from the old *Nancy Drew* series, like *The Secret of the Old Clock* or *The Sign of the Twisted Candles*. Or maybe Hazel had even kept the box of *Nancy Drew* books she'd given Kit years ago. After discovering the tubs of old childhood memories in Hazel's basement, Kit supposed the house might contain more mysteries than she would have guessed.

The day spent relaxing around the pool at their rented home was exactly what she'd needed.

It was probably a good thing my book didn't keep me reading past my bedtime last night, she thought as she waited behind the wheel on Friday morning for her slower friends to get moving.

They'd agreed to leave the house by seven to beat the crowd on the Road to Hana. It was ten minutes to seven. She remembered Dean's comment the morning they were due to meet her grandmother for breakfast, claiming she was always at least ten minutes early for everything. He knew her well.

But how well did *she* know *him*?

The interior of the rental was already stifling so she started it and turned on the air, hoping her friends would be out soon.

She checked her cell phone again for any calls or messages from Dean. Nothing. She still hadn't talked to him since she'd bolted from his apartment. He hadn't bothered to respond to the voice messages she'd left earlier in the week and she feared the spotty service wasn't to blame.

Actually, maybe this was good. Maybe both of them needed the time to decompress after her shocking discovery. In her quiet moments, when she considered her options, she realized that perhaps discovering Dean was already a father didn't have to spell the end of their relationship. Never being able to give him the child he wanted had been the biggest stumbling block, at least in Kit's mind, that was holding her back from marriage. But didn't this clear their path?

She fiddled with her ring, deciding she was glad she hadn't gotten ahold of Dean. They should talk in person.

Knuckles rapped against the passenger-side window. She jumped. She hadn't noticed the way the windows were starting to fog over—no doubt given the high humidity and climbing temperature outside versus the now cooled, air-conditioned interior of the SUV. Jackie looked impatient on the other side of the glass. Kit searched for the button to unlock the door.

Once seated next to Kit in the front, Jackie snapped her belt in place and blew on her steaming to-go cup of coffee.

"It's nice of them to keep the kitchen stocked with lidded cups," Kit said, setting aside the heavier topic that was never far from her mind. She knew she needed to tell Jackie what was up, but today had to be free of distraction. The adventures they'd planned for this final "touristy" day of their vacation would include a road purported to boast over fifty hairpin turns and plenty of one-way bridges.

Lynette had offered to drive again, but Kit knew she couldn't stand another day in the backseat. Besides, her friend's defiance of the universe the night before might come back to bite them all if they let Lynette drive the tricky road today. Never underestimate karma—Lynette was always saying as much.

Jackie switched her cup from one hand to the other. "Man, that's hot. Styrofoam works better, but biodegradable paper products are much easier on the environment. No one wants paradise to be littered with a bunch of nearly indestructible white cups. Did you know that scientists estimate it could take five hundred years for one of those Styrofoam cups to break down?"

Kit picked up her own cup and took another sip before responding. "Jackie, I *am* a scientist. I know all about how pollution is killing our planet."

"Oh. Right. Sorry, too little sleep and too much wine last night. You turned in earlier than the rest of us. How do you feel this morning?"

"I feel ready for anything," she replied, checking her watch again. "Which is probably a good thing, since I hear this road is tricky. Where are the other three? We should get going."

"Chill." Jackie let her head fall back against the headrest and closed her eyes. "Renee can't find her glasses, and since she's into reading the brochures about the different stops on our way to Hana, she didn't want to leave without them. They'll be out in a minute."

"Did you guys pick the spots you want to stop at? We can't hit them all in one day. But it didn't make sense to stay in Hana overnight to make it a two-day event since we're already paying for this place."

Jackie opened one eye and looked at her. "You did a great job selecting this rental. It's been perfect. Thanks again."

Kit smiled. "I did good, didn't I?"

"Careful, or you'll get stuck planning next year's trip, too."

"No way. That wasn't the deal. We should talk about where we want to go next year, though."

Through the fogged windows she saw the three stragglers heading down the driveway toward the SUV.

"I agree," Jackie said. "Let's talk about it tomorrow. I'm glad we left tomorrow wide open to just relax. Today will be fun, but I'm getting too old for all this running around."

The back doors opened in the middle of Jackie's comment.

"I thought we agreed we were going to remove the phrase 'too old' from our vocabulary," Lynette said as she took her seat behind Kit.

"And *I* thought we agreed I didn't have to sit in the middle every dang time," Annie muttered.

Kit grinned at the new arrivals in the mirror. "Who's ready for another adventure?"

Two hours later, Kit and Jackie scanned the small turnout for a parking spot while the three women in the back exclaimed about their beautiful surroundings.

"There!" Jackie cried, pointing to a midsize Chevrolet with its backup lights on. "Just wait here and you can pull in once they leave."

As Kit inched their big vehicle into the now open spot, she said, "Good thing I learned to park the Mustang in tight spots as a kid. Thank you, Grandpa!"

"Thank you, Gus," Jackie said, glancing through the windshield toward the sky.

Amid laughter, Renee said, "Gus? Who's Gus?"

"Gus was Jackie's favorite goldfish," Lynette said. "She won him at the fair in one of those carnival games when we were . . . what . . . freshmen in high school, maybe? She was the only one of us who could land a ping-pong ball in a fish bowl of water to win the darn thing."

"That's because I was the only one who took my softball seriously," Jackie reminded them, earning groans from her fellow passengers, Renee included.

"Anyway," Lynette went on, "none of us thought the fish would survive the trip home in its little plastic baggie."

"But Gus *did* make it home, and I kept him alive until our senior year in high school, thank you very much," Jackie said. "When he died, we kept his memory alive by praying to him every time we needed a little help to snag a parking spot at the beach. And he's been my go-to helper for parking ever since."

Renee laughed.

"I admit I've used the old 'ask Gus for help to find a parking spot' trick, too," Annie shared as they all climbed out of the car. "Especially on those rare occasions when I hit the Mall of America. I need to get a close spot at that place or I'll forget where I left the car."

The five women wove their way around other parked cars, letting the sound of rushing water guide them.

"This one is the Upper Waikani Falls," Renee said. "Also known as the Three Bears Falls. Most people consider it the most scenic waterfall on the Road to Hana."

Kit grinned as Renee continued to motion toward the breathtaking scene in front of them. "Hey, Renee, if that whole resort-and-retreat gig doesn't work out for you, you should consider being a travel guide for your next career reinvention."

But Renee shook her head emphatically. "No, thank you. I doubt I'd be up for another life overhaul of that magnitude. Running Whispering Pines has taught me more than I ever wanted to know about the hospitality industry, and I'm still learning!"

As the group reached the low concrete railing in front of the falls, Kit whistled. "Three waterfalls for the price of one!"

The majesty of the sight before them silenced them all as they took in the three rushing columns of water, running side by side to crash into the pool below. The falls varied in size.

As a car drove behind them, moving slowly in deference to both the foot traffic and nature's beauty, the sound of tires on wet pavement pulled them out of their reverie.

"I can see where the name Three Bears comes from," Lynette said, pointing to the falls. "One is big and loud, one is small and almost soundless, but the third is . . ."

"Just right," Kit chimed in. "Like Baby Bear's bed."

"I sense a theme here," Annie said, leaning over the railing for a better view of the pool at the base of the falls. "Nancy Drew last night, and now child nursery rhymes. Are we regressing?"

Jackie laughed. "No! We're working our way back into the world of kids' books to help you prepare for your new grandma gig."

Annie straightened, her smile growing. "I'm looking forward to that title. *Grandma.* Or maybe 'Nana.' I haven't decided which I prefer yet. And I can't wait to read 'Goldilocks' to her. But since I'm not quite an old rickety grandma yet, I really want to climb down by those people at the base of the falls. How do we get down there?"

Kit followed Annie's finger, surprised to see people below. She couldn't see an obvious trail down.

Renee looked skeptical. "The travel book says you *can* climb down there, but it can be tricky climbing over wet, moss-covered boulders. Coming back up can be even harder. It would be fun to see the falls from there, but I'm not sure it's a good idea."

Annie stepped back from the railing, hands on hips, eyes scanning the vicinity. "I want to go. Look! Those people just climbed up over there. I'll go ask them how they got down."

As she watched Annie skip away, Kit shrugged. "I'll try it. As Lynette is so fond of saying, we aren't old yet. How about the rest of you? We used to climb all over the area around Diamond Falls at summer camp. How hard can *this* be? We should follow Annie down. I thought she was nuts when she convinced us to try ziplining, and I ended up loving it. She might be on to something here, too. I think we should try. What could go wrong?"

Kit regretted following Annie's lead. The hazardous path down to the base of the falls left her with a mysterious rash on her lower legs and earned Lynette a twisted ankle. Renee even lost her cell phone during the challenging descent. The stop at the falls turned out to be problematic, but additional stops during the drive between Waikani Falls and Hana resulted in no further injuries or lost items. Now hunger was making them all irritable. Kit knew food would help everyone's mood and was happy to pull into Hana around lunch time.

"You jinxed us, Kit, with that question about what could possibly go wrong," Lynette said, hobbling her way to an open picnic table near a small collection of food trucks in Hana.

"Oh, no—I'm not accepting all the blame on this one. Weren't you the one flipping the bird to the universe last night? How do you know *that* wasn't what jinxed us?"

Jackie shook her head as she eased down onto the bench. "You two are way too woo-woo for me. Everything that happened makes perfect, logical sense. That path down to the base of the falls was tough."

Renee snorted. "I wouldn't call that a *path*. When we get home, you guys have to promise to share all your pictures with me. I can't believe I dropped my phone. Then you wouldn't even let me go look for it."

Kit brushed a seed pod off the bench seat, grimacing when a sliver of red paint flaked off and stuck under her thumbnail. "Did you seriously want to ignore that huge warning sign posted right next to where your phone skidded down the rocks and into all that vegetation, Renee? You know what was likely down there? *Snakes.* And spiders the size of your fist. Maybe even bodies of hikers who didn't abide by that DANGER-STAY AWAY sign!"

Renee sighed. "I read somewhere that there aren't snakes on Maui, but fine. You're right. I had no business digging in the underbrush, even for my phone. Thanks for talking some sense into me. But I feel naked without it."

"You should have talked me out of climbing on that boulder for a better shot of the four of you in front of the falls," Lynette said. She gingerly lifted her leg onto the bench, her injured ankle hanging off the edge. "I wonder if I can get a bag of ice for this."

Kit gasped at her first good view of Lynette's ankle. "You poor thing! Do you think you broke it? First that scrape on your stomach and now your ankle. Maybe we should hurry back so we can find somewhere you can get that looked at."

"Nah. I know it looks bad—and it hurts—but this isn't the first time I've rolled that ankle. I slipped on the ice about eight years ago, and ever since then it's given me some trouble. It'll be fine. I packed one of those tight elastic sleeves just in case. Tomorrow I'll keep it iced and elevated, and hopefully before too long I'll be good as new."

The rash on Kit's lower legs was really starting to itch. "Anybody have any itch cream?"

Annie unhooked a fanny pack from her waist. "Matter of fact, I do. I keep a little first-aid kit in here. When you work with teenagers, you learn a thing or two about being prepared. All that would fit were some Band-Aids, itch cream, tiny tweezers, and a few spare aspirin tablets. Sorry, Lynette, I don't have a wrap for that ankle."

"I'll take the tweezers and cream," Kit said. "I've got a sliver, too."

Jackie threw her hands up in exasperation. "For God's sake, you sound like a bunch of old ladies. Can we just suck it up and get some food? I'm starving."

As she stood up and marched toward a food truck with a line long enough to suggest the food was tasty, the other women yelled at her retreating back, in unison, *"We are not old!"*

Kit was interested in checking out the small boutique she'd spied nearby. She still needed to pick up a little something for her grandmother. Hazel had mentioned that, back in the '50s, this road had been the highlight of her honeymoon. It wasn't even paved back then, and Kit couldn't imagine how much harder that would have made the drive.

Lynette wanted to rest her ankle and Annie claimed to have spent too much already on her new grandbaby, so the two stayed at the picnic table while Kit, Jackie, and Renee went to explore.

"There aren't many shops around here," Jackie said as they approached the lone boutique. "I doubt Annie would have spent much more money in here."

As Kit pulled open the door for her two friends, Renee gave a low whistle. "There are some cute things in here. I'll probably pick up a few more souvenirs, too."

"Actually, I'm glad Annie didn't come," Kit said, heading straight for a rack of decorative items.

"Is she wearing you out with all of her adventure-seeking? I swear, she's in denial of becoming a grandma. Not that I can blame her," Jackie said. "When I think 'grandmother,' I picture my two. One puttering around in her garden and the other in the kitchen, both bent over and looking old beyond their years."

Kit's eyes caught on a wooden tube; both ends were nicely finished with brass bands. She wanted a closer look, but she worried she might break something if she reached for it. She spied the shop's proprietor in a far corner, visiting with the only other customer in the place, and decided to wait.

She turned back to Jackie. "No, I could never tire of Annie. She's fun. But did you remember that it's her birthday on Sunday? The day we fly home? I thought we could pick up a little something for her. When I ordered groceries, I included a cake mix and frosting. It won't be fancy, but we should have a little party for her tomorrow while we're relaxing by the pool."

Jackie clapped a hand to her mouth. "Oh my gosh, I completely forgot! That sounds perfect. We haven't celebrated our birthdays together since we were kids!"

Renee, having overheard their conversation, stepped closer and said, "Since I wasn't around the four of you as often when we were all kids, I missed those celebrations. I'm so happy to be with you for Annie's now. Did you have any gift ideas? It can't be too big, or she'll see it."

"I might..." Kit wagged a finger at the wooden item above their heads. "If that's what I think it is, it'll make the perfect gift for Annie."

Chapter Nineteen

K IT COUGHED AS POWDERED cake mix spewed from the waxy bag, tickling her throat. "This kitchen could sure use a pair of scissors."

Jackie laughed. "Our grandmothers wouldn't feel too sorry for us. They had to make all their birthday cakes from scratch."

Kit dumped the yellow cake mix into a mixing bowl. "Hazel still does." She brushed the spilled powder from the granite countertop into her palm then headed for the garbage can.

Jackie stepped out of her way. "No one makes homemade chocolate cake like dear old Hazel."

"Yes, and she taught me many things, but baking wasn't one of them." Kit brushed her hands off against her orange terrycloth swimsuit coverup. "I wonder how she's doing at Marge's."

Jackie picked up the empty cake mix box, squinting as she tried to read the small print of the baking instructions. "It was great of Renee to take Annie on a walk so we can surprise her, but once she smells the cake, the birthday girl will know something's up. How hot should I set the oven?"

"Here, let me see . . ." Kit took the box from Jackie and pointed to the instructions in a large font on the top. "Three-fifty for about thirty minutes." She set the box back on the counter. "I think Annie already suspects something is up. When I met her coming out of the bathroom this morning, she reminded me she doesn't do chocolate."

"I can't imagine a world without chocolate," Jackie said.

"I can't either, but that's our Annie. I don't think she's allergic to it, but she's never been a fan. Not even Hazel's cake could convert her when we were kids."

Jackie put the nearly empty carton of eggs back in the fridge. "Where's Lynette?"

Kit handed her the large container of vegetable oil to return to the cupboard. "Conference call in the back study. We won't disturb her from the kitchen."

"On a Saturday? God, I don't miss those days."

After pouring the thick batter into a cake pan, Kit started preparing sandwiches for a simple lunch. "What are you talking about? You work weekends all the time!"

"Yes, but the dogs seldom talk back, and we're only open till noon. It's my most peaceful time of the week. I wonder how Lynette's business is doing. I know she mentioned trouble with her board of directors. She doesn't seem as excited about work as she was last summer. Remember how she practically glowed over wine and cheese on my parents' porch when she told us about her latest collection? She was excited to source her caftans from a small group of industrious women in an African village."

Kit slathered mayonnaise on bread for two sandwiches. "This bread is getting stale. Good thing we leave tomorrow."

The oven beeped, telling them it was finished preheating. Jackie slid the cake in and set a timer.

"I'd gladly eat stale bread if it meant we could stay here for another week. I feel like I've been living in a slice of paradise." Jackie topped off her coffee mug with the last dregs from the pot. "How did the time go so fast? I feel like we still have so much to catch up on."

Kit knew she couldn't avoid telling Jackie about the wedding invitation she'd discovered any longer. It was just the two of them now, so maybe it was the perfect time to discuss it. She had already told Annie, but of all her friends, Jackie knew Kit and Dean as a couple the best. "Grab your sandwich and let's go sit by the pool. Something happened with Dean, and I've been meaning to talk to you about it."

Jackie nodded knowingly. "I've wondered when you'd get around to this." She tucked a bag of chips under her arm before picking up her coffee and plated sandwich. "Is it your engagement? I know you haven't wanted to set a date. Be honest if you don't want to marry him. He deserves that."

Kit snorted. "That's rich. He deserves my honesty? You might sing a different tune when I tell you what I discovered just before we left. Come on."

A tiny bird hopped over to peck at Jackie's sandwich where her plate lay abandoned on the ground next to her chair. "But I don't understand. That doesn't sound like Dean. I can't believe he never told you! I mean, I believe you, but it's just so out of character for him."

Kit shook her bare foot at the scavenger bird, but it didn't scare easily. "If you plan to eat the rest of that, you better pick it up."

After an absentminded glance down at her lunch leftovers, Jackie shook her head. "I'm done."

While Kit watched the jerky movements of the bird as it snatched a piece of crust from Jackie's plate, she caught herself cracking her knuckles. It was another nasty habit she only fell into when her stress was too high. "I wonder if we're done, too."

"You and Dean? Is that what you really want? You two seemed happy. I've always thought Dean helped fill in the empty places inside your heart."

That rankled. "So now I'm not a complete person without Dean?"

Jackie rested her head back against the wooden slat of her lounger and sighed. "That isn't what I meant. I know this is hard, but you don't have to be defensive with me. I'm trying to help. I'm still in shock over your bombshell news. It just doesn't sound like the Dean we know at all."

"That's the hardest part in all of this," Kit said. "He knows kids have always been a sticking point in our relationship. He knows how I've struggled with guilt over keeping him from having kids. How could he keep this from me?"

Jackie didn't immediately reply. Kit pushed out of her chair, gathered the remnants of their half-eaten lunch, and headed for the house. "Be right back. The birds are freaking me out."

She balanced the two plates and empty coffee mugs as she opened the sliding door into the kitchen. Once inside the cool, shaded house, she shivered at the extreme difference in temperatures. The tile felt cold under her feet. Part of her wanted to slip back into bed. Maybe if she slept long enough, her mess of a life would sort itself out.

"Not likely," she whispered.

But she knew she couldn't sleep through this. Neither her shock over Dean's secret nor her problems with Mia would just go away. She would need to deal with both situations when she returned to Minnesota.

There was beeping again as Kit re-entered the kitchen, and she realized she'd forgotten all about the cake. She yanked the oven door open, relieved to see it looked perfect. At least she hadn't burned Annie's birthday treat in her distracted state.

It surprised her that Annie and Renee hadn't returned from their walk yet.

Hopefully Jackie would give her some helpful advice, at least where Dean was concerned. Her friend had been through her fair share of relationship drama and was usually helpful when Kit was feeling overwhelmed. Her own parents were a terrible example of what beneficial relationships could look like, so she appreciated Jackie's perspective. But even Jackie might need a few minutes to process everything Kit had dumped in her lap.

This was their last full day of vacation, so that meant it was the perfect time to dip into the frozen concoction she'd prepared upon their arrival. Frozen pineapple, cream of coconut, and orange juice—plus a splash of rum and soda—would make for the perfect drink to sip while spending the afternoon around the pool. They might not have hunky male servers keeping their glasses filled like they'd had at the luau earlier in their trip, but this would be the next best thing.

By the time Kit returned poolside, Jackie had slipped off her coverup, and she was swimming laps, stroking gracefully from the shallow to the deeper end of the pool.

Kit raised a glass and shook her head. "That looks too much like exercise. It's the last day of our vacation!"

Pausing at the far end of the pool, Jackie wiped the salt water from her face. "Technically we still have tomorrow. Our flight doesn't leave until almost midnight. What time do we have to be out of this house?"

"Eleven. But don't worry, I have a fun day lined up for us tomorrow. It will go fast." Kit handed her friend one of the two plastic martini glasses full of the creamy white slush before resuming her seat, angled to face the sun.

Jackie managed to sip her drink while treading water, then she set the glass on the side of the pool and swam back toward Kit.

"That will melt fast in this heat," Kit warned. She wouldn't let Jackie make her feel guilty for sitting on her butt and relaxing. This was supposed to be a vacation.

Jackie headed back for the deep end. Once there, she hoisted herself out of the water, picked up her glass, and joined Kit in the warm sunshine. "It'll be good, even after it melts." After helping herself to another sip, she finally looked ready to talk about Kit's dilemma.

"What should I do, Jackie?"

Before she could answer, the back gate opened. Annie and Renee strolled through, laughing about something.

"It looks like you ladies had fun," Kit said, torn between the distraction their arrival meant for her discussion with Jackie and loving to see the two women laughing.

"We did!" Renee said. "This place is so beautiful. But if I don't use the bathroom this minute, I'm going to wet my pants. You should have seen our birthday girl here when an overly friendly rooster followed us home."

Annie shivered. "I've always hated birds. I was afraid he was going to peck my eyes out!"

Renee snorted. "He may have pecked at your hand, but your eyes were never in danger. Be right back."

"Where do I find one of those?" Annie asked, pointing at the slushes.

"Freezer. Here, freshen mine up, will you?" Kit passed hers to Annie, who headed to the kitchen.

Jackie laughed. "Pace yourself, Kit. These things are a little strong."

"I need liquid courage. I want to figure out what to do, and I need you to help me do that."

By the time Annie returned with more slushy drinks, Lynette had wrapped up her work call and joined them. Renee was back, too.

"Tell me you plan to turn that lovely, plain cake in there into the 'better than sex' version before you frost it," Annie said, handing fresh glasses to Renee and Lynette after giving Kit her refill.

"I'm not sure it'll qualify for being better than sex since you won't let me use *chocolate*, but yes, I'll poke it and add caramel sauce and sweetened condensed milk as soon as I finish my drink."

"Nummy!" Annie grinned as she sank into the last open chair. "You know that's overrated, don't you?"

Kit choked on her sip of slush. It felt like a sliver of coconut was stuck in her throat. "*Sex* is overrated? Oh, honey, you've been married too long."

Color flooded Annie's cheeks. "Says the woman who's still engaged. But no, I meant *chocolate* is overrated. Though now that you mention it, sex isn't all it's cracked up to be anymore, either. Maybe I'm just getting old."

"Hey, we're not allowed to utter those words. Remember? We are still on vacation."

She gave Lynette an apologetic look. "Sorry. I slipped. Easy to do when you're turning forty-nine. I still can't believe next year we'll all be *fifty*. Doesn't it seem like we should still be eighteen?"

"Some days," Kit agreed. "But not the day we went ziplining. I felt my age that day."

Annie pointed at her with the same hand that held her slush. "But you still did it!" Some of the drink sloshed onto her lap.

"Don't waste that," Lynette teased. "This is delicious, Kit. I need the recipe."

Kit nodded. "I'll text it to you. It helps that the pineapple and coconut are so fresh."

Jackie set her empty glass aside and folded her hands over her middle. "I agree. Those are great. But I have to take these slow if I want to last, so no refills for me just yet. Now, where were we, Kit? If you don't mind pulling these lovely ladies into the conversation."

"I can use all the help I can get," Kit said with a shrug. She downed the rest of her second glass, hoping she wouldn't regret it in twenty minutes, and brought everyone up to the same page where Dean was concerned. Lynette was the first to start peppering her with questions.

"Have you talked to him since you left?"

A wave of unease passed through her. "No. I've tried. And I've left him messages. But maybe he's pretty rattled by our fight."

"How did you leave things? Does he know how mad you are about this?"

"Trust me, he knows."

She wondered again why she still hadn't heard a word from him. It wasn't like they never fought. But this was different. This was a life-changing issue.

"I suspect Dean is just giving you space," Jackie chimed in. "He knows you are in good hands, and he'd know what a blow this is for you."

"It sounds like you think I should forgive him."

"I said nothing of the sort. Only *you* can decide whether to forgive him. My only advice is to give yourself time to decide whether you can live with this latest information. His daughter is obviously a grown woman now if she's getting married."

"She's only twenty," Kit said. "No one is *grown* at twenty."

Jackie shuddered. "I agree. But my point stands—the girl is old enough to marry. I'm guessing she wants to be part of Dean's life if she invited him to her wedding. Dean gets to decide if he wants that. You also have a choice to make. I know it won't be easy, but if you decide to stay with Dean, you don't want this to taint your future relationship."

Annie swirled her glass. "Maybe this is actually a good thing."

"A *good* thing? How can dishonesty be a *good* thing?"

"Jeez, Kit, take a breath. Don't be so defensive. You wanted to have a discussion."

Kit felt bad for snapping. "I'm sorry, Annie. You're right. I need to talk about this, and I trust you all to give me sound advice. It's just that I've always hated dishonesty."

Annie snorted. "Trust me, no one should tolerate dishonesty in a partner."

The look that passed over Annie's features had Kit wondering if her friend was struggling with her own issues in her marriage. As she glanced at each of her four friends and the concerned expressions on their faces, she felt a surge of love for each of them.

"You got that right," Lynette said before taking a noisy slurp of her drink. "I *love* these."

Kit laughed, appreciating her friends more than she could ever express. "And I love all of you. Thank you for listening to my problems. Look. I promise I'll give it more thought. I do miss him. I'm leaning toward forgiving him . . . maybe even asking Dean if I can go to the wedding with him. Maybe I need to meet this girl. And her mother—again. I just feel like I'm operating from a place of secrets, and I don't *do* secrets. But I don't want to talk about me all day. I've told you the whole ugly truth, and now I think it's time to celebrate the birthday girl."

"My birthday isn't until tomorrow," Annie said with a shake of her head. "And, like I said, I'm not super excited about being one year older. Fifty doesn't feel far enough away anymore."

Lynette waved her free hand dismissively. "It doesn't matter what our technical age is, what matters is that we are happy and healthy and growing. And knowing you, Annie, I suspect you have all three things down pat."

Annie paused before responding. Then she pushed out of her chair, drained the rest of her slush, and wandered over to a nearby hibiscus plant, plucking a bloom from the plant and tucking it behind her ear. She turned back to the others. "Today I'm happy. This trip has been amazing. And I'm doing what I can to stay healthy, though I have to admit that it's getting harder than it used to be to keep the weight off."

Every other person around the pool nodded or spoke their agreement.

"Turning fifty isn't for the faint of heart," Jackie said.

"Oh no, not quite fifty yet," Annie shot back.

Kit stood. "Give me a minute to finish the cake so it can set up. We'll have it after our shrimp dinner later. But I want to give you your gift now. We're all pretty excited about it, actually."

As she headed into the house again, she heard Annie exclaim that they shouldn't have gotten her a present. Kit smiled. She was glad she'd stumbled on the perfect gift for Annie. Every girl deserved presents on her birthday.

Renee snorted at the sight of Annie carefully folding the turquoise tissue paper. "Are you really saving that?"

"It reminds me of the color of the ocean," Annie said, smiling as she tucked the neatly folded tissue between her outer thigh and the chair. "I want to remember this amazing trip forever."

They all watched as she lifted a wooden tube-like item from the gift bag. Kit felt a surge of pride over her find. It really was just perfect.

"Oh, my . . . I *love* it!" she exclaimed, grinning as she held the kaleidoscope up to her eye and twirled the tube. "This will make a beautiful addition to my collection."

"Do you still have the one we made at summer camp that year?" Lynette asked.

"Of course!" Annie handed her birthday gift to Lynette. "Check this out. The colors are so vibrant!"

Lynette took the instrument reverently. "I don't know that I've looked into one of these since I was eighteen."

Annie looked appalled. "You've been missing out!"

"I have," Lynette said as she held the wooden tube to her eye and rolled it. "These patterns are truly amazing. I wonder whether my designer could capture this effect and incorporate it into next year's summer line."

"If you figure out how, I want to buy your first piece," Annie said. "The Kaleidoscope Girls live on!"

"We sure do!" Lynette handed the instrument to Renee. "You ladies have no idea how much I appreciate taking this trip with all of you. Having this to look forward to really kept me going."

Renee gazed through the kaleidoscope, grinning at what she saw. "Have you ever thought about how our lives are like these patterns?"

"What do you mean?" Kit asked.

"Life is always changing . . . shifting . . . you know? When you twist this, the patterns change. Like when you take action in life, things change. But it isn't just that." Renee shifted so she could point the kaleidoscope at the flowering vegetation surrounding the pool area. "If you change how you look at something, you might find a blessing instead of problems."

She sighed, then passed the instrument on, like a baton at a relay race.

Jackie looked through it. "Like the way you took your aunt's resort and turned it into a new career?"

"Exactly," Renee said. "I wasn't sure where to turn after I got laid off. But then I learned Aunt Celia had left Whispering Pines to me, and I decided I'd never forgive myself if I didn't at least give it a chance."

"How did it work out?" Annie asked, though her smile spoke volumes, as if she already knew the answer.

"I've never been happier," Renee confirmed with a grin of her own.

But the bird that nibbled on Jackie's sandwich earlier was back. "God," Annie said, kicking her foot to shoo away the bird. It flew off, but it didn't go far, landing on a nearby branch and keeping a close eye on the group around the pool. "First a rooster, and now that thing. Next year we might want to go somewhere without so many birds."

"Speaking of next year, where should we go?" Kit asked. "And remember, one of you gets to do the planning for the next round."

CHAPTER TWENTY

K IT LOCKED THE FRONT door of the rental house, then laid her palm against the rich, dark wood. The intricate floral design inlaid in the door was an impressive work of art. She wished she knew what kind of wood the craftsman used. "Thank you for the wonderful stay," she whispered before turning away.

"Who are you talking to?" Jackie asked. She was snapping pictures of the fragrant, brilliantly colored flowers lining the walking path.

"The house. I was thanking her for her hospitality."

Jackie grinned. "If most men heard you talking like that, they would think you were insane. Although those same men probably call their cars 'she.' Go figure. But I actually whispered my thanks to the house when I had my morning coffee on the back lanai this morning. And you're right—this house is all about the feminine energy. It was perfect."

Kit yanked the retractable handle of her suitcase up and lugged her bag toward the vehicle, the hard plastic wheels thumping across the cobblestones. "Don't you have enough pictures yet?"

"Renee wanted a few more shots of these," Jackie said, pointing to a bush covered with vivid purple blossoms. "Remember, we need to send her our pictures when we get home since she lost her phone. They look so bright! Probably because the sky is gray today."

"I wonder whether my geraniums survived the week. I checked the weather, and it's been hot back home."

Jackie pocketed her phone into the cardigan she'd thrown on against the light mist of the early morning. "Won't Dean have watered them?"

"I sure *hope* he's been by my place. I'm not worried about the flowers, but Chloe can't go this long without fresh food and water."

Jackie followed her to the car. "Dean loves that cat. He'd never abandon her."

Kit reached the SUV and shoved the handle of her suitcase back down. Once she had the back door open, she moaned. "I bet this baby is overweight now, after all the shopping I did. I'm not sure I can hoist it up into that spot you guys left me."

"Here, let me help."

Together, the two heaved the bulky bag into place, giving it one last shove before slamming the back hatch closed.

"We'll have to be careful when we open that back up," Jackie said. "I don't know what all you have in that bag, but if it falls on someone's head, it could kill them."

Lynette tapped the horn. She stuck a hand out her open window, waving at Kit and Jackie. "Come on, ladies! My phone says we're a good forty-minute drive to the plantation, and our tour starts in forty-five."

Kit, noticing Annie had already taken the front passenger seat, bit back a groan. "I shouldn't have eaten that omelet this morning."

Jackie paused with one hand on the door handle. "Why?"

Kit made a silent gagging motion, then nodded toward their driver. "I love her, but she's a little jerky on the steering wheel. I'm not sure my stomach can handle forty minutes if the road is curvy."

Jackie giggled. "Don't worry—I have a barf bag in my purse. I never travel without one. Even though I've never gotten carsick, my twins sometimes do, and it's just a habit that stuck. I've got you."

Laughing, Kit shoved Jackie into the middle and snagged the window seat. She put the window down before she even snapped her seat belt. The rain might get in, but it would be better than having to use Jackie's barf bag.

The rest of the day went quickly. *Too* quickly. Kit wasn't ready to leave their tropical paradise. The low-level clouds had cleared by the time they reached the pineapple plantation, and they'd spent a pleasant hour roaming around the grounds. The air smelled of sweet fruit, and by the time they'd stopped for lunch at a food truck offering fish tacos and fruit smoothies, she'd have given anything for a Canadian bacon and pineapple pizza.

Hoping the fish taco wouldn't mess with her stomach around the time she had to board the plane later that night, Kit dug in. Lynette waited next to her for Jackie to return with her order.

Lynette had managed the tour without too much difficulty, but her ankle was swelling again. Although she never complained, her friends noticed her limp, and Jackie had insisted on grabbing her lunch while she got off her feet.

Renee and Annie had opted for a different food truck offering fried chicken and weren't back yet.

"Thanks again for the beautiful rooms you surprised us with, Lynette," Kit said. "Between the resort and the house, I'd say our accommodations were perfect."

Lynette yanked at the hair band she'd used to catch her strands during their plantation tour. Her curls bounced around her shoulders in the light ocean breeze. "I'm only sorry I missed the first day. After waiting thirty years for this trip, it went too fast. I know we talked a lot, but I feel like we were just scratching the surface. We've all lived lots of life since high school, and I haven't been as good about keeping in touch as you, Jackie, and Annie. And I'm sure glad Renee joined us. This trip was about perfect."

"What would have made the trip better for you?" Kit asked, curious. "I'm sorry about your ankle. And that you had to work some."

Lynette shrugged. "I'm lucky that I get to travel with my business, but I never unplug completely. Maybe if I could do that, I'd end the vacation feeling completely recharged. I suppose that's the price of owning your own company. You can't get away."

Kit thought surely a business owner could structure things so she could be out for a week, but who was she to judge? She had no experience in work like Lynette's. "What is it like?"

"What's what like?" Lynette asked, rubbing at her ankle.

"Running a super successful online business? It has to be exciting. To get to be creative at work—designing beautiful clothes and hearing from appreciative customers. Jackie got me a pair of your bamboo pajamas for Christmas, and I think I need to buy myself a few more pairs so I can chuck all my old crap. Those are amazing."

Lynette dropped her foot, shaking her head. "Believe me, it isn't nearly as glamorous as everyone thinks. I can't remember the last time I sketched out a piece of clothing, let alone run a sewing machine. It seems like all I do these days is hire and fire people . . . oh, and talk to my lawyers when someone threatens to sue. Maybe I should have *let* the board kick me to the curb instead of cleaning house and starting fresh."

Kit picked a piece of cilantro out of her taco. She thought the green garnish tasted like soap. "Why would your board do that? The company wouldn't exist without you. You *founded* it, for crying out loud!"

Jackie came by and slid a basket of fish and chips in front of Lynette. "I'll be right back with our lemonade. I couldn't carry everything."

Lynette's eyes trailed her as she returned to the truck. "Sometimes I wish I was in the same place as Jackie."

Kit looked between her two friends, confused. "Like Jackie? What do you mean?"

"Oh, you know how things feel when you start something new. It's *exciting*. It can be both exhilarating and terrifying to build something from scratch, but early on is when you have the most freedom."

Kit thought about this as she took another bite of her fish taco. "I think you should have complete freedom to do what you want to do *now*. You own the company, Lynette. Wait—does your mom have an interest in it, too? Beyond just wanting to support you, I mean."

"She has a fifteen percent interest," Lynette clarified. "Enough to keep her interested, but not enough that she can make significant changes within the business on her own. The woman isn't overly focused these days."

Kit laughed. "She never has been. Still, it must be great to work with your mom."

"It is—most of the time." Lynette accepted a cup of lemonade from Jackie. "But you know how moms can be. She knows how to push my buttons, and sometimes I think she does it just to spite me. I know my success has always bothered her a little."

Kit wondered what Mia knew about the work *she* did. Probably nothing—unless Hazel paid more attention than she seemed to and passed what she knew on to Mia.

"What did I miss?" Jackie asked, settling on the bench across from them.

Kit dug out another piece of cilantro. "I asked Lynette about work."

Their conversation drifted to other topics, eventually landing on the state of Hazel's house following the summer storm.

"When the contractors come in, I'll go back. I couldn't find anyone to help get things back in order until early August, though. Hopefully Grandma and Marge don't kill each other. And I hope my mother doesn't show up out of the blue again. I think Marge would flip."

Jackie took a bite of her taco, nodding but waiting to talk until she'd swallowed her food. "Do you really think your mom is coming home?"

"It's possible. Grandma insists she's been clean and sober for years, but can you blame me for doubting that? I mean, Grandma wouldn't ever outright lie to me, but there's just something about the mother–daughter relationship. I could see it in Grandma's eyes. She misses Mia. Despite everything she's done to me. To our family."

Jackie squirmed on the bench. "I suppose I can see her point. At least a little. As a mother, I can't imagine ever losing complete contact with one of my girls. It would kill me."

Kit nodded, thinking again that maybe she'd been a little selfish through the years. She'd hated her mother for the way she'd hurt her and her brothers, but maybe she hadn't ever considered the impact it must have had on Hazel. "I'm not sure what I'll find in Ruby Shores . . . but first I'll need to deal with the mess with Dean in Minneapolis."

The other two women nodded.

"Have you decided to forgive him?" Jackie asked, looking hopeful.

Kit grinned, despite her exasperation over her friend's apparent siding with Dean.

"What I've decided is I want to meet this bride. Because I think you're right. She must want something from Dean if she reached out after all this time. And I think Dean needs to build a relationship with his long-lost child. What will that type of dynamic do to our relationship as a couple?"

"What would you wear?" Lynette asked.

"Wear? What do you mean?"

"To the wedding. What would you wear if Dean is open to taking you with him?"

Kit shrugged. "I have no idea. I haven't thought that far ahead. I doubt I have anything in my closet that would work."

Lynette dunked a fish stick into her tartar sauce. "Nonsense. If you are going to the wedding of your lover's long-lost daughter, and *his* old lover will be there as the bride's mother, you need the perfect dress."

Kit paused at this. Lynette was right. She'd need to look her best if she was going to that wedding with Dean. If he even wanted her there.

"Let me send you something," Lynette said. "I know the perfect one."

Kit wrapped the soft shawl around her shoulders. Lynette had surprised each of them with one that night, as parting gifts. The darkened cabin was quiet except for the occasional snore or whisper. Most passengers slept, but a few unfortunate souls like herself couldn't doze off.

If she had remembered the medication her doctor prescribed for her restless legs syndrome during her last annual physical, maybe she wouldn't feel like she wanted to crawl out of her own skin.

How had their week passed so quickly? What would she come home to? Was her cat all right? Or had something happened to Chloe, and that was why Dean wasn't answering her calls, afraid he'd ruin her vacation?

Knowing she was being ridiculous, Kit gave up on sleep. She folded her shawl, stowed it in her carryon, then pulled out her phone. A colleague had sent her a new report the Friday evening before the weekend of the big storm back home. She'd downloaded it when it came through, intending to look at it after the weekend, but forgot all about it in the chaos that followed the storm. She might as well review it now, since she'd be back at work on Tuesday. If Lynette could sacrifice vacation time for her career, Kit could, too.

"What are you doing?" Jackie said, her voice raspy with sleep. "Are we landing?"

"Unfortunately, no," Kit said. "We have about two hours until we land in Chicago. Go back to sleep."

With a nod, her friend shifted positions, and Kit could hear her soft snores again within minutes. What she wouldn't give for two hours of sleep. But she was too wired.

She pulled up the report she'd downloaded to her phone earlier. The latest monarch counts in the southeastern part of the United States were disheartening. Were they fighting a losing battle? There was talk in the scientific community that the butterflies might become endangered in the next few years if things didn't improve.

Kit laid her head back and closed her eyes as she tried to remember how many monarchs she'd noticed while in Maui. Not many. She'd spied one or two in the trees while ziplining. While walking through the pineapple plantation, she'd noticed a few more.

The thought brought her back to her first summer of camp. It was where she'd met Jackie, Annie, Lynette, and Renee. Annie and Lynette were kind to her from the start, and she'd found a kindred soul in Renee, since they'd both felt like outsiders that first year, but Jackie had been determined to bust her butt at first, when she'd found Kit snooping in their cabin.

It was funny how her friendship with Jackie had felt the rockiest in those first days, but eventually, they became the closest.

That was also the summer when she first became fascinated with the monarch butterfly. She remembered the way the park ranger explained the complicated process of metamorphosis in a way that a twelve-year-old would find fascinating.

Kit would love to go back and thank that woman. Despite all of her struggles in her personal life, she'd found satisfaction in her career of choice as a scientist, studying the fascinating creatures.

She thought about how she'd transformed from a frustrated kid at that camp to the accomplished, grown woman she'd become. It wasn't all that different from the metamorphosis the caterpillar experienced, with plenty of mess and chaos in the middle.

But just when Kit thought she was emerging from her cocoon, complete with a husband-to-be and satisfying career, that wedding invitation had sucked her right back into the muck again.

At least her lifespan was longer than that of the monarch.

How could she still be struggling to figure out her life?

Their time in Maui had reminded her that she wasn't the only one with problems. Her girlfriends were also experiencing different crises in their own lives. Kit suspected no one ever figured things out completely, because life keeps throwing curve balls. She could either play along, or throw up her hands and lose at the game.

A dinging noise filled the cabin and Kit's eyes popped open. She must have drifted off after all. She even felt a little rested.

Their Chicago layover would be short. The four of them might have to run to catch their Minneapolis connection, while Lynette headed for a different gate for her flight to New York City. Kit would hate to miss their flight. She needed to get home as soon as possible.

She missed Dean. They needed to talk.

CHAPTER TWENTY-ONE

DEAN EYED THE SHIMMER of heat above the Iowa cornfield. The mirage reminded him of the distortion a jet's exhaust causes during its final taxi leading up to takeoff. He checked his watch. Kit was due home today. She might be in the air right now.

He wouldn't be there to meet her when she landed. Would she expect him to pick her up?

Was it a mistake to give her this much space?

He hadn't talked to her since she blew out of his apartment after he'd completely bungled his attempt to tell her about Summer. She'd called from Maui and left a few terse messages, but he didn't want their first conversation after that scene to be over the phone. They needed to be eye to eye if he wanted to maximize his chances of convincing Kit that they could make it through this together.

He should have at least told her why he wasn't taking her calls.

"You know, bro, it's cooler inside. Mom says you need to come in before you suffer heat stroke."

Dean nodded but didn't get off the porch steps. "She realizes we used to spend every summer day, from sunup to sundown, out in this heat, doesn't she?"

His brother grunted, sinking onto the top stair next to him. "It's not the heat that worries her."

"I know." Dean plucked a tall blade of grass from beside the stairs and twirled it around a finger. "It's the sun."

Ever since their father died of melanoma, their mother barely left the house. If she had her way, her grown sons would live their days inside, too.

"What are you doing out here, anyhow? It's not like you to sit around moping."

When the tip of his finger turned purple, he loosened the blade of grass. "I'm not moping. I'm enjoying the view. You have a great place, Nick."

His little brother pulled a knife out of the front pocket of his jeans and used it to dislodge a dried chunk of mud from the sole of his boot. "We do, don't we? And here you thought I was a lost cause."

Dean snorted. "You would have been if your wife hadn't saved your sorry ass."

"I'll give you that," Nick said. "I think we both got lucky in the wife department. At least, I thought you were lucky, too, until you messed that up."

The twinkle in the younger man's eye told Dean he was kidding, but he was also correct. Dean *had* screwed things up where Kit was concerned.

"I knew I'd regret telling you what happened," he said. "Don't you dare tell Mom. Remember your promise."

Nick slapped both hands on his knees, causing a cloud of dust to rise from his worn jeans. "I won't tell her, but she might weasel it out of you yet. You can't show up here without an explanation. *I* might have let it go and tolerated your company, but that isn't my wife's style. Or Mom's."

"You can say that again," Dean said, thinking back to the grilling he'd received from his sister-in-law on their drive from the airport the day before. "But I needed to talk to someone, and I appreciate the advice the two of you gave me. I have a lot to think about."

High above them, the thin white slash of exhaust from an airplane cut across the brilliant blue.

"I don't suppose that's her plane now?" Nick said, eying the sky.

"Not likely," Dean said. "I don't remember her exact flight times."

The screen door behind them creaked open then slammed shut, followed by giggles and the scurrying of small feet. Dean braced himself for the onslaught.

"Uncle Dean!" squeaked his four-year-old nephew as the boy slammed into the back of him.

Dean reached around and pulled the wriggling child onto his lap, rubbing his knuckles across the top of the kid's tight black curls. "I thought you might sleep all day!"

The boy squirmed out of Dean's arms, then jumped into his father's lap and wrapped both arms around his neck, nose to nose with the man. "Daddy, my ear is all better now. No doctor. Please . . ."

But Nick shook his head. "Sorry, bud. We have to check those tubes. Where's your mother?"

"Going potty. I went first, then it was her turn. She made me leave. *Women*," the boy said with a dramatic sigh. He reminded Dean of Nick at that age.

Dean bit his lip to keep from smiling and caught his nephew by the hand. "Mason, it's important for us men to show women respect. That wasn't respectful."

Little Mason laid a hand on top of Dean's. "I'm a man?"

"Yes. A miniature one. It's never too early to learn how to be a gentleman."

The child pulled his hand away and touched it to his chest. "Should I go say sorry to Momma? Maybe I slammed the bathroom door. I didn't mean to inspect her."

Dean chuckled at the boy's attempt to sound grown up, despite his erroneous word choice.

"Yes," Nick cut in. "Go tell her you're sorry and that it's time to go. We don't want to be late."

The boy turned. "*I* could be late," he muttered, and then disappeared into the house again.

The two men sat in silence following Mason's exit.

Nick got to his feet. He cleared his throat. "Dean, I love Kit. I really do. But raising a kid of your own has always seemed like your destiny. Things happen for a reason. Maybe this is a sign. If you can't smooth things over with Kit, you can still have that chance. It isn't too late for you. You're old, but not *that* old."

Dean leaned forward, resting his forearms on his knees. "You forget. I *am* a dad already. But since my only child is getting married, I'd say I missed the boat on raising her."

Nick shrugged, then sauntered down the steps. "I didn't forget. Hell, maybe that girl starts a family of her own soon. She's only, what, twenty? You could jump right to Grandpa and skip the dad role. Either way, you always tell me that things have a way of working out, even if it's not in the way we'd hoped."

Dean dropped his head onto his knees. "I'm too young to be a grandfather."

"Technically, you're not. But don't worry. I suspect you'll be raising a kid or two during your lifetime. It's fate."

Dean dug around under the kitchen sink, hopeful that his sister-in-law stored a spare flower vase there. After his brother drove off with his little family for Mason's appointment, he'd wandered into a nearby shelterbelt for the shade it offered. He knew his mother was inside Nick's house. Mason had said she was mending his favorite stuffed elephant, but Dean was afraid she'd want to talk about what brought him home unexpectedly, so he'd stayed outside for a while. He'd skirted a fallen tree, its trunk so deteriorated that he suspected it might be home to a family of racoons or other wildlife. He'd spied a trail cam and deer tracks as he strolled.

Despite the struggles both Dean and his mother had suffered during Nick's rebellious years, he knew their father would finally approve of the path his youngest son was on. The old farmstead where he lived with his wife and child had been in her family for a century. They worked as a couple to keep the tradition alive. Dean could picture a slightly older Mason, climbing trees and playing hide-and-go-seek back here with friends—maybe even a sibling or two. Farming was hard work, and Nick confided to Dean that he felt in over his head now that his father-in-law was dead. But the couple seemed happy. They were figuring things out.

He also appreciated that Nick didn't live far from their mother and so visited her often. She helped watch Mason during the school year when his wife taught. Her presence back at the house wasn't unusual, and Dean knew he'd stayed outside long enough. His mother would know he was avoiding her, and she wouldn't appreciate it. When he'd spied a wild swatch of white daisies, he'd picked a handful, knowing it might help soothe her potentially ruffled feathers.

If I could just find a vase . . . somewhere in here . . .

"What are you looking for?"

He jumped at her voice, knocking the cupboard door hard.

"Nick will skin you alive if you give him one more thing to fix in this rickety old house."

Dean straightened, trying but failing to hide the flowers behind his back. "I thought you loved this house."

She entered the kitchen and set Mason's well-loved elephant on the small luncheon table under a bank of windows with a view of the fields behind the house. "I do love it. It keeps Nick out of trouble because there is always so much to do." She smiled at her eldest son. "Are those for me?"

He sighed and set the loose bunch of flowers on the table. "Of course. But I can't find a vase."

She nodded and opened a narrow cupboard next to a refrigerator that looked as old as the house. Over her shoulder he glimpsed an array of glassware on the shelves inside. She selected a slender white one with little nubs all over it and handed it to him. "Fill this with water."

Once the bouquet of wildflowers sat in the middle of the table next to Mason's toy, Dean motioned to his mother to take a seat. He'd decided during his walk that he should be upfront with her, and he wanted to get it over with while the house was quiet.

"Are you finally going to tell me what's going on?" she asked, pulling out one of the three wooden chairs. "You never just show up like this. And I haven't had the privilege of seeing you alone, without Kit, since your fortieth birthday party."

She wasn't going to make this easy.

"I thought you liked Kit," he said, noting the way the chair squeaked under his weight. He hoped it would hold him. Nick should tighten up the chair's screws, maybe try some glue.

"I like your girlfriend just fine. She's a smart, funny woman, and I know she loves you."

His mother said the right things, but her inflection could never hide what she was really feeling.

"Mom, she's my fiancée, remember?"

"So you say. But until I hold an actual wedding invitation in my hand, I won't believe it. She's in no hurry to marry you. I think deep down she knows that she might not be the right woman for you."

Dean wanted to bang his head against the table in frustration. But all that would do was give Nick another thing to fix. It would do nothing to fix his mother's true opinion of Kit. Nothing could, and he didn't have the energy to try. Her mention of a wedding invitation reminded him of what he stood to lose when he wasn't honest.

His mother deserved to know she had a granddaughter.

"Kit *is* the right woman for me, Mom. But that isn't what I want to talk about. There's something else I want to discuss."

His mother's already pale face lost any hint of color. "Oh, no. You're sick, aren't you? I knew something was seriously wrong when you showed up without warning yesterday."

Dean took a deep breath—something he'd learned to do in the years after his father died and his mother would suffer her irrational panic attacks when one of her sons had an issue. "I'm fine, Mom. There's nothing wrong with me, at least physically. But I have carried a secret for too long, and I apologize for not talking to you about it sooner."

His mother slid her chair back. "I'll get us something to drink. Lemonade? Does that sound good? It's too blasted hot for coffee."

He nodded. That was another of his mother's habits. She needed to move whenever she faced the prospect of disturbing news. He wondered if he would have known so many of his mother's idiosyncrasies as well as he did if his father had lived. The man's death had changed so much.

Once they each had a tall, iced glass of lemonade in front of them, she sat back down.

"You look like you feel at home in Nick's house," he said, appreciating his first sip of the sweet drink. "I'm glad."

She stared at him from across the table. "Nick has really turned his life around. All right. Now. Tell me."

He wasn't sure where to start. There was so much to tell. How much detail should he give about the brief relationship he'd had with his coworker so long ago?

His mom gave him an impatient look, and he almost laughed. He always needed to give her time to prepare for bad news, but once she was ready to hear it, he'd learned that it was best to get straight to the point.

"I have a grown daughter, and she's getting married next month."

He wasn't sure what he'd expected, but her whoop of delight wasn't it. She flew to her feet, hurried around the table, and wrapped her arms around his neck, much as little Mason had done to Nick earlier. Her hip bumped the wobbly table, sending lemonade sloshing over the lip of both glasses.

"Little Summer is getting married?" she said, tears welling in her eyes.

"Summer?" Dean said, confused. Maybe it was the lack of oxygen reaching his brain because she was squeezing his neck so hard. He couldn't think. "Mom . . . I didn't say her name."

His mother froze, arms still tight around his neck.

He reached up and pried them off. "Belinda Marie Adams. What do you know?"

She drew a deep breath as she made her way back to her chair. Once seated, she mopped at the spilled lemonade with a napkin.

"Mom . . . you've known all along, haven't you?" he said as awareness dawned. He watched her reaction for any sign that his suspicions were correct. "How?"

"Erin told me." Her words held a hint of apology—but just a hint.

"*Erin?!* How do you know Summer's mother?"

She shrugged. "I don't. Not really. I met her once. She told me about the baby but didn't want me to say anything to you about her visit."

Dean's stomach churned with a mixture of anger and confusion. How could his mother have kept this from him for all these years? He'd thought he bore the weight of his guilt alone. No one else was supposed to know.

But as the anger took hold, he realized that this was probably how Kit felt. He hadn't been honest with her, either, but he'd thought his silence was justified. Maybe his mother thought the same about her own silence.

"Erin . . . came *here*?"

His mother dabbed at the damp table with her wet napkin. "Well, not *here* exactly. But to my house."

"Obviously," he bit out, fighting to stay calm. "When did she come see you?"

"Years and years ago. The baby wasn't even born yet. She was pregnant, confused, and looking for guidance."

"That took a lot of balls for her to come see you."

His words earned him a frown, but she didn't reprimand him, even though she hated coarse language. "As a mother of four boys, I always worried that one of you would get some poor girl pregnant. Imagine my shock and disappointment when it was you."

"You never said a word."

She shook her head. "A promise is a promise. Erin needed to know about our family. I think part of the reason she sought me out was to determine what your father died from at such a young age. She knew how seriously you took your role as a quasi-parent to your brothers. Though I wish now that I hadn't allowed you to take on so much. You deserved to live your life, too, Dean, and my weaknesses prevented you from doing that. Maybe if I wasn't so needy, you could have built a life with Erin and your child."

Dean didn't want to talk about his mother's guilt around her parenting style. This was supposed to be about *his* child. "Erin told me she didn't need, didn't even *want*, me involved in her child's life. Part of me has always wondered why she even bothered to tell me she was pregnant."

His mother folded her hands and looked out the window. Was she trying to remember a conversation that took place over twenty years ago? "I could tell Erin was a capable young woman," she said. "She had career aspirations, a strong family network on the East Coast, and no interest in being tied down."

"Mom, a *baby* ties a woman down. How could you be sure she'd do right by my child?"

She tossed the sodden napkin into the garbage behind her. "That's a fair question . . . and I don't know if you'll understand . . . but I just knew she would make a wonderful mother. Maybe it's a woman thing. Or a mother thing. Like kindred spirits, you know?"

He didn't know, but he wanted her to keep talking, so he simply nodded.

"Erin loved that child, even though she barely had a baby bump to show for it that day. We decided you had a right to know about the baby, but it would be up to you whether you wanted to be part of his or her life. Erin wasn't going to push. I admit, it surprised me when you never said a word about the baby to me. I knew that meant you had made your choice."

He could hear the disappointment in her voice. A fresh wave of guilt washed over him.

"I'm sorry, Mom."

"No need to apologize to me, Dean. You'd given up enough of your life already, helping me raise your brothers. If you weren't ready to be a father, and Erin didn't care to involve you, who was I to say anything? I guess we all have our share of secrets."

He wondered again if this was how Kit felt. Like you never really know someone as well as you think you do.

But there was still something he didn't understand.

"If Erin only came to see you once, how did you know she had a girl named Summer?"

His mom shrugged. "Just because you chose not to be that girl's father doesn't mean I couldn't be her grandmother."

Dean was so shocked by her statement that it felt like the floor had fallen away beneath him. When his mother hovered over him with a panicked expression, he realized it wasn't the floor falling in his imagination, but the old chair he was sitting in had truly collapsed under his weight. Dazed, he gave himself a second to catch his breath, then he climbed back to his feet.

His mother took a step back to give him room, and when his eyes caught hers, he saw a sparkle of amusement there, replacing her fear for his well-being.

"Don't you dare laugh," he said, rubbing his backside.

Then the absurdity of everything hit, and a chuckle slipped out. His mom laughed, and before long, both had tears streaming down their faces.

When she could finally speak, holding her sides because they ached from laughing so hard, she said, "Nick is not going to be happy that you broke his chair."

"That really wasn't funny," Dean said, wiping at his eyes. "I could have broken my neck."

"Not likely," she said, using another napkin to wipe her nose.

The screen door screeched, and Nick strode in, his eyes going straight to the busted chair. "What the hell happened? Did she break that thing over your head when you told her?"

Dean shook his head, throwing his arms up in the air. "She already knew."

"About your kid?"

"Yep," Dean confirmed.

It was Nick's turn to shake his head in amazement. "Of course Mom already knew. I could never get away with a damn thing, either."

Both Dean and his mother scoffed at that. Nick had gotten away with plenty.

CHAPTER TWENTY-TWO

K IT CLIMBED OUT OF the backseat of the Uber, relieved to escape the cramped vehicle. Five more minutes and she'd have left a three-star rating for the guy, even though he'd been friendly enough, chatting with Jackie in the front seat during the drive. Both Renee and Annie had dozed off enroute. The red-eye had taken a toll on everybody.

"Good thing Lynette split off in Chicago. There was no way all five of us would have fit in that tin can," Annie said, shaking out her legs after getting stuck in the backseat again.

Renee laughed as she grabbed her bag from the driver. "If Lynette was along, we probably would have been in a stretch limo."

Impatient to be off, the driver slammed the trunk and sped away.

Jackie watched him go, then turned and spied a car parked in Kit's driveway. "Now *that's* an amazing surprise! Kit, did you let them know when we were getting in?"

"Who?" Kit asked, struggling to pull her suitcase up the curb after their driver left it in the street. "Whose car is that? It isn't Dean's."

"My girls!" Jackie said, not bothering to move her own suitcase off the street before running toward Kit's front door. "That's the new vehicle Todd bought for Mack. Their father should be good for *something*."

Kit shook her head as she grabbed Jackie's suitcase and wheeled both toward the door. "Annie. Renee. You're welcome to come in, even if you just need to use the bathroom before you hit the road."

But both women declined her offer, eager to get home.

"I have to stop for gas," Renee said, giving both Kit and Annie a quick hug before heading toward her parked car. "Tell Jackie goodbye for me. I'll call her soon. And Annie, remember—my vote is for somewhere warm again next year. I hope you don't mind handling the logistics for us!"

"Ha-ha," Annie said, waving Renee on her way. "I was sure my hand would hold up, but then you pulled that blackjack."

Once Renee was out of earshot, Annie turned to Kit. "I'm not convinced I actually agreed that whoever lost the hand has to plan next year's trip, by the way. But I won't let you down. Now, I need to hustle. Relic sent me a text. He's the starting pitcher tonight, and he was hoping I'd get home in time for his game. I hate goodbyes, so I'm just going to hop in my car and head on down the road before I get all sappy."

When both women were out of sight, Kit turned back to her townhouse. At least she wasn't coming home to the empty house she'd feared. She'd given Jackie's girls the code to get in through the garage, back when Jackie had stayed with her the previous winter. It warmed her heart that the girls would feel comfortable letting themselves in to her home.

The curtains on her bedroom window twitched, and Chloe came into view, eyeing her with a look of disdain. The cat was always cool toward her whenever she first got home from a trip. She was glad to see Chloe was alive and well, though she'd never really doubted Dean. He might avoid Kit's calls, but he'd never put her cat at risk.

She wondered how long he'd keep dodging her, now that she was home.

Her bag's wheels caught on the grass, and over it went, pulling Kit with it.

"What are you doing out here, Aunt Kit? Did your suitcase break?"

She straightened, trying to pretend she didn't just trip and nearly sprawl across her front lawn. Why was she always so clumsy? "Hailey! It's so good to see you! Come here, girl. Give me a hug and help me with your mother's bag, will you? She left the dang thing on the street."

The young woman laughed from the doorway, then joined Kit on the sidewalk. "She was excited to see us. You'd think we haven't seen each other for a year by the way she's acting. I barely escaped her bear hug to come out and check on you."

"I'll take one of those hugs now," Kit said, ignoring the bags for a moment to catch one of Jackie's twins up in a hug of her own. "Chloe didn't give you any trouble, did she?"

Hailey shook her head. "Haven't even seen her, though we could hear her meowing from the back part of your house. There's still a little food in her bowl and plenty of water, so Dean must have checked on her not too long ago."

Once they'd stowed both heavy suitcases in Kit's foyer, they went in search of Jackie and Mackenzie.

"I love your new kitchen, Kit," Mack said. She rushed forward to give Kit a hug, just like Hailey had done outside.

"If I'd known you were coming, I would have planned to cook for you," Kit offered, to which both girls laughed.

"That's just what you should do after a week in Hawaii. We have a better idea. Come out for an early dinner with us! I bet you don't have any food in the house. Or do you have plans with Dean? I'm sure he misses you."

Kit wasn't so sure about that, but before she could think of a reply, her stomach rumbled.

Hailey giggled. "I heard that. Come on, it'll be fun! We haven't seen you in *months*, Kit. We want to hear all about your trip and your wedding plans. There *are* wedding plans, right?"

Chloe picked that moment to saunter into the room and rub against Kit's shin, as if welcoming her home.

"Huh," Jackie said. "I've never seen her show so much affection."

Kit bent over and picked up the cat, snuggling her. Chloe allowed it for a few seconds, then arched and squirmed until Kit had no choice but to set her down or drop her. The cat streaked out of the room.

"You call that affection?" Mack asked with a grimace. "Now I know why we're dog people."

"I probably shouldn't leave her again so soon," Kit said, feeling a pang of guilt.

"Her? The cat? Trust me, she won't mind," Hailey said. She checked the time on her phone. "Come on, ladies. Chop, chop! I made reservations, and we only have twenty minutes to get there. Kit, we won't take 'no' for an answer. You're hungry, and we've missed you."

Kit sighed. "Fine. You win. I can't pass up time with my favorite girls. But let me at least give the cat fresh food and change my clothes. Your mother drooled on my shoulder during the flight last night. I'll drive separate so you don't have to bring me all the way back home later. I'm sure Jackie is ready to get home, too. It was an amazing trip, but it always feels good to sleep in your own bed."

After pulling one last promise out of Kit that she wouldn't change her mind, her best friend and her two precious daughters cleared out, leaving her alone with her thoughts for the first time in a week and a half.

She filled Chloe's bowl—though it wasn't even completely empty yet. Hailey was right. Dean had stopped by within the past few days. She wondered where he was now and what he was doing. They'd never gone this long without talking.

As she stooped to put the cat food back in a lower cupboard, she noticed a sheet of paper on the floor beside the kitchen island. She picked it up and flipped it over, her heart skipping a beat at the sight of Dean's handwriting. Chloe must have knocked it down. She wasn't supposed to jump up onto the countertops, but the cat had a mind of her own.

Hey Kit, hope you ladies had an amazing time. Thirty years is a long time to plan something. I hope the trip met all your expectations. I know we need to talk. You'll be home tomorrow, but I'm heading to Nick's for a few days. I'll let you know when I'm back in town. Take care, D.

Kit pulled out a nearby stool and sank onto it, reading through Dean's words again. No mention of missing her, no request to call him to let him know she got home safely, not even his usual "luv ya" before his name.

Was he even more upset about her reaction than she was to learn his secret?

Her phone pinged with a text from Jackie.

Are you in the car yet?

Yes, she replied, knowing her friend would likely see right through her little white lie. When she eventually reached the restaurant, she'd claim heavy traffic held her up.

She wasn't really in the mood to go out for dinner, even though she had to since she'd said she would. She'd rather take one of the sleeping pills her doctor had prescribed and crawl under her covers. She'd never taken one before and hated the notion that she might become dependent on them if she did. But right now, slipping into a dreamless oblivion sounded like the perfect solution.

If she did that, she would also have to set her alarm, of course. Vacation was over.

Her boss was likely to fire her if she missed any more work.

A crash sounded from the back of the house, pulling her off the stool with a groan. She'd heard the sound before. She shouldn't have lied to Jackie, but now she'd have a legitimate excuse for being late. Chloe was mad at her for being gone so long, and she'd knocked over the spider plant again.

"I thought maybe you tumbled onto your bed and fell asleep when you went back to change," Jackie said when Kit finally found them at their outdoor table.

After so much time in airplanes, airports, and cars, it felt delightful to sit in the warm summer sunshine and smell the fresh air—even if it was missing the tang of salt water and tropical flowers. "No, but excuse me if I get sleepy in this cozy spot," Kit said, relaxing in her chair. "Did you order?"

"We did," Jackie confirmed. "Don't worry, I got you your favorite. Thanks for joining us, Kit. I know you're exhausted. I'm sorry you couldn't sleep on the plane. You have a lot on your mind."

Mack set down her drink. Kit spied a green olive in the bottom of the martini glass. It felt so weird to see the girls drinking. How could they be old enough already?

When a waiter passed by, she waved him down. "I'll take one of those," she said, motioning to Mack's glass. "But make it light. I'm driving. And tired."

"Will do, ma'am," he said, smiling at all four of them. Kit thought his eyes lingered on the two younger women.

In Maui, she had enjoyed the occasional flirtations with waitstaff as they served their table of five laughing, mature women. She raised her water glass to Jackie. "I guess it's back to the real world."

Jackie tapped her beer bottle to Kit's glass, a sparkle in her eyes. "I guess."

Kit knew Jackie could read her mind. Just like that, they'd become invisible again, especially with two beautiful, fresh-faced young women beside them.

She didn't really mind. It was fun while it lasted, but she'd never been one to want attention from random strangers.

"What is Dean up to?" Mack asked. "You could call him and have him join us."

The waiter delivered Kit's drink, and she fished the olive out of it. "He's out of town," she said, before popping it into her mouth.

"Really?" Jackie said, surprised. "He didn't have a work trip scheduled, did he?"

"Nope. And it isn't work. He's at Nick's."

Jackie sat up straighter and set her bottle down. "As in his *brother*, Nick? Back home? When was he last home?"

Hailey—always the more perceptive of Jackie's twins—looked between her mother and the woman she often said was more fun than her mother. "Hey, did you and Dean have a fight? Because you two are acting weird."

Jackie tipped her bottle up again, mouthing the word *sorry* to Kit before hiding behind it.

Kit made a split-second decision. Maybe the twins could help with her dilemma. Besides, she was sick and tired of secrets. These two loved her and they'd always liked Dean.

"Dean surprised me with something, girls, just before we left for Maui. It was a huge revelation, and I'm not sure what to do with it."

"Kit . . ." Jackie said, her voice low. "Are you sure you want to talk about this? With them?"

Mack slapped her mother's arm. "Hush, Mom. This sounds juicy. Go on, Kit. What were you going to say?"

"Mackenzie, knock it off. This is serious. If Kit feels compelled to bring you into her confidence, the least you can do is act your age."

"It's fine," Kit said. She didn't want the evening to dissolve into a mother-daughter squabble. "I found out that Dean actually has a daughter, and she is about the same age as you two. A year younger, actually."

That shut them both up.

Their food arrived, helping to fill the awkward moment.

Eventually, eyes full of sympathy, Hailey asked, "How could he keep that from you? And how did you find out?"

Kit picked up half her sandwich. She pulled out the slice of tomato.

"Sorry, forgot you don't like those," Jackie said.

"I went to his house to pick up a suitcase before we left. And I found a wedding invitation on his desk, which confused me, but then he rushed in, afraid that I would see it, and everything fell into place. Or maybe it all fell apart. I honestly don't know for sure. I feel like our relationship is on extremely rocky ground at the moment."

Jackie still looked unsure about Kit bringing her daughters in on such a delicate subject. But Kit needed their input.

"The invitation was for his daughter's wedding. They haven't had any type of relationship up to this point. At least, that's what he told me anyway. But he loves kids so much, I'm having a hard time believing that."

Mack dipped a fry in ketchup, looking deep in thought. "He must have just found out about her, too," she said.

Kit shook her head. "He said he knew about her. The whole time."

"Weird," Mack said.

"I'm sorry this is happening, Kit. Secrets are tough on a relationship," Hailey said.

Out of the mouths of babes, Kit thought, smiling at the young woman.

"Secrets *can* be a bad thing. I grew up with a mother who struggled to be honest with me, so I hate secrets and lies. But I love Dean. I need to figure out what to do."

Hailey reached across the table and touched Kit's hand. "How can we help?"

Kit's vision blurred and she had to blink back a tear. "When did you two get so grown up? And I'm not just talking about the alcohol. I'd like your input, since the bride-to-be is roughly your age. Dean said Summer—that's his daughter's name—wanted to invite him. If he goes to the wedding, should I go with him? If *you* were the bride, would you want to meet me, or would you think I was imposing? I saw the invitation. It listed his name and 'guest.' Hell, I don't even know if he'd want me along."

Jackie shook her head. "Of course he'd want you there for moral support . . . if he goes. He loves you, Kit."

"Then why haven't I been able to reach him since we left for Hawaii? And why did he run home to his mother before we could talk? He just left yesterday. It's like he's avoiding me."

Jackie opened her mouth to respond, but closed it again.

"Exactly. I'm getting lots of mixed signals here," Kit said, pushing the food around on her plate. Her appetite was deserting her—just like her fiancé.

Mack tapped her fork against her plate. "I think you're overthinking this, Kit."

Despite the ache in her heart at discussing this embarrassing turn of events with the twins, Kit couldn't help but smile. "Do tell, Mack. How am I overthinking it?"

She shrugged. "Do you love him?"

"Well, sure, but . . ." Kit's words trailed off when Mack held up one hand.

"But nothing. Dean is a great guy. Look, Hailey and me, we pretty much grew up without a dad because our father is nothing like Dean. If he has a kid and he never told you about her, there must be a good reason. And if this girl, this daughter, reached out to him, I'm sure she'd love to meet you, too."

Hailey nodded in agreement with her sister. "Yeah, what's not to love?"

Kit looked to Jackie. "Maybe they're right. Maybe I'm making this into a bigger deal than it is. Dean must be upset, too, and my reaction couldn't have made things easier for him."

Jackie nodded. "These two are always good for a reality check. We should finish up so you can go home and try him again. You two will work this out. You always do."

Kit nibbled on the corner of her sandwich, her hunger overpowering her nervous stomach. "I hope you're right. I would make a wonderfully wicked stepmother, wouldn't I?"

They met her half-hearted joke with a round of sincere laughter. Mack ordered a second drink, and when Jackie disapproved, they assured her Hailey would drive Mack's new vehicle home. Jackie had her own car.

"It's great to have my moms home. I missed you both," Mack said, bestowing both Jackie and Kit with a wink and a grin.

Kit grinned back, loving the feeling of inclusion.

Chapter Twenty-Three

B Y THE END OF Kit's first week at work, she and Chloe had fallen back into their routine. After being away from her desk for nearly three weeks, Kit had plenty to keep her busy during the day. Evenings were more difficult while she waited for Dean to return from Iowa, but it was time she probably needed. She knew she should go into their discussion with some idea of what she wanted.

Lynette's comment during their vacation about Kit's need for control was more on point than she'd like to admit.

As a scientist, Kit was used to working with probabilities. Here, she was eighty percent sure she wanted to convince Dean to let her attend Summer's wedding with him. But there were too many factors over which she had no control—a fact she disliked immensely.

She needed Dean to explain to her why he'd kept Summer's existence a secret. How could he, when the subject of children was such a sticking point in their relationship? When he'd proposed, he'd declared he was choosing her over the opportunity to have kids of his own. It was the only way, he knew, that she would accept the ring.

But, deep down, had she really believed him? Even if he thought he meant it, was it fair for her to expect him to give up something so integral to his own deepest desires?

She'd put off setting a date because she thought her stance meant Dean had to give up too much.

Disgusted with the never-ending loop of guilt and anger, Kit tossed the throw pillow she'd been hugging onto the concrete slab of her patio and pushed herself up to her feet. The roof of the small porch on the front of her townhouse protected her from getting wet as a light summer rain pattered against it. She felt pulled toward the tiki totem pole she'd shipped back from Hawaii. It now stood in the front corner of her covered patio, overlooking her driveway.

Purchasing the two-and-a-half-feet-tall statue had been an impulse buy, fueled by encouraging friends—and one or two cocktails—but Kit didn't regret it. She'd opted for an unpainted version that sported an eagle on top with the face of a man carved into its belly, which sat atop another heavy-featured face of a scowling man. When she'd arrived home from the office to find the wrapped package on her front step, she'd held her breath, fearful a wing might have broken off in transport. But the decorative statue was solid, and still in one piece. Would Dean laugh when he saw it? Would he find it gaudy? Did she care? All she knew for sure was that it made her smile, this unique art she'd brought home from her long-awaited trip.

Her finger traced the backside of one wing that stuck out of the pole's top. From the back, it looked like the letter *T*. She'd opted for the cheaper version that only sported carvings on one side. Could the *T* stand for "trust," or maybe "truce," in this difficult situation in which she and Dean found themselves?

As if her very thoughts might have summoned him, a familiar car pulled into her driveway. She stayed where she was, watching. Now that Dean was finally here, she couldn't decide if she should run inside and hide beside Chloe—sure to be under the bed as thunder rumbled overhead—or if she should run to Dean.

No matter how mad she was at him, she'd missed him.

He turned off the car but stayed where he was. The motor made a ticking noise for a few moments, then quieted completely.

Maybe he was every bit as unsure as Kit.

Her eyes found his through the windshield, and even with the bug-spattered glass between them, she thought she could see uncertainty there. Then she noticed it wasn't just the windshield that was filthy. The front bumper and car hood were peppered with bugs.

The driver's side door opened and Dean climbed out, looking nearly as worn as his vehicle. The rain picked up just then, and he stood there with his face to the sky, letting the water run over his features.

Kit's heart caught in her chest. Her feet took her across the grass, over the hot, wet concrete of the walk and driveway, and straight into Dean's arms. There may have been the slightest of pauses before he pulled her in tight, but she didn't care. They were both hurt, and regardless of where they landed on the big issues between them, they couldn't fight the natural urge to comfort each other.

The rain fell harder, but neither made a move for shelter until a loud crack of thunder jolted them apart. She grabbed his hand and pulled him under the protective cover of her front patio. Once there, she released it, stopping instead to pick up the pillow she'd discarded earlier. She held it against her stomach and eyed Dean. His gray T-shirt looked soaked through, and he seemed to be avoiding her gaze.

"Do you want to go in and switch out your shirt? You have a few spares in the laundry room."

He didn't seem to hear her. Instead, he walked over to the backside of her new totem pole and spun it around so he could see the carved portion. When his eyes reached the lowest carving, the corners of his mouth twitched upward.

"This guy bears an uncanny likeness to my first boss. When that heavy brow of his furrowed, you knew you were in trouble." He finally met her gaze. "I presume you picked this up on your trip?"

She nodded. "Call me a sucker, but I couldn't resist. I picked it up at a luau in a town called Lahaina."

He spun the statue back to face the driveway. "That thing would scare the crap out of anyone foolish enough to come sneaking around here after dark."

"It wards off evil spirits." She hated how stilted their conversation felt. "Chloe doesn't make much of a guard dog, so I thought this was the next best thing," she joked, hoping to ease the tension.

Dean shivered, despite the warm, sticky air.

Kit dropped her pillow on the bench and headed for the house. "Come inside and get out of that wet shirt. I have leftover chicken and rice if you haven't eaten."

To an outside observer, the two might have looked like any other couple, going about a typical Friday evening. Nothing could be further from the truth. The time had come for the discussion she'd been dreading. She couldn't put it off any longer.

Dean disappeared, then reappeared in a dry shirt and a wrinkled pair of shorts. At her raised eyebrows, he shrugged and said, "Better than wet." She wondered where he'd found the shorts.

"Are you hungry?"

He shook his head as he meandered around the kitchen, avoiding her gaze. "Haven't had much of an appetite. Kit . . . we need to talk."

"I know. I wondered how long you'd stay away from me."

That stopped him in his tracks. "I told you I'd be gone for a few days."

"But I wasn't sure you'd come here when you got back." She could hear the anguish in her voice but couldn't stop it. "You've never gone completely silent on me before. Chloe knocked down your note, I think. If I hadn't found it on the floor, I'd have no clue where you disappeared to. Dean, I'd have been terrified. Thank you for taking care of Chloe while I was gone, by the way."

As if the mere mention of the cat was enough to kick off his allergies, Dean sneezed. He chuckled as he wiped at his nose with the back of his hand. "I forgot my allergy meds at home. My nephew has a cat, too. It's been a rough week, in more ways than one. Look, Kit, I knew I was taking a risk going silent on you like that, but this is too important. I didn't want to have this conversation over the phone. I needed time to think through things. And I think you did, too."

She nodded. In hindsight, the break was indeed what she'd needed, even though it hadn't felt like it in the middle of it. "Let's go sit in the front room," she said.

She led the way out of the kitchen and back to her main living area. Her bare feet registered the transition from the cool tile she'd had installed in her updated kitchen to the thick area rug she'd splurged on to mark her tenth anniversary at her job. The rug was soft and cushiony beneath her toes. Would this critical discussion with Dean result in a soft landing, too, or would the day end with the hard, cold reality of the possibility of Kit living out her days alone, much as the other women in her family all seemed to do?

She stepped toward the solitary swivel chair covered in supple, cream-colored leather, but Dean caught her hand and pulled her with him to the couch, upholstered in a light fabric. When she first bought the furniture a half dozen years earlier, Jackie had joked that this was a grownup's room, one that would never suit family life. Kit remembered thinking it was perfect then, because that was what she wanted: a life filled with responsible adults she would never have to take care of. But now it looked cold and stark.

"Sit by me," he said, his expression earnest.

Once they were both settled, he released her hand. "Can I start?"

She nodded, curious where he'd want to begin.

"Kit, I've made so many mistakes . . ." He bent forward at the waist to rest his forearms on his knees, his eyes on his clasped hands. "I know that the thing you value most is honesty, and I failed you there. At first, I didn't appreciate the magnitude of the error I was making by not telling you I had a kid out there in the world. It felt irrelevant to our relationship. Yes, I still thought about that baby I'd walked away from so long ago, but it had no bearing on us. Or so I thought. I can see now that I was wrong about that."

Kit slid forward on the couch, her knee bumping his. "Dean, you knew how conflicted I've always felt about the differences in our desires to have kids. You wanted them. I didn't. Given such a huge disparity, I was never as sure as you were that we could build a life we would both be content with. You can't imagine how shocked I was, after all this time, to learn you were already a father."

He relaxed his clasped hands and gently dropped one on her knee. The small, intimate gesture was so automatic, it made Kit's heart ache at the simplicity of it. He sighed. "I think my trip home gave me a better appreciation of how shocked you felt. I got a shock of my own there."

"Another one? I thought the wedding invite came as a pretty big shock to you."

"Oh, it did. But the surprises didn't stop there. I thought my secret of never claiming my child was something I bore alone. Well, aside from Erin and Summer—they knew, of course. But I was wrong. Mom knew. And that she never admitted as much to me until this week . . . it felt like a huge betrayal. It didn't take me long to figure out that was how you felt, too."

She fought to make sense of his words. "Wait. Your mother knew you had a child out there somewhere, but she never told you? How?"

He squeezed her knee, then released it and ran his hand through his already mussed hair. "Apparently Erin went to see my mother while she was pregnant."

Kit thought back to the limited interactions she'd had with Dean's mother. They'd never clicked, and she always sensed that the woman found her lacking. Dean admitted once that he'd confided to his mother that Kit didn't ever want children. His mother hated that he was willing to go along with Kit's wishes. Learning that the woman knew he was already a father threw a new light onto things.

"Did she stay in touch with Erin?" she asked, shocked. Then another idea occurred to her. "What about the girl? Does your mother consider her a granddaughter?"

He shrugged. "Well, she admitted to some ongoing communication with them through the years . . . but she didn't know Summer was getting married, so they can't be overly close. She seemed excited at the news."

"She wasn't invited to the wedding?"

He shook his head. "Guess not."

Kit hadn't considered how Dean's extended family might be impacted if he built some kind of relationship with his long-lost daughter. This was getting more complicated by the minute.

Dean rubbed at his eyes, and she wasn't sure if he was getting emotional or if it was his allergies. His eyes were glassy, but the look he gave her as he again captured her hands in his, pulling her to face him head-on, was one of determination.

"Kit, I'm confident we can see our way through this mess with Summer, if that is what we choose to do. But I need to know what *you* want. I've known for a long time that I want to build a life with you. We're good together. No one gets everything they want out of life. That's just a cold, hard fact. But . . . if we're lucky, we get to decide what is most important to us . . . and for me, that's you. Can you forgive me for not telling you about Summer until now? Because if you can't, none of the rest of this matters."

Can I forgive him?

Since finding that invitation, she'd asked herself that exact question what felt like a million times.

Her grandmother's face flashed in her mind: sitting on the park bench, her eyes reflecting the pain she'd endured for decades around her own daughter, Kit's mother. She suspected Hazel's mind and heart were fighting an internal battle. Kit had learned at an early age that there was always a cost to loving someone. She'd concluded the cost of loving her own parents was too high, and she'd shut down, refusing to forgive them for their many faults. She'd also felt betrayed by her grandmother when, despite everything, the older woman let Mia back into her life again. Mia had betrayed them all, but Hazel seemed willing to forgive her.

Kit couldn't forgive her mother for all the heartache she'd caused, but this man sitting next to her was different. He'd proven his loyalty to her over the years. Yes, his lie of omission was a big deal, but she could see how genuinely sorry he was for it.

If she couldn't forgive him, she'd lose him.

That was too high of a cost. She didn't want to end up all alone. She still wanted to build a life with this man. If that life now included an adult daughter, Kit could help him navigate those uncharted waters. It wouldn't be easy for Dean, either.

Chloe jumped up on the arm of the sofa, surprising them both. She fixed her eyes on Dean, as if the feline was also struggling to decide whether to allow him to stay. Kit felt the low rumble coming off the cat before she could even hear it, and leaned back when Chloe pranced across her lap, over Dean's, and paused for a split second to rub her head against his shoulder. He reached to pet her, but she darted off the couch, landing soundlessly on her feet before sauntering out of the room, her head and tail held high.

The cat's message was unmistakable. She'd forgiven Dean for an indiscretion against her mistress.

Now it was Kit's turn. As she picked a stray cat hair off Dean's shirt, she met his eyes. "Dean, I'm sorry for how I reacted when you tried to tell me about Summer. I know you well enough that I could see how much you were hurting, but I felt so betrayed. You never told me about her. I wish you would have . . . but I forgive you. I'll let you take the lead on what type of relationship you want to build with your daughter. But I want you to know I support you, no matter what you decide. And if you want to go to her wedding, I want to be your plus-one. I'll accept the girl's presence in your life, but not Erin's. I have no intention of letting that woman get her claws into you again."

Relief flooded Dean's eyes, and he yanked Kit hard against his chest, his arms tight around her. "You mean it? I haven't lost you over this? Because I know how much I hurt you, and I promise I'll never, ever hurt you like that again."

Kit wriggled until she could pull up her trapped arms, laying her palms against his chest. She pushed back slightly until she could once again search his face. "Dean, I've been around a long time, and if life has taught me anything, it's that the people we love will always hurt us. Unfortunately, you will hurt me again. I will hurt you, too. But that's the price we have to pay. Thank you for helping me see that sometimes forgiveness is the best course of action."

He grabbed her hands again, his thumb stroking the engagement ring on her left hand. "I'm tired of being engaged, Kit. I want to make this official. We aren't kids anymore. I want you to be my wife. Now that all our dirty laundry is out in the open, can we just tie the knot already?"

She considered his heartfelt request. She could finally admit that the one thing holding her back had been Dean never being able to be a dad. While the solution had come as a complete, and painful, surprise, he was in fact a father already.

It was time she was a wife.

But not until after Dean became someone's father-in-law.

"Let's get through Summer's wedding first, and then we can plan our own. But, I warn you—I want simple. As in, justice of the peace or something. No big extravaganza with flowers and a crowd."

Dean's face glowed with relief at her words, and he got to his feet, pulling her with him. This time when he pulled her in, he met her with a kiss that spoke of a myriad of feelings ranging from relief, to joy, to a deep wanting. As she sank into the oblivion of the moment, feeling at home again in his arms, a crash reverberated through the house.

She pulled back and let her forehead fall to his chest, her shoulders shaking with barely repressed laughter.

"What the hell was that?" he asked, his eyes still cloudy with passion.

"That, my dear, was the third member of this family. I think she's letting us know she approves of our decision. But I admit I'm getting tired of cleaning up that dang spider plant she's using to communicate with me."

Dean slung an arm around her shoulder and turned her toward the master bedroom. "Are you sure she isn't trying to warn you about me?"

Kit captured his hand on her shoulder and kissed his fingers. "Oh, no. You spoil her rotten. If she wanted anyone kicked out of here, it would be me. You are exactly where you belong."

Chloe was standing just inside the bedroom door, next to a pile of dirt and the toppled plant stand. Dean shooed her out the door and closed it gently behind the pet, promising her a treat if she'd just give them a little time to plan their own wedding in private.

Chapter Twenty-Four

K IT FIDGETED IN HER seat as she peered through the windshield of Dean's parked car. Wedding guests were streaming into the old-fashioned church, visible between bouts of heavy traffic. Even on a Saturday afternoon when all the office workers were off enjoying their weekend, downtown Minneapolis was hopping.

Her mind flashed back to that first restless night in Hawaii. In her dream, the wedding guests sported loose, tropical clothing in bright colors, and everyone was barefooted. *Sand-filled shoes are no fun.* The guests at this real-life celebration appeared to be wearing subdued finery. Only the bright sprays of blooms festooning the main doors bore any resemblance to her imaginary destination wedding. The gray sky matched the hue of the masonry covering the church.

Is this a wedding or a funeral?

"Maybe this was a mistake," Dean said, nervously tapping the steering wheel with both hands. "We won't know a soul."

Kit nodded. She'd suffered similar doubts ever since dropping the RSVP in the mail. "You know the bride's mother." She was still uncomfortable saying Erin's name out loud. "Maybe some people you've worked with are here. But, Dean, remember—we aren't here for us. We are here because your daughter wanted her father to attend. She wants to meet you."

He sank back against the driver's seat with a sigh and tilted his head to gaze out the sunroof above them. "At least she didn't ask me to walk her down the aisle. Wouldn't that have been awkward? I wonder who will do that today. Who do you suppose she views as her father figure?"

She could hear the pain behind his questions. "You need to stop beating yourself up over this, Dean. I bet her mother did a wonderful job raising her. You can't change the past. But I'm proud of you for taking a chance on changing your future."

He turned his head and caught her hand in his. "We are both taking a chance. Thank you again, Kit, for agreeing to come with me today. For *suggesting* it. I know it can't be easy. But I'd be terrified if you weren't by my side for this. You look gorgeous today, by the way. I'm sorry I didn't say anything when I picked you up . . . I'm just so damn nervous. New dress? I've never known you to wear that shade of silver. It's so elegant."

His eyes looked sincere, alleviating a smidgen of the apprehension she was feeling. Today, she needed to look nice on his arm. But her normal wardrobe, full of bright colors, had felt wrong. Her usual attire would have looked more appropriate at her imaginary beach wedding. Besides, her recently completed Hawaiian vacation, with all the delicious food and tasty cocktails, had contributed a couple additional pounds to her weight.

"Lynette came through for me," she said, smoothing the shimmery fabric of her skirt across her lap. "She wouldn't even let me pay her for it. The woman works miracles, designing clothes that flatter all different shapes and skin tones. I see why she's so successful."

He nodded, grinning at her. "Let her know I approve of this. You look stunning. And not at all like the wicked stepmother you joked about."

"Oh, I wasn't joking," she deadpanned, but when he looked confused, she let him off the hook with what she hoped was an encouraging smile. "Fine—I'm not overly concerned about what any of them think of me. I just want you to enjoy this opportunity to meet the bride. Decide where you want to take things after today. Maybe you'll find a connection. Maybe you won't. Even if nothing more comes of this, you will finally feel some sense of closure. Now, come on—we might miss the bride's entrance if we don't go in. That wouldn't make the best first impression."

Dean's eyes skipped from hers to the clock on the dash. "Let's do this," he said, though his words lacked any excitement.

Kit's heart went out to him. She'd moved beyond most of her anger over his lack of transparency, and she truly wanted this to be a special day for him. Would he get the chance to feel like a father, or would it be a complete disaster?

She climbed out of the car and looped the chain of her purse strap over her shoulder. A strand of hair caught in her necklace, and she stopped to pull it loose.

Dean rounded the car and noticed her struggle. "Need some help?" he asked, stepping to her side.

"My hair is caught . . ."

She felt his fingers on the back of her neck and dropped her hands.

"It's wrapped around the clasp," he said. "Stand still."

"Just yank it if you can't get it out," she said, trying not to grimace. How could the hairs on the back of her neck be so sensitive?

"There," he said, straightening the necklace. He fingered the tiny silver butterfly before letting it fall back against her skin. "Where did you get that? I don't recognize it."

Kit's hand came up, absentmindedly touching the charm. "Believe it or not, I've had it since I was a girl. I'd forgotten all about it. It was in a drawer in my jewelry box. When I found this necklace, I knew it would be perfect. Lynette gave me this, too, actually. The night of our senior prom. She gave all of us one. I thought it was a good sign. It'll be a little like having the girls in my corner today. No matter what happens."

He smiled and offered his arm, their eyes nearly level thanks to the heels she'd worn. "I suspect I owe your friends a thank-you," he said as he turned them toward the church.

"Why's that?" she asked, stepping carefully so her heels wouldn't sink into the strip of grass between the car and the sidewalk. A puff of wind ruffled her short hair and sent a solitary leaf floating down in front of her.

He patted her hand where it rested on his forearm. "I'm sure you discussed this whole wedding-and-hidden-daughter mess with your girl-friends on your trip."

She shrugged. He knew her too well. She couldn't deny that she'd turned to her tribe for advice.

"If they hated me for what I did," he went on, "or what I'd failed to tell you, I know that could have swayed your decision."

"They have given me some pretty good advice in the past." She was unable to hide a grin. "If any of them had felt as betrayed as *I* did over this whole mess, I may have kicked you to the curb. But they know you. You are a good man, and they were quick to remind me we all make mistakes. They helped me see we could get through this. So," she said, giving his arm an extra squeeze, "here we are. But you need to know something. If you ever keep a secret of this magnitude from me again, they'll *help* me bury your body."

Dean chuckled, but his eyes were already scanning the church and fellow guests. She wished she could tell what he was thinking. As they reached the sidewalk at the base of the massive steps leading up to the church doors festooned with colorful flower sprays, he squeezed her arm in his.

"There are no more secrets, Kit. I promise. Now, if you're ready, I want to go see what kind of bride my long-lost daughter makes."

Kit nodded, placing a foot carefully on the bottom step so her spiky silver heels wouldn't trip her up. She didn't want to fall on her face as a stepmother, either figuratively or quite literally by stumbling on the stairs on the way into the girl's wedding.

The atmosphere inside the church was brighter than the overcast day outside. Heavy doors creaked as they swung behind them, closing with a thud. The aroma of flowers blended with the recognizable scent of incense. A pianist tickled keys from a hidden corner somewhere, the soft notes hauntingly familiar to Kit's ear.

She eyed a guest book on a small table near the entrance. The woman in front of her finished signing and straightened, handing her a white feather pen. Before turning to one of the nearby ushers, she smiled and said, "Aren't you just so thrilled for the happy couple?"

A wave of guilt flushed through Kit as she took the over-the-top writing instrument. Would it shock the woman if Kit confessed that she'd never met the bride or groom, but was in fact engaged to the bride's long-absent father? That would surely throw the older woman for a loop. She bent over the guest book, but as pen touched paper, her eyes snagged on a framed photograph at the corner of the white linen-covered table.

The couple in the picture looked so young, so . . . *happy.*

Kit froze. The girl had Dean's smile. Kit had never been one of those people that picked out similarities between parents and children, but this one couldn't be missed.

Suddenly she couldn't force the pen across the paper to sign the guest book. She was an imposter, standing in the entrance to this beautiful old church, half filled with guests, all of whom loved the couple in the photograph. Their hushed whispers held a note of excitement as the pretty piano music underscored their muted conversations. She stepped back and passed the pen to Dean. She suspected he correctly read the doubt in her eyes, because he dropped his free hand to her waist and offered her a reassuring squeeze as he signed on their behalf.

She needed to pull herself together. She was supposed to help Dean get through the day, not fall apart on him. She allowed him to lead her to another of the ushers, a young man waiting to escort guests to their seats.

"Are you a member of either the bride's or the groom's family?" the closest usher asked. "We have reserved rows up front for family."

Kit held her breath, unsure how Dean would respond. He *was* family, but admitting as much to this young stranger might draw confused attention from other guests.

She pulled her arm out of Dean's, reaching instead to take his hand and offer a reassuring squeeze. His palm, normally warm and dry against hers, felt clammy with sweat, reminding her that she wasn't the only one nervous about making an entrance. His fingers pumped hers with nervous energy, but she doubted an outside observer would notice his discomfort.

As she watched, Dean nodded, then shook his head. "Just an old friend of the bride's mother," he said.

His words caused a pang deep in her heart. He wasn't yet ready to claim the bride as his own daughter. Appropriate under the circumstances, she knew, but would today change that?

Kit noticed a stack of folded programs on a table behind the back pew and helped herself to one as the young man headed down the main aisle, his steps quieted by the blue-and-wine-patterned carpet underfoot. He stopped two pews shy of those in the front third of the church, which was festooned with glowing lanterns held in place with bows and sprays of flowers that matched those on the heavy front doors.

Their pew already held other guests, so Kit and Dean sat close to the aisle. She was happy he'd have an unobstructed view when the bride made her way toward the altar and a new life.

As the ushers continued to seat other guests and the piano music droned on, Kit studied the pamphlet in her hands. Her eyes skimmed the names inside, but aside from Erin and Summer, none looked familiar. It reinforced her feeling of unease, like they were crashing this wedding. A tiny part of her had wondered if Summer might list Dean in the program, but of course his name wasn't there. That would be asking too much.

How must the bride be feeling right now? She was so young. Was she nervous about getting married? She might even be wondering if Dean was in attendance, despite their RSVP.

She tapped him on the arm with the wedding program. He took it, and she watched for any hint as to what was on his mind as he perused the names inside, but he gave little away.

Finally, the tempo of the music changed, and all eyes shifted to the back of the church. A handsome couple made their way to the front and took a seat in the first pew across the aisle. Kit guessed them to be about her age—likely the groom's parents. Then the wedding party filed in, each glowing with the light of youth. Dean sneezed just as Kit caught a whiff of eucalyptus.

She elbowed him, then whispered, "I thought it was only my cat you're allergic to."

He gave her a one-shouldered shrug and a smile that didn't quite reach his eyes. It was then that she noticed those eyes held a telltale sheen of moisture, and she wondered if it was allergies or emotions behind the unshed tears. He was blinking fast to remain stoic as he waited for his first glimpse of the daughter he'd never claimed as his own.

Finally, the piano faded to silence, and for a moment the only sounds were the guests getting to their feet in anticipation of the bride's entrance. Kit suspected Erin would walk the girl in, since she hadn't yet caught sight of the woman.

Kit held her breath, anxious for her first glimpse of Dean's daughter. Strains from an organ in the loft above floated through the air, and she recognized the familiar chords of "Here Comes the Bride."

As they waited, Kit's mind flitted back to another wedding, so long ago. She'd waited at the front of the church, her stomach fluttering with nerves, excitement for her best friend, and an unbidden sense of apprehension as her eyes were drawn to the man waiting for Jackie. Kit had secretly worried he wasn't the right man for Jackie, and unfortunately she'd been proven right.

Aside from her grandparents and Annie, Kit couldn't think of anyone she was close to who had stayed married. Even Annie was on her second husband. Were the poor track records she'd witnessed another reason she was so hesitant to marry Dean? Fear of following that same path?

The bride stepped into view, flanked on both sides by someone in silver.

A shiver of apprehension wriggled up Kit's spine.

The woman on the bride's left wore a shimmering, floor-length silver gown that sparkled in the sunlight streaming through stained glass windows. While the style differed from Kit's dress, the fabric looked identical, at least from a distance. On the bride's right, also holding her arm, was a man in a dark gray suit.

The bride appeared calm, her eyes on the young man waiting for her at the front of the church. The term "old soul" flashed through Kit's mind as she watched Summer, despite how young she looked with her blond curls and serene face. She'd tried to imagine how it would go when Dean and his daughter would first see each other. But the bride kept her gaze on her groom, as if the rest of the world had faded away.

There still was a flash of recognition, but it was between Dean and the bride's mother. As the trio reached their pew, Erin's eyes snagged Dean's, and Kit would have sworn the woman stumbled ever so slightly, though the moment passed so quickly she couldn't be sure.

They continued on, the bride unfazed and still focused, and Kit expelled a breath she hadn't realized she'd been holding as the congregation settled back into their seats and the ceremony began.

"She's beautiful," Dean whispered into Kit's ear.

"My dress is too much like hers," she whispered back, watching the back of Erin's head. She was mortified that her own outfit so closely resembled that of the bride's mother. She'd thought Lynette had dressed her in a way that Kit looked pretty but wouldn't outshine the mother of either the bride or groom.

Dean frowned, confused. "Like Summer's? I didn't think you'd bought a wedding gown yet."

Of course, Dean only had eyes for the daughter he'd never met. He'd probably barely noticed what Erin was wearing.

Kit needed to remember that today was all about Summer—was about her and her father—and not her own petty insecurities.

"Never mind," she whispered. "Your daughter looks beautiful, Dean."

Chapter Twenty-Five

An hour later, Dean and Kit joined the stream of wedding guests on the short walk to the reception hall. The gray skies had given way to a drizzle, and Kit was thankful for the light shawl Lynette had included with the dress.

The Catholic service had included a full mass, and Kit was starving. She wasn't sure what made her more uncomfortable: her aching toes or grumbling stomach.

They hadn't yet met the bride and groom, though Erin had caught them on the way out of the church, exclaiming her delight over their presence. Kit suspected it was really only Dean the other woman was happy to see, and she didn't miss Erin's double take when she spied Kit's dress. She knew she was being petty in comparing herself to the bride's mother, but she imagined Lynette whispering in her ear, assuring her she was rocking her version of the silver gown.

Once they were inside, Kit watched as Dean scanned the room. "Are you nervous?"

He glanced over at her. "What, to finally meet my daughter? Of course I'm nervous."

"She's going to love you," she assured him. And she meant it. She loved the man at her side, and she knew Summer would, too. He was kind, generous, and fun.

He sighed. "There are so many people. Not exactly the environment I pictured for our first meeting."

She could feel the tension radiating off him. "Do you want to go? We could hunt Erin down and give her some excuse. Then you could set up a more private meeting with Summer later?"

He considered her suggestion, but then squared his shoulders and shook his head. "No. Summer might be disappointed. She wanted me here. I can't leave without talking to her. Let's go find our seats, and we'll wait for the bridal party to arrive."

Kit was feeling better thirty minutes later after getting off her heels for a while and munching on a bag of marshmallow-coated popcorn from one of the snack stations provided to keep guests occupied until dinner could be served. The flavor combination took Kit back to her first summer at camp.

What she wouldn't give to have Jackie sitting next to her right now. The wait was tying her nerves in knots.

A commotion by the front doors meant the bride and groom and their entourage had finally arrived. Kit smiled at the ridiculously corny but admittedly cute skit announcing all the members of the wedding party. Then, two host couples began releasing guests by table to fill their plates at the buffet-style food lines. Kit found it all a bit over the top. She couldn't imagine the amount of coordinating—not to mention cost—of pulling off a celebration of this size.

No wonder she was hesitant to plan her own wedding.

"This really is something, isn't it?" Dean said, polishing off the last of his chicken breast and potatoes.

For a moment, that petty streak reared up inside of her again. Dean's comment didn't sit well with Kit. Erin and her fiancé must do well if they paid for all of this. "Maybe the groom's parents helped pay for some of it, too."

"Maybe," he conceded. He gave her a sideways glance. "You don't like this, do you?"

She pushed her plate away, despite her earlier hunger and the half-eaten meal that remained. "It isn't that I don't like it. It's nice, if you like this type of thing."

Dean settled back into his chair. "What's wrong, Kit?"

She dropped her linen napkin onto her plate and crossed her legs. She rubbed at her sore calf muscles, avoiding his eyes. "I suppose all of this just makes me feel . . . I don't know . . . overwhelmed. Is this the type of ceremony you envision for our wedding?"

Chuckling, Dean sat forward and dropped an arm across the back of Kit's chair. "I just want to be your husband. I prefer to think about what our day-to-day will look like. This is nice and all, but I'd love to skip to the good part. The *marriage*."

She felt her shoulders relax for the first time in hours. "You wouldn't be upset with something simple, like that quick trip to see a judge at the courthouse that I mentioned earlier?"

Before he could answer, Kit saw a flash of ivory silk. The time had come for Dean to meet his daughter, face to face. The discussion about their wedding plans would have to wait. Again. She gave him a warning nod, alerting him to the bride's approach. As if he could read her mind, he gave her a reassuring wink, stood, helped her to her feet, and together they turned to face the approaching bride.

Despite the throng of people around them, she approached them alone, uncertainty in her eyes. It reminded Kit of how young this girl still was, despite the wedding trappings all around them. Dean stood slightly ahead of Kit, so she couldn't see his expression as his daughter approached.

"Dean?" Summer said, her voice hesitant.

He extended both hands toward the bride in welcome. Kit knew the man would do everything he could to make this meeting comfortable for his daughter.

"Summer," he said, his tone holding a note of awe. "It's wonderful to meet you. Finally."

Kit shifted her stance so she could see his face. When Summer reached them, she allowed Dean to take her hands, and the two stood eyeing each other while mixed emotions played across their features.

Someone bumped into Summer. The woman tried to start a conversation with the bride, but Summer seemed rattled. Dean pulled her close and gently set his arm across her shoulders.

"Why don't we go find someplace quiet to talk?" he said.

Summer nodded, then looked to Kit. "You must be Kit. Dad's fiancée? I love your dress, by the way. It's like Mom's, only a little better. But *please* don't tell her I said that. I—I *shouldn't* have said that."

Kit felt a rush of some inexplicable emotion as the young bride stumbled over her words. It felt oddly . . . protective. "It's nice to meet you, Summer. Come on. I like Dean's idea. Is there somewhere quiet you can talk?"

Another guest hurried by, this time jostling Kit. The venue was small for so many guests.

Summer nodded and headed for a door that Kit hadn't noticed. Soon, the trio stood together in a hallway that ran alongside the reception room.

The bride looked anxious again. Kit couldn't imagine what the girl was thinking. She had to be exhausted, meeting her biological father for the first time on top of an already emotionally charged day.

Dean hesitated, as if he wasn't sure where to start. Neither of them did.

So Kit stepped forward. "You look beautiful, Summer," she said, hoping to get the conversation started. "And the ceremony was exquisite. You were probably worried about the weather, but you know what they say about rain on your wedding day. There are riches in your future."

The young bride seemed to visibly relax at this, and a calm smile graced her features. "I already *feel* rich. Today I married the man of my dreams . . . and now I get to meet my father. Fin can't wait to meet you, but I wanted to talk to you by myself for the first time. With you here, the day couldn't get any better."

Kit's first thought was, *You aren't even old enough to know what kind of man is right for you.* But then she realized she was being cynical again.

She hoped Summer's childhood had been happier than her own, and that she grew up with a confidence in her mother's love. Kit had never felt such a thing, but she wished it for Summer. The girl in front of them now was nervous, but her essence radiated a sense of peace and happiness. In that moment, Kit felt a sense of awe as she looked at Dean's daughter. Erin must be very proud of the young woman Summer was becoming.

Finally, Dean spoke. "Thank you for inviting us, Summer. The invitation was a surprise, I'll admit. But I'm glad to be here."

Summer laughed, the sound light and full of joy. "I bet it was. Maybe I should apologize. I probably should have called you. But sending you the invite took about all the courage I could muster. It was too scary to call you from out of the blue. I hope you'll forgive me."

Dean took a deep breath. "Don't ever think you have to apologize. I'm the one who should apologize. I've missed so much."

The bride shook her head so hard that the dangling pearls in the small, bejeweled hair clip over her right ear jangled. "No. Please. Today is my wedding day. Regrets have no place here. What's done is done. It wasn't always easy, but Mom was amazing. I'll admit I missed having a dad growing up, but I don't want to dwell on that. Let's start fresh today."

When he didn't immediately reply to Summer's heartfelt words, Kit swung her eyes to Dean. He was squinting, studying his daughter's face. As the silence stretched, Kit bumped him lightly with her hip. As if the contact had knocked him out of a stupor, Dean shook his head, his smile returning.

"Forgive me. For a moment there, you reminded me of my dad. He died long before you were even born, but you sound like his wisdom somehow found a way into your heart. He was quick to forgive and focus on the future."

Dean seldom talked about his father. Kit knew he'd loved his father deeply, and she'd often wished she'd gotten to know the man, too.

She watched Dean and Summer as they slowly got to know each other under these unusual circumstances, and it suddenly struck her. Like Kit, both had faced their own unique heartaches growing up. But that was where the similarities ended. Kit had let her parents' betrayal fester. She didn't need a therapist to tell her that the ache prevented her from living a life free of shadows. Dean and Summer didn't seem to suffer the same fate. Both appeared willing to move ahead with a new relationship, unfettered by the past.

What would that kind of freedom feel like? she wondered, as Dean launched into a discussion with his daughter about the life she was planning with her new husband.

Maybe it was high time Kit threw off the chains of her past and lived a little, too. She didn't want a big wedding like the one they were attending, but she thought she was finally ready to be this kind man's wife. She resolved right there and then that she'd call Jackie first thing in the morning and ask her to help plan something simple.

As if on cue, the silver-beaded handbag on her wrist vibrated with an incoming text. Probably Jackie checking on how the big meeting between father and bride was going. Synchronicities like that happened all the time. Especially between friends.

Kit turned from Dean and his daughter to give them a minute while she checked her phone. But it wasn't a text from Jackie. It was from Marge. Kit's heart stopped for a beat at her aunt's words.

Your grandmother had a spell. They are admitting her now. I'll keep you posted.

CHAPTER TWENTY-SIX

K IT SPUN TO FACE Dean—but froze when she caught the look on his face as he gazed in wonder at Summer. The bride was gesticulating wildly as she described how one of her bridesmaids' toddlers dumped an entire basket of rose petals on the floor of the church's basement and said no to wearing her flower girl gown. When the strong-willed child refused to cooperate, the wedding had to proceed without the youngest member of the bridal party.

Dean laughed. "I have a nephew about that age, and once he decides about something, there's no changing his mind!"

Kit fingered her phone, torn between her instinct to fly out the door to go be with her grandmother and her desire to not interrupt the happy exchange in front of her.

Dean glanced her way and his smile slipped.

Her racing heart twinged. She didn't appreciate Dean's perceptive nature often enough.

"Everything all right?" he asked.

She hated to do it, but she knew she'd forever regret it if she didn't rush to her elderly grandmother's side and the "spell" turned out to be serious.

"I'm so sorry. Family emergency. It's Hazel."

"Hazel?" Summer echoed, looking between Kit and her father. "Whose family?"

That simple question drove home the complexity of the situation they all found themselves in. The poor girl was probably wondering if this Hazel woman was *her* family, too.

"Is she all right?" Dean asked, ignoring Summer for the moment.

Kit shrugged. "Marge sent word. They're admitting her. I assume that means to the hospital. She said she'll keep me posted, but . . ."

"But you need to go," Dean finished. He turned to Summer. "I'm sorry to have to run. Meeting you exceeded all I'd hoped for, but Kit's grandmother is old and frail. She lives in Ruby Shores, a couple hours from here. This probably can't wait."

Stepping forward, Kit laid a hand on Dean's forearm. "I could Uber home and grab my car. You don't have to leave."

But Dean's head shake was definitive. "No. Summer needs to get back to her other guests, anyway. Hopefully we'll be able to continue talking after today. But we need to hurry."

Summer nodded. "I'm so glad you both came. I know it couldn't have been easy. The gift opening is tomorrow, and I was going to invite you both. It will be a much smaller affair at the hotel we are staying at. It would give you a chance to meet a few others in my family."

Dean captured his daughter's hands and brushed a quick kiss on her cheek. He pulled out his phone. "Give me your number. I'll let you know about tomorrow after we find out more about Kit's grandmother. But regardless, I want to keep in touch."

The bride plucked the phone out of Dean's hand and fiddled with it for a moment. "There," she said. "And I'll completely understand if you can't make it. Now, go. And thank you!"

After giving Kit a quick finger wave, Summer spun away in a swirl of tulle and ivory lace, leaving them alone.

"Dean, I'm serious. I know how much you've been looking forward to tonight. I can take care of myself."

With a barely perceptible shake of his head, Dean took her arm and firmly but gently turned her toward the exit. "We both know you can take care of yourself. But when are you going to figure out that I *enjoy* helping you? Now, how about you take those blasted heels off, and we'll make a run for the car? It sounds like that drizzle might have turned into a downpour."

Kit followed his finger as he pointed to the ceiling, noticing the *rat-a-tat-tat* above them for the first time. The sound elicited a flashback of that stormy night in early July when she rushed to her grandmother's side, only to find her relatively unscathed.

Would the elderly woman be that lucky this time?

Kit shifted from foot to foot while Dean tried to ease the zipper down the back of her dress. She was anxious to get on the road.

"This wasn't what I'd envisioned for tonight when I thought about helping you out of this," he said, his fingers warm against her skin.

"Believe me, this wasn't how I thought our evening would end, either. Dean, I'm so sorry to pull you away from Summer's wedding. I know you were enjoying yourself."

He sneezed, managing to cover his mouth with a forearm. "Damn. I forgot to take my allergy pill."

"That reminds me," she said, holding the shimmery fabric to her breasts with one arm and hurrying toward her bathroom to retrieve the top and jeans she'd worn earlier in the day. "Regardless of what the deal is with Grandma, I'm sure I won't be back until at least Sunday night. Work won't be pleased if I have to miss more days next week. But can you pop over to check on Chloe? I know she'd probably be all right, but I don't like to push my luck."

"Of course. Are you sure you don't want me to go with you? I don't care about the gift opening tomorrow. I mean . . . I care . . . but I'm sure it'll be awkward, especially if I go alone. Besides, I'm worried about Hazel, too."

Kit slipped out of her dress and into her other outfit, mildly cursing for leaving it in a heap in the corner of the bathroom. It was wrinkled. She hung her silver dress on a hook on the back of the door, hoping the rain didn't damage it. "I want you to go to the gift opening," she replied as she ran a quick brush through her damp hair. "God, why didn't you tell me my mascara was running down my cheeks?"

She pulled a makeup-remover wipe out of the top drawer and ran it all over her face, hoping the limited effort would make her presentable again. She needed to get on the road. Grabbing a few pairs of underwear from her top dresser drawer, she tossed them into the open, partially packed duffle bag on her bed and zipped it shut.

"I could tell it was important to Summer that you come. I know she said she'd understand if you didn't, but trust me, she invited you, which means she wants you there."

Dean held out a hand. She gave him the bag, then searched the floor for her everyday purse and quickly transferred her wallet out of the silver handbag.

"Can I at least call ahead and get you a hotel room, or will you stay at your grandmother's? You said most of the cleanup from the storm was done, right?"

"Right. Pretty much. Grandma already had a new bed on order for my old room—even though I wish she wouldn't have spent the money for that—and they set it up when they delivered it from the furniture store. Since we had to toss the twin mattresses in the boys' room, Marge offered a full-size bed from her basement, but we haven't found someone with a pickup yet to move that in. And the tree is gone. Other than the mattress, the one thing left to do is to rebuild the front porch."

"So you don't need a room?" Dean asked, following her out to her car.

"I'll be fine. Right now, all I care about is getting to the hospital."

The two entered the garage, and Kit hit the opener.

Dean popped the trunk and tossed her duffel bag in. "Do you have your phone? And your charger?"

She patted her purse before tossing it onto the passenger seat and climbing behind the wheel. "All good. Sleep here, unless your allergies are too bad. But either way, lock up for me, will you?"

He leaned in to give her a quick peck on the lips, then stepped back and slammed her door.

Once she'd started the car, she rolled down her window before backing out. "I really am sorry, Dean. I'm sure you weren't ready to leave the wedding yet."

"Quit apologizing," he said, wiping at his left eye. "But I better head over to my apartment. I'll never be able to sleep here tonight since I forgot my pill. Now, go! And text or call me the minute you know anything more about Hazel."

For a split second, Kit almost relented and let him jump in with her. Two hours alone on a dark highway, worried about her grandmother, sounded awful. But he'd already given up enough for her. Shifting into reverse, she blew him a kiss. He tapped the roof of her car before heading back for the house.

As Kit drove through her neighborhood, she noticed lights on in many windows. It wasn't even nine yet, but the overcast sky made it appear later. At least the rain had let up again. After a quick stop for gas—and a soda to help keep her awake—she found a favorite podcast on her phone and synced it to her car speakers to help pass the time. She considered calling Jackie, who wanted to hear all about the wedding after it was over, but then she remembered her friend had plans tonight. Neither of them had expected that Kit and Dean would leave the wedding early.

As she entered the interstate, she turned down the podcast so she could pay attention. Despite the hour on a Saturday night, traffic was heavy in the city and the pavement slick from rain. It took nearly fifty miles before things thinned out and she could relax and tune back into the podcast, though her mind kept drifting back to what condition she'd find her grandma in at the hospital.

By the time the town of Ruby Shores showed up on the sign along the highway, she could see the glow of lights on the horizon. The cloud bank was low, and things looked hazy. Few other cars were on the road, and it was nearing 11:30 at night. The initial traffic had slowed her down.

Her cell phone buzzed in her cupholder. It was a text from Marge. She hated to take her eyes off the road for long, knowing this stretch of road was notorious for deer crossings at night, so she shot off a quick *10 min*, then dropped her phone back down. She clicked off her radio, realizing she'd heard little of the podcast.

There was a smattering of vehicles in the parking lot at the small local hospital. Visiting hours were long over, and Ruby Shores wasn't exactly a hotbed for nighttime activity that would keep an emergency room hopping, but she supposed there was always someone needing medical assistance, even in such a small town.

As she pulled into a spot under one of the tall lights, she glanced around the parking lot and noticed Marge heading in her direction. Her aunt must have been watching for her from the entryway. Even from a distance, Marge looked upset.

A ripple of fear passed through her.

Kit took a deep breath, tossed her phone in her purse, and got out, flipping her lights off. She slammed her door, used the fob to lock it, then turned to face her aunt.

"Is Grandma all right?"

"I think she'll be fine. I swear, the old bat has nine lives."

With a sigh, Kit let herself relax back against her car. She could feel the heat from the motor. Out of nowhere, a low sob popped out of her, surprising both herself and Marge.

"Wow, honey, I'm sorry if I scared you," Marge said, pulling her into her arms. "I really think she'll be fine."

Kit, never much of a hugger, patted Marge on the back then pulled away. Tears she hadn't even realized were right at the surface leaked down her cheeks. She swiped them away, shaking her head. "I believe you. Because you're right—Grandma is tough. And I'm sorry I'm crying. I'm not even sure why."

"I hope I didn't pull you from something important," Marge said, turning and leaning against Kit's car, mirroring her niece's stance.

"Only Dean's daughter's wedding," Kit said, instantly wishing those words hadn't slipped out.

What is going on? She was not normally an emotional person.

Marge looked confused. "Since when does Dean have a daughter? And one old enough to get *married*?"

As if on cue, Kit's phone buzzed inside her purse. She pulled it out, holding up a finger to Marge. "Let's just say it's a skeleton in Dean's closet. I'll tell you about it later. But I need to let him know I made it to town."

After a quick text, she pushed away from her car. Her emotions were feeling steadier, now that she knew her grandmother hadn't done something awful like die on her while she was driving to be at her side. "I want to go see her."

Marge grabbed her by the arm. "Speaking of skeletons in closets, I ran down here so I could warn you before you came up to Mom's room."

"Warn me? About what?"

"It's Mia. She's here."

The sound of her own mother's name on Marge's lips stopped Kit in her tracks. She wasn't sure her emotional state could handle yet another massive wave of drama today. First, it was her fiancé's secret daughter's wedding. She thought she'd handled that quite well. Brilliantly, even. Then it was the scare about Grandma Hazel. Tough as it was, she'd arrived to good news.

But her mother? Here? Now?

"Kit, your mom is here," Marge repeated. "She's in there with Mom. I'm sorry. Mom had me afraid that this might be it. Much as I hated to do it, she asked me to call Mia while we waited for the ambulance. Her number was in her phone. I couldn't very well deny her the chance to talk to her daughter, maybe for the last time. Much as I wanted to . . ." Her words faded away as she tilted her head back to study the starless sky. "I'm not even sure I can go back in there. I can barely stand the sight of her."

Kit had known this day would come. Ever since she'd found the old items from their childhood—things only Mia could have still possessed—in her grandmother's basement the morning after the storm. An entire decade had passed since she'd last seen her own mother, but Mia was infiltrating their world again.

She was like a bad penny. She just kept showing up.

Kit pulled her shoulders back and looped her purse strap cross-body-style. "I didn't drive all this way to have that woman scare me off. I came to see Grandma. Whatever's going on with her medically, it could be serious. Hazel isn't getting any younger. I need to see that she is doing all right."

With that, she forced her feet to move, and she covered the distance between her car and the doors to the hospital quickly, before she could change her mind. As she pulled the heavy door open, ignoring the automatic button, she glanced behind her. Marge wasn't far behind.

They made their elevator ride to the second floor in silence.

The hustle and bustle on the upper floor surprised Kit. Three nurses looked busy at the central station. Someone in street clothes with a cup of coffee in hand was entering a room labeled by a small metal sign: "Family Waiting Room." Marge took the lead, and Kit peeked into the waiting room, dismayed to see half a dozen uncomfortable-looking chairs and little else. It didn't look like somewhere one would enjoy sitting and waiting for news. With luck, she wouldn't be spending the rest of the night in there.

Marge took a right turn ahead of her, into one of the hospital rooms. Kit pulled back, taking a moment to collect herself before going in. While she wanted to see Hazel, seeing her mother again was a different story.

The *hiss* of a wheeled cart bearing some type of medical device whirred past her, and the young man in scrubs pushing it nodded a quick greeting in her direction, but his speed told her he was in a hurry to get somewhere.

It reminded her that life-and-death battles were a constant in this place, and while her history with Mia was painful, these types of awkward reunions between estranged family members probably weren't all that uncommon here.

Steeling herself against whatever might await her inside, Kit walked into the room her aunt had entered moments before, her eyes searching out her grandmother.

She wasn't sure what she'd expected, but the welcoming smile from her bright-eyed, white-haired grandma wasn't it.

"Kit, dear, I'm sorry you had to be bothered to come all this way late at night. I seem to make a habit of this, and for that I apologize," her grandmother greeted her, one hand extended in her direction. "I hope I didn't pull you away from something important."

Marge, standing right behind the upper corner of the hospital bed, snorted. Kit shot her a look. She did not have the energy to go into detail about where she'd been earlier in the evening.

She grabbed her grandmother's extended hand, squeezing the icy fingers as she bent down to drop a kiss on her wrinkled forehead. The skin there felt cool, dry.

When she straightened, she caught the way the old woman's eyes flitted to the corner of the room, and she knew without turning who

Hazel was looking at. While it was probably childish, Kit intended to ignore her mother for as long as possible.

After all, wasn't that what the woman had been doing to Kit for her whole life?

"Grandma, what happened? Did you fall? Is it your heart? I'm glad to see your bruises from the night of the storm are almost gone."

Her grandmother shook her head. "I guess it takes a long time to heal up after you pass the ninety mark. I'm not sure they'll ever fade entirely."

Two healthcare workers entered the room right then. "How are you feeling, Hazel?" the older of the two asked. "We're still waiting for your test results, but I wanted to stop in and check on you one last time before I call it a night. I'm leaving you in this capable doctor's hands."

Kit suspected the woman talking was a full-fledged doctor, while the fresh-faced younger one couldn't be more than an intern.

"But she's only a child."

"Mom!" Marge gasped. "Don't be rude."

The older doctor chuckled. "Hazel, Dr. Lance is one of our most talented new doctors. Promise me you won't give her too hard of a time tonight."

Kit grinned. Hazel's one-shouldered shrug didn't convey much of a commitment, but the younger doctor looked like she was taking it all in stride.

"Tell me this then," Hazel said. "How long until I can go home? I've got tomatoes and peppers to harvest in my garden. They won't keep."

Dr. Lance checked the various monitors attached to her patient. "Let's see how your test results come back, and then we'll discuss the next steps. I bet one of these three ladies could get your vegetables picked if you're worried about them going to waste."

"Ah, yes, my three girls. Doctor, you wouldn't believe how long I've waited to get the four of us in the same room again. Darn near had to kick the bucket to make it happen."

Her grandmother's comment felt odd to Kit. As if the woman had somehow contrived to make this happen. She squinted her eyes, inspecting Hazel's expression.

She wouldn't. Would she?

The older doctor checked the watch on her wrist before giving her hands a single clap. "If your blood pressure wouldn't have been so high when they brought you in here, Hazel, I'd wonder if you designed this little family reunion. But science doesn't lie. You are all related, aren't you? You certainly have similar enough features."

Unable to resist, Kit stole a glance at the woman in the corner. Ten years and a hard life had taken a shocking toll on her once beautiful mother. But if she'd expected Mia to look ashamed over her extended absence from her life, the woman's ramrod position and the way she held her daughter's eye told a different story.

"Hello, Kit."

"Hello, Mia."

Kit heard her grandmother's *tsk-tsk* behind her, but Mia had lost the right for Kit to call her anything more endearing than her given name.

Perhaps sensing the tension in the air, Dr. Lance cleared her throat, snagging their attention. "Hazel, you had a scare tonight, and I need you to get some rest. I know it won't be easy, as nurses will be in and out of here to check your vitals tonight, but I'm going to ask that your visitors all head home now. Marge, we have your number, and if there are any changes, I'll be sure to call you. Otherwise, come back when visiting hours start in the morning at eight."

The older doctor left, but it was clear from Dr. Lance's crossed-arm stance she wasn't leaving until Hazel could rest alone.

Mia sighed dramatically, got to her feet, and left the room without a word.

"You girls should talk," Hazel said, her tone light, as if the three of them were due for a lighthearted chat over a glass of wine.

Marge rolled her eyes, then motioned to Kit to exit the room in front of her. "I have to work in the morning, Mother, so Kit will be up for you tomorrow if you are well enough to go home. You'll still be here then, won't you, Kit?"

Kit noticed Marge didn't mention her sister, who may or may not have left the floor by now.

"Of course," Kit said. "Night, Grandma. Behave for the doctors and nurses."

Mia hadn't left the floor. She was waiting for the two of them by the elevator.

"I'm glad she's doing better," she said, nodding back toward her mother's room. "Thank you, Marge, for calling me. That couldn't have been easy. Mom is right. The three of us need to talk. But it's late, and it won't be a quick conversation. Mother told me she has a new bed set up in my old room, back at the house, and told me where she put a spare key if I ever needed it, so I think I'll go back there now. Kit, are you coming with me?"

Mia's take-charge attitude was throwing Kit off. Why did she suddenly feel compelled to follow Mia's directive, like a child? She'd be fifty years old in a matter of months, and this woman hadn't acted like an actual mother to her in decades. Come to think of it, she'd *never* acted like one.

The bedroom with the new mattress was a perfect example. Mia called it *her* bedroom, as if oblivious to the fact it had been *Kit's* room since she was twelve years old.

Marge must have read the discomfort on Kit's face. "Kit will come with me. She doesn't want to sleep in Mother's bed, and the third bedroom at the house has no beds right now. I agree with you on one thing, Mia. We are *not* going to talk tonight. Kit, come, I prefer to take the stairs."

With that, Marge spun on her heel and headed down the hallway, away from the elevator. Kit had no idea where the stairs were in this place, but her aunt appeared to, and her already overloaded system would never tolerate even a ten-second elevator ride alone with Mia.

Mirroring this near-stranger's stance, Kit straightened her spine, gave Mia one curt nod, then followed Marge, wishing with all her might that she could drive right on by her aunt's house and head home to Minneapolis. The alternative was a conversation tomorrow that she'd have preferred to put off for the rest of her life.

Chapter Twenty-Seven

K IT WOKE TO A strange gurgling noise. White curtains over the windows of Marge's spare bedroom—just off the kitchen, where the gurgling noises seemed to be coming from—did little to block the morning sunlight. "What time is it?" she yelled, too tired to even check her phone on the small table next to the bed.

The door squeaked open. "Sorry. Did I wake you? It's 6:15. I should have been at work by six, but I let Evelyn know I'd be late. She can handle things for a bit. I'll be there before the Sunday morning rush."

Kit groaned. "Who rushes anywhere on Sunday morning?"

"Lots of people," Marge said, backing out of the room but leaving the door open. "Coffee's ready whenever you are. But we didn't even get to bed till after two. Go back to sleep. No news is good news from the hospital, and they said not to come back before eight. That doesn't mean you have to *be* there at eight. I remember when Dad was in. That joint operates on a whole different schedule. If they send Mother home today—which I'm not convinced is a good idea—I bet it won't be until at least early afternoon."

Kit stared at the ceiling and debated whether to get up. The heady aroma of freshly brewed coffee sealed the deal. Besides, she wanted to talk to Marge before her aunt left for work.

The older woman was emptying the dishwasher when Kit joined her in the kitchen. "Marge, how much longer are you going to work at the Crystal Café? God, Mia is almost seventy. What does that make you?"

Marge shoved a stack of plates into an upper cupboard, then spun to face her niece. "Sixty-seven. Working, it keeps me young. What else am I going to do? Besides, Neil's hospital bills cut into what little we had for savings. If he hadn't gone quick, he'd have left me with nothing. If I could find good help down at the café, maybe I would work a little less, but that's easier said than done."

Kit thought about this. She'd always sensed Aunt Marge struggled financially, especially since Uncle Neil died, but they'd never discussed it. "Do you ever think about selling?"

"My house? Or the café?"

"Either, I suppose."

Marge pulled two mugs out of the top rack of the dishwasher, filled them with coffee from the old-fashioned percolator, and set them on her small kitchen table. "You take it black, right?"

"When it's yours," Kit said, sinking into a chair and taking a deep sniff of the potent brew. "It took me a second to place the sound your coffee pot was making this morning."

Marge smiled. "I can't seem to get those newfangled jobs to make a decent cup. Are you hungry?"

"No, coffee is all I usually have at this hour. How long do you work today?"

Marge eyed her over the rim of her cup as she sipped. "I've got two out on vacation. The summer is winding down, and if I don't give them some time off before they're back in school, they might quit on me, and I can't have that. So no, I'm not going to be able to run interference between you and your mother. As far as Hazel goes, it's about time Mia makes some of those tough decisions where our mother is concerned. I've been doing it my whole life. Well, at least since Dad died and Mom's gotten older. I don't like to complain, but it gets to be too much sometimes."

The two sat in silence for a moment, each lost in their own thoughts.

"I don't know if I can forgive her," Kit finally said, knowing that if anyone understood, it was this woman.

Marge considered this for a beat, then sighed. "Honey, no one is saying you have to forgive Mia. *I* certainly have no intention of forgiving her. I'll do my best to be civil in front of Mom—God knows this has all been incredibly hard on her, too—but that's it. There is no reason we'll have to have any kind of relationship after Mom is gone."

Sometimes Kit felt the same way. But lately, the things her grandmother shared with her a few weeks back near the water fountain in the city park kept stealing into her thoughts, chipping away at her resolve. "How much do you know about what happened to Mia when she was still in high school?"

The question seemed to surprise Marge. "More than Mother thinks I know."

It was an evasive answer, and Kit supposed that maybe her aunt didn't want to share secrets that weren't hers to tell. She didn't have any such qualms. Mia had broken Kit's trust so many times, she didn't owe her any loyalty. "Do you know a boy raped her, and then Mia had an illegal abortion that almost killed her?"

"Yes, I know all about that. Mother thought she was so good at hiding Mia's secrets and faults, but sisters know."

Kit nodded. She didn't have any biological sisters, but even with her oldest girlfriends, she often knew things about them that a more casual friend would never notice. "You don't think those things excuse her behavior in any way?"

"We all live through some kind of trauma. Mia's was awful, and no one should have to endure those things. But I gave her so many chances through the years. I tried to help her, but I'm wondering now if there was ever any chance of redemption, or if she's just evil through and through."

Kit squirmed in her chair. Mia was an awful screwup, but she couldn't believe she was pure evil. If her mother was rotten to the core, what did that make Kit? And her brothers, Tony and Pete?

Marge must have realized how her words landed, because her expression softened. "I'm sorry, Kit. I shouldn't go on like that. Things happened later between us that are unforgivable. None of that is any reflection on you."

Kit swirled the coffee around in her white ironstone mug, taking in her aunt's words. "Marge . . . why do you hate her so much?"

A barking dog beyond the kitchen windows snagged her aunt's attention, and Kit wasn't sure she'd get an answer. But eventually Marge took a deep breath and swung her eyes back to her.

"Mia came to me on my wedding day and told me my Neil, the man I was marrying in exactly two hours, might be the father to your youngest brother."

Kit choked on her coffee. "To *Pete*?"

"Of course, it was all a lie. She was drunk. As usual. Mother was mad at me because I wouldn't let Mia be in my wedding. But she had some strange fascination with Neil. He was two years older than me, in her class. When I asked him about it, knowing that she might be lying because that's what she always did, he admitted to me he'd dated her once, when they were juniors. He took her to a movie, but they had nothing in common, and he thought that was that. She kept after him. Eventually, she started dating this other kid to make Neil jealous. This guy was bad news. He's the one who ended up beating her. Raping her even, if that part of her story was true."

"Wait, stop," Kit said, struggling to keep up. "Your husband . . . Uncle Neil . . . he *knew* the guy who raped Mia?"

"A little. They played football together, at least until the other kid got kicked off the team. He had a mean streak a mile wide. Mia was pretty innocent back then, but he did a real number on her."

Kit was finally understanding why Marge's bitterness toward her sister ran so deep. She and her brothers weren't the only ones Mia betrayed. "She tried to ruin your wedding?"

"Our wedding. Our marriage. Even our twenty-fifth wedding anniversary. I'm lucky Neil never left me because of that psycho sister of mine."

"Do you think it was because she never got over the crush she had on him in eleventh grade?" Kit asked, thinking that seemed like extreme behavior, even for Mia.

"Oh, it was more than a crush. In her mind, Neil was her first love, and her little sister stole him away from her. When her mind got so warped with all her drinking and drug use, it twisted her actual memories into some kind of fantasy."

"Does Grandma know?"

Marge shrugged. "I honestly don't know. She knew when Mia went to the movies with Neil, way back when, and she knew Mia pouted for weeks afterward when nothing came of it. I didn't go out with Neil until years later, when he got back from Vietnam. Let me tell you—Mia didn't like it."

Kit did the math, remembering from her history classes that the Vietnam War ended in the seventies. Pete was born in 1974. She had to ask. "Do you think Mia and Neil got together like she claimed?"

"Absolutely not. Besides, the joke was on her. Neil got hurt in the war. We knew he could never father children. We kept that tidbit to ourselves. Mia has been sick for years. I doubt I'll ever trust another word she says."

The telephone on the wall next to the refrigerator rang, jarring Kit. "You still have a landline? But you have a cell phone."

Marge pushed away from the table. "Yep. Got both. Neil is the voice on my old answering machine. Can't seem to give that up. Hopefully that isn't the hospital calling."

Kit watched Marge take the call, her mind racing with everything she'd just learned. She could tell from her aunt's end of the phone conversation that someone was calling from the café. The call was brief.

Marge hung up, then grabbed her coffee from the table, took one last swallow, and dumped the rest down the drain. "Gotta run. Are you going to be okay? I know I dumped a lot on you. Maybe I should have taken that nasty business to the grave, but I wanted you to understand why I have such a problem with your mother. It has absolutely nothing to do with you or your brothers. I suspect Mother is going to welcome Mia back with open arms. I've already decided how I'll handle it. Now it's your turn. Have that talk with your mother. Then decide for yourself. You need to make your own decisions, and if they are different from mine, I'll understand. We only have one mother."

Kit accepted the quick side-hug Marge gave her on the way out the door, then remained seated at her aunt's kitchen table until long after her coffee had gone cold, thinking about everything she'd learned about her mother.

As Kit drove back to the hospital, she kept playing over the many things both her grandmother and Marge had shared with her about Mia. She knew Mia's actions through the years hurt Hazel. What mother wouldn't feel conflicted, furious, and sad if one of her children made such a disaster of their life? She'd known there was a deep rift between Mia and Marge, too, but she hadn't thought much about that. Almost all of Kit's bitterness she'd felt over the years was for how Mia had failed her and her brothers. Even how Mia had failed Kit's father. She blamed her mother for the man's ultimate fall from grace, too.

Her fingers tapped nervously against the steering wheel. It had taken her practically fifty years to understand that the dynamics of her family were so much more complicated than she'd ever imagined.

Today, she would try to get some answers ... directly from her mother.

Even just the thought of airing all the dirty laundry between them made her feel like throwing up. She probably should have taken Marge up on her offer of breakfast, but it was too late now.

She pulled into the hospital parking lot. This time, no one came out to greet her. If Mia was already here, Kit would find out soon enough.

Once on the second floor, she returned to her grandmother's room—and felt a wave of panic when the room was empty.

A nurse's aide came in right behind her. "If you're here for Hazel, they took her down to run a couple more tests. You're welcome to wait in the family room if you'd like. Just off the elevator."

Kit didn't *like*, and she was hungry. Maybe she could check out the hospital's cafeteria. Every hospital had one, didn't they? "Do you have any idea when she'll be back up, or when the doctor will be by to update us?"

The aide shrugged, tightening her high ponytail. Kit guessed she was a high school or early college student, exploring the world of healthcare from the bottom rung. "On the weekend the doctors don't usually start rounds till ten. It could be a couple hours. If you'd like, I can take your phone number and call you when it's a good time to come back up."

Kit nodded, grateful for an option other than the uncomfortable chairs in the waiting room on an empty stomach. She provided the information, then headed for the elevator. She should have asked where the cafeteria was, but she hadn't thought to. She'd head down to the information desk near the front entrance. It wasn't like she had to hurry.

When the elevator doors slid open, she came face to face with Mia.

"How's Mom?" Mia asked.

"Good morning to you, too," Kit said, considering whether she should get in the elevator when her mother got off and ditch her. Tempting as it sounded, acting on that immature impulse wouldn't solve anything. So instead she moved away from the elevator, giving Mia room to step into the hall.

Mia rubbed her face with both hands. Kit didn't think her mother looked as stoic as she had the night before. "I'm sorry, Kit. Good morning. I'm just worried. Seeing you again is hard. I've waited for this for a long time."

"Have you?" Kit asked, unable to resist her forceful tone. She didn't have to be one hundred precent mature. That would be asking too much.

Mia's shoulders drooped. "I understand why you might not believe it. Is Mom all right? It looked like you were leaving."

Kit shoved her hands in the front pockets of her jeans. "They took her downstairs for more tests. I gave them my number. They said it could be a couple hours, so I was going to go find the cafeteria."

Mia looked torn. "I could eat . . ."

Kit had to bite back a snarky retort, since she hadn't invited her mother to come with her for breakfast, but they might as well find a quiet place to talk. "Fine. Follow me."

"I'll meet you there. I brought a lounge set for Mom," Mia said, turning toward Hazel's room, a shopping bag Kit hadn't noticed hanging from her fingers.

Fifteen minutes later, the two women took cafeteria trays out to a small concrete patio behind the hospital and found an empty picnic table near the grass.

Kit took her time buttering her pancakes and wrestling with the cover on the small plastic container of syrup. Mia nibbled on a piece of buttered toast, but acted as if her appetite had deserted her, much as Kit's had. She waited to see if Mia would start their conversation.

She didn't have to wait long.

"Mom told me you found my things in her basement," Mia began. "I'm sure you have questions for me. I asked her not to tell you they were down there, or even that we were talking again, but I can see now that I shouldn't have done that. It wasn't fair to put her in that position."

Kit gave up on the syrup and cut off a piece of the pancake with her plastic fork. A tine snapped. "It wasn't fair to put Grandma in that position? Since when have you cared about the position you put any of us in?" She paused to take a deep breath, picking the broken piece of plastic out of her breakfast.

"Kit . . . I know I failed you. You *and* your brothers. There's nothing I can do to change the past. I made terrible choices, and my family paid the price."

She wanted so badly to lash out. To hurt this woman like Mia had hurt her. She needed answers, but she wouldn't get them if she couldn't be civil. It was hard to know where to start, and even harder not to let go of the tight grip she was trying to keep on her temper.

"When was the last time you saw Dad?"

Mia snorted. "Your father?"

Kit's mind filled with conflicting images of her dad: the kind man she thought she knew as a young girl versus the thug who came to her grandmother's house the day after Kit's senior prom. "It seems you always made terrible choices where men were concerned. Even before Dad."

Mia picked at her toast, shredding it. "You have no idea."

Kit popped a bite of pancake into her mouth, nearly gagging but hoping that once it hit her stomach she'd stop feeling queasy. "Why don't you tell me, then? Mia, I'm almost fifty years old. You are almost seventy. Don't you think it's about time we dispensed with all the secrets?"

Some of the starch she'd noticed in her mother's posture the night before seemed to return. "It isn't a pretty story, Kit. Are you sure you want to hear this? I'll tell you everything, if that's what you want."

She considered the question. Maybe letting Pandora out of her box was a terrible idea. But Kit was pretty sure there was nothing left to salvage anyhow, so why not?

She nodded.

"All right then," Mia said. "Forgive me if this gets a little disjointed. It isn't a pretty story, and I know there are things I don't even remember.

Not only because of the booze and drugs. Some of it happened a long time ago, and my mind has lost it. I'll do my best to share with you what I remember. I want you to know that I've been clean for ten years."

She must have seen the doubt on Kit's face, because she paused. But when Kit stayed silent, she went on.

"I had to be as sure as I could that it was safe to rebuild any kind of relationship with my family. I know my sobriety is tenuous, and I'll live with that knowledge until the day I die. I'm doing all right now."

Despite her resolution not to care about this woman sitting across the table from her, Kit felt a glimmer of something akin to relief at Mia's words. Still, she didn't interrupt.

"I know I can't ask for your forgiveness, Kit. But maybe after we talk, you will at least understand me a little better."

"I'll be the judge of that," Kit said, no longer able to remain quiet. She thought back to her conversation with Hazel in the town square. She did her best to remain calm. "When Grandma told me what happened to you after I found your things in her basement, it helped me see you a little differently. No one should have to go through that. But you married Dad. You had us. And after Dad went to prison, you vanished on us. Where did you go?"

Kit hated the anguish she could hear in her own voice, the way it cracked.

Mia sighed. "I was only nineteen when I married Duncan. I had you at twenty. Then Tony and Pete a few short years later. I was so young . . . I didn't understand what was happening. But now, after literally decades of counseling and treatment, I believe I had severe postpartum depression, and it got worse with every baby."

Another tine broke off her fork at Mia's words, so Kit gave up on the pancakes, pushing her plate away. "If you think you are going to blame any of this on us, I will get up and walk out of here right now, Mom, and you will never see me again."

Mia reached across the table and grabbed Kit's hand, holding on tight. "No. I didn't mean to imply that. I just think my screwed-up hormones contributed to my inability to stop self-medicating with booze, sometimes drugs. Duncan did his best to hold our family together for the next ten years. I know you loved your dad, and you thought he could do no wrong. I'm thankful you kids didn't see his mean streak. He hid it well, but it was very real and very scary."

Ten-year-old Kit wouldn't have believed that. Forty-nine-year-old Kit, on the other hand, did. She pulled her hand away from Mia's, remembering when her father showed up that awful day demanding Kit turn over her keys to the Mustang. He was a different man than the one who went away to prison. She could see now that her father, like so many people, wore a façade that she hadn't seen through as a younger child.

"Mia . . . what really happened that day? When Dad had the accident and that little girl died?"

Her mother nodded. "I know you deserve the truth about that. Duncan *was* drunk when he hit that little girl . . . but *I* was the reason he was behind the wheel in the first place."

"What do you mean?" Kit asked, but she was scared to hear the truth. It was a subject no one would ever discuss with her.

"I caught him with another woman. I'd suspected he was having an affair, but I wasn't sure until that day. I followed him. I'm ashamed to say I left you kids home alone. He pulled into this dive motel, and I saw the two of them get out of his truck and go inside a room. He was carrying a bottle of whiskey. I was so mad. I parked right next to his pickup and walked to the bar across the street. I must have gotten obnoxious, because they kicked me out eventually, but not until after I'd had too much to drink. I guess I passed out in my car, because next thing I knew, Duncan was pounding on the hood, screaming about you kids."

"About us?"

Mia laughed, but there was no joy in the sound. "He always was a better parent than me."

"That isn't saying much."

"Do you want to hear this or not?"

Kit suspected she might know where the story was going now that she knew how it started. But she had to know for sure. "Yes."

Mia took a sip of her orange juice, but some of it sloshed out on her shirt because her hand was shaking so badly. "People started poking their heads out of motel doors. I was just sober enough to realize that if I didn't leave, someone was going to call the cops. I pulled away, but Duncan got my door open, and we damn near crashed, fighting over the wheel. I finally gave in and crawled over into the passenger side and"—she shrugged—"I let him drive."

Kit knew she didn't want to hear the rest. She held up a hand.

Mia nodded. "Right. I'll spare you the worst of the details. It took me years of professional help before I could sleep without nightmares. It's my fault that little girl died that morning. Kit . . . she was on her way to the school bus. We both should have gone to prison after that. Duncan should have swerved to miss her. Even if we would have hit a tree and died, it would have been what we deserved. We'd become miserable excuses for human beings. But life doesn't work out like that. Too often it's the innocents who suffer. Like that little girl. Like you and your brothers."

Kit felt stunned as her mother shared the horrid details of that long-ago day. It amazed her that the woman could remain dry-eyed through it all. "Mia, we don't have to keep talking about this. We can go check on Grandma."

"No," Mia said, shaking her head. "I want to get this all out, and then we'll see where we go from here. The accident happened a long time ago, and lots more happened between then and now. Can I keep going? Please?"

Kit nodded, not trusting her voice.

"The authorities didn't have anything solid to charge *me* with, so they convicted your father for that awful tragedy. We both knew there was no way our marriage could survive it, so when he had his lawyer start divorce proceedings about a year after he went to prison, how could I fight it? I'd failed our little family again. I couldn't bring myself to tell you or my parents. Besides, I figured, he wouldn't get out for years, so no one needed to know. But secrets like that will eat at a person. Things got so bad, I knew I was out of control and at risk of losing all three of you forever. But I couldn't stop drinking."

Kit was familiar with this part of the story. "That's when Pete and Tony and I ended up in that awful dormitory-like place with social services. I still have nightmares about that night we slept there."

"I had to convince my folks to take you in," Mia went on, as if she hadn't heard Kit. "Once I knew you were safe, I snuck out of the live-in treatment center my dad got me into. I didn't want to go on. I was on my way to the lake, intent on ending it all. I don't know if I'd have actually gone through with it, but I knew I had to swing by the house and say goodbye to the three of you. You all were just leaving when I got there. I think you were going to that summer camp?"

Kit felt like she'd been punched in the gut. She'd never been so mad at her mother as she was when Mia showed up that morning, out of the blue. She hadn't even wanted to go to the stupid camp in the first place, but it was all she had, really, and how dare her mother mess *that* up for her, too?

Mia continued with her sad tale. "Thank God someone called the cops. They got me somewhere safe, locked me up so I couldn't hurt myself, until I was in a better place emotionally."

She stopped speaking, picked up the apple on her tray, examined it, then took a bite. She looked lost in her thoughts. Kit's stomach rumbled, and she forced herself to eat the banana beside her inedible pancake. After eating half her apple, Mia started back up again.

"I decided it was best if I stayed away from you and your brothers. I knew you were safe and well taken care of with Mom and Dad. I wanted all of you to graduate—maybe even go on to college, the way I used to think *I* would after high school."

Kit rolled up her banana peel, thinking back to her years in the Ruby Shores school system. "You came back that one Thanksgiving. You weren't there long. I remember you fighting with Grandma and Grandpa, and then you were gone again. Later, Grandma told me that was when you gave them back the title to the Mustang. Was it even yours to give anymore? Dad claimed you gave it to him in the divorce proceedings."

Mia shook her head. "I don't think I did. Your father is a liar."

"You needed money," Kit prodded, deciding she'd never get a straight answer on whether her father had any legal claim to her vintage car. She had what the world thought was a clear title to it now, and that was one thing she vowed to not worry about anymore.

Mia nodded. "I needed money. The Mustang wasn't drivable, and I knew I'd never have the money to fix it. It was a good solution."

Kit would give her that. It had ultimately worked out. Her father showed his true colors over it, which was awful, but it allowed her to see for herself what he was really like.

Then she remembered another terrible time when her mother was absent. "You didn't come home for Grandpa's funeral."

Mia's eyes, dry all this time, finally welled up with tears. "Kit...I didn't know. I was living on the streets. After I found out Dad was gone, I got myself help again. I got serious about attending my AA meetings, and it helped. For a while. Then there was another guy."

"Of course there was." Kit smiled, and for the first time since they'd sat down at the table, they both laughed without the shadow of cynicism.

"I told you—I suck at men. He helped me stay clean for a while, even encouraged me to go back to school. I got hired on as an LPN, and I wasn't too bad at it. That lasted until he fell off the wagon, convinced me to steal drugs for him. And when a coworker caught me red-handed, *that* guy made me sleep with him to stay quiet."

Her words left Kit dumbstruck. She'd never really allowed herself to consider the horrors her mother could have lived through because of her addictions.

"The next five years were a blur. I still can't believe I didn't wind up dead in some alley somewhere." She shook her head, as if pushing away an ugly image in her mind. "The next time I saw you three was at Marge's twenty-fifth wedding anniversary. That was a mistake. I fought with Marge . . . again . . . but seeing you three kept me going."

Kit considered telling Mia that Marge had told her the actual, full story behind all of that over coffee earlier in the day, but she decided against it. She didn't want it to shame Mia into silence, not now when she was finally sharing. There was something that confused her, though.

"Mia, if you were sometimes homeless through the years, how do you still have all that stuff from when we were little?"

She shrugged. "I'd stashed some boxes in a friend's old garage. No one bothered them. Eventually I found other work. Survived and did my best to stay clean. Then, in my mid-fifties, I looked your father up."

The shocks kept coming.

"No," Kit whispered.

"I did. I'm such a fool. Looked him up on Facebook, if you can believe that."

"He's on Facebook?!" Kit yelped.

"Probably not anymore. He isn't so different from me. He's had a few good years here and there, but mostly, his life has been a catastrophe, too. The two of us, we're like poison together. My temporary sobriety took a hit when we reconnected. Three years later, Marge's Neil died, so I came home again. Do you remember that? You and I fought that time. You were finally old enough to stand up to me, I suppose. I deserved every awful thing you said to me, Kit. I crawled back to my lonely apartment, and I knew I'd finally reached the point where, at fifty-nine, I either had to clean up my act once and for all . . . or die. There was no more space left in the in-between."

Kit's mind ticked through the life events. "Uncle Neil died ten years ago."

Mia nodded. "And I swear I've been sober ever since."

"What finally worked?" Kit asked, wanting to trust the apparent sincerity behind her mother's words.

"A friend of a friend took pity on me and hired me as an office assistant for a CPA. I couldn't be around any drugs or other addicts. I earned enough for a simple life. I'm painfully aware that my sobriety is always at risk. In 2016, when I was sixty-six years old, a larger firm bought out the company I worked for. I was out of a job and had to move from my one-bedroom to an efficiency apartment. I didn't have room for everything, and Mom agreed I could store some of my things in her basement. She invited me to move back home then, but I worried I'd fall back into my old habits."

A cafeteria employee stopped by their table and offered to take their trays. Once he was gone, Kit stared at her mother for a minute.

"You're back now."

"I'm back now," Mia said. "As awful as it was to share all of this with you, I'm glad we talked about it. I'm not proud of any of it, but it is my story. As my daughter, you deserve to know. The only thing I ever did right in my life was to have you and your brothers. Now, if you'll excuse me, I need to use the bathroom. They should call about Mom soon."

As Mia walked away, Kit checked her phone. She'd lost all track of time while listening to her mother's story, so it shocked her to see it was ten minutes past ten. Her phone rang just then as she stared at it, and she nearly leapt with surprise. The nurse on the other end suggested Kit come upstairs. Hazel was back in her room, she said, and the doctor should be in shortly.

"I hope Mom hurries up," Kit muttered, realizing she'd begun thinking of Mia as *Mom* for the first time since she was a kid.

Chapter Twenty-Eight

WHEN KIT AND MIA walked into Hazel's hospital room, yet another doctor stood next to her bed. The young man glanced their way, and Kit felt a hint of recognition.

"Good morning," he said, but his focus was obviously on his patient as he listened to her chest with his stethoscope.

"I wasn't sure which of you would be here today," Hazel said, earning a stern look from her doctor. "What?" she asked as she met his eyes. "You people have been poking and prodding me all morning. I want to go home."

With a sigh, the doctor straightened and shook his head with a glance toward Kit. "You have a feisty one here."

Kit grinned back at him in agreement. "Aren't you Owen's boy? You helped Grandma the night of that big storm that ripped through town. I apologize for not remembering your name."

Hazel slapped her bed with a soft thud. "That's right, Kit! I thought those baby blues looked familiar."

Kit would have sworn the man blushed at this.

"Apologies for not recognizing you," he said. "That was a crazy night, but I certainly remembered Hazel. I'm Adam Jameson. You know my father?"

"A little. We went to school together. And that was a long time ago. My friend Jackie was much closer to him."

He nodded. "Sure. I know who Jackie is. And now I recognize you. Hazel is your grandmother, right?"

"Right. And this is Mia, Hazel's daughter," Kit said, motioning behind her where her mother waited just inside the door. "What's going on with Grandma?"

Her question elicited a frown out of the young doctor. "Your Hazel is in remarkable health for her age."

Hazel scoffed from her bed. "Why do all you doctor types have to ruin every positive comment with a reference to my age? I didn't have time to eat dinner last night, that's all. I got a little light-headed and wobbly on my feet."

Mia approached the hospital bed. "Mother, when Marge stopped to check on you after work, you were on your kitchen floor and unresponsive. That's certainly more serious than a dizzy spell."

Hazel crossed her arms over her chest stubbornly, and Kit noticed that all the wires protruding from her the night before, appeared to be gone. She hoped that was a good sign.

Adam studied his patient, as if still trying to decide for himself how serious things were. "All of your tests have come back either negative or inconclusive. So far, I'm not finding anything of great concern. But I am worried about your weight loss."

"Weight loss?" Kit said. "Grandma, aren't you eating?"

"Of course I'm eating, child," the old woman in the hospital bed insisted. "I'm eating more for lunch, though, because I'm tired by evening, and heavy meals make it harder to sleep."

The doctor didn't look convinced. "I'm concerned that Hazel isn't getting enough nutrients in her diet. Or enough calories. Hazel, you've lost ten pounds since the night we saw you in here for your bumps and bruises after the storm. I'm not finding a specific medical reason for the weight loss, aside from the fact you said your appetite isn't what it used to be. In my professional opinion, your blood sugars dropped dangerously low last night, probably because it had been too long since you ate a substantive meal."

"I'll be sure to restock her pantry with easy-to-prepare items this afternoon," Kit offered, hating the idea that her dear grandmother wasn't eating enough.

"That would be a good idea," Adam conceded, looking only slightly less concerned. "I know how much you want to go home, Hazel, and to continue living on your own, but I'm afraid I can't release you unless I know someone will be there with you. Maybe not indefinitely, but at least until your weight stabilizes and these swings in your blood pressure are under control again."

Kit and Mia exchanged glances. Kit wished Marge was here, since she was the only one of the three of them who actually lived in Ruby Shores. But then her mind bounced back to her discussion with her aunt over coffee that morning. Marge still worked lots of hours, and that didn't seem like something she planned to change soon.

"I'll stay with her," Mia offered, shocking Kit.

"Mia, you were just saying that you didn't feel ready to come back here," she reminded her mother.

Mia held up a hand. "I said I wasn't ready three years ago, when I moved to a smaller place. But you heard the doctor. Mom can't be alone right now. Marge has her own life. And so do you, back in Minneapolis. I need to do this. I owe her."

"I'm still right here!" Hazel interjected. "Don't talk about me like I'm some feeble old woman. Mia, we've talked about this before and you weren't comfortable living in Ruby Shores. You have your own routine that I know is very important to your own . . . er . . . health. While you know I'd love to have you, are you sure that's such a good idea?"

Mia took a deep breath, then turned to address the young doctor directly. "I'm an addict, ten years sober. I've gotten sober before, but something always threw me off track. I've learned to be extra careful. I think I'm strong enough to do this, and Mom needs me. Tell me, will she be on any medication that might tempt me, should I find myself in a weak moment?"

Adam checked the computer on a tall stand next to Hazel's bed, then shook his head. "I appreciate your honesty. And no, there is nothing here that I'd be concerned about for you. I'm not your mother's regular physician, though, so be sure to keep having this conversation as needed."

Mia nodded firmly. "All right then. It's decided. Mom, I'm moving in with you for as long as it takes, and we are going to get you your strength back. That way you can still come home, and we can avoid any discussions—at least for now—about you moving somewhere where you can get more professional, constant care."

"I can take care of myself," Hazel said, but Kit caught the happy twinkle in her grandmother's eye. The woman couldn't hide her joy that her eldest daughter was finally coming home.

Kit agreed that it seemed the only logical solution, but she prayed it wouldn't backfire.

Despite Dr. Jameson agreeing to release Hazel with Mia's assurances that the older woman wouldn't be left alone, the process to actually release her into their care took time. Mia had stayed at the hospital while Kit slipped away to buy groceries and then returned to pick the two women up. Her grandmother needed a nap, and dinner would be ready in two hours, so grandmother and granddaughter were making their way up the stairs of Hazel's home. There were no bedrooms on the main floor, and Hazel refused to sleep on the couch.

Kit was happy with how well her grandmother handled the stairs, noting that she seemed only slightly winded by the time they reached the upstairs landing, but Kit insisted she should not go to her room without help. When Hazel opened the door to her bedroom, Kit remembered the scene she'd walked in on the morning after the big storm.

"Oh! Grandma, I forgot to ask you. Why did you have so many clothes spread out on your bed a while back? You know, when I was here after the tornado?"

"Ach, child, I was assessing the state of my wardrobe."

Hazel walked straight over to her dresser and slid open a drawer in the old jewelry box that had sat there since Kit was a child. Her grandmother's steps were slow but steady. Kit knew Hazel was making sure her wedding ring was still there. It was another age-old habit. Arthritis caused Hazel's knuckles to swell, forcing her to stop wearing the ring, but it remained a kind of touch point for her. Kit was sure the woman pulled that drawer open to check on the ring at least once a day. She found it sweet, but she doubted Hazel even realized how often she did it. God forbid anyone ever break in here and steal the old set of rings. But the rings weren't something to be locked away for safekeeping. Their real value was in the comfort they still gave Hazel.

With a sigh, Kit went to the closet and opened the door. "The state of your wardrobe, huh? Would you like me to take you shopping sometime? I know the old dress boutique downtown finally closed. Is there anywhere decent to buy clothes around here anymore?"

Hazel shrugged. "The thrift shop."

Kit laughed. "I can do better than that. Tell you what—you get your strength back, and I'll bring you back to Minneapolis with me. We can have a sleepover at my place, and I'll take you shopping for some new clothes. It'll be getting cold again before you know it. A few new sweaters and warm slacks might be nice for you."

"I had sleeveless blouses in mind . . . and maybe a new dress . . ." Hazel muttered, closing the drawer on her jewelry case.

"Yeah, I'm not ready for winter either, but this is Minnesota."

Kit shut the closet door. At the look on her grandmother's face, she paused, hating the idea that skittered through her brain that buying more summer clothes might be a waste. With luck, this woman would still be with them for many summers ahead.

"I should probably get that nap in," Hazel said, turning down the coverlet on the bed. She had dressed in the comfortable lounge set Mia had brought with her to the hospital that morning, so she didn't need to change clothes again.

"That would be good. I need to call Dean and give him an update. He's been worried sick about you."

Hazel smiled as she got into bed. "That Dean is a catch. You hold on tight to him, you hear?"

"I hear," Kit said. At some point she needed to update Hazel on Summer, but that could wait for now. "Can I get you anything else?"

As Hazel adjusted a pillow, she nodded. "Yes, dear. Get me my cell phone and charger, please?"

Surprised, Kit nodded. "Sure. But who are you going to call? Marge is working a double today."

"*You* need to update Dean. *I* need to update Floyd. He'll be wondering why he hasn't heard from me today. We usually talk every morning at eleven. He has enough to worry about with that boy. I don't want him to worry about me, too."

"That boy? Do you mean Isaac?" Kit asked, thinking back to the helpful teenager who came back after the storm and helped her get the wet mattresses out of her brothers' old room. "Why? What's going on with him? He seems like a nice kid."

Her grandmother lay back against her mound of pillows. "He is a very nice kid who has had to face more than his fair share of tragedies at too young an age. Floyd is doing his best, but it isn't easy."

Kit reached for the doorknob. "You're right. Raising a teenager is tough at any age. The stories Jackie would tell me about her twins used to give me nightmares—and they're good girls."

"Isaac is a good boy, too," Hazel said, her tone defensive. "But he has a hard road ahead of him. Now, get me my phone. I need to make that call and get a little sleep before attempting to eat your mother's cooking. It's been a very long time, but when she was a kid, she burned boiling water."

Chuckling, Kit left her grandmother to go find the cell phone. She supposed it was nice that Hazel was in regular contact with someone her age, but was this turning into some kind of boyfriend–girlfriend relationship? At their age?

"What would be wrong with that?" Kit asked herself, her mind jumping back to the discussion she'd had on the beach in Hawaii with the woman who called herself Nancy Drew.

No one should ever think they are too old for love.

CHAPTER TWENTY-NINE

D EAN PULLED THE TWO steaks out of Kit's refrigerator that he'd picked up on his way over after work. Thursday nights were his nights to cook. Once unwrapped, he sprinkled the generous cuts of sirloin with his favorite seasonings, then pushed the plate farther back on the countertop to rest and fired up the grill.

Chloe better stay off the countertop, he thought. Knowing the cat would ultimately do whatever she felt like doing, he covered the steaks just in case.

After returning from Ruby Shores, Kit had been enduring long days at the office and wasn't home yet.

He took a swig of his cold beer, taking in the modern elements that Kit—along with Jackie's help—had incorporated into this kitchen during the recent remodel. Kit had sought his input throughout the remodeling process, so there was nothing he disliked about the updates. The aesthetics were in stark contrast to his brother's farmhouse kitchen, a place that continued to be on his mind after his impromptu visit, but both rooms were homey in their own way.

He appreciated that Kit always kept bottles of his favorite beer and the two percent milk he preferred on hand, even though she said it made her gag, but he still thought of this place as *hers*. Could he live here?

Could they make it feel like their place, or would he always feel like the townhouse was still Kit's domain?

The lease on his apartment had flipped from an annual term to month-to-month. It was costing him more in rent, but he'd hesitated to give notice with Kit's unwillingness to set a wedding date.

His mother's words came back to him from their discussion in Nick's worn kitchen. She still wasn't sure Kit was the right person for him. Even Nick, who usually kept his opinion on personal matters to himself, had brought up the whole *kid* topic. His little brother had his doubts about her, too, even though *he* liked her.

So his family had doubts about Kit. That was probably his own fault for not insisting that they all spend more time together. When he'd attended his daughter's gift-opening celebration the previous Sunday morning, he'd met an extended family made up of what one might term *nontraditional* relationships. Summer's new sister-in-law was there with her wife and two adopted children. Erin's fiancé, a man Dean liked from the moment he met him, treated Summer like a daughter. Instead of all of this bothering Dean, he realized the new bride was lucky to have so many people who loved her.

Family didn't have to be blood. Love and loyalty could be the basis for a strong family, too.

While he hated to admit it, Kit knew him well, and deep down, maybe he *had* been worried he was giving up too much if he married her. But after meeting Summer and the rest of her family, he was realizing he could let go of the antiquated version of what family meant.

But he couldn't let go of Kit.

He hadn't forgotten Kit's comments about finally being ready to get married, too, but just not with a splashy ceremony like Summer's wedding. Maybe he could broach the subject over dinner. But he wouldn't push. Kit was worried about her grandmother, and she was stressed about the return of her long-estranged mother. When he and Kit had grabbed a quick dinner after work on Monday, she shared a little about the conversation she'd had with Mia, but there was so much more for them to discuss.

When he opened a bottom cupboard to retrieve a bowl for the salad, Chloe sauntered into the room and wove between his feet. Luckily, he'd remembered to take his allergy medicine that morning, so the cat didn't send him into a sneezing frenzy this time. She wanted to be fed, and Kit stored her food in the cupboard next to the bowls. He dropped a quick hand across Chloe's back, then fished out one tin of her food.

"Why do you only suck up to me when you're hungry?" he asked.

But he loved that Kit's cat no longer hid under a bed the whole time he was in the house. He was finally making inroads with both of the females in this home.

The sound of the garage door opening didn't fill the room until after Chloe licked her bowl clean and Dean had the salad pulled together. Chloe bolted at the screech of metal on metal, and Dean remembered he still needed to fix the garage door track Kit had bent when she rammed it with the handle of her bike.

It felt nice to be needed.

"Hey there," Kit greeted him as she thumbed through a stack of mail she'd brought in with her. "Here's that magazine you ordered on vintage cars."

He grabbed a second beer from the fridge, popped the top, and exchanged the bottle for the magazine. He glanced at the cover, smiling at the classic red-and-white Corvette, then set it aside so he could finish preparing dinner. "Hope you don't mind that I used your address."

"Course not," she said. She took a long pull of the beer before sneaking a crouton from the top of the tossed salad. "When are you going to move in here officially? Isn't your lease up?"

He caught her around the waist before she could head back to her bedroom to change into something more comfortable, which she did first thing every day after work. "I was just thinking about that before you walked in, actually. Are you good with me giving notice?"

She nodded, then gave him a peck on the lips. "I thought that's what we decided. Now, release me, you big brute, so I can get out of this bra."

Laughing, he stepped back. "Lucky for you, I need to get these steaks on."

It wasn't long before the two of them were relaxing at the small table on the back patio, enjoying the simple meal Dean had prepared.

Kit moaned. "This is *amazing*. If you didn't cook for me, I'd never have a decent steak. I've never figured out how to grill one properly."

Dean stabbed a sweet pepper from his bowl of salad, waving it on the end of the fork at her. "We can thank dear old Dad for that. He made sure I knew my way around the grill before I was a teenager."

Kit shook her head, her expression sobering as he popped the pepper into his mouth. "I wish I could have met your dad. I know how much he meant to you."

Once he swallowed, he gave her a big grin. "He'd have loved you."

"Your mother doesn't love me," she pointed out.

It was his turn for the sober expression. "She just doesn't know you well enough yet."

Kit added more dressing to her salad. "Dean, we've been together for five—no, *six* years. I should know your mother well by now."

She was right. "Let's see what we can do to rectify that. I feel like we should make more of an effort to spend time with my family. You won't believe how Mason has grown. And Nick finally seems to have pulled his life together. His wife is good for him. And speaking of family, when do I get to meet Mia?"

"Ah, yes . . . Mia." Kit set down her fork. "Last weekend was exhausting. I was so glad to hear you at least had fun at Summer's gift opening. I'm ready for a fun, drama-free weekend at home. But, unfortunately, I don't think that will happen *this* weekend. I've been meaning to ask you if you'd be up for running back to Ruby Shores with me again."

The invitation came as a surprise. "Of course. Has Hazel had another setback, or is this about her house?"

Kit snorted. "No. Neither. She seems to feel fine. In fact, she's insisting we have a nice dinner with guests on Saturday afternoon. She already has Mom working on the menu. Grandma wants to invite her friend Floyd and his grandson over. Apparently, there's something important she wants us all to discuss. I swear, Dean, if she says she's marrying that old fart, I'm going to lose it."

He laughed, almost spewing his beer, and his nose burned when things backed up. By the time he caught his breath, Kit was laughing, too.

"You don't really think *that's* what she wants to talk about, do you?"

Kit sliced off a bite of her steak, shaking her head. "No. But with my mother living back at home with Grandma, I kind of feel like I'm in *The Twilight Zone*, so who knows?"

Dean noticed Kit was referring to Mia as her mother more often these days—something she'd seldom done before, but he thought it wise not to mention it. It was best to tread carefully where Kit's relationship with her mother was involved.

He raised his beer in a toast. "Here's to both of us getting to know each other's mothers a little better."

The first thing Dean noticed as he followed Kit up the porch steps and through Hazel's front door was that she seemed ill at ease. Nervous, even, as she fiddled with the small diamond stud in her left ear. Kit didn't fidget. The second thing he noticed was the stench of burnt food. He could hear voices coming from the back part of the house—probably the kitchen—but the living room was empty.

"Since when do we use the front door?" he asked, keeping his tone light. "Isn't this your home away from home, babe?"

She spared him a glance, but the tempo at which she rubbed her hands together didn't slow. "Grandma said she hoped, now that they'd rebuilt her front porch, that people would start using the front door instead of the back. And, trust me, if Mom is back in the kitchen cooking dinner, that's a mess we want to avoid."

He nodded. "It *does* smell like someone might have hit a little snag in the cooking department."

"Grandma says Mia can't even boil water. I wouldn't know. We probably should have eaten something before we came." The hand rubbing stopped, but he watched her begin to pace. "I should find Grandma. I think her guests are supposed to arrive in an hour, and I may need to figure out a contingency plan to feed them."

Sensing her tension ramping up, Dean debated between offering his assistance or escaping the potentially escalating drama between the women in the house. "Would you like me to stick around and help, or should I get out of your hair? The mechanic working on your car asked me to swing by the shop the next time I got to town, and they are open on Saturday afternoons."

Kit looked toward the kitchen, anxious. Words between Hazel and a voice Dean didn't recognize gained in volume. "Go. I should get back there. Let me get things calmed down before I introduce you to Mia for the first time. Please be back by four, when Floyd and his grandson are supposed to get here. With any luck, there will be decent food and engaging conversation. But I'll warn you, *luck* and Mia don't go hand in hand. Unless it's *bad* luck."

"You sure?" He was sensitive to the fact he didn't want to upset Kit further by leaving.

"Trust me. It's fine. Go see how they are doing with my Mustang. Maybe they'll finish in time for us to drive it up the north shore to see the colors this fall."

Dean grimaced. "That would be early. They're pretty backed up, and your birthday isn't until February, so I wasn't pushing them. But I do like the idea. Call me if you need me to pick up anything, and I promise I'll be back in an hour."

By the time he stepped onto the front porch, he could already hear Kit's voice mingling with the others. Instead of neutralizing things, it sounded like she might be throwing more gas on the fire. All the more reason for him to go now, before things got more heated.

He drove slowly, knowing his stop at the shop wasn't likely to take long. It would have been fun to bring Isaac with him again, but since the boy and his grandfather weren't due at Hazel's yet, and Dean had no idea where Floyd lived, it wouldn't be possible today. Maybe next time. The kid seemed to love the shop when Dean took him there after the storm.

He pulled into the parking lot in front of Wolff Gibb's shop, but he had to wait for someone else to leave so he could park. Things were hopping. Maybe Gibb wouldn't even have time to talk to him. He probably should have warned him he was stopping by.

Once inside, Dean noticed a food buffet set up near the front windows. They had moved all the vehicles that were usually on display in the showroom. Plenty of people were milling about, some with plates of food in their hands, but no one looked like they were working. There was chatter, plus music from Dean's era playing in the background, but the sounds that usually emanated from the back shop area were noticeably absent.

He caught the sound of a familiar voice and turned to catch Gibb saying goodbye to an older couple as they made their way toward the front door. Hoping to catch him quick to weigh in on the red paint color he'd phoned about, Dean approached him, hand extended.

Gibb looked happy to see him. "Hey there, my man! You picked the perfect day to swing in."

Dean motioned around them. "Yeah. It looks like you're having a party, but my invitation must have gotten lost in the mail."

Gibb chuckled. "We *are* having a party. For all past customers, plus my staff. We do this once a year. Same weekend every August. No fussy snail mail invitations. Just a quarter-page ad in the paper—which I'll probably skip next year, since the paper is only a few pages these days due to a dramatic drop in readership—plus an email blast. I probably don't have your email in our system yet. But be sure to grab a plate before you go!"

Dean thought back to the smell of burnt food at Hazel's and decided grabbing a little something here might be a smart idea. "I'll do that. Hey, I'm sorry I didn't call first, but I ended up coming back to town this weekend with Kit for a deal with her family. I thought I'd try to catch you and have a look at those two paint colors you were debating between. If you don't have time, though, with your shindig and all, it can wait."

He would have loved to prod Gibb to get the Mustang's renovations done sooner than they'd initially agreed, given Kit's comment about a drive to see the fall colors. But timing was everything, and Gibb had his hands full at the moment. Dean knew that.

"Nah, it's not a problem. Let's go take a quick peek. Actually, there's something else I wanted to visit with you about, too, so I'm glad you stopped in."

At the shop owner's last words, Dean imagined even more dollar bills flying out of his wallet to pay for the updates on the Mustang. Or make that *hundred*-dollar bills. Vintage car restoration was an expensive business.

"Follow me out back," Gibb said, and Dean had to hurry to keep up with the shorter man's purposeful stride. "I shuffled all the cars around, and the Mustang is back by my second building. But don't worry, it's safe back here. The fence keeps the riffraff out."

Dean wasn't concerned. "Are you kidding? If Kit's Mustang hadn't been safely stored here with you, it would have been annihilated during that storm."

Gibb slowed as he approached the Mustang. "That's right. I remember you mentioning Kit's grandmother's garage coming down. Well, here she is. Check out the interior. I had an expert come through town a couple weeks back, does a great job on old leather, and I convinced him to get your Mustang knocked off the list."

When Gibb swung the door open, Dean leaned in. Sure enough, the improvements were impressive. He could smell new leather, though the seats still displayed the patina he knew Kit loved. Plus, new seat belts draped neatly over the repaired seats.

Straightening, he gave Gibb an appreciative nod. "Those look amazing!"

"They do, don't they?" Gibb nodded, obviously pleased with the quality of work his team provided. He took two paint swatches off the dash. "We've started doing the body repair work, but as you can see, there's more to be done. She isn't ready for that paint job yet, but I'd like to at least get the shade nailed down so I can be sure to have enough on hand when the time is right. Here are two that I think would work nicely."

Dean accepted the rectangular cards from Gibb, each as big as his hand, and together the two men debated the merits of each, eventually deciding on the brighter hue.

"This old girl deserves to shine," Dean said, tapping the roof. "And my wife will look great in it."

"Wife, huh? Last I heard, you hadn't set a date yet. Congrats, man!"

He opened his mouth to correct Gibb, but then closed it. He'd slipped, using the term "wife," but hopefully, by the time Kit got to take the Mustang for the first spin after the renovation was done, they *would* be married. He hoped he wasn't tempting fate. Maybe he should call Jackie. He suspected she'd love to help him plan something simple—just the way Kit said she wanted it.

And they could start living as man and wife once and for all.

Trying to keep his attention on the task at hand, he took a deep breath and prepared himself for bad news. "You mentioned there was something else you needed to talk to me about. So? Lay it on me. What other expensive repairs have you discovered? I knew to keep a few extra dollars in reserve for contingencies, but I'm hoping you aren't going to break me with your news."

His question seemed to confuse Gibb for a minute. Then the man laughed. "Actually, it doesn't have anything to do with your Mustang."

"That's a relief. My wallet thanks you," Dean joked. "But if it's not about the car, what did you want to talk about?"

"About Isaac."

"Isaac?" It was a surprise to hear Gibb say the name. "The kid I brought in here with me last time? God, tell me he hasn't been hanging around and causing trouble. If so, I apologize for introducing him to your place."

Gibb shook his head, waving a hand to interrupt. "It's not that. I don't know if you remember, but I invited him to stop back anytime. Not for an actual job—he's too young—but because he seemed interested in the cars, and I really respected his old man. Shame the way he died. Hits a little too close to home for me, if I'm being honest."

Dean thought back to what little Isaac had shared with him. "What actually happened to his father? I know he's dead, but that's about all I know."

The shorter man grimaced. "A jack failed, crushing Kane, Isaac's old man, to death under a car. To make matters worse, Isaac was the only one around, and he had to run for help. Kane shouldn't have been doing work like that alone."

Horrified, Dean let this sink in. "Wait . . . you said Isaac was there. So he wasn't alone."

"A young kid like that doesn't count. Around here, no one can work under one of those big jacks without someone else nearby, in case there's trouble. Learned that the hard way. Damn near the same thing took my dad out."

"Wow," he said as the shocks kept coming. "I had no idea."

Wolff Gibb jammed a thumb toward his office. "I saw you looking at my graduation certificates on the wall behind my desk. Didn't you ever wonder how a law student from Stanford ended up in a joint like this?"

Dean paused, taken aback, but nodded. "Honestly, yeah, the thought crossed my mind."

Gibb shrugged. "It all happened a long time ago. When my dad died, I had to figure out what to do with this place. I decided this was a better fit for me than a courtroom. But back to Isaac. He took me up on my offer, came in for an hour or two almost every day. I was concerned, to be honest. Worried he was helping out too much instead of just observing. I felt guilty about the free labor—I can't put him on the payroll at his age. When I talked to him about it, he begged for me to let him keep coming. Said something about learning the basics because he has big plans to work on vintage cars after engineering school. Do you know anything about that?"

"A little. The kid has some good ideas. Honestly, he's got me intrigued enough to do a little digging of my own. Believe it or not, I'll be seeing Isaac and his grandfather right after I leave here."

"Really?" Gibb said, sounding surprised.

Dean pulled his phone out to check the time. "Yeah, and actually, I need to get going. Isaac and his grandfather are joining us for dinner at

Hazel's. Do you need me to convince him he can't spend so much time here? Is he getting underfoot?"

Someone hollered out the back door for Gibb. One of their top customers was inside waiting to see him. Gibb held up a finger, then turned back to Dean.

"Nah. It's not that. He's fun to have around. At least, he *was*. But I think something might be going on with him. It has me a little worried."

"All right," Dean said, stowing his phone again. "I'm listening."

"About a week and a half ago, I caught him going through my desk. It was really odd, and when I asked him what he was looking for, he got belligerent. All red and flustered. Completely out of character for the kid. At first I thought he was looking for a pen or something, but he acted guilty, which shot my BS antenna up. Haven't seen much of him since. When he stops in, it's obvious he's trying to avoid me, but it's almost like he can't help himself. Like he *needs* to be around the cars. Last time I saw him was Wednesday, and I told him to stop by today. Look, my gut tells me he's getting into something he shouldn't be. I feel for the kid. Trauma does a number on anyone. But I don't know him outside the walls of this place. I thought you'd want to know, since you're the one who brought him in. See what you think if you talk to him later. That's all I ask."

Dean's phone vibrated in his back pocket with an incoming text. "I'll do that. Thanks for looping me in. I'll give you a shout if I find anything out. Poor kid. He has so much potential, but maybe not enough of a support system."

"Happens to too many kids these days," Gibb said, shaking his head.

He followed Gibb back through the main showroom, and it wasn't until he was back in his vehicle that he remembered he hadn't grabbed any food off the buffet.

His stomach growled. Hopefully Kit had managed to get something edible on the dining room table for Hazel's little dinner party.

CHAPTER THIRTY

Kit hoped Floyd and his grandson wouldn't stand Hazel up. It was already ten minutes past four, but there was no sign of them yet. Dean was late, too.

She hated it when people weren't on time. It felt so . . . disrespectful.

After the burning of the brownies, Mia had been more than content to turn the reins for the dinner party over to Kit.

A car door slammed, and by the time she'd drained the pasta, heavy footsteps pounded up the stairs leading into the back porch off the kitchen. Dean strode in, a guilty flush on his cheeks.

"I'm here," he said, hurrying to her side and dropping a kiss on top of her head—something he wouldn't have done if they weren't alone in the kitchen. "I'm sorry I'm late. I know you hate that. Things were hopping at the shop today. Some kind of customer appreciation deal. Plus I got caught up in a longer discussion with the owner than I'd expected."

Kit dumped the drained noodles back into the heavy pan and covered it to keep things warm. "Is everything all right with my car?"

"It is, and boy, is she going to look *preeeeetty* when she's done," he assured her, helping himself to a breadstick on a nearby platter.

She slapped at his hand.

"What? I'm starving! Where is everybody? It smells good in here now. What did they burn?"

"Just the brownies. Marge is dropping off cookies, so we'll still have dessert. Our guests are late." She shrugged, trying to act nonchalant about this. "Mom and Grandma ran upstairs to change, and I don't know what's taking them so long. If Floyd and Isaac stand Grandma up, I will not be happy. She's excited about this."

Dean tore off a hunk of bread and popped it into his mouth, talking around the bite. "You're cute when you're feisty. I love it when you get all tough and protective of Hazel."

"She *had* to be tough," another voice joined them from the archway between the kitchen and Hazel's dining room. "Unfortunately, my daughter learned early on that too many people have a tendency to disappoint you and your loved ones."

Mia stepped into the room, and Kit thought she looked a little more like the woman she remembered. She'd washed and styled her hair, and she might have even bothered to put on a little makeup. The understated, knee-length blue dress she wore looked appropriate for a casual, late summer dinner party.

"Hello. You must be Dean. I'm Mia. The feisty one's mother."

Dean looked momentarily taken aback, glancing between mother and daughter, but then he dropped the breadstick and stepped toward Mia, one hand extended. "Dean Adams. It's nice to meet you, Mia. I have to say, I can see the family resemblance."

Kit hoped he wasn't going to offer the standard line that he'd heard so much about her, because most of what she'd shared with him about her mother wasn't exactly flattering. But she needn't have worried. Her fiancé was self-aware enough not to step on *that* landmine.

Mia gave a soft smile. "That might have been true once, but while my daughter here has bloomed into a beautiful woman, I'm afraid the life I lived sucked plenty of life out of me."

When he frowned, she made a sniffing sound. "Come now. Let's not pretend Kit hasn't been bending your ear for some time about all the troubles I've caused this family. To be honest, it was probably even worse than she described. I can't change the past, but I'm here now, and I vow to do my best to live a better future."

Kit blinked, distracted by Mia's declaration and thus forgetting to turn the burner down under the spaghetti sauce that was boiling hotter than necessary. A wayward bubble of the sauce popped, splattering her wrist with the steaming liquid. She pulled her arm back, taking a sharp breath. Dean hurried to wet a dishcloth.

Hazel yelled something from upstairs.

"You see to her, Dean," Mia said, pointing at Kit's wrist, "and I'll run upstairs to see what Mother needs. Her guests should be here shortly."

"Are you sure they're still coming?" Kit asked, flicking the sauce from her injured arm.

Mia nodded before turning away. "Floyd called. He apologized for their tardiness, but they'll be here by 4:30."

As her voice faded, Dean captured Kit's left hand and dabbed at the small red welt forming on her wrist. "Are you all right?"

She pulled the wet rag from his hand and held it against the spot. "I'll be fine. It's nothing. So, there she is. My illustrious . . . or should I say, *notorious* . . . mother. What do you think?"

He paused, as if trying to decide what kind of answer she wanted out of him.

His reaction struck her as funny, and she smiled as she turned the burner down under the roiling sauce. "Wait. Don't even answer that. I know she seems, I don't know . . . *normal* . . . right? Maybe that'll last. Probably it won't. But let's try to do like you said: give it time and get to know our mothers better. Besides, tonight is for Hazel, and I just want this to be a nice dinner. For her sake."

The back door opened, and Marge rushed into the kitchen carrying one of those aluminum tins that is such a staple of summer. "Oh, good! Here are those cookies. They're Mom's favorite. I'll see you later!"

Kit watched, surprised, as her aunt headed back out. "Wait! Where are you going? Aren't you going to stay and eat?"

Marge stopped with one hand on the door. "No. I've had enough of my big sister for a while. Besides, I have plans tonight. You kids have fun! Oh, and hello, Dean, it's good to see you again."

With that, Marge was gone.

Dean stole a peek at the cookies, then opened the cupboard that held plates. He'd spent enough time at Hazel's through the years to be comfortable in her kitchen. He counted out a stack and moved them down to the counter. "I take it the sisters still aren't seeing eye to eye?"

The doorbell rang.

Kit hung the dishtowel she'd been using on her burned wrist over the oven handle, straightening her blouse. "I'm not sure that will ever happen. Now, whatever happens tonight, I'm glad you're here. It's nice to know I have someone in my corner."

She suppressed a sigh when she spied him sneaking one more bite of his pilfered breadstick, but was appreciative when he followed her to the front entry.

"I've always got your back," he whispered behind her, and, knowing it was true, she smiled. She still didn't trust Mia for an inch, but she knew the blowup with Dean over his secret daughter was one storm they'd weathered together.

She just hoped this evening wouldn't blow up another storm. Their summer had been eventful enough.

Hazel and Floyd chatted like old friends over the spaghetti and breadsticks. Kit wondered how long they'd known each other. Both made obvious efforts to include the rest of them in their conversation, but Kit sensed the two senior citizens might be up to something.

Isaac was in a sullen mood. The teen responded appropriately when spoken to, but he wasn't the same talkative kid who'd helped her move out the water-soaked mattresses in late June. She could tell that Floyd was working extra hard to bring the boy out of his shell, but nothing seemed to work. Dean shot her a worried look, and she wondered if he'd noticed the teenager's change in behavior, too.

Mia, having no frame of reference for any of the happenings at her mother's home, was relatively quiet, but at least she was a more active participant in the discussions than Isaac.

Once everyone had finished the main meal, Kit rose to clear the dishes. The people Hazel and Floyd were gossiping about were strangers to her, and she noticed Isaac discretely fiddling with his phone.

"I'll help with dessert," Dean offered, getting to his feet.

They scraped the plates and put them in the sink to soak while Hazel and Floyd kept the conversation going at the table. Kit caught Dean over by the coffeepot, away from anyone's line of sight in the dining room. She leaned in close and kept her voice down.

"I think things are going all right, don't you?"

He nodded, but then, as if reconsidering, shrugged. "Except for Isaac."

She was glad he'd noticed, too. "I know. I'm a little worried about him. He's like a different kid tonight."

Dean lowered his voice even further. "I meant to tell you something I heard this afternoon about the boy, but I forgot."

"Really? About Isaac?"

"Yeah . . . remember how I took him with me to the shop where they're fixing your Mustang? It was the morning after the big storm. The owner over there actually knew Isaac's dad, if you can believe that. They ran in the same car circles. Anyway, on that first visit, Gibb saw that the kid has this fascination with muscle cars and invited him back. I guess Isaac went back lots of times after that. But lately he hasn't been himself. Gibb is worried about him, too. Apparently the kid has a dark past. Lots of tragedy."

"What are you two lovebirds doing in there?" Hazel yelled from the other room. "I'm ready for one of Marge's famous orange cookies you promised!"

"Be right there, Grandma," Kit called, then turned back to Dean. "I hope Isaac's okay. He seems like such a great kid."

"I hope so, too . . ."

Kit watched him retrieve the disposable container Marge had brought the cookies over in and retreat to the dining room, wishing he sounded more optimistic. She remembered some of Dean's stories about helping his mother with his three younger brothers and knew he had plenty of experience with sullen young men. She threaded her fingers through as many coffee mugs as she could with one hand and picked up the pot with her other, following him out of the kitchen.

Isaac had downed two of the orange treats before anyone else had coffee or cookies.

"Should I tell Marge you approve of her orange drop cookies, then?" Kit asked, offering him what she hoped was a warm smile.

Isaac shrugged. "Sure. Whatever. Hey, Gramps, can I go? Jason said he can swing by and pick me up."

"Jason who?" Hazel demanded, even though Isaac had been speaking to Floyd.

"Jason Carbo."

Both Mia and Hazel stiffened. Dean must have noticed their reactions, because he looked Kit's way, but she shrugged. The name didn't mean anything to her.

"Just curious," Hazel said, but now she looked flustered all of a sudden. "Floyd, why don't you let the boy go?"

"Really?" the older man said, looking surprised.

Hazel nodded, and Floyd sighed.

"Fine. You can go. But you have to be home by ten."

"Ten?" Isaac shot back. "I'm *fifteen*, and summer is almost over! Why do I have to be home so early?"

Kit admired the unflinching stare Floyd gave the boy. "Because I said so. I can't stay awake past ten, and I have to make sure you are home."

"Fine," Isaac bit out, leaving the table. Kit doubted his ride was here yet, but the teen had apparently had enough of Hazel's dinner party. He took two steps toward the front door but stopped and came back, helping himself to a couple more cookies. She caught the boy's eye, and for the first time since he'd arrived, Isaac's face lit up with the same smile he'd worn the day he'd helped her at the house. "Tell Marge her cookies are great."

The knot of worry in her chest over the boy's behavior loosened. If anyone had asked her why Isaac's surly attitude concerned her, she couldn't have explained herself, but that quick smile helped her relax all the same. The front door opened and closed, and she pushed her chair back, but her grandmother held up a hand to stop her.

"Sit, Kit. I'm not finished with my coffee yet."

She sank back down, noticing her grandmother hadn't even touched her coffee, and she remembered her earlier intuition that something was ... *brewing*. Did Hazel have an ulterior motive for gathering them all for this dinner? As if this question summoned the answer, the older woman cleared her throat, then looked to both Mia and Kit.

"Floyd and I want to go on a trip."

"A trip?" Kit said, caught off guard. "You two want to take a trip together? Why?"

Hazel frowned. "Why does anyone want to travel? To have fun! To see some sights. It's been a tough summer, what with the storm damage around here and all. Besides, Floyd and I have been talking about going to Branson for months."

"Branson, Missouri?" Kit remembered the clothes she'd found laid out across her grandmother's bed. "Wait ... were you packing to go to Branson the night the storm hit?"

"I was," Hazel confirmed. "Floyd even had a friend lined up for Isaac to stay with. I hadn't mentioned it to you, Kit, because I thought you might try to talk me out of it. You hadn't even met my Floyd yet."

Kit didn't miss the "*my* Floyd" part of her comment, and based on the looks exchanged across the table, Dean and Mia caught it, too.

"But then that blasted storm blew through here and messed everything up. The folks at the hotel down there allowed us to reschedule, but they said it has to be within sixty days. Kit, when you got back from Hawaii, you told me how much fun you had with your friends. I want to experience that, too, while I still can."

Mia cleared her throat and leaned forward, hands clasped around her empty mug. "Branson sounds fun, Mother, but you just got out of the hospital. I'm not sure it's a good idea. What if something happens? Are the two of you driving?"

Hazel pointed in Floyd's direction. "He'll drive. I understand your concern. But when you get to be my age, you realize you can either keep moving and squeeze every ounce of living out of life, or you can sit and wait."

"Wait?" Kit repeated. "Until what? Wait until you're well enough to travel?"

"No, dear girl. Wait until you *rot*. Until you fade away."

Her smile meant she was kidding, but Kit didn't see the humor.

"Don't joke about that, Grandma."

Hazel shook her head. "Dear girl, I'm not really kidding. Someday you'll understand. But to be clear, this isn't up for discussion. We *are* going. We just need help with one thing."

"Isaac?" Mia said.

Floyd inclined his head toward Mia. "That's right. My friend is unavailable next weekend."

"Next weekend?" Kit asked. "So soon?"

"Yes, Kit, next weekend," Hazel confirmed. "We only had sixty days, remember? And they didn't have much available."

Mia helped herself to another cookie. "Isaac can stay here with me so the two of you can go, Mother."

Kit balked at the idea. "Here? But there isn't even a *bed* for him! And, no offense, Mia, but what do *you* know about monitoring a teenager?"

Mia eyed Kit as she took a bite of her orange cookie, considering this harsh comment, then set the cookie on her napkin and offered a small smile.

"I guess I deserve that, Kit. I wasn't here for you or your brothers when you were kids. But maybe this is where my ill-spent teen and young adult years might serve us all. I know the tricks. I know the trouble kids can get into. And it just so happens that I know the family of the boy Isaac is hanging out with—which needs to change. Floyd, you may not know the Carbo family, but I do, and so does Hazel. This kid might be a couple generations removed, but the Carbo I knew almost killed me. That is *not* a family you want your grandson having anything to do with. Maybe if I tell Isaac the truth about what happened to me, it'll scare him straight."

The ruddiness in Floyd's cheeks paled.

"You are right, Mia," Hazel said. "Tonight is the last night Isaac can afford to hang out with that Carbo boy. As far as our trip goes, I was hoping you'd offer to help with Isaac." She reached out and tapped the top of Mia's hand. "Thank you, dear. That settles it, then. We leave next Friday! I'm confident you can keep Isaac out of trouble while we're gone."

Kit couldn't sleep. The hotel bed was smaller than her king-size one at home. Dean was uncomfortable and restless. She'd been staring at the strips of light that undulated across the ceiling for hours, watching them shift ever so slightly when the curtains waved softly in the cool stream of air pushed out by the air-conditioner.

They should have planned to drive home after dinner instead of staying a second night.

"What's wrong?" Dean asked, his voice husky with sleep as it floated up in the darkness.

"This bed sucks," she said, though she knew that wasn't the real reason sleep eluded her.

She felt him shift to face her. The light on the ceiling didn't reach them down below.

"Since when does an uncomfortable bed keep you from sleeping? Remember the way you could sleep like the dead on your old mattress in your room at Hazel's?"

Kit sucked in a breath. "You mean the room that is, once again, my mother's, with a new bed to boot?"

He chuckled. "Yeah. That room. Look, Kit, I'm sorry that having your mom back home is so hard on you. I'm sure it's hard on her, too. It's never fun to go back and face your demons."

She sighed. He was right. She knew that, and part of her even admired her mom for trying to reconnect with them again after the countless times she'd screwed up. But she was also pretty sure that it wasn't her mother who was costing her sleep.

"I'm worried," she admitted.

"About Hazel and Floyd? Honey, I think they'll be fine. I'm not crazy about Floyd driving all that way, but they can take as many breaks as he needs to."

"I know. I don't even think it's their trip that's bothering me. I'm worried about Isaac. Tell me everything that guy from the old car place told you about him."

The mattress shifted as he fell back against the bed. Either his eyes were closed, or he was staring up at the black-and-light pattern on the ceiling, too.

"I will. I promise. But can it wait until morning?"

She tapped the face of her phone on the bedside table. "Technically it *is* morning."

He groaned. "Fine. But you are going to owe me."

She grinned and snuggled into the side of his warm body. "I'll figure out a way to repay you."

So he repeated it all, and Kit pressed herself even closer to his side as the horrors poor Isaac had faced sent shivers through her. When he finished, silence settled across the dark room again.

She didn't know what to say. No child should have to experience the horrific losses of both parents the way Isaac had. The fact he'd been present for both deaths elevated the tragedies tenfold. Before Dean had repeated what he knew of Isaac's background, she'd been thinking Isaac reminded her of her brothers: absentee parents, grandparents doing their best to guide a lost kid. Now she knew Isaac's situation was so much worse.

After a while, Dean's breathing evened out, and she thought he might have fallen back asleep.

As she lay there in the dark, she continued to worry about the teenage boy. Had he made it home by ten? Why was he hanging out with a kid from the wrong side of the tracks? Was the Carbo kid the reason Isaac seemed to be losing his sunny disposition?

Mia thought she might be able to help the boy, but Kit had countless doubts in that arena.

As the light of dawn framed the ineffective curtains, Kit wished she could sit Isaac down, give the kid a hug, and assure him that everything would be all right. But she had no business making a promise like that. He had a tough road ahead of him.

Maybe she should call Annie and tell her about all this. Isaac would start at her school in a few short weeks. And as principal, she might have some insight into the Carbo boy. Isaac needed a firm ally in his corner. Kit remembered how she used to wish she had someone like that—besides her grandparents, who always tried their best.

Sleep finally found her, but just before she dozed off, she wondered if *she* could ever be that person for Isaac.

Chapter Thirty-One

A WEEK LATER, KIT worried she would suffer through another restless night, given her concerns about Hazel being on the road with Floyd and whether Mia could handle Isaac, but sleeping in her own bed made a big difference. Dean wasn't home with her. He'd worked late packing things up over at his apartment. He planned to move most of his things over to her place the next day.

Ring-ring-ring! The jarring noise from her cell phone yanked Kit out of a sound sleep.

Kit groped for her phone in the dark as her sleep-sodden mind struggled to function.

Had something happened to her grandmother? She never should have agreed to that ridiculous road trip.

But as the cobwebs of sleep cleared, Kit knew it wasn't her decision to make. Hazel didn't need anyone's permission to take a trip.

Her breath hitched when she saw the name displayed on her phone.

Why would Annie be calling her at . . . *two thirty* on a Sunday morning?

"Hello?" she said, doing her best to sound awake.

"Kit? It's Annie. I'm sorry to call in the middle of the night, but I thought you'd want to know."

She sat up and flipped on her bedside light. Chloe jumped up on the end of the bed, watching her as if also concerned. No news delivered at such an ungodly hour could be good.

"What's happened, Annie?" she asked, hearing the panic in her own voice but not caring if Annie noticed.

A staticky sigh. "Probably nothing more than typical teenage shenanigans. But you made me promise to let you know if I heard anything that could involve Isaac this weekend."

"What did he do?" Kit swung her legs over the side of the bed. She wished Dean was next to her, helping her keep calm, instead of sound asleep at his apartment.

"Wait," Annie said, her voice taking on a steadier note. "I didn't say anything was wrong. Look, I'm on a standard text blast that goes out anytime the police encounter something serious with my students. A text came through about ten minutes ago. They just broke up a huge kegger on the west side of town, out near the lake. In fact, it might have even been on the old Camp Barefoot land."

"You mean Owen's land?" Kit asked, trying to follow.

"Maybe. If not on it, then close. The police wrote up a bunch of kids. Some got warnings, some will face charges for minors with alcohol."

Kit sighed, rubbing at her eye. "And you think Isaac was there? That's why you're calling?"

She heard someone say something in the background, and Annie said, "Sorry, that's Henry. He's sick of me waking him up at all hours. Unfortunately, with the school year starting in a couple weeks, there will be more of these. Anyway, back to your question. I don't know if Isaac was there. But they specifically mentioned Jason Carbo, the kid you'd asked me about. He resisted arrest, so he'll be in a bigger heap of trouble than most of the kids. I don't know if Isaac is part of this mess, but if he is, and his grandfather is out of town, who would the police even know to contact? Man, remember when we almost got caught at that keg party when we were seniors? Am I ever glad we got away. I always thought we had Owen to thank for that, the way he drove us out of there right before the cops arrived."

Annie's words conjured up a long-forgotten memory of good music, disgustingly warm keg beer, and hot summer nights. Kit couldn't help but smile. "I guess none of us were perfect, were we?"

"Nope!" Annie laughed. "But some of us were smart enough not to get caught."

Kit's phone buzzed with another incoming call. "Oh, God. Mia is calling. I gotta go."

"Keep me posted!"

She hit the button to accept her mother's call. "Mia, what's going on?"

At first, all she could hear was a soft, muffled crying.

"Mom!" she yelled, unable to help herself. "Is it Isaac? Is he there?"

"No. He's gone. And I have no idea where he is," Mia sobbed. "I never should have offered to watch him."

Kit wanted to scream *I TOLD YOU SO!* through the phone. It took every ounce of restraint she could muster, but she calmly told her mother to sit tight, that she'd be there in two hours.

She called Annie back immediately, her stomach sinking, and asked that she make a special call to the police. If they had Isaac, or had seen him at the bust, could Annie please explain the unique situation to them and let them know Kit would be there just as soon as she could?

Then she called Dean. He was at her door before she was even dressed. He'd insisted on going with her when she called to let him know that

Isaac was missing. It was a huge relief to have him at her side as he drove them through the darkness toward Ruby Shores.

Ruby Shores. She really had to stop with these late-night dashes back home.

"But what if something awful has happened?" Kit whined, not for the first time.

Dean shook his head. "Stop thinking the worst. Even if he got caught up in the keg bust, we'll help get it straightened out."

"But didn't you say that Floyd isn't even technically his legal guardian?"

Dean sighed as he flipped on the windshield wipers. It was sprinkling. "Isaac hinted at that, but I'm not sure what the real story is."

"I can't believe Mia let him go! We never should have trusted her to keep an eye on a teenager."

A flash of lightning illuminated the car's interior, but Kit couldn't hear any thunder. She caught the disapproving glance Dean sent her way.

"What?" she demanded. She didn't want to be cross with him, but her nerves were stretched taut.

"Kit . . . you and I have never raised a teenager."

She snorted. "Actually, we've *both* had to fill the parent role."

"What do you mean?"

"Think about it!" She adjusted the car's air vent because it was drying out her eyes. "I usually felt more like my brothers' mother than their big sister. And when your father died, you had to step into his shoes and help your mother raise your younger brothers."

"Hmm . . ." But he didn't say more, seemingly lost in his thoughts.

The minutes ticked away. Kit kept battling with her own imagination, trying to not think the worst.

"It's different," Dean said finally, his words echoing within the quiet confines of the car.

"What's different?" she asked, startled out of her musings.

He ran a hand around the steering wheel, then dropped it onto the seat between them. "Our situations. We were never the ones ultimately responsible for those kids. In your case, the buck stopped with your grandparents. Yes, I know you were a huge help to them, but you weren't alone. And it was the same with me. Dad's death shook Mom to her core, and sometimes I resented how much she relied on me, but she was still *there*, you know?"

Kit considered this. He was right that neither of them was the last word for their younger brothers. But Mia only had to keep Isaac safe for one lousy weekend, and she hadn't even been able to do that. "I knew Mia couldn't handle it."

Dean blew a raspberry. "I get why you're disappointed. I bet it feels like you take two steps forward with her, but then another step back."

She nodded. She thought he'd summed up her current relationship with her mother perfectly.

"But . . ." he started, his words fading off.

"What? Don't tell me I need to cut her some slack. I did that for the first thirty years of my life, and look where it got me."

"No," he said, waving his free hand. "That isn't what I'm saying. I just don't think we should be so quick to judge when we've never truly parented a teenager ourselves."

She snorted. "*We* could do better."

But she caught his shrug out of the corner of her eye.

Their headlights fell on the sign for Ruby Shores, and she had a sense of déjà vu.

He flipped on his blinker. "You sure about that?"

It looked like every light burned in Hazel's house when they pulled into the back. Kit used her key to open the door between the back porch and the kitchen.

"Isaac, is that you?" Mia hurried into the room but came up short at the sight of her daughter, deflating. "Oh. Kit. It's you."

"I told you I was coming."

She nodded, then caught Kit up in a surprise hug.

Kit froze at her touch. Her mother hadn't hugged her since she was twelve years old.

"I'm so sorry," the woman mumbled against her hair.

Dean stepped into the kitchen. He would know that Mia's touch would make Kit extremely uncomfortable, and she was thankful when he cleared his throat. When Mia didn't loosen her grip, he did it a second time. Finally, she dropped her arms and took a step back.

"Oh. Hi, Dean. I didn't know you were coming with Kit. But I'm glad to see you. We need to find Isaac. I refuse to call Hazel and Floyd and admit to them that I lost the boy."

Kit dropped her purse on the counter, fishing out her phone. "You still haven't heard from him yet, or anyone else?"

Mia narrowed her eyes at her daughter. "Who else would I hear from? You promised you wouldn't call Floyd yet!"

"Oh, stop it," Kit admonished her mother as she hit the *return call* button for Annie. "Haven't you done enough? The last thing we need is for you to get all hysterical on us."

"Kit . . ." Dean said.

She caught his warning. She couldn't get hysterical right now, either.

She was relieved when her friend picked up. "Oh, thank God, Annie. What have you learned? Was Isaac at the party?"

"What party?" Mia asked. But she could only hear Kit's end of the conversation.

Annie reported that the police had nothing on Isaac.

"Really?" Kit asked. "He wasn't there? I was so sure that was where he disappeared to. Maybe he gave the police a false name?"

As she listened to Annie explain that the police always check identification if the kids are old enough to drive, she noticed Dean pull out his phone and hold it up to his ear. Maybe it was Isaac on the other end of the phone, calling Dean.

"I appreciate you checking for me, Annie. I'll keep you posted, too."

Mia had also noticed Dean take the call, and both women waited, watching as the man nodded, a look of relief stealing across his features.

When he hung up, he held up both hands. "I know where he is. And he's okay."

"Thank God," Mia said, stepping back and fumbling blindly for a chair at the dining table. She collapsed into it.

"Who was on the phone?" Kit said, not as quick to celebrate as Mia.

"Wolff Gibb."

She looked at him blankly. "Who the heck is that?"

He closed the distance between them and looped an arm around her waist. "Breathe, Kit. Isaac is fine. Wolff Gibb is the guy who runs the shop where they're fixing your Mustang. Remember? That was him on the phone. He has motion detector cameras in his parking lot. They went off, and when he checked them from his computer at home, he could see someone wandering around. He hustled down there to see what was going on."

"Did he call the police?"

"No. Gibb is the kind of guy who will handle that type of thing himself if possible. He said he wasn't all that surprised to see it was Isaac. The boy was on the ground next to your car."

Her relief was tinged with confusion. "He found him by my Mustang? Why?"

"Gibb isn't sure. Isaac didn't have his phone with him, and he couldn't remember his grandfather's cell number. Mia's either. So Gibb called the only number he thought might work. Mine. He was shocked to find out I was in town."

His words were finally helping Kit to feel a little better. "Are they still there? At the shop?"

"They are. I told him we'd be right over."

Kit snagged her purse and headed for the back door. "Stay here, Mia. We'll bring him back."

If her mother didn't like that plan, Kit wasn't about to wait around to find out. She ran out the back to Dean's car. When he didn't immediately join her, she tapped the horn.

Two minutes later, he yanked open the driver's-side door. "Christ, Kit! I had to use the bathroom. The sun isn't even up yet—your grandma's neighbors are going to call the cops on *you* for the horn! You've got me running all over like a chicken with my head cut off. Chill!"

As he yanked his seat belt on, Kit glanced his way, and, absurdly, despite the tension on Dean's face and their worry over Isaac, she couldn't help but laugh. But her unexpected reaction did nothing to calm him down. Still, she couldn't stop herself. By the time they'd exited the alley onto the street, her eyes were streaming.

"Are you laughing," he said, "or are you crying?"

"I'm laughing because your zipper is down. I'm sorry I rushed you."

Dean immediately anchored the steering wheel with one knee while he zipped up his pants. The sight of this caused Kit to burst in a whole new wave of laughter.

"I'm honestly not sure why I'm so emotional," she admitted when she had control of herself again. "I'm mostly just relieved. Dean, we barely know this kid. Why was I so scared?"

"He's a special kid."

They'd arrived, and Dean pulled into the rear parking lot behind the shop.

"There they are!" Kit cried, pointing through the windshield and flinging her door open before Dean reached a full stop.

She ran toward Isaac. The boy was seated on the ground next to a guy she didn't recognize. That must be Gibb, the man who called Dean. She skidded to a halt in front of them and searched Isaac's features, as if she couldn't be sure he was all right until she saw it for herself.

"Hey, Kit," he said, a sheepish look on his face.

She heaved a massive sigh, then dropped onto the ground beside him. "You scared me to death, Isaac!"

"Jeez, I'm sorry. What is everyone so worked up about? I couldn't sleep so I went for a walk. Mia was snoring, and I didn't want to wake her. I had an idea that kept gnawing at me, so I headed down here to check it out." The boy paused when he saw Dean walk up. "Dean! Hey, I didn't even know you guys were back in town tonight until Gibb told me."

Dean crossed his arms over his chest, gazing pointedly at Isaac. Even Kit could feel the displeasure radiating off him. There was no way the teenager could miss it.

"We weren't," Dean said, his voice low.

Isaac flinched. "Oh."

"Yeah. Oh." Dean dropped his hands, then turned to Gibb. "Thanks, man. I owe you. Hope he didn't cause you too much trouble."

Gibb got up off the ground with a grunt, slapping dust off the seat of his pants. "Hell of a lot less trouble than some prowler would have been. Remember, Isaac, my invitation to drop in 'anytime' meant between the hours of eight a.m. and six p.m. And only after three on a school day. There may be a fence, but I don't want you down here at night. It isn't safe. Obviously, the fence did nothing to keep *you* out. I need to go inside and reset the cameras. We good here?"

"We will be," Dean assured the man.

"Night, then."

Both Dean and Isaac watched Gibb head inside, then Dean held out a hand to the boy. "Get up."

Isaac groaned, but he clasped the offered hand and allowed Dean to hoist him to his feet. "I'm really sorry if I put you guys out. I can't believe you drove all the way from Minneapolis."

Kit shifted onto her knees, then rose to her feet. "I was afraid you might have gotten arrested, Isaac. A bunch of kids got busted at that keg party tonight, and I thought maybe you were there with your friend. With Floyd out of town, I didn't know who the police would even call."

Either Isaac was a great actor, or he didn't know anything about a kegger getting broken up.

She sighed. "My friend Annie called me. I'd told her a little about you, and that my mom was babysitting you this weekend."

This drew a grunt out of him. "I'm too old for a babysitter."

"You know what I mean. Anyway, she's the high school principal, so she's in the know if any kids get in trouble with the law."

"Still don't see how that has anything to do with me," Isaac said, falling in behind Dean when he motioned for them to follow him back to the car.

"It was a big party. The police broke it up, and a lot of kids are getting charged with a variety of things. Your buddy Jason Carbo got thrown in jail for resisting arrest."

At this, Isaac stumbled over his awkwardly large feet. "I've decided I can find better company than Carbo. Mia helped me see that."

"Really?! *Mom* convinced you the kid is bad news?"

Dean opened the door and motioned for him to get in. Isaac ducked into the backseat. Kit took her seat up front.

"It's not like we were friends or anything," he said, clicking his seat belt on.

"But you were hanging out with him last weekend," she said.

Isaac was smart. If he knew they didn't approve of the Carbo kid, he might deny spending time with him, true or not.

"First and last time," the boy said. "Dean, turn the air on, will you? It's stuffy back here."

She shifted to look back at him. "You really weren't on your way to the kegger and just hadn't gotten there yet?"

He dropped his head back against the seat. "I *swear*. I was just going for a walk. My phone was dead, and I forgot to bring my charger to Hazel's.

I wasn't going to any stupid keg party with a bunch of kids I've never met. Chill."

She noticed Dean grin when the teen used one of his favorite words. She shook her head, then let it rest against the cool glass of the window.

Isaac was safe, and she was exhausted.

They drove off. When they got back to Hazel's, all three exited the vehicle just as the sun's first blush of pink tinged the sky.

"I think I'll be able to sleep now," Isaac said, hurrying for the back of the house.

Kit leaned against the car, watching him go. Once he'd disappeared inside, she turned to Dean, who was waiting on the other side of the vehicle.

"I'm sorry."

"For what?" he asked, pushing away from the car and wandering around the front to her side.

She held her arms out to him and rested her forehead against his chest. "I'd make a terrible mother." Her words were muffled against his favorite T-shirt. "Always overreacting . . ."

He threw his head back and laughed. "I beg to differ. You're caring, you're brave, and you don't take any crap. You'd make a wonderful mother."

As he rocked her gently against him, his words seemed to echo through her heart.

Chapter Thirty-Two

J UST A FEW HOURS later, as she entered the Crystal Café, Kit caught her aunt's eye. She was ringing a customer up at the register, but she pointed toward the back of the restaurant. There Kit found Jackie and Annie huddled over steaming mugs of coffee, so intent on whatever they were talking about that they didn't even notice her until she pulled out a chair. Both jumped back, and Kit would have sworn they looked guilty.

"Why do you look surprised to see me? You two invited me for coffee. What did I miss?"

She'd barely taken a seat before an efficient waiter appeared with a fresh coffee for her. When the other two women stammered, she knew she was on to something.

"All right. You two look like a couple of kids who got caught sneaking downstairs early on Christmas Eve."

Jackie looked at Annie. "We should just tell her."

"Tell me *what*?" Kit's intrigue was increasing. Whatever they were talking about, they looked excited about it.

Annie shrugged at Jackie. "Fine . . . if you don't think he'll be mad."

"He? Who?" Kit asked.

As they continued their vague back-and-forth, she opened a creamer and dumped it into her coffee. She normally took it black, but after her middle-of-the-night wakeup call and yet another mad dash back to Ruby Shores, this was at *least* her fourth cup of coffee today. She may have lost count.

"I don't think he'd care . . ." Jackie said.

Kit slapped the table. "I'm right here! Spill!"

Finally, Jackie looked at her, a wide grin enhancing the smile lines around her chocolate-brown eyes. "I talked to Dean this morning."

Kit shrugged. "I know. I was the one who told him to call you." She had been jumping in the shower when Dean's boss called to ask if he could stop in later that afternoon for an all-hands-on-deck meeting, even though it was Sunday. She remembered Jackie saying she was coming over to Ruby Shores to see her folks for the weekend, and thought maybe he could head back and she could ride home to Minneapolis with Jackie later. "I wanted to stick around here a little longer."

Jackie scooted her chair closer to the table. "You didn't hear what else we talked about, then?"

"While I was in the shower? No. Why?"

Her friend took a deep breath. "I hope it's all right for me to tell you this. I don't think Dean will mind . . ."

Kit could feel the beginning of a headache behind her eyes. "Jackie, our friend Annie here woke me up at two thirty this morning, and I haven't shut my eyes since. Don't play games. What else did Dean want? I'm not in the mood to guess."

"Jeez, fine, don't get crabby on us! This is too fun of a topic."

Then Kit had an idea. "Oh. Wait! I bet I know. Were you picking his brain about where we should take our next girls' trip? Dean travels for work, and he's been to some neat places."

"No," Annie butted in. "It's *my* turn to plan our trip, remember? But it's a great idea to talk to Dean. I'm actually thinking we might need to go around spring break next year, instead of waiting until summer. My spring and summer are going to be crazy. Would that work with both of you? I'd call Lynette and Renee, too, of course."

It was Jackie's turn to slap the palms of her hands on the table. "Ladies. Focus. Yes, Annie, as long as you'll plan our next girls' trip, I'll make the timing work. But let's pull this conversation back to my talk with Dean."

Then a different idea occurred to Kit, and she narrowed her eyes at Jackie. "Did he talk to you about wedding plans?"

"Ding-ding-ding!" Jackie said, rubbing her hands together. "He told me you're finally ready to move ahead. *Tell* me that's true."

Kit thought back to the last few weeks, how she'd felt so much closer to Dean. "It's true. I know you both think I've been dragging my feet for too long, but there were just some things I've been grappling with. Mainly I was worried that Dean would have to miss out on having kids if he married me."

"But now we all know he already *has* a kid. How are things going with his daughter, by the way?" Annie asked.

Kit grinned. "It's only been a couple weeks since the wedding—even though it feels like it's been a year with everything that's been going on over at Hazel's. But I think things are going really well between Dean and Summer. They talk often. He attended their gift opening, even though I had to miss it, and they have dinner planned in a week or two. It isn't exactly how I pictured him being a parent, but that doesn't make it any less special."

One of the waitstaff slid three caramel rolls onto their table, and Kit looked up at her in confusion. The woman shrugged. "Marge told me to."

Kit's stomach grumbled over the welcoming scent of vanilla, brown sugar, and fresh bread.

"Please tell her she's a saint," Jackie said, picking up a fork and diving in. "Keep going, Kit."

Kit picked up her own fork and joined in. "That's about all I have regarding Summer. I like her, too, and really think we'll all be able to build a relationship together."

"So, see? Dean is a *dad*! Now, about your wedding," Jackie tried again, poking her fork in Kit's direction.

"Jackie, I'm not sure what he told you, but I want simple. His daughter's wedding was beautiful, but almost the exact opposite of what I want. I mentioned the justice of the peace to Dean, because that would be easiest, but that might be a bit too extreme."

"I agree," Annie said between bites of her roll. "We can do better than that. We have an idea."

"For what part?" Kit asked, moaning at the scrumptiousness of her first bite.

"The location."

Jackie nodded. "You don't want to wait, right? Are we safe to think this wedding could happen any time now?"

Kit cut another bite off with her fork. "I don't see why not. But, the problem is, any place would require some notice. I picture a small outdoor wedding, but not in the ice and snow. Why? What were you two thinking? Because you seemed awfully excited about something when I got here."

Annie and Jackie exchanged yet another look.

Jackie set her fork down. "What would you think about getting married near Diamond Falls?"

Kit blinked. "Diamond Falls? As in the falls we always visited at summer camp?"

"Exactly!" Jackie cried, earning herself a dirty look from a neighboring table.

"You think I should marry Dean next to Diamond Falls?" Kit asked, stunned by Jackie's suggestion.

"Why not? You mentioned to Dean something about the fall colors. If we planned this wedding for, say, early October, I bet the leaves would look beautiful out there then."

Kit frowned. "Jackie, Owen isn't even doing anything with that land right now. At least he wasn't last year when we went out there and looked around. Has something changed?"

"Nope, not that I know of," Jackie said with a shrug. "And to be honest, I haven't cleared this with him yet. I wanted to talk to you first. But Dean asked me to help him plan something simple, and I think it could be beautiful. If we can't do it at Diamond Falls for some reason, I'll check with Renee to see if we could try Whispering Pines instead."

"You keep saying 'small' and 'nothing fancy.' How many people do you think you'd invite?" Annie asked.

Kit suddenly felt like they were wading into the details, and her appetite deserted her. She set her fork down. "I don't know . . . I haven't thought about it."

Jackie gave her a smile, as if she could sense the way their questions were making Kit's pulse jump. "Don't get spooked. We'll keep this simple. I promise." She dug a pen out of her purse and pulled a clean napkin over for notes.

Kit took a deep breath, knowing she had to face this at some point if she wanted to get the wedding itself behind her. She helped Jackie tally the small number of family and friends she'd want to invite. "Oh, and I'd like to invite Floyd and Isaac, too," she finished.

Jackie paused. "Who?"

"You met them the morning after the big storm, remember? Floyd is Grandma's friend, the one she's in Branson with now. And Isaac is his grandson. The reason I rushed back here?"

Annie pushed her empty plate away. "Speaking of Isaac, I was so relieved when you let me know he wasn't one of the kids involved in that party. I already suspected that was the case when the cop I talked to couldn't find his name on the list. He's back at Hazel's now, and Mia knows to keep a closer eye on him."

Jackie set down her pen. "I feel so out of the loop here. Come on, ladies, what did *I* miss?"

Kit smiled when Jackie's words mirrored the ones she'd said when she'd first joined them for coffee. She gave her the abbreviated version of both the events of the previous twelve hours, but also of the terrible things that brought Isaac to Ruby Shores. When she stopped to take another bite of roll, Jackie was looking at her with an odd expression.

"What?" Kit asked, not liking the look in Jackie's eyes. A bit of caramel dribbled onto her chin, and she wiped at it.

"If I didn't know better, I'd think you were feeling some maternal instincts toward this kid," Jackie said. "You never thought you had it in you to be a mother, but I always knew better. You were so great with my girls when they were growing up."

Normally, Kit would have stopped Jackie right there and told her she was crazy. But, as so often happened in conversations with her oldest friends, they seemed to see through any bluster, right to the core. Maybe it was because of their shared history.

No one—not even Dean—knew her like these girls did.

Though it scared her to say the words out loud, she needed to get something off her chest. "I actually think you're right, Jackie. Can I ask you guys something . . . and you promise you won't laugh?"

Both women made crosses over their hearts.

"What would you say if I told you I've been wondering what it would take for Dean and I to become Isaac's foster parents?"

Jackie's mouth hung open in shock.

Annie recovered quicker. "I'd say that Isaac is one heck of a lucky boy. And I've got some contacts through work that might help."

"You don't think I'm stark raving mad to even suggest it?" Kit asked, shocked at the relief she felt, now that the thought that had been rolling around in her head for some time was out in the open. "I haven't even mentioned it to Dean yet, but something tells me he'd at least consider the idea."

Jackie seemed to recover from her initial shock. Her face lit up and she stood to grab a small stack of napkins off a nearby counter. She held her pen high in the air. "Now we not only have to plan a wedding, but we have to figure out how you can become a foster parent, too. And we've gotta move fast, because school starts in two weeks in Minneapolis, and Isaac needs to be in the same town as his new parents!"

Kit laughed for a second until the truth behind Jackie's words registered.

Parent . . . Had she lost her mind?

EPILOGUE

K IT HELD UP HER left hand, enjoying the way the sunlight glinted off her new wedding band. Diamond Falls provided a stunning background. She smiled, thinking back to the warm glow in Dean's eyes as he'd slipped the set on her finger during the intimate wedding ceremony that was playing out even more perfectly than she could have imagined.

"You did good, Kit Adams," she whispered. She liked the sound of Dean's last name coupled with her first. It felt right to shed her maiden name—a name forever tied to the heavy burdens of her tough childhood. It had taken her nearly fifty years, but she finally felt equipped to set those burdens aside along the bank of the river and let nature sweep them away.

Jackie had helped Dean select the perfect wedding band. Of course, the single stone in the engagement ring would always represent her new husband and the life they were building together. But could he have guessed what the wedding band's five smaller diamonds would symbolize for her?

As if in response to this thought, sunlight glistened, and a tiny prism of color shimmered above her ring. It was almost like wearing a kaleidoscope on her finger. Her family situation had always been tenuous, but her best friends were a consistent force, helping her navigate life.

If not for those four women—her forever friends—Kit wouldn't be standing on the banks of this lake now as a new bride. The same lake where she'd first splashed during summer camp. The Kaleidoscope Girls had helped show her it was safe to build a life with Dean. With their help, she could finally accept that she was worthy of him and his love.

"What are you doing over here, all by yourself?" Jackie stepped up to stand beside her and handed her a fluted glass of champagne.

Kit sighed, then held up the brimming glass, as if toasting the waterfall. "Just thinking about how far I've come since the first time I visited this place. How far we've *all* come, really. How much we've endured, how much we've overcome. How much we've grown."

Jackie smiled. If anyone understood the depth of wonder Kit was feeling, it would be her.

"Thank you for helping Dean pull all of this together so quickly," Kit said. "It's perfect."

"It's the least I could do after you took me in last year." Jackie sipped her champagne. "I was so lucky you were there to help me get back on my feet after I blew my career apart."

While Kit appreciated Jackie's gratitude, she knew *she* was the lucky one. But she didn't press that fact. "When we were kids, did you ever imagine coming back here like this, as adults?"

Jackie considered this, then shook her head. "Not exactly. Once we stopped coming here for camp, I never thought I'd be back. But I never doubted that we'd still be friends."

"I didn't doubt that, either. We'll always have the Kaleidoscope Girls! Sunshine and friends. What more could a girl want?" Kit laughed.

Jackie shrugged. "Well, it turns out there are a few things beyond those basics that we need to live a happy life. But sun and girlfriends certainly provide a strong base. Now, we should probably get back so you can spend time with your guests."

"I suppose you're right."

Together they wandered over to the tables set up along the shale-covered beach of their childhood. A simple meal was available in a buffet-style line—catered by her aunt's café—and ready whenever the bride and groom wanted to eat.

The other three Kaleidoscope Girls sat at a table nearest the water. As Kit approached, she heard snippets of Annie's tale as she shared the old story of the relay race they'd won as a team during that first summer when they were all together. Lynette added her recollections as the tale went on. Annie's and Renee's husbands listened with polite smiles, but Kit knew the two men could never grasp the excitement they'd felt that long-ago day. She loved hearing about the special memory all five of them shared.

After accepting congratulatory hugs from her besties, plus Henry and Matt, Kit moved on, joining her new husband beside the table that held the members of his family who could make the trip on such short notice. Young Mason, Dean's four-year-old nephew, perched on Belinda's lap so he could reach his plate that held tiny squares of cheese, crackers, and mints. It was enough to keep the child from getting crabby with hunger, and also away from the softly lapping waves along the beach that would be tempting to any young boy.

Kit eyed her new mother-in-law with a bit of apprehension—she knew the woman still held reservations where her oldest son's new wife was concerned—but Belinda offered her a tentative smile in return. Not that she blamed Belinda. Kit had dragged her feet on making wedding plans for more than a year after accepting Dean's proposal. But while Belinda's "Welcome to the family" came with a touch of reserve, Dean's brother Nick showed no such qualms as he caught Kit up in a boisterous hug and swung her off her feet. Nick's wife, Candace, laughed as she pulled at her husband's arm, insisting he put Kit down before he made her sick. Kit sent her sister-in-law an appreciative smile once her feet were on solid ground again. She knew she'd found an ally in the younger woman, and perhaps she would help provide the bridge Kit might need to build a solid relationship with Dean's mother.

"Auntie Kit, are we going to eat pretty soon? I'm *starving*," Mason whined, scrunching his little face up in mock dismay and eliciting laughter from other guests.

Dean walked to his mother's side and swung Mason out of her lap and onto his shoulders. The boy whooped in delight. Kit was only sorry that Dean's newly married daughter and his other two brothers hadn't been able to make the wedding on such short notice. Luckily, Belinda was already planning a large, family-filled Thanksgiving where everyone could toast the new couple.

Kit suspected the quiet holidays she'd grown accustomed to might be a thing of the past.

Someone tapped her on the shoulder, and she turned to find Owen standing there, dressed even more casually than her guests. She'd insisted he attend the wedding as a guest, but he'd respectfully declined, choosing instead to stay in the background and make sure the festivities went off without a hitch, since they were using his property. Jackie had reported Owen's initial surprise, followed by his gracious agreement to allow them to plan Kit's small wedding ceremony here.

"Everything going okay, Kit?" he asked. She noticed a circular pouch dangling from his fingers, its outside marked with a diagram of cables hooked up to a battery. "I need to run a quick errand, but I wanted to make sure the caterers have everything they need."

She nodded. "Marge gave me a thumbs-up a few minutes ago, so I think we'll probably eat shortly. Are you sure you won't join us? I can't thank you enough for allowing us to hold our wedding here. I'm sure it was a pain for you to get the grounds looking so nice."

Owen shook his head, grinning. "It's my pleasure. I love how much this place means to all of you. Maybe one of these days we can all sit down and you can help me brainstorm ways to use it. I keep meaning to do more out here than just mow and repair cabin roofs, but I'm still waiting for that spark of inspiration. Anyway, I appreciate the invite to sit, but I need to run. And not to rush you, but remember, night falls earlier now, and it'll cool off pretty quick. You might want to start serving dinner soon."

Kit pulled the soft ivory shawl her Grandma Hazel had crocheted for her a little tighter around her shoulders. "Of course. I'm just going to speak with my family quick, and then we'll eat. Should I be worried that you are holding a set of jumper cables in your hand?"

Owen's eyes skittered toward Dean, still bouncing a noisy Mason on his shoulders, before coming back to meet hers. "No, no worries, Kit. As far as I know, that old Mustang of yours is running like a Swiss watch. It's Logan, actually. My youngest. He's having car trouble back at our house. Again. So, I have to run. But just in case you haven't heard it often enough yet today, you make a beautiful bride. Dean is a lucky man." He dropped a quick kiss on her cheek before turning away with his jumper cables.

Kit felt relief at his words. They had plans for the Mustang.

"We'll eat soon," she said to her in-laws' table, then she walked the last few steps toward the table that housed her family.

Everyone there seemed enthralled as Hazel told the story of how she and Floyd had been a day late getting home from Branson because he'd insisted on stopping to help a young family stranded along the side of the road.

"Strangest thing I've ever seen," she was saying as Kit approached. "All four tires, flat as pancakes. Who knew lightning could do that to a minivan? Do you know they had to put that thing up on a trailer and haul it into a garage so they could use a special wrench to remove the tires? Those young parents had their hands full with three little kids. We couldn't leave them stranded without a vehicle. They were a little leery of accepting our help at first, but eventually they could see that we meant them no harm."

Kit shook her head. Each time her grandmother told the story, the tale got a little taller. The first time she'd heard it, Hazel had said the father flagged them down. She was really playing up their roles as good Samaritans. But she'd never quell the woman's enthusiasm. She suspected both Hazel and Floyd loved the feeling of being needed. At their ages, they were usually the ones needing help, and that had to grate on them.

"There you are, Kit," her brother Tony said, capturing her arm and pulling her closer to the table. "Grandma was just telling us about the family they helped after lightning struck their van."

Kit laughed at the way he wriggled his eyebrows, as if to beg her to save them from having to listen to the entire story again. She squeezed his hand and let her head fall to his shoulder. "I can't tell you how much it means to me that you could get here for this. I only wish Pete could have made it."

Tony released her arm and wrapped his around her shoulders, pulling her close. "Nothing could have kept me away from my big sister's wedding. A day I wasn't sure would ever come. Glad to see Dean is finally going to make an honest woman out of you."

Kit pretended to push him off with a giggle. "You and me both. Say"—she lowered her voice—"have you talked to Mom at all?"

Tony's smile slipped. "I see you aren't calling her Mia anymore?"

"Only when she ticks me off. Which still happens plenty. But overall, she seems like she might have it together for once. What do you think?"

He dropped his arm and stuck both hands in the pockets of his dress pants. "I invited her to ride out here with me from the house, so . . . yeah . . . we talked a little. I told her about my family, her grandkids she hasn't met yet. It was hard. But I think we're making baby steps. She seems like she's clean. Time will tell if she stays that way."

Kit nodded, her eyes finding the woman she used to refuse to call "Mom." She was visiting with Isaac, the two of them laughing about something. It seemed she and the teenager had bonded during their week together.

There'd been no additional trouble with Isaac after the awful night when Kit and Dean raced home to help find him. In fact, Kit's idea about possibly acting as foster parents for Isaac had mushroomed into a real thing. Dean had warmed quickly to the idea when she'd broached it with him. Floyd had as well, admitting he wasn't as up for the challenge of raising a teen as he'd hoped. His relief was great over the suggestion of a different, but still safe, option for the boy he thought of as family. Floyd had even reached out to his daughter, the boy's legal yet uncommitted guardian. The woman had a life of her own that had never included a teenage son of a man she'd only been married to for a short time. Kit struggled to understand how the daughter of someone with Floyd's compassion could be so heartless, but Dean's cautionary advice floated back to her whenever she judged the woman.

Raising a teenager was tough for anyone. Hazel's struggles with Mia were a prime example of that.

Kit couldn't know what other things were going on in Floyd's daughter's life.

Her willingness to pass the responsibility for Isaac off to someone else was ultimately a gift to Kit and Dean. Isaac's initial skepticism when they first sat him down to talk about what they were considering didn't last long. The teen was back to his old self—usually smiling, but still peppered with the moodiness Kit knew every teen felt.

Tony raised a hand in greeting to Nick, pulling Kit's attention back. Her brother knew they were working on becoming Isaac's foster parents, but she had yet to hear his thoughts on the matter. As if he could read her mind, he motioned toward their mother and Isaac as he spoke. "Looks like they enjoy each other's company. Isaac seems like a great kid . . . but are you sure you're taking him on for the right reasons?"

"What do you mean?" She studied Isaac's smiling face. "He *is* a great kid."

"I'm sure he is." Tony sighed. "Kit, you've always said you didn't want kids. Taking on a teenager is a lot of work. And you actually kind of already did that with me and Pete. I know we weren't easy on you."

She shrugged. "*You* weren't too bad, but Pete was a bigger challenge."

They both laughed at the dig against the brother who wasn't there to defend himself.

"Why are you doing it?" Tony asked.

Kit wasn't sure how to respond when the answer was so complicated. "It feels like there are more good reasons to do it than bad reasons to scare us away. Isaac needs stability. And I think we can give him that. Dean has always wanted to be a dad. I didn't think I ever wanted to be a mom, but I can see that was my trauma talking. *Our* trauma. I like the idea of helping Isaac figure out how to navigate this world."

Tony nodded, then gave her a quick hug. "I guess that's reason enough. I wish you luck, sister. Now, I see dear Aunt Marge over there by the food, waving madly at us to get this party started. What do you say? Should we eat?"

Kit glanced toward the buffet table, then noticed her mother getting to her feet. "In a minute," she told her brother. "Please go talk to Marge. Tell her to let her team know we'll eat in five minutes. And remind her she's a guest, not the hired help today."

"I'll try." Tony winked. "Good luck with Mom."

Knowing she had to hurry, but feeling drawn to her mother, Kit joined the woman along the shoreline. The two remained silent for a minute, both of them gazing at the horizon.

"I'm glad I could be here today to help you celebrate," Mia finally said. "Dean is a wonderful man. And he's lucky to have you."

"I'm the lucky one," Kit said, feeling a prick of self-doubt and hating herself for it.

Maybe Mia sensed it. She nodded. "You're both lucky. Marriage isn't something to be taken lightly. I learned that too late. But you, my dear, have always been much smarter than me."

Kit tried to let the words sink in. She wasn't used to receiving compliments from her mother, and she wished the woman wasn't so filled with her own self-loathing. "I'm glad you're here for this, too," she said.

"Are you, really?" Mia asked, her eyes locked on Kit's. "Because you could have sent me away. I'm afraid I'll screw this up again."

Despite the sincerity behind the words, Kit gave a soft laugh. Something told her, finally, after all these years, that even if Mia screwed up again, she would figure it out.

It was a gift for Kit to realize she no longer had to feel responsible for the woman. And that felt like a solid start to a different, and hopefully better, type of relationship with her mother.

Two hours later, the sun was setting. Volunteers had magically swept away their presence along the beach. Matt and Henry had slipped away after the meal, so Dean went off to find them, whispering to Kit that he hoped they weren't sticking an obnoxious "Just Married" sign to the back of her Mustang.

Most of the guests had headed home, including Isaac. He'd spend the weekend with Hazel and Mia, while Dean and Kit meandered through the Minnesota countryside in her newly refurbished Mustang, enjoying what remained of the fall colors. It was the only honeymoon they could fit in right now, since Isaac had already started at the high school nearest their townhouse in Minneapolis. There would be time later for a longer vacation with her new husband.

Only Kit, Jackie, Annie, Lynette, and Renee remained.

"Thank you again for all your help with Isaac, Annie," Kit said. "I'm not sure we could have pulled off getting him enrolled in a new school and starting the legal steps of fostering him without the contacts you gave me."

Annie nodded. "He's a good kid, and I didn't want to see some of the boys he was starting to hang out with get their hooks into him. I hate to say that about students at my school, but it's reality. To be honest, the year is off to a rough start already. I'm going to be more than ready for our annual girls' trip come next February. Now, all of you are sure that timing will work for you, right?"

"Works for me!" Lynette said. "Summers are always so busy, so escaping the dreariness of winter with you lovely ladies will be a great change."

"Winters are actually an easier time for me to get away," Renee chimed in.

"And we've already told you we'll make it work," Jackie said, motioning between herself and Kit.

Kit caught herself twirling the new wedding set on her ring finger. She wasn't yet accustomed to the weight of it. "I know you'll plan something fabulous, Annie. If you haven't picked the location yet, can you make sure there's plenty of sun wherever we go? Something tells me I'll need a hit of both warm weather and friendship by February. I'm thrilled we're incorporating Isaac into our family, and building a relationship with Summer—not to mention my mother—but I suspect all these new dynamics are going to leave me ready for some relaxing time with all of you again. I just hope planning the trip doesn't prove to be too much for you, Annie. You have a big year ahead of you, especially once that new grandbaby of yours arrives."

Annie shrugged. "That won't happen until after our February trip. Besides, it's my turn to play travel agent, and fair is fair."

Jackie smiled. "You've been saying that since we were kids."

"I know, and life seems to keep testing my commitment to that philosophy."

Kit knew she meant it as a joke, but was more convinced than ever that something was up with Annie. It was almost like the woman was trying too hard to make it look like everything in her world was as it *should* be.

Kit knew that was a dangerous charade.

A horn tooted off in the distance, drawing smiles out of all of them.

"I'd recognize that sound anywhere," Jackie said, bending down to put her low-heeled sandals back on. "I'm so happy they finished the Mustang in time for today! It sounds like Dean is ready to get your little honeymoon started, Kit."

Jackie took a step toward the worn path that would lead them back past the old cabins that were such an integral part of their summer camp days. "I've learned I can do pretty well in life without a man, but they sure come in handy sometimes."

They all laughed, and Lynette chimed in, "Spoken like a true divorcée!"

"Wait!" Annie said, grabbing Jackie's hand and pulling her back. "I'm going to miss all of you so much. How can I make it to February without seeing any of you again? Did you guys realize Jackie turns fifty the week of Thanksgiving? What would you think about everyone coming back here to Ruby Shores for the holiday. We could throw a party?"

Kit groaned. "I can't. Dean's mom is already planning a big celebration for us back in Iowa over Thanksgiving for his family that couldn't get here today."

Renee grinned. "I'm afraid I wouldn't be able to come at Thanksgiving either. Aren't we all turning fifty over the next year? I suggest one big party in February, when we are all together again."

Jackie squeezed Annie's fingers, then pulled her hand away. "That sounds like a great idea, Renee. I will be the first to hit the half-century mark, but none of you are too far behind me. I'd rather we all celebrate this milestone together."

Annie held her arms out in surrender. "Fine. That'll work, but if any of you *do* get back here for Thanksgiving or Christmas, I expect a call. Now, come here. We need a group hug to top off this spectacular day."

The five women came together, laughing, and Kit accepted another round of congratulations from her dearest friends.

The Kaleidoscope Girls still knew how to celebrate.

She watched, then, as Annie and Renee fell in step behind Jackie and Lynette, leaving her alone on the beach. She turned back to the horizon one last time and smiled as the bottom edge of the glowing orange sun that had warmed her wedding day disappeared into the cool blue water.

The sun would dip from view for a while, and her old friends might be gone from her day-to-day for the next few months, but they'd all be sitting together in the warm sunshine again soon, debating and helping guide each other through this crazy thing called life.

She could hardly wait.

AUTHOR'S NOTES

I hope you enjoyed this second book in *The Kaleidoscope Girls* series. It was so fun to write **Sunshine and Friends**. I'm glad I could kick off their annual girl's trips with a big adventure!

Eleven years ago, we took our three kids on a family trip to Maui. Our oldest was a senior in high school, and we suspected trips together would become much harder to schedule once he headed off to college. We surprised them with Hawaiian-themed tree ornaments and travel guidebooks at Christmas that year, then boarded our flights less than two months later. We lost one day to a winter storm and flight delays, but we packed plenty of fun into the rest of the trip. There was ziplining, snorkeling, and even the luau in Lahaina. I plan to dig out some of our old pictures to share, even though the ziplining helmets were not flattering!

If you thought the storyline about Nancy Drew was improbable, guess what? It's true. Well, at least the part where we met a helpful older woman named Nancy Drew while snorkeling on that trip to Maui. Our youngest was afraid to get in the water, but the kind woman gave her plenty of pointers and encouragement. It worked!

Someone also scratched their belly across some coral, just like Lynette in **Sunshine and Friends**, but I can't remember exactly who suffered that mishap.

In my first draft of this book, I glossed over any details of the luau, but my editing team pushed me to expand on the scene. I tried to take the lazy route because many of the details were hazy after all this time, but I'm so glad I eventually dug deeper. YouTube is a wealth of fun videos, and watching a clip recorded at the Lahaina Luau took me right back to that long ago night when we sat right up front with our kids. Was I a terrible mother for laughing at how uncomfortable the skimpy costumes on some of the dancers made our then eleven- and fourteen-year-old daughters?

Traveling back into my memories to write the various fun-filled scenes of the Kaleidoscope Girls' first official annual trip makes this book extra special to me. I hope you enjoyed coming along for the ride, too!

Each of the five Kaleidoscope Girls is starring in a book of her own in this series. Next up will be Annie in **Five Golden Friends** (Book 3). The friends are turning fifty and Annie gets to plan their sun-kissed birthday bash, complete with black sashes and gold birthday balloons!

From an outsider's perspective, Annie appears to be one of the only friends in the group to actually have her life figured out. She's excelling in a career of her choice, her husband spoils her with first-class flight upgrades, and she enjoys a close relationship with all three of her young-adult kids. She'll even gain the title of Grandma before her fiftieth birthday.

But does anyone ever really have life figured out? Years ago, Annie was forced to make some tough choices that still hold the power to fracture the one thing that is most important to her. Her family.

Like Annie, family is also the most important thing in my life, too. If you've read my *Celia's Gifts* series, you'll likely have picked up on that theme. If you haven't yet read the seven books in that bestselling family drama, don't miss out! It starts with **Whispering Pines** (Celia's Gifts Book 1).

I'll also continue to weave Renee, her wonderful extended family, and her very special Minnesota lake resort into this friendship series.

You'll find more information on all my books and links to them on various storefronts on my website. While you're there, be sure to sign up for my newsletter so you never miss the latest news, including release dates, glimpses into what goes into creating my books, and more.

Thank you for coming on this writing journey with me. I love reading and writing alongside you!

www.kimberlydiedeauthor.com

THANK YOU!

Dear Reader,

I would like to thank you for taking the time to read **Sunshine and Friends**. I am so grateful you selected it and I hope you enjoyed this second book in my *Kaleidoscope Girls* series.

If you don't mind taking a few more minutes with this book, I'd appreciate it if you would leave a review. Reviews are extremely helpful and much appreciated.

Next up in this fun series is **Five Golden Friends (Book 3)**. A girls' trip to sunny Arizona will give Annie and the rest of the Kaleidoscope Girls a warm escape from the northern winters to celebrate turning fifty. Pack your bags and come join the party!

For links to all of my books and to sign up for my newsletter, please visit my website at www.kimberlydiedeauthor.com.

Wishing you my very best,
Kimberly

Preview Five Golden Friends (Book 3)

Can these forever friends recapture their zest for life together?

Annie Pierce knows the best part of turning fifty will be raising a glass in a toast with her oldest friends. As long as there is water, wine, and warmth, plus time to reminisce and reconnect, everyone should be happy. Fun with friends is a great way to escape life for a while. And Annie *needs* the escape. Will a week in Arizona be enough to quell her growing trepidation?

She'd expected to enjoy her empty nest, but the house is too quiet and regrets are piling up over decisions made long ago. The rift within her blended family feels like a chasm. Her husband is pulling away, her ex is back, and loyalties are in question. Frustrations at work aren't helping. A favorite student is making stupid choices and putting lives at risk. As she awaits her first grandchild, Annie would give anything to bring her family back together.

How can this soon-to-be grandma muster the energy to save both her family and her students? She'll need the support of her best friends if she's going to move forward through these paralyzing midlife struggles.

She used to be fearless. Now she's frozen.

Can Annie begin to thaw under the Arizona sun with a little help from her friends?

Enjoy a fun-filled girls' trip with this welcoming group in **Five Golden Friends**, book three of *The Kaleidoscope Girls* women's friendship series by Kimberly Diede. Life is a compilation of yesterday's choices, but hard-earned wisdom plus a little courage *can* lead to new pathways and fewer regrets.

Treat yourself to **Five Golden Friends** for a reminder that we can do more than survive. We can thrive.

You'll find information on where to purchase books on my website at https://www.kimberlydiedeauthor.com.

ALSO BY KIMBERLY DIEDE

THE KALEIDOSCOPE GIRLS SERIES
BETTER WITH FRIENDS (BOOK 1)
SUNSHINE AND FRIENDS (BOOK 2)
FIVE GOLDEN FRIENDS (BOOK 3)
with additional books to come...

CELIA'S GIFTS SERIES
WHISPERING PINES (BOOK 1)
TANGLED BEGINNINGS (BOOK 2)
REBUILDING HOME (BOOK 3)
CHOOSING AGAIN (BOOK 4)
CELIA'S GIFTS (BOOK 5)
CELIA'S LEGACY (BOOK 6)

WHISPERING PINES CHRISTMAS NOVEL
CAPTURING WISHES (BOOK 3.5 OF CELIA'S GIFTS)

FIRST SUMMERS NOVELLA
FIRST SUMMERS AT WHISPERING PINES 1980

About the Author

Kimberly Diede writes contemporary novels that weave together family, friends, hope, and romance. She writes family sagas, suspense, and women's fiction that you'll find hard to put down. She truly believes we are never too old for second chances in life.

Kimberly enjoys spending the short months of her Midwest summers on the lakeshores of Minnesota and North Dakota. Nothing beats writing and hanging out with family and friends at their cabin. Her love of tradition and all things vintage comes through in her decorating and her stories.

Be sure to follow Kimberly on social media to catch glimpses of the junk she drags home to repurpose and to get updates on her latest books.

Website: https://www.kimberlydiedeauthor.com/
Facebook: https://www.facebook.com/KimberlyDiedeAuthor/
Instagram: https://www.instagram.com/kimberlydiedeauthor/
BookBub: https://www.bookbub.com/authors/kimberly-diede